Acclaim for Bob Rogers'

First Dark: A Buffalo Soldier's Story

The Gripping saga of Isaac Rice is a hero's journey. [Don't] be surprised if *First Dark* ends up as a popular movie. It's also a darn good read.

-- *Baltimore Post-Examiner*

First Dark captivated me from page one as the novel became my time travel machine into another world. Protagonist, buffalo soldier Isaac Rice, is confronted by natural and man-made catastrophes that make the book a real page-turner. *First Dark* is a top-notch work of historical fiction.

-- Dr. Shelley Kirilenko, author of *The Blue Kimono*

I thoroughly enjoyed *First Dark*, a roller coaster thriller about the life of Isaac Rice, a former slave. The book is rich in historical detail and scenic descriptions that allow you to taste, feel, smell, see, and hear the events in the book.

-- Dave Miller, CEO,
American Red Cross National Testing Laboratory

First Dark is a powerful story of the underbelly of American history that has been carefully researched and written. It covers the horrors of bigotry from the points of view of several different characters and brings everything together at the end of the story. Characters are well-developed and believable, and the dialogue and description throughout the book are brilliant.

-- *Readers' Favorite*

First Dark is a well researched work of historical fiction, set during and just after the Civil War. This engaging story centers on Isaac Rice, a run-away slave who eventually joins a Buffalo Soldier's unit of the U.S. Army in the West and intertwines his life and experiences with those of such diverse people as plantation owners, U.S. congressmen, army units operating behind enemy lines, hostile Indians and Mexican combatants. It accurately reflects the attitudes and prejudices of the times and presents both villains and heroes.

-- E.S. Tennent

FIRST DARK:

A BUFFALO SOLDIER'S STORY

FIRST DARK:

A BUFFALO SOLDIER'S STORY

Bob Rogers

Also by Bob Rogers

Hitting Life's Curveballs

Lieutenant Flipper's Trial – The Play

The Laced Chameleon

Sacrifice at Shiloh Church

Dedication

For the descendents of
Rachel Patterson, Samuel Rice, and Isaac Rogers.

11 If I say, "Surely the darkness shall cover me,
and the light around me become night,"
12 even the darkness is not dark to you;
the night is as bright as the day,
for darkness is as light to you.
Psalm 139:11-12

12 Their hearts were bowed down with hard labor;
they fell down, with no one to help.
13 Then they cried to the LORD in their trouble,
and he saved them from their distress;
14 he brought them out of darkness and gloom,
and broke their bonds asunder.
Psalm 107:12-14

Contents

Foreword

Imagine riding along a bucolic dirt road on a pleasant spring morning with birds singing among the budding trees. Then the peace is shattered by rifle fire. With that opening, Bob Rogers had my full attention and drew me into the lives of nineteenth-century families whose stories he used in *First Dark* as a contribution to the discussion Americans are having today about how things got this way in our country. After reading the last line in *First Dark*, the struggles of lead character Isaac Rice and his young contemporaries continued to fill my mind with questions about our troubled national past and its effect on the future of our country.

First Dark is one of the few books that fully seized my attention and kept it until I read the last line of the last chapter. I admit that *First Dark* also altered my usual routine, for I found it difficult to set aside reading Isaac Rice's journey when other important life duties demanded my time. Once these duties were satisfied, I immediately returned to Isaac's exciting tale. My wife commented that she had never seen me so taken by a book as I was with *First Dark*. Bob Rogers did a tremendous job of detailing scenes that thrust readers right into the 1860s where they find themselves in the middle of the Deep South, plantation living, slavery, and America's Civil War. Once Rogers snatches you into the lives of his characters, you will be compelled to reflect on the state of race relations in America today and more importantly, how we got to where we are now. If you are an American, this book will speak to you because no matter your heritage, you are connected to the successes and failures of our nation that are directly connected to slavery and the setting of Isaac's nineteenth-century story.

Even though the Buffalo Soldiers were a key part of early American history, there is still little written about those heroic African Americans who helped defend white settlers and Indians alike. This is an unpleasant part of our history that is still difficult for many of us to sit and have an eye-to-eye conversation about today. Bob Rogers takes this history in novel form and vividly illustrates the difficulty of those times through the lives of several families whose struggles touch and are touched by Isaac Rice. *First Dark* is a moving and effective work that successfully revisited for me the historic horrors related the "Negro and Indian problems."

Bob Rogers was a United States Army captain who served with distinction in the cavalry. He knows the tactics of fire and maneuver when engaging in close fighting because he is a combat veteran of the Vietnam War. Rogers visited the locations where many events in *First Dark* took place. He walked the land where these characters walked and listened to many elders, historians, and curators who shared their knowledge. For example, he stood where historic and fictional characters of the Third Louisiana and Thirty-Eighth Mississippi Infantry Regiments stood in trenches at the Battle of Vicksburg. He did the same in West Texas on a battlefield of the Victorio War. As a result, *First Dark* has a strong feel of authenticity.

I can appreciate the struggles and successes of Isaac Rice as a soldier; for I, too, can identify with the perils of war – especially when bullets are flying all around you. In the Vietnam War, I flew fighter aircraft, many times in support of the army on the ground. During my tour of duty in Vietnam, I flew two-hundred sixty-nine combat missions, seventy-nine over North Vietnam. Witnessing Isaac's every hard earned promotion caused me to reflect on the high value pioneering task performed by Buffalo Soldiers – the first

African Americans in the "peacetime forces" of the United States. Isaac's and his comrades' triumphs contributed to the path leading to four-star promotions in the twentieth century for Chappie James, Colin Powell, J. Paul Reason, and others – including me.

Additionally, I felt an immediate connection to Isaac in that I also grew up near Charleston, South Carolina. Rogers' vivid description of local flora and fauna took me home. Typical of those days for many black people near Charleston, Isaac Rice was born and grew up on a rice plantation. The first black man Isaac saw in a military uniform was the day his father was accidentally killed by a group of black Union soldiers as they ambushed a Confederate supply convoy. Isaac was sixteen at the time. He was so impressed by the black army men that he immediately tried to imagine himself wearing the blue and red uniform of United States Colored Troops (Second South Carolina Volunteer Infantry Regiment). The black Union soldiers apologized to Isaac for accidentally killing his father because their target was the Confederate soldiers escorting the convoy. After learning from a black soldier that they were stationed at Port Royal, South Carolina, Isaac decided that one day he would be a Union soldier. Becoming a member of the Union army was a sure route to freedom and more than anything, freedom was what Isaac Rice wanted.

After quietly gathering key intelligence about his route, Isaac plotted his unusual waterborne escape on rivers from Tiffany Plantation near Charleston to the Union army regiment at Port Royal. When he arrived, he learned that he was too young to join the army. However, he got work as a stoker on the Union Army steamer known as the *John Adams*. These ships were sometimes used by the Union Army to raid plantations and bring slaves to freedom. Shoveling coal into a furnace in the boiler room of one of these ships was hard work but Isaac found it far better than remaining enslaved.

The story moves to the Bender Plantation near Montrose, Mississippi where we meet a slave family of four that Rogers uses to illustrate the latter stages of the Civil War in the South, life under the infamous Black Codes, and new liberties that came with the Reconstruction Era. They had one special secret in this family, Rachel, their daughter, could read. It was illegal for a slave to be taught to read and write in those days. As a child, Rachel was secretly taught by a white playmate. One evening, Union soldiers came to Bender Plantation for food, horses, and to bivouac for the night. These soldiers constituted the Union cavalry brigade that conducted an unsung but daring romp of destruction through central Mississippi. Known as "Grierson's Raid," we witness the incursion deep into Confederate territory through the eyes of a white Union soldier, James, who went on to play pivotal roles with both Rachel and Isaac.

After several years of working on as a stoker on army, then navy ships, and finally after the war on commercial ships Isaac was old enough to join the army. Isaac and his best friend joined the Tenth Cavalry within two months of Congress' first authorization (1866) of colored men in the peacetime military. In the decade that followed, the Tenth Cavalry and sister all-black regiments became known as the Buffalo Soldiers. His service took him throughout the Southwest. He fought Indians, Mexicans, white rustlers of Indian livestock, and of course racism. Through their skill and professionalism, Isaac Rice and the Buffalo Soldiers helped make the West safe for white settlers. Even though Isaac grew up in slavery, he believed in the traditional values of America and proved this through his loyalty and service as a Buffalo Soldier. He fell in love several times during his life. He married a woman who nursed him back to health after suffering severe injuries during a battle with Mexican Revolutionaries.

Bob Rogers successfully broadened Isaac's story to encompass the viewpoints of a literate enslaved black woman (Rachel), a Confederate guerilla (Billy) who refused to accept defeat at Vicksburg, an Englishman (James) who joined the Union cavalry, a Mescalero Apache warrior (Ortega) who followed the great Chief Victorio, and a Mexican farm girl (Alejandra) who matured into a nurse who also performed surgery. Isaac's saga engages and enlightens as readers learn more about early influences on how things got to be the way they are.

There is no question, Bob Rogers, who has written other prodigious books, has hit the target center mass again. He did the research, collected the history and wrote a compelling story that caught and held my attention. Rogers explores an important time in the history of our nation. The story of Isaac Rice, Buffalo Soldier, reminded me of my own service to our country and my commitment to try to make the nation better for *all* citizens. I thoroughly enjoyed reading *First Dark* and I am sure you will as well.

Lloyd W. "Fig" Newton
General, US Air Force (Retired)
Lithia, Florida
August 7, 2015

Preface

"Proud to Serve" is a painting by the noted artist-historian, Don Stivers (1926-2009). I am grateful to Don's heirs for permitting me to use his painting on the cover of *First Dark*. The lone African American Buffalo Soldier shown in the painting is leading his horse forward while looking back over his shoulder. Don's young soldier was immediately a reminder for me of reasons to reminisce. The soldier's backward glance drew me in to examine possible reasons for his checking the rear. The result became a shared retrospection of his life and people – friends and foes – who made things the way they were for him and America.

A memorable look back in search of "how things got this way" for me was my 1967 arrival in Vietnam when I was assigned as commander of a platoon in the First Squadron of the famed Tenth Cavalry. Within an hour of reporting for duty, the First Sergeant handed me a fistful of mimeographed pages and taught me the history of the Buffalo Soldiers – a history that did not appear in my history textbooks or other sources available to me. How was this part of American history kept hidden from the general public?

Growing up during the Jim Crow era in South Carolina, I learned lessons that fed a need to know "how things got this way." Apartheid was the law and clear red lines existed in the sand – destroying social, psychological, and educational development of nonwhites. Economic opportunity, self-esteem, and even aspirations and core individual beliefs also suffered. It was evident among those experiencing privilege because of race and those oppressed because of race. The impact of that era has had lasting effects on the meaning of being an American in the minds of Aboriginal, black, brown, white, and yellow peoples in the United States.

In 1991, Don's African American Buffalo Soldier in "Proud to Serve" and my wife prompted me to give the man in the painting a name and tell his story. His name is Isaac Rice. Readers meet Isaac and learn his story as he touches, and is touched by, his perceived friends and enemies – Aboriginal, black, brown, and white. Isaac's journey is American history that resulted from twenty years of research in hundreds of pages of nineteenth-century documents and more than one hundred books that enabled me to follow the trails and trials of nonfictional characters in Isaac's story on behalf of readers.

The epic of Isaac Rice establishes him as the patriarch of a family whose lives will be bared in coming volumes that follow *First Dark* and Isaac's descendants well into the second half of the twentieth century. The story of Isaac's descendants is America's story of "how things got this way" – the way Americans experience the twenty-first century.

Bob Rogers
Charlotte, North Carolina
August 8, 2015

Acknowledgements

My inspiration to write *First Dark* came in 1991 from a noted military artist and historian, the late Don Stivers. I am very thankful to Don's heirs for giving me permission to use his inspiring painting, "Proud to Serve", on the cover of *First Dark*.

Many people contributed to the development of this book. First, I want to thank my able, experienced, and highly competent editors, Rosemary Wellner Mills and Barbara Jean Perry Grainger, for keeping me on the straight and narrow. I offer my thanks to the National Parks staffs at Vicksburg, Forts Concho, Davis, Gibson, and McKavett, and the museum staffs at Forts Bliss and Sill.

Along the way, Ellyn Big Rope, Apache historian at Mescalero, New Mexico told me where to find the real Mescalero Apache story. Dekoka Davidson took time from her busy day in Ruleville, Mississippi, to show me how to grow rice. Milburn Crowe, historian, gave up a vacation day in Mound Bayou, Mississippi to dig through his documents and find what I needed to know about Ben Montgomery and his descendents from Joe and Jeff Davis's plantations at Davis Bend. Richard Ryan of the National Park Service at Fort Gibson gave me the inside story on laundresses marrying Buffalo Soldiers, a matter not printed in history books. Johnny Stringer grows beans in Jasper County, Mississippi, and owns the farm where the Bender Plantation stood in 1863 when Colonel Grierson and a thousand Union cavalrymen bivouacked for an evening. Johnny welcomed me to his property and allowed me free rein to explore. In 1997, Johnny also introduced me to the then eight-five-year-old Chester Thigpen, who gave me an oral history of Jasper County.
George "Bubba" Bolm, curator/director of the Old Court House Museum in Vicksburg, Mississippi and his able assistant, Neal Brun, hosted me for two days and provided copies from their archives of the personal accounts of General Grant's siege of Vicksburg written by two Confederate soldiers in the Thirty-eighth Mississippi Infantry

Regiment. For the special help given with Gullah matters, I present special thanks to Alphonso Brown of Charleston, SC's GullahTours.com. I give many thanks to Jaielynn Williams, Valerie Perry, and archivist Karen Emmons of the Historic Charleston Foundation for unfettered access to the Aiken-Rhett House and the unpublished papers and letters of the late South Carolina governor, William Aiken, Jr. and his family.

I offer my thanks to the following people for their kind support, loan of books, advice, or some other help: Lew Berry, Reverend Henry Midgett, Pastor, First Baptist Church of St. Louis, Missouri, James Guercio of St. Mary's Cathedral in Natchez, Mississippi, Shelley Kirilenko, Pam Harrison, Veronica Rogers, Jennifer Stubbs of the Ruidoso Public Library in New Mexico, Claudia Rivers of the University of Texas at El Paso, Bill Cummings, Director of Music Ministries at Charlotte, NC's Friendship Missionary Baptist Church, Linda Palafox, Melvin Herrera of the Mescalero Tribal Museum, Edgar Carrasco, Lois Hawthorne, Zelan Liu, Mississippi historian Isiah Edwards, and Louis Skrmetta, Operations Manager of Ship Island Excursions in Gulfport, Mississippi.

Salute to my comrades in arms who provided encouragement and counsel, including Colonel Leroy Zimmerman, Artillery, US Army Retired, and the late John Craig, former US Army sergeant and co-founder of the Baltimore chapter of the Ninth and Tenth (Horse) Cavalry Association.

Though I am much obliged to many, any errors herein are mine.

Bob Rogers
Charlotte, North Carolina
August 8, 2015

Map of the Travels of Isaac Rice and Friends – 1863-1882

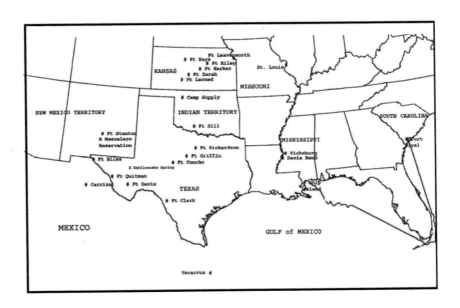

Legend:

\# Cities, towns, or Forts

R Indian Reservations

X Major Battle Site

Chapter 1: Isaac

Mark screamed, "Git down!"

Less than a second later, a bullet slammed into his chest. The bullet, a French-made minie ball, shattered a rib and ripped away the left ventricle from his heart before exiting through his back. Bone splinters pierced his aorta and left lung. The team of four mules Mark was driving bolted. The reins slipped from his fingers. Mark fell backward onto the burlap bags of rice in the cargo bed of the wagon. Birds replaced singing with screeching. In a rush of flapping wings and rustling green leaves, blue jays, robins, warblers and wrens fled.

With their opening volley, the ambushers had cut down two of the six Confederate soldiers escorting the Charleston-bound convoy of eight wagons loaded with rice, corn, and fodder. Mark drove the lead wagon. The convoy bore contributions to the war effort made by the owners of Tiffany and Jehossee plantations – the largest rice plantations on the Pon Pon River. The owners regularly allowed the use of their drivers, wagons, and mule teams to transport rations for Confederate troops and fodder for their animals.

When the first shot rang out, Mark's last words were, "Git down!" It was then that Isaac dove, headfirst, from the wagon's bench seat beside Mark to the gray-brown muddy roadway below. Isaac splashed into a puddle and rolled himself into the ditch beside the rutted dirt road. From there, he scrambled out of the murky ditch water and crawled into the woods.

The firing intensified. Isaac looked back to see the mules running away and Mark's head rolling from side to side atop a sack of rice. In horror, he screamed, "Pa!" Amid the bullets whizzing overhead, he stood and turned to chase the runaway wagon. Abruptly, he felt himself pushed onto the wet leaves and undergrowth. Isaac had been grabbed from behind and forced down by a large black soldier wearing a thigh-length dark blue tunic and red trousers. In the soldier's right hand was a long Enfield Pattern 1853 rifle-musket, the first Isaac had seen close up.

"Stay deh! Stay down!" The soldier spoke the same Gullah dialect as Isaac.

Isaac was bewildered. He nodded and obeyed. Peering through vines and a wild azalea bush covered with spent blossoms, Isaac could see that more black soldiers, led by two white soldiers, had stopped the runaway mule team. He could no longer see Mark. It was quiet again. Light rain continued falling. The smell of gunpowder and the blue smoke from the rifles still hung in the air.

About them, more blue and red-clad soldiers emerged speaking Gullah. The large soldier stood and spoke again. "Son, I'm so sorry we hit your pa. We meant oonah and him no harm."

Still shaken, Isaac nodded and rose. "N-n-now, suh, can I go see about my pa?"

"Why, yes. I'll go wid oonah."

Stumbling along the road from Tiffany Plantation, Isaac could not keep his eyes off the black soldiers rounding up red-faced Confederate prisoners. The soldiers laughed and guffawed and reveled in their work. The soldier who grabbed Isaac now walked beside him. The rain had stopped and the morning sun broke through the fog and clouds. The warmth from the sun felt good through his wet shirt. His ever-present straw hat rested on his back, held in place by the cord around his neck. But the sun would not dry his shoes anytime soon. Because Isaac was apprenticed to the plantation blacksmith, he wore shoes – high-topped leather shoes with wooden soles.

* * *

Three bodies lay at their feet. Mark's upper torso and head had already been wrapped in a piece of the tarp used to cover the rice and corn. His blood had soaked through the tarp where it covered his chest. The bodies of two Confederate soldiers were still uncovered.

Isaac sank to his knees beside his father's body and wept. His tears were a flood – but silent. Isaac swayed from side to side while laying his hands on his father's chest. The soldier with Isaac explained to his comrades that the dead black man was Isaac's pa. He wore three chevrons on his sleeves. They stopped talking and removed their caps. At length, the sergeant directed the soldiers to cut one mule out of a team and secure Mark's body across the beast's back for the trip back to the plantation.

Isaac turned to the sergeant. The man's stubble revealed several short silver hairs on his chin. Isaac stuttered. "S-s-suh, w-who oonah people?"

The soldier sucked in his middle and expanded his chest. "Oh, we're the 1st South Carolina Infantry Regiment of Volunteers (Colored). We're in the Union army."

"Where'd oonah come from?"

"Not far. Mostly we came from plantations on James Island and Johns Island."

"Eh, suh, I mean where'd oonah come from dis mornin'?"

"Oh-h-h. Yisdiddy, we came up from Port Royal by steamboat. Fus, we trabel on de Coosaw River and den up de Combahee. Followin' Missus Harriet's plan, we's been raiding plantations along de Combahee. We wuz marchin' on our way to the Pon Pon River when we heah your convoy a comin'. We planned to destroy the ferry connectin' the Jacksonboro-Charleston Road across the Pon Pon 'foe we head on back to Port Royal. Instead, looks lak we'd best be gittin' all dis heah booty back to our boats."

"Who Missus Harriet?"

"Boy, don't oonah know nothin'? Dat be Missus Harriet Tubman."

* * *

As they walked along the road to Tiffany, except for Luke, the men who had been drivers of the other seven wagons talked quietly, but excitedly, about having seen black Gullah-speaking men like themselves in Union army uniforms executing a perfect ambush – no matter that they were the victims. Most of the men were from Tiffany. The remainder came from Jehossee Plantation, just down the river. The men from Tiffany would take them back to Jehossee on a flatboat, passing under the cannons of the Confederate artillery battery atop Willton Bluff. Luke walked in silence beside Isaac, as

Isaac led the mule bearing his father's body at the head of the procession.

After a time, Isaac spoke. "Eh, Mister Luke, my pa didn't know when he was born. But I wanna 'member dis day. What day is dis?"

Luke cleared his throat. "Why, dis be Monday, the fourth day of May in de year ob our Lawd 1863."

"Mister Luke, in your trabels wid Massa, have you seed Port Royal?"

Luke was in charge of the livery at Tiffany. He occasionally spelled his master's regular carriage driver.

"Surely, I hab. Dat was 'fore de war started."

"How far is it from here?"

"Oh, it a fur piece from here if oonah go by de road or ober land true de woods. Dere be many swamps, streams, and wide ribbers to cross – wid snakes and 'gators, too. But tain't all dat fur by boat – maybe a day's trabel."

Isaac was silent for a long time. The sun was climbing toward midmorning and bringing with it a hot and humid low-country day. There were deep woods on both sides of the road. Along the ditches, five-starred wild roses and honeysuckle released their sweet scent. Gnats buzzed in swarms that looked like black columns surging to and fro in midair. Yellow flies circled and attacked with dazzling speed. Isaac slapped one as it bit into his arm. The mule shook its head, wiggled its ears, twitched its shoulder skin, and swished its tail trying to get rid of the flies.

Luke remained quiet until they reached the ornate brick and wrought iron gated entrance to Tiffany Plantation. They were still surrounded by deep woods of pines, palmettos, cedars, several varieties of oaks, and the odd wild magnolia – regal with shiny dark green leaves and large bright white blossoms. Giant cypress trees stood in low swampy places. Beyond the gate, the woods had been cleared away. Along each side of the road, evergreen live oaks stood like mighty sentinels. Each live oak was draped in Spanish moss that hung like generous tufts of gray hair from the gnarled branches. The live oaks were evenly spaced; between each tree, azaleas stood in front of rhododendrons. The blossoms on the azaleas were spent, but a few rhododendrons still held the last of their lavender and white flowers. The foreground daffodil blossoms had long since died and their stems swayed to and fro in the gentle breeze.

A whitewashed rail fence separated the flowering bushes from small orchards of apple, plum, peach, fig, and pear trees, whose blossoms had already fallen. Soon, the trees would be loaded with tiny green fruit.

Isaac would usually cast an admiring glance at the new hinges on which the main gates were mounted since he had helped the blacksmith, Big Gus, forge those hinges. Today, Isaac didn't even look up.

Tiffany Plantation's rich land lay on both sides of the Pon Pon River, about six miles south of Jacksonboro in Colleton District, where the river was nearly one thousand feet wide. Three hundred twenty-three souls lived on the grounds of Tiffanys – three hundred ten of them enslaved. People and livestock had flourished here since 1741 when William James Tiffany, grandfather of the current owner, John Bartholomew Tiffany II, arrived from Barbados with a few slaves. The elder Tiffany soon learned that his Barbados sugar plantation slaves from West Africa were experts with rice crops. In 1863, rice was still, by far, the most important crop raised in Colleton District, and especially at Tiffany Plantation.

Luke cleared his throat again. He moved closer to Isaac and whispered, "Ni, Isaac, oonah know Mark wuz ma frien'. So I's gonna tell oonah lak mine own son. I seed de way oonah eyed dem soldiers back dere. I seed wanderlust in yo' eyes. I ain't gonna say dis but jes once. If oonah thinkin' 'bout runnin' tuh Port Royal, don't walk – ride. And, for Gwad's sake, don't talk 'bout when oonah goin' wid nobody – not even me."

Isaac stared at Luke in amazement. He asked himself, how'd he know? He felt warmth and kinship for this man who was no kin.

Isaac glanced over his shoulder at the men walking behind them and again made eye contact with Luke. "Yessuh." Isaac thought again about the colored soldiers taking up arms to help the Yankees win the war. "Mister Luke, I heard you tell Uncle Jacob dat Mister Lincoln's proclamation ain't gone be worth a hill a beans in Colleton

District 'til the Secesh are defeated. Well, all de news oonah bring back fuh two years say de 'Cesh are winnin' most ever' battle. Sounds to me lak de Yankees can use colored help. Ain't we got a pony in dis heah race?"

"Son, oonah's right on all counts. I ain't sayin' go or don't go. I jes tellin' oonah, though dangerous – berry dangerous – taint likely no white man gone cotch you goin' by water."

Isaac thought for a long minute. "Yessuh. I sees yo' point."

They didn't speak again until Luke reached for the reins. "Oonah go on and tell yo' ma. I'ma take Mark's body on ober to Aunt Ella's so she can lay'im out on her coolin' board and get'im ready."

"Yessuh. Thank you, Mister Luke." Isaac handed the reins to Luke and went off to deliver the bad news to his mother, Eve.

Once he passed the big house, Isaac saw the reflection of the sun shimmering on the surface of the water that covered the neatly banked squares that made up Tiffany's vast rice fields. Isaac turned west and followed the sound of voices coming from the provision crop fields. While the waters of the stretch flow covered the young rice crop, the workers were hoeing weeds from among the corn and vegetables planted the previous month during the time that the sprout flow waters covered the rice fields. When that happened, only the few trunk minders patrolled the rice fields. Isaac thought of his best friend, Caleb. He knew Caleb would be somewhere along the rice canal banks with Uncle Jacob learning from his mentor how to read the weather, the river, and the needs of the all-important rice plants. Isaac smiled as he recalled Caleb and Uncle Jacob playing their fiddles and harmonicas at jigs and campfires.

"Nigger, what the hell is you doin' heah?" It was Jeb Foster. Isaac turned and met the gaze of the overseer's oldest son. Deep in thought and grief, Isaac had not heard the approach of Jeb's horse. "How cum you ain't wid dem wagons dat left heah dis mornin'?"

Isaac's reply was even and monotone. "We wuz bushwhacked by Yankee soldiers. My pa is dead. I'm on my way to tell my ma."

"Yankee soldiers? Heah? Boy, you lying! Taint no Yankees 'round heah."

Isaac ignored Jeb. "Dey kilt my pa. I'm on my way tuh find my ma."

Jeb was four years older than Isaac. Both were a couple of inches under six feet. Though he was only sixteen, Isaac's muscles and upper torso were the better developed of the two from swinging large hammers at the smithy. Isaac was ambidextrous and used a hammer or machete equally well with either hand.

Jeb scratched the few blond hairs on his chin. "Well, I don't reckon you'd lie 'bout yo' pa being kilt. Yo' ma's down yonder on the low end of dis heah cornfield. I'ma let it go dis time on account o' yo' pa. Next time don't forget tuh say, 'suh.'"

Isaac bit his lower lip – hard. "Yessuh."

* * *

Isaac found Eve hoeing in a row beside her best friend, Hannah. He took a deep breath, preparing to speak. Eve looked up and Isaac heard her usual cheerful greeting come from her smiling face. In an instant and before Isaac could speak, Eve's smile vanished. Suddenly, she was unsteady on her feet. She waivered as if she had received a blow and leaned on her hoe. Eve searched his face. Her scorching gaze caused Isaac to cast his eyes down. "Isaac, what's wrong? Why oonah here? Where's Pa? What's happened?"

Isaac reached with both arms to hug his mother. "Ma...."

Throwing the handle of her hoe to the ground, she backed away, holding up both hands – palms out. Eve shrieked. "No! Don't oonah tell me dat! No! I no yeddy dat! No! Taint true!"

Isaac hugged Eve. At first, she pushed halfheartedly against his chest and then leaned on him. She began wailing in a loud voice with tears streaming down her face. Isaac's tears were warm on his cheeks. He tried again to speak: "Ma...."

She shook her head. "Taint true! Taint true! Not my Mark!"

Hannah stepped over her row of young corn plants and joined Isaac in hugging her friend. Eve wailed and gasped for breath. She sagged and her weight was supported by Isaac and Hannah as they gently laid her between the rows of corn plants. They revived Eve with water from Hannah's clay jug. On her feet again, Eve draped her arms around the shoulders of Isaac and Hannah. Both held Eve about her waist and walked her to the cabin she shared with Mark and her children.

* * *

Aunt Ella, the sick house minder, midwife, nurse, and undertaker, arrived shortly after Hannah made dinner. "Chile, what oonah want me to sing tonight?" Aunt Ella smoothed her silver hair, drawn back into a bun, and looked expectantly at her patient. Eve blinked and, after a moment of reflection, looked up from her pallet on the floor at Isaac. "Son, what do oonah tink 'bout 'I Wanna to be Ready'?"

"Ma, dat be fine. Pa always lak dat song."

"Aunt Ella, please also sing 'Lawd, Remember Me' – speshly fuh me."

"Why sho', chile. I'll git young Caleb to help me raise both o' dese songs. Now oonah jes res' easy. Hannah will fetch anything oonah need and mind the girls."

* * *

Isaac and Aunt Ella arrived at George's carpentry workshop as Big Gus and Tom Foster approached. Inside there was the fresh smell of fresh-cut pine. Sawdust covered the worktables and the floor. Big Gus's hand dwarfed the blue glass jar of nails he handed to George. He offered the same hand to Isaac. "Son, I was mighty sorry to heah dat oonah lost yo' pa."

Isaac blinked back tears. He watched his hand disappear into Big Gus's. "Thank you, suh."

Tom Foster was the head overseer. He did not offer his hand, but did mumble condolences. He turned to George. "You gonna be finished here by nightfall?"

"Yessuh. It'll be ready, now dat I hab de right size o'nails fuh dese heah planks." George rubbed a hand over the one completed side and frame of the coffin he was building for Mark's body. George appeared to admire his handiwork. His skills were renowned in Colleton District and as far away as Charleston. He was often loaned or hired out to other plantations for cabinetry and building projects.

Tom asked, "Aunt Ella, will the body be ready in time?"

"Yessuh, Mister Tom."

* * *

After supper, family and friends sat by the body into the night singing and praying until time for the funeral to begin in the slave section of the plantation cemetery. Some of the men held torches to light the way. A neighbor brought two ladderback chairs with woven grass string bottoms for Eve and Isaac. They were the only people seated during the funeral. Isaac's youngest sister, Mary, stood beside him. Deborah was patting her mother's shoulder. Most of the time, Eve leaned her head on Isaac's shoulder and continued shedding silent tears. Mark's coffin had already been nailed shut.

Aunt Ella and Caleb raised their voices together and led the community in song. Aunt Ella was sometimes accompanied by Caleb's harmonica. Isaac reckoned that there were more than two hundred members of the community present. Tom Foster spoke on behalf of the Tiffany family, since they had already moved to their Charleston townhouse to avoid the "fever season." Uncle Jacob repeated words from the Bible he had heard the visiting white Episcopal preacher recite. He ended with the 23 Psalm and a long prayer. "...and bress Eve and her chillums. Prop dem up on ebber' leanin' side. Hep dem make it true dese tryin' times.... Amen."

Following the internment, with Mark's head facing the east, members of the community took turns hugging Eve and Isaac while offering their private condolences. After a while, the people made their way back to their streets and cabins by torchlight.

When the final torch was extinguished, Bianca stepped from the shadows, grabbed Isaac's hand, and pulled him from the street. In a shadow again, she whispered, "I'll never forget what oonah did for me and my Andrew last year. Please let me know if there's anything I can do for oonah."

Slowly, she turned to face him, toe to toe. In the dim light of a quarter-moon, Isaac saw beauty in her eyes and lips. Her smile revealed perfectly even teeth that he had not noticed in all the years since he first met her. She moved closer and laid her head on his chest. She put her arms around Isaac and pulled him tight against her body. He caught her scent and inhaled deeply. Isaac felt Bianca gently slide her thigh between his legs. She whispered, "Anything. *Anything* at all."

Through his shirt and her white cotton dress, Isaac felt her rigid nipples against his midsection and the soft flesh of her shoulders under his hands. He experienced surprise, confusion, and the sensation of blood rushing to his loins. He knew she felt his erection. In a moment, Bianca was gone.

* * *

Wide-eyed, Isaac lay on his pallet in the attic of his mother's cabin. He called the attic a loft; he had slept there since he was eleven years old. He lay awake, staring at the dark rafters above his head. Bianca's scent remained in his nostrils and he could still feel her flesh in his hands. He thought of his brief friendship with Miriam – of the one kiss behind the smithy, her almost constant sickness with severe stomach and muscle pain, and finally her death at age fourteen. Isaac thought he would've ask his father about the feelings Bianca stirred – or, maybe, not. But he was sure he would not discuss it with Caleb. His mind drifted to the sight of Bianca's beautifully proportioned body nearly naked as she was beaten by Jeb Foster while the community was forced to watch. His mind returned to the embrace. Isaac relived that embrace several more times. He fell asleep without answering his question of what he should say to Bianca.

* * *

Isaac smelled bacon. He bounded down the ladder from the loft. Eve had his breakfast of bacon and cornbread ready. He stepped outside and washed his face with cold water from the small wooden hoop basin on the shelf next to the door. He thought of how he used to wait for his pa to finish with the basin first. With the memory came an ache in the middle of his body. He thought, *just yesterday,*

10

Pa was right here beside me. The sun was not up yet, but in the early morning light Isaac knew his mother could see his tears. Eve walked over and put her arms around Isaac. She drew a deep breath. "Son, I know it hurts. It allus hurts when we lose a person we love."

In a low, but steady voice, Isaac replied, "Ma, thank oonah for your kind words."

"Your pa was a fine man. Oonah remind me so much of him...." She sniffed and sighed. "It's getting late. You bes' git on to wurk now."

"Ma, I can still hear his voice in my head...."

"I know. I know. But now it's time to git. Out you go." Isaac could see that Eve was fighting back tears. Blinking rapidly, she hugged him again. "Try to smile some today. Talk to Caleb and Uncle Jacob."

"Yessum."

Isaac was glad Caleb could not see him letting his mother hug him or observe him crying. He took the cornbread and bacon that Eve held out. He noticed right away that she had given him an extra piece of bacon. He smiled and dried his eyes.

As he turned to go, Eve said, "I know today is a sad day for you. But, Pa would say that a smile looks good on you."

Isaac was out the door when he shouted over his shoulder, "Bye, Ma!"

He didn't follow the street to the smithy. As usual, he was almost late. Isaac trotted along the worn path between the gardens that separated the back of the cabins on his street from the ones facing south. He was eating bacon from his right hand and cornbread from his left. There would be no time to lose when he arrived at the smithy. He would immediately start the fire in the furnace – which should have been started already. Big Gus wanted it hot by the time he arrived in the mornings. Isaac pushed the last of the bacon into his mouth as he reached the smithy's front door.

Flames were starting from yesterday's embers and the dry pine splinters Isaac had thrown into the furnace when he heard the horn blow first call for the field crews. Final call would be sounded in sixteen minutes and Big Gus and Tom Foster would appear in the doorway. Isaac especially did not want to be yelled at this morning for not having the fire going on time. He had put the first logs on and was pumping the bellows furiously when Big Gus arrived. Tom Foster was not with him.

Big Gus stood in the doorway, blocking the daylight. He was half a foot over six feet and weighed almost three hundred pounds. He counted as two men in the tug-of-war games they had at harvest time celebration. Big Gus was also the blackest man Isaac had ever seen. His skin sometimes had a bluish glow. He stood there looking at Isaac for a long moment.

Finally, Big Gus spoke. "'Mornin', son. Com'ere."

It was then that Isaac noticed the leather lines in his right hand. He left the bellows saying, "Mornin', Mister Gus." He knew that sometimes Big Gus had been ordered by Tom Foster to flog an enslaved worker for some infraction of the rules. As he drew nearer, Isaac could see that the leather lines were attached to the bridle of a large bay horse standing quietly to the left of the door. Isaac exhaled. "Yessuh, Mister Gus?"

Big Gus reached out, put a big hand on Isaac's shoulder, and said, "Son, I'm still saddened by the loss of your pa. If I could, I would tell oonah to take the day off."

The gentleness in the man's voice surprised Isaac. He managed to say, "Thank you, suh."

Big Gus cleared his throat. "Isaac, I want oonah to start work on the replacement hinges for the corral gates and barn doors this mornin'. I'm goin' down to the main gate to measure the post hinges for new tie rods. Be back 'fore dinner time. Oonah be careful with dat fire." Big Gus took his leave.

It was unusual for Isaac to be in the smithy working alone. He was pleased that Big Gus had shown confidence in him. He thought; *wait 'til I tell Pa....* Isaac shook his head and said aloud, "Pa, it may take awhile to stop missin' you so much." The thought of his father brought back the ache deep inside. Isaac went about selecting pieces of iron and taking down tools from Big Gus's neat wall pegs for the hinge job. Today he just did not feel up to putting forth the effort and doing the good work that he knew would earn Big Gus's praise.

His fire was roaring and he was in his leather apron pounding out a hinge plate when in a glance he noticed his best friend, Caleb, with Tom Foster in the doorway trying to get his attention. This iron plate was glowing red and yellow and Isaac didn't want to stop now, so he pretended not to see them. It was only midmorning, but sweat covered his face and dripped from his chin. He continued to strike the hinge plate with mighty blows. His hammer and the anvil could be heard ringing far outside the smithy. He finished the plate and, with his long tongs, immersed it in the water trough.

While the plate made a loud hissing sound in the water and with steam rising, he looked up. Caleb was waving and calling his name. Isaac knew that neither Caleb Jenkins nor Tom Foster would come close while he was hammering because of flying bits of hot iron and the heat from his furnace. This was the only time he could make Foster wait.

Isaac shook his head and sweat flew from his face. He grinned and greeted them. "Mornin', Massa Foster. Mornin', Caleb."

Caleb said, "Mornin', Isaac."

Foster did not acknowledge the greeting, yet he would have expressed displeasure if he had not received one. Foster went directly to business. "Are you working on hinges for the barns?"

"Yessuh."

"Well, I want you to shut down here as quickly as you can. I need you over in Liberty Square to fix a trunk dock – a bolt on a pulley broke. I want you two boys to get over there real soon. I need that trunk holding water out of that square today without fail."

Foster continued, "Take a canoe with you and go by the front gate and tell Gus to come on back to the smithy. Then you two start out for Liberty Square. Take the tools you think you'll need. I'll meet you there."

Both said, "Yessuh."

* * *

When Foster was gone, Caleb turned to Isaac and said, "I'm real sorry about yo' pa. I know oonah miss him awful bad."

"Thanks, Caleb. I'll say the last thing I imagined was losing my pa to a Yankee bullet."

"Is it true? Mister Luke say dey be black Yankees from James Island."

Isaac looked toward the door to be sure Foster was not returning and said, "Yeah. And Johns Island too."

Caleb looked over his shoulder through the open doorway before asking in a low voice, "Dem Yankees need big help. Dey still gittin' dey asses kicked in evah big battle – 'cept maybe Shiloh. You still wanna join'em?"

Bianca flashed through Isaac's mind. He hesitated. Frowning, he spoke. "I think so. Oonah still goin' wid me?"

Caleb dropped his head and fidgeted. "Naw. I see bad signs. Oonah still wanna go?"

"Well, let's talk while we walk. I want to be sure no one hears what we say." Isaac began putting tools in the big wooden box under the worktable next to the anvil. Some, he hung on wall pegs. He put a bolt and the tools he thought he would need to fix the trunk dock pulley into a burlap bag.

"Okay, while oonah finish shuttin' down, I'll git a canoe."

"Git ol' Della, too, while oonah gittin'."

"What oonah want with dat ol' retired mule?" Caleb had taken a step toward the door, but now he stopped.

"Surely oonah didn't think I was gonna help carry dat canoe all de way to de front canal?"
"So tell me how's ol' Della gettin' back to the stable, or is oonah plannin' to take that dusty ol' mule in the canoe?"

"Caleb, jes write her a pass so the patty rollers won't bother her and she can come back by herself!"

Caleb let go with a loud guffaw. He was walking backward, laughing, and saying, "Yeah, like either one of us can read or write. You're as silly as yore Brer Rabbit..." when he tripped over a log stool and tumbled against the wall. Barrel hoops hanging from wooden pegs on the wall near the door fell on Caleb as he struggled to get up. One was around his neck. Isaac would have doubled over laughing at this scene last week. But today he felt sad and his head

14

felt strange – almost like having a band tied too tightly around his head just above his eyes. He went over and helped Caleb clean up the mess. Isaac managed to smile while Caleb repeated the hilarity about ol' Della, the rollers, Brer Rabbit, and the hoop around his neck.

They tied the canoe onto two skinny pine poles like a patient to a litter. With one end draped over Della's shoulders, they let her drag the ungainly apparatus. When the boys passed the kennel, they heard Foster's hounds snarling and barking.

"Caleb, dem dawgs allus remind me o' de time we walked past here and spotted dem patty rollers dragging Bianca and Andrew back here. Do oonah 'member?"

"I'll neber forget it. Dat wuz jus lak the time my ma and pa and me got caught tryin' tuh run in '51. They beat us and sold us 'way from de Jenkins Plantation on James Island."

* * *

The first time Jeb Foster had beaten a slave, he had done so while his father was away in Charleston. Bianca, who had assisted Caleb's mother in the kitchen house, and her husband, Andrew, had escaped from Tiffany in the spring of 1862. Isaac had learned later from Caleb's mother that the couple was convinced that the Confederates would win the war and had decided to go to Canada. Isaac had passed the corral with Caleb and discovered Bianca and Andrew stripped to their waists and on their knees, their wrists tied to the split-rail fence of the corral. Their arms were spread apart and tied so they could neither sit nor stand. The practice at Tiffany was to leave any enslaved person who had violated a rule tied to the corral fence until the end of the workday, when all the community was forced to watch punishment meted out.

From Isaac's workplace at the smithy across the street from the corral, he saw Aunt Ella twice give water to the couple during the day – an act that itself was an infraction of the rules. Aunt Ella knelt in the mud and dung beside Bianca, and then Andrew, giving each of them water from a brown clay jug. Isaac was afraid for Aunt Ella. She was beloved by the community and respected by the Tiffanys and Tom Foster. Yet Isaac sensed that no such respect was held by Foster's sons for any black person.

* * *

When the community gathered, they were somber and quiet. While his younger brother sat his horse, Jeb Foster greeted those assembled with a warning. "Ni, I ain't no speechifyin' fella lak my pa. And I ain't usin' ma pa's whip. So I'ma let my lil' toy kitty cat heah do the talkin' for me." He held up his new cat o'nine tails. It was handsomely constructed from a hickory handle wrapped in leather that bound the stick to three ropes, unbraided into three strains each, with three small knots of leather tied to each strain. The whole cat was a bit over three feet long. At the sight, the crowd murmured. Jeb grinned. "Ni y'all watch what happens to niggers who run off."

Jeb turned and stood over Andrew. Jeb took a deep breath, drew back his cat, and swung it hard down against Andrew's bare back, drawing blood on contact. Andrew snapped his head up and gasped. He struggled against his bonds, his fingers making gripping motions. Though Bianca was not struck, she screamed, "No!"

Jeb turned and struck Bianca. "Shut up, you black bitch!"

Bianca screamed louder. He hit her again. Blood trickled down her back. Tears and mucus streamed from her face onto the mud.

Jeb struck Bianca again and again until he heard Andrew yell, "Stop it, damn you! Son of a dog, leave her be! I'll take her beatin'."

Jeb stopped. He snarled. "Well, you kin have yo' wish!"

Jeb turned and struck Andrew fast and hard. After a time, Andrew's body went limp. His head slumped so that his chin rested on his collarbone. Jeb did not stop.

Aunt Ella yelled. "Enough!"

Still standing over Andrew's bloody back, Jeb glared at Aunt Ella. His face was flushed and sweat ran down his brow and the top of his nose. "You wanna be next, ol' woman?"

Bianca pleaded through her tears. "Stop. Oh, please stop. Can't you see he's passed out?"

Jeb's response was to lash Bianca across her back. One of the nine knotted tails of his cat reached around her back and ripped her left breast, barely missing her nipple. Blood dripped from her breast.

Several women in the crowd screamed. Isaac scampered over the corral fence and ran to Jeb. Isaac stopped when he was less than a foot in front of Jeb's face, hands akimbo. They were standing toe to toe. Neither Isaac nor Jeb said a word. A hush fell over the crowd. Isaac stood between Jeb and Bianca. Then, he folded his arms across his chest and watched Jeb's perplexed face. Jeb lowered his cat and took a step back. Isaac took a step forward, gazing into Jeb's eyes.

"Mister Foster, yo' pa woulda stopped already."

Jeb snapped his head around to see who had spoken and had to look up into Big Gus's eyes, two feet away. Big Gus continued. "Yo' pa would know better'n to damage Massa Tiffany's property like dat."

Aunt Ella was already cutting Andrew loose from his bonds.

Jeb's face was flushed from his exertion. Now it turned an even brighter pink. He walked away in a huff.

* * *

Aunt Ella sent Luke for the white Dr. Pritchard from Jacksonboro. In spite of Aunt Ella's and Dr. Pritchard's best care, Andrew's back festered, turned blacker by the day, while it produced more and more yellow pus. His fever never broke. Andrew died five days later. Dr. Pritchard said it was gangrene.

* * *

Isaac hid a smile as he savored the memory of his brief tender embrace with Bianca less than twelve hours before. He was surprised by the intensity of the memory. He could almost feel her flesh. Isaac asked Caleb, "How old is Bianca?"

"Ma say she be 'bout twenty-three. Accordin' to Ma, Bianca still refuses to take comp'ny – no matter, young man or old man. I've often wondered, what wuz oonah thinkin' when oonah jumped into dat corral? Evahbody thought oonah done lost *yo'* mind."

"I didn't think. I jes jumped. I neber seed nobody beat anyone lak Jeb did dat day. I thought it was Jeb who'd lost *his* mind. If he beat me, I didn't care if I died. Oonah 'member, dat wuz only a few days after my sweet Miriam had died."

They lapsed into silence, Isaac in his private thoughts about the consequences of running away from Tiffany – or any plantation. They walked at a brisk pace on opposite sides of Della's head without leading her. Caleb glanced at the sun. Isaac looked down at the shortening morning shadows. Isaac knew it was time to be well on their way to Liberty Square. He didn't want to be on Tom Foster's list today. He was sure Caleb didn't either. Isaac grimaced and shook his head as he remembered Bianca being struck again and again. He tried to remove from his mind the sight of blood flowing from her back and down her side from her injured left breast. He bit his lip and kicked the dirt.

They passed the smokehouse, the commissary, the guard station and bell stand, and the row of three overseers' houses before Caleb broke the silence. "Don't oonah think Bianca and Andrew getting' caught is a bad sign for runnin'?"

Isaac said, "Talkin' 'bout dem gave me a new idea. I'll tell you 'bout it after we pass the big house."

The street headed west and joined a large circular avenue directly in front of the big house. They smelled the roses as soon as they turned the corner. The inner circle was lined by a low hedge. The green leaves of the hedges contrasted with the brown pine needles that covered the ground in a neat circular row from the roots of the hedges out to about three feet by Isaac's guess. Caleb worked with Uncle Jacob to tend the vegetable gardens of the big house and the flowers in the front circle.

Isaac glanced over his shoulder toward the big house before saying, "So, here's my idea. Ni oonah can still go wid me."

Caleb cast his eyes down. "Naw, man. I best stay heah."

Isaac took a deep breath. "Well, I'm changin' up my plan. On a night wid no moon, I'll run to Jehossee and hide in the winnowing house."

"What? Oonah loco?"

18

Isaac thought Caleb's face showed stunned disbelief.

Della raised her head and quickened her pace when Caleb spoke loudly and sharply to Isaac.

"Listen. The reason so many of us get caught is because we didn't listen to our own Brer Rabbit and Brer Fox stories."

"Isaac, oonah good as dead. Naw, man. Please don't go."

Isaac ignored Caleb's protests. "First, like Brer Rabbit would do, I send them running in the wrong direction."

"Oonah don't look much like no Brer Rabbit to me."

"Think about how the rollers caught every runaway you've seen them drag back here."

"I don't have to think too far – jes to my own family."

"I know. And you were a little tyke. But think about it. Your family, and most of the others, did something the rollers expected you to do. All of you's took off through the woods goin' north or west. The rollers got on your trail with their dawgs. None of you's had any help. There was no place to rest, no any food to be had along the way. Once dem dawgs and rollers on dey hosses had the trail, it was only a matter of time 'fore dey caught you's."

"Okay. Oonah right. So what oonah get by runnin' to the Jehossee Plantation? It ain't but three miles away."

"De thing is, Jehossee is south of here. De rollers expect us to go north or west toward Beaufort. Second, I'll go by canoe after walkin' west to the canal that runs to the Ashepoo River. Third, I doubles back over de same ground draggin' brush. De dawgs won't know if I was goin' or comin'. Dawgs only know a scent trail. When dey git to the canal, dey'll take the dawgs up and down tryin' to find where I woulda come outta de water. Meanwhile, fourth, I'm in a canoe on another canal goin' south to Jehossee. What I get is a place to lay low 'til they stop lookin' and think I drowned or somethin'. Can't let nobody else in on the plan. Even the rollers and overseers can't make a body tell what he don't know." He thought, *including Bianca*.

"Whoa! Man, that's a great idea. They'd neber look for oonah dere. Oonah *is* loco – like Brer Rabbit!"

"When I get to be seventeen, I might be as smart as oonah and Della."

"Now don't be puttin' me in with dis dusty ol' mule jes 'cause we the same age. I got another idea for you – since you got me thinkin' like Brer Rabbit."

"So what's that, Brer Caleb?"

"Go with the ebb tide down the overflow canal past Liberty Square and into the Pon Pon. That way, oonah won't have to start so early and use all your strength gettin' there. Oonah can git seen by the overseers far past fus dak jes by bein' round and 'bout as usual. By the time oonah put in at Jehossee, it'll still be a long while before fus call. Ebb tide two nights from now is an hour or two past midnight. That will give oonah time to leave a canoe near the overflow canal."

"Okay. When it is time for me to run from Jehossee, I'll go at ebb tide in the night. Dat time I'll have much further to go."

Suddenly puzzled, Caleb asked, "Somethin' ain't right 'bout this. Where oonah thinkin' 'bout puttin' in at?"

"I think Port Royal Island. Dat's where Luke said the Yankees camped."

"Yeah, but that's not what's botherin' me. Oonah got to put in somewhere and rest. I 'member goin' down the Pon Pon to fish in the sound with Uncle Jacob a few years back and we stopped somewhere."

"I've been down there too. Everybody fished the sound back 'fore de war."

"Yeah, now Massa Tiffany and Massa Aiken 'fraid dem Yankees will snatch us." Caleb laughed softly, but Isaac only smiled. Caleb frowned, perplexed again, and continued, "No, there's some danger in this plan and it ain't the rollers. Your plan has'em foxed."

"Well, what then, Brer Fox?"

"I can't get my hand on it. Maybe it'll hit me after we leave the gate. I don't want Big Gus to hear."

The massive black wrought iron main gate at Tiffany Plantation hung from gate posts made of brick. The posts were part of a brick wall. Isaac could not ever remember seeing the gates closed. A guard house made of brick was built into the west wall, but was used only when the Tiffanys held a large social event. It was then manned by servants and liverymen dressed like butlers in uniforms topped by fine coats with tails and shiny buttons. The guard house was almost completely covered by green moss.

When William James Tiffany built this grand entrance, it was the talk of Colleton and Charleston Districts. Over the years, the elite of the South Carolina low country, visitors from Washington and Europe, and several governors regularly attended winter socials at the plantation. The walls were eight feet tall at the posts and sloped to four feet where they joined the whitewashed rail fences that ran beside the orchards. The walls, guard house, and gates were just south of the bridge over the front canal. Isaac thought this canal was a useless decoration, for it did not provide water for the rice fields like the maze of canals on the rest of Tiffany.

Big Gus was finishing his measurements early. As he put away his tools, he smiled and called to them, "When I saw the likes of oonah comin', I said, 'here comes trouble.'"

"Aw now, Mister Gus. Are we all that bad?" Isaac asked with a big grin. His grin suddenly faded. He was confused about the strange feeling he had each time he smiled while in the presence of his mother or Caleb or Big Gus. He thought he would feel sad every minute for a very long time after his pa was buried. He pushed the feeling aside and tried to smile.

Big Gus had started a chuckle and Caleb was laughing, but before anyone could say another word, they heard the thunder of distant hoofbeats and the sharp rattle of an empty buckboard moving rapidly toward them. They turned and saw two fine black horses in full gallop on the road from Jacksonboro. It was not a runaway. The driver was not trying to slow his charges, he was urging them onward. He was yelling and snapping his lines. The white foam from the mouths of both horses contrasted with their black coats, glossy with sweat.

Big Gus said, "Why, that's Luke. He's runnin' that rig like he's got a bee in his bonnet. Com'on boys, give'im room." Big Gus took his bay by the halter and led him and his two-wheeled work cart away from the gate. Isaac moved Della and the canoe aside.

Now they could hear Luke yelling to them, "Make way! Make way!"

Isaac thought Luke might not clear the turn just before the bridge. Isaac watched with widening eyes as Luke hit it without slowing. Luke and the horses leaned in unison into the turn. The buckboard's rear wheels skidded, throwing dirt up from the road. Luke's hat was bouncing on his shoulders in the breeze, pulling the cord taunt that held it around his neck. Sweat glistened on his forehead. The rear of the little buckboard snapped back into line behind the horses and clattered across the wooden bridge over the canal and through the gate. Luke, the horses, and the rig soon disappeared down the avenue toward the big house in a cloud of dust.

Isaac looked wistfully down the avenue and said, "I wish I could drive like dat Mister Luke."

Caleb said, "I wouldn't drive *dat* fast 'less somethin' was powerful wrong."

"Well, boys, Luke only drives like that when he has news from Massa Tiffany."

Isaac and Caleb gave Foster's message to Big Gus while untying the canoe and securing Della's lines to the tailgate of Big Gus's cart for the trip back to the stable. They walked and half slid down the bank to the water beside the bridge. They took the oars out and were quickly under way toward Liberty Square. The decorative canal, adorned with ivy and white roses, took them past the cornfields that helped feed Tiffany's people, livestock, and, of late, Confederate troops in Charleston and Colleton Districts. They rowed steadily without talking and were soon making the turn into the overflow canal that held reserve water for Liberty and Independence squares and adjacent rice fields on the west bank of the Pon Pon River. Isaac imagined he saw his pa standing beside the canal waving to him.

They were quiet for a time. Isaac's mind drifted back to Bianca's embrace. Now he wanted to stay and see what might develop with her, not run. But he still wanted to join the Yankee army.

Suddenly, Caleb remembered what had bothered him about Isaac's runaway plan, "Hey, Isaac, I got it!"

Reluctantly, Isaac left the secret place in his mind. "Got what?"

"Listen to me. Dat thing that bothered me about your plan is dis: Leaving Jehossee on an ebb tide with miles to row – by yo'self –

22

across the mouths of both the Combahee and Bull rivers, you'd be very tired. By the time you reach the Coosaw River, the tide would be goin' out again. You'd have to row up the Coosaw *against* the current *and* the tide to Port Royal Island. You could be swept out tuh sea!"

Isaac sat up straight and stared at Caleb for a long moment. "Well I do declare. Oonah sounding more and more like ol' Brer Fox everyday. Look out Brer Rabbit! So, what should I do, Brer Fox?"

Caleb motioned for Isaac to stop talking. He continued his instructions. "Leave Jehossee two hours *before* tuh end of ebb tide. Go down the Pon Pon and drag yo' canoe over the shortcut through the narrow neck over tuh the Ashepoo and continue into the sound. By the time oonah git there, the tide will start comin' in again. Oonah will be able tuh cross the mouths of the Combahee and the Bull wid ease. Oonah should reach Port Royal Island by the next ebb tide."

"Whoa. Thanks. And I thought I had it all planned. My pa allus said, 'two heads better'n one any day'. Oonah a big help."

"If you ask me, I say, don't go. Dis still a dangerous plan."

Isaac reflected on those dangers. He concluded he would be safer with Bianca. His eyes narrowed and he pumped a fist into his palm. "I'm goin'! Mister Lincoln needs me."

Caleb raised an eyebrow and sighed. "Well, okay. I'll fetch the tide times from Uncle Jacob."

"Thanks, Brer Fox."

"Oonah welcome, Brer Rabbit."

Chapter 2: Bianca and the Ball

Bianca smiled and waved. Luke called out, "G'mornin'!"

The horn for second call sounded. Isaac and Big Gus yelled their greetings and waved from the doorway of the smithy. She heard Big Gus's booming voice above Isaac's. "And a mighty good Thursday mornin' to y'all!" In the distance, Bianca saw work crews, armed with hoes, on their way to the provisioning fields.

Luke's fine black duo pulled his buckboard at a smart canter. Besides Bianca, his cargo included two wooden hoop barrels of catfish, still swimming in their home waters from the Pon Pon River, and a burlap bag of rice. Luke and his sons had caught the catfish the previous afternoon and left the barrels mounted on the buckboard overnight in the corral. Now, with Bianca in tow, Luke was well on his way to fulfilling instructions sent the day before by Mrs. Margaret Tinsley Tiffany from the family's Charleston townhouse.

Bianca's mind drifted. She could still picture Isaac as a young boy playing marbles or baseball with his friends. That memory competed with reliving his firm embrace from a few nights before. Bianca smiled at the realization that Isaac was a small boy, spending his days at the little children's house, when she had her first menses. Remembering the small boy and now the boy-man were the two thoughts at the top of her mind when she spoke to Luke as they drove through the front gate. "You know, Mister Luke, I was born on Tiffany Plantation. This is only the second time I've been off the plantation. I don't think Andrew could imagine that someday I would ride away in a buckboard."

"Now, gal, looka heah. I hope oonah ain't thinkin' on runnin' again heah t'day." Luke's frowning face showed he was serious.

"Oh, no suh, Mister Luke! I wouldn't do dat and git oonah in trouble. Besides, I want to see Charleston, do dis work for Missus Aiken, and git on back home."

Luke let out a sigh. "Well, okay. Den in dat case, I drives oonah a 'round 'bout way in the city for a look 'fore we reach the townhouse."

Bianca clasped her hands together. "Oh, thank you, Mister Luke! Dat will be wonderful! How old is Isaac?"

"Huh? I no yeddy."

"How old is Isaac?"

"Oh, dis year he be sixteen summers."

"Will oonah stay in Charleston until after the big Saturday night ball?"

"Yeah, I stay to run and fetch stuff. Den, Missus says I take oonah back to Tiffany de day atter de ball."

Bianca smiled as she reflected on how cleverly she had dropped her question about Isaac in the middle of a different conversational topic. She continued. "What do oonah think dey really want me to do?"

"Oh, chile, I don't know. My guess is dey want oonah to do more'n chop food and hep in de kitchen."

Bianca was puzzled. "Like what?"

"Oonah a comely lass. I guess oonah be servin' 'mongest the guests at de ball. Dat give the Tiffany family som' braggin' rights. Dem and the Aikens allus tryin' som' clever way to outdo one another." Luke added a small knowing laugh.

"Well, thanks, Mister Luke. But that can't be the reason Missus sent for me. Why, oonah said yesterday that an Aiken servant just gave birth and I'm to replace her."

"Yeah, dat be Dorcas. And Missus latched on dat chance to slip you in wid an offer o' catfish and rice to show off Tiffany hepin' out the Aiken family. O'course when oonah gets right down to it, the Aikens don't need no hep from nobody. But dat way Missus Margaret can show guests how close friends she be to Missus Harriet. Oh, I kin heah it now." Luke laughed and raised his voice into a falsetto. "In front o' dey friends, Missus Margaret say, 'Chile, you know dat cute little negress in the tasteful uniform over dere was trained at Tiffany.' Den Missus Harriet say, 'Oh, isn't she marvelous! And she so clever and moves wid sich grace.'"

Bianca doubled over laughing at Luke's imitation. Luke laughed and slapped his knee. The horse on the left flinched.

"Who is Missus Harriet?"

"Oh, dat be Gobernor Aiken's wife."

"How is Gobernor Aiken de gobernor when all 'e do is sell de rice his Africans grow?"

"Chile, 'e ain't de gobernor no mo'. He was gobernor back in de middle '40s when oonah was a babe."

"Well, how cum peoples still callin'im 'gobernor?'"

"Ni, I don't know dat but dey do – even atter he served in de Congress o' de New Nited States in de '50s."

* * *

At Jacksonboro, they turned east on the Charleston-Savannah road. Within a mile, they crossed the Pon Pon River. Luke turned to Bianca. She inhaled. Bianca was sure she saw a twinkle in his eye, but was completely unprepared for what came next.

Luke smiled and pushed up the brim of his straw hat, exposing his salt and pepper hair. "Bianca, I think Isaac would be a right nice catch for oonah. And he'll hab a trade too. Oonah know his pa wuz ma frien'. I'm sure, Isaac will make fine man too, jes lak 'e pa. Ni y'all's ages ain't gonna matter much in a few years. Oonah might not do better'n him."

Bianca's jaw dropped. Now she realized that Luke had seen through her attempt to hide her interest in Isaac. She could think of nothing to say and she stared at Luke, unaware that her mouth was open.

* * *

Three horsemen urged their mounts up the steep slope from the ditch beside Bee's Ferry Road. Water dripped from the lips of their horses. Once on the road, the men used their horses to block the way. Bianca cast an apprehensive glance at Luke, who looked unperturbed. One horseman pulled a Colt .44 revolver from his belt. Bianca felt foreboding enveloping her. Luke eased back on the reins and his black duo slowed.

The tall man made the first move. He held up his hand and signaled Luke to stop his rig. His long hair was the color of wheat straw. A curving scar extended from his left ear nearly to his

26

unshaven chin. He and his comrades sat their horses, evenly spaced across the road. They wore butternut colored trousers like many Confederate soldiers, but their shirts were of various colors. Bianca heard her heart thump loudly and rapidly. She glanced again at Luke and was amazed at his apparent calm.

The scar-faced man nudged his horse's sides with the heels of his boots. The large brown animal snorted and moved forward, then danced sideways as Luke brought his team to a stop.

The scar-faced man spoke. "Boy, whar you steal dem fine hosses?"

"G'monin', suh. Dese hosses b'longs to Massa John Tiffany. Dey a lil' skittish, but dey good hosses."

Bianca was relieved when the scar-faced man's eyes betrayed an instant glint of recognition at the mention of the Tiffany name. Still, she fidgeted with her interlaced fingers on her lap.

The leader waved his revolver toward the rear of the buckboard. "Well, you don't say. Mister Tiffany's rig, eh? How do I know you ain't haulin' a couple o' deserters in dem barrels?"

"Oh, no suh. Massa Tiffany won't 'llow nothin' lak dat. We's hauling fish."

"Keep'em covered, boys." The scar-faced man put away his revolver. "Nigger, lemme see yo' pass."

"Yessuh." Luke stood and reached slowly into his pocket, retrieved a pass, and handed it over. The scar-faced man glanced at the upside-down pass and rode to the back of the buckboard and lifted and reclosed the lid on one of the barrels.

"Boy, you seen any deserters 'long yo' way?"

"Oh, no suh."

"Say, dese hosses a lil' skittish, huh? Well, fellows, whata ya say we have a lil' fun for our trouble?"

Bianca pressed her lips together and held her breath.

One horseman grinned and put away his rifle. "Yeah, boss. Good idée." He and his comrade cleared the road as the scar-faced man raised his whip to strike Luke's horses.

"Er, suh. Please, suh, please don't...."

"Shutdap, nigger!"

He brought the whip down hard on the romp of the left horse in Luke's team. The startled animal reared and alarmed its set horse.

Luke yelled to Bianca. "Hold de seat wid one hand in front and de otter in back!"

Laughter from the three Confederate conscript hunters was ringing in her ears as she grabbed the buckboard seat and held on for dear life. Luke's team surged forward, and after three steps was in full gallop. Bianca heard a gunshot behind her. The two horses went even faster. With terror in her eyes, Bianca turned to Luke. "C-c-can you stop them?"

Luke looked over his shoulder. When he saw that they were not being chased, a smug smile crept across his face. Luke held the reins, but with slack. Then, to Bianca's complete surprise, Luke laughed. Bianca said nothing. She knew she could not be heard above the rattle of the buckboard moving so fast over the rutted dirt road. Luke spoke soothingly to his charges. He did not pull back on the reins, but moved them on the horses' backs like a gentle rub. Soon they dropped from a gallop to a canter. When the horses returned to their normal gait, Bianca felt exhausted. Slowly, she released her grip on the seat and relaxed her shoulders.

Bewildered, she asked, "What was so funny?"

"Dem 'script hunters neber know me and dese hosses regular run faster dan most any rig in dese parts." Apparently delighted with himself, Luke laughed again.

Hands akimbo, Bianca drew up her shoulders and smiled. "Oh no not the briar patch!"

They both doubled over laughing loud and long.

Bianca took a deep breath. She fanned herself with one hand. "Well, de whole matter nearly made me faint."

After a pause, she asked, "What about de pass? Dat bad man never gave it back. Is dere goin' to be trouble gettin' into Charleston?"

"Naw. I got me two mo' passes in my pocket. Massa and Mister Foster allus give me three since dis done happen b'fore."

Bianca sat shaking her head.

* * *

It was late morning when they arrived at Bee's Ferry. Luke showed his pass and paid the ferry operator. Standing aboard the ferry, Bianca stared at the river's brown water. It reminded her that she felt grimy from the dust kicked up by the galloping horses. It was a warm day and she had begun to perspire. The road dust clung to her exposed skin – her face and neck. She used her gloved hands to brush at her long-sleeved dress. She wished for some cool river water to dab away the grime.

After the crossing, she turned and found Luke checking the wheels and axles of the buckboard.

"Say, Mister Luke, what ribber is dis?"

"Why, dis be de Ashley. By the by, I need oonah to keep 'e ears open at dat ball."

Bianca's fear returned. "M-m-me? What oonah think I can find out?"

"I don't know 'xactly. But try to stay near de tree main mens. Dat be Gobernor Aiken, Massa Tiffany, and Gen'l Beauregard."

She had no idea how she could do what Luke suggested. "What do I listen fuh?"

"'Member anything dey say 'bout de war."

Bianca smiled at the prospect of conspiring with Luke to spy. "Well, maybe I can do dis. B-b-but, I don't know…. What we do wid what I hear?"

"Dis week, me and Isaac met a cull'rd Yankee sergeant. De sergeant say he know dat famous Missus Harriet Tubman at Port Royal. I figure some way to git word o' what oonah heah to'em."

At the mention of Isaac's name, Bianca blushed. Her fear dissipated and her countenance brightened. Having no need to hear anything further, she blurted, "O'course, I'll listen for oonah and report all I heah."

"Ni dat's mighty fine. You best be careful, though, and not be caught eavesdroppin'."

"Yessuh, Mister Luke."

* * *

Luke detoured through several streets on his way to the Battery at the southern tip of the Charleston peninsula, pointing out along the way the homes, or former homes, of freed blacks of note. The first were the educators, Thomas S. Bonneau and his student, and later a famous educator himself, Daniel A. Payne. Luke spoke with admiration about men he called spiritual leaders, like Morris Brown and Richard Holloway, Jr. He mentioned Jacob Weston as an example of a free man of color who was a successful businessman. He said nothing about what enslaved blacks had to say about these men.

Driving north on Meeting Street from the Battery, they left behind the Friday afternoon hustle and bustle of downtown Charleston. As they approached the Manigault house on the east side of the street, Bianca pointed. "Dat is a beautiful hotel!"

Luke chuckled. "Dat house be de home of de Manigaults."

Bianca looked again at the house and shook her head in disbelief. "Oonah sho'?"

"Sho' 'nough."

As they passed, Bianca turned about in her seat for a better look at the rear of the Manigault house. Luke turned east on John Street and north again on Elizabeth. After a short distance, Luke stopped his rig and pointed out Wragg Square Park on his left and the Aiken mansion ahead on their right. At her first sight of the Aiken's three-story brick double house, Bianca gasped and held her hands, one over the other, against her collarbone. "Oonah mean dis huge house is jes fuh one lil' family – Gobernor Aiken, Missus Harriet, and one daughter?" She marveled at how the house sat high above the ground over a cellar with half windows and large wraparound piazzas on two sides at the first and second levels. The white columns and rail spindles of the piazzas gleamed in the bright sunlight, contrasting with the brick of the house and the greenery of the front garden and trees.

"Yeah. Jes dem three. And, a few years 'fore de war started, dey added another room biggen my house in de back to show off all de stuff dey done brung back from Europe." They sat for a moment comparing the Aiken and Manigault urban mansions, first to the more modest Tiffany townhouse she saw a few minutes earlier and finally to the small cabins built for their families and friends at Tiffany Plantation. Bianca continued shaking her head as they drove past the main entrance of the Aiken house on Elizabeth Street. She thought the Tiffany's big house on the plantation was grand, but the urban homes of the Aikens, Manigaults, and others now caused her to feel bewildered and think, how can dese families become *dat* rich?

Luke turned east on Mary Street and stopped at two tall wooden gates mounted on taller brick columns. He pulled a chain that rang a bell in the livery. The livery building was a part of the outer wall on the Elizabeth Street side of the Aiken's urban plantation where its first level served as quarters for horses and coaches. In the upper level, coachmen and drivers lived in small dormitory rooms facing the garden and courtyard that were accessed by a narrow wooden spiral staircase. On one side of the second level, hay was stored for horses, which was dropped through chutes into feeding troughs below.

The gates opened and they were greeted by a coachman named Charles Jackson. Bianca saw before her a short avenue, brick paved between the kitchen house and the mansion and flanked by five magnificent magnolias with brilliant white blossoms. Brown-red chickens and white hens scratched about and pecked in the dirt of the courtyard. Between the magnolias and the Elizabeth Street wall stood two cows eating hay in a small brick shed. On the opposite wall were a brick chicken coop and a small spice and vegetable garden. Ahead on the left was a two-story masonry kitchen house. The kitchen was on the first level in the end closest to the main house, with a laundry sharing the remaining space. The Aiken's domestic enslaved families occupied the second level, living in one-room apartments, each equipped with a fireplace.

Standing at the livery, Bianca asked, "What are those rooms in the back corners of the wall?"

Charles and Luke laughed. Charles pointed to one. "Guess oonah neber seed a brick outhouse b'fore. Dat un be fuh men. De otter fuh 'oman."

Bianca flushed, though neither man could see. "Is there one for de Aikens?"

Both men guffawed. When Charles recovered enough to speak, he explained. "No, gal. De Massa's family use chamber pots set inside fine m'hogany chairs dat hab a hole in de seat jes lak de outhouse."

"Oh."

* * *

Washed and refreshed on Friday morning, Bianca stood beside a long preparation table in the kitchen wearing a crisply starched servant's dress. The cook was telling Bianca what she needed her to do as the stand-in chop chef when Ann, the head maid, entered from the courtyard in a huff. Bianca and the cook stopped talking and waited while Ann took a couple of deep breaths, her breasts heaving. The scowl on Ann's middle-aged face made Bianca feel apprehensive. With her arms firmly folded, the older woman looked Bianca up and down as she had done when they first met.

Ann let her hands slip akimbo. Bianca felt Ann's piercing eyes as she commanded, "Hold your arms up and turn about – slowly."

Bianca hesitated, but did as she was told. To prevent Ann from seeing her hands tremble, Bianca squeezed her extended fingers together until no light shone between them. With her back to Ann, Bianca became aware that her forehead and buttocks felt warm, accompanied by a new flutter in her stomach. When she faced Ann's stare again, she wished she could change her figure to fill a dress as wide as Ann's.

Ann turned to the cook. "Well, there goes your chop chef. Missus wants to show off our new little 'miss gal' serving at the ball tomorrow night. What me and you decided don't mean a thing."

The cook shrugged and ambled toward the red brick and iron range built into the chimney at the corner of the kitchen. "Nothing we ever call ourselves 'cidin' never did, or ever will, matter. You know dat." She cast a look over her shoulder at Ann. "Futhermo', dis chile ain't name no 'miss gal.' I'ma call her Bianca, lak I s'pose her ma does."

Bianca turned toward the cook, but kept her place. She had the urge to run and hug the short plump cook. At once, the flutter in her stomach was gone. She took a deep breath. Bianca watched Ann drop her head and tap her foot several times. Ann gave a sigh and returned her hands akimbo. "All right, *Miss* Bianca. Let's git you ready. Before we go look the house over, here are a few rules you mus' neber violate in the Aiken household."

Bianca let her hands fall to the front of her dress and locked her fingers together. "Yessum."

"First, make yo' self invisible. Be there, but neber so much that Massa, his family, or his guests notice you're there. Be jes lak dem plants in dere."

"Yessum."

"Next, neber met the eyes of the men – especially the younguns. And, for Gawd's sake, if something drops, don't bend over; crouch down to pick it up, swayin' yo' knees to one side."

Bianca flushed and felt like a steak – medium rare. "Yessum."

Ann did not pause. "When dey see a body like your'n, some o'dem will drap somethin' jes to see you bend over and give'em a better look at yo' tits. And who knows whether dey might act later on notions dey take up while dey looking at yo' butt."

Bianca felt much warmer. She squirmed and put one foot on the other. She saw the cook cast a look, covered by a furrowed brow, at Ann. But Ann ignored the cook and continued her instructions.

* * *

From her position in the first parlor by the door to the piazza, Bianca watched guests arriving at the top of the marble stairs from the grand entrance on the Elizabeth Street side of the house. The butler announced the arrival of each guest. Every family name Luke had mentioned during their tour of the city and more were announced, some several times, including Alston, Ball, DeSaussure, Drayton, Grimball, Heyward, Huger, Jenkins, Laurens, Manigault, Middleton, Pringle, Ravenel, Rutledge, Tiffany, and Vanderhorst. There was a stir among the guests when applause erupted upon the arrival of General Pierre Gustave Toutant Beauregard, the hero of the

Battle of Bull Run, who had, five weeks prior, successfully defeated a Union attempt to capture Charleston.

Bianca was surprised by the youthful appearance of General Beauregard, splendid in a perfectly tailored gray tunic festooned with eighteen brass buttons arranged in two columns and a high priest-like collar bearing the stars of his rank. She smiled as she thought, *it won't be difficult to find him again.*

* * *

On a signal from Henrietta, the Aikens' daughter, the orchestra struck Robert Alexander Schumann's Piano Quintet in E flat major. A hush fell in the first parlor and all eyes followed Henrietta to the stairs from the living quarters on the third floor. Slowly descending the stair was her mother, Harriet. The assembled guests gasped, then applauded. Harriet wore a serene smile as she fairly floated from the stairs into the parlor. Diamonds on the front of her blue brocade gown were attached to silver threads woven into its fabric. Harriet's dress left her shoulders bare and was form-fitting down to her knees, so that it flattered her almost perfect figure. Below her knees were black mesh-covered slits on each side and a pleated train that trailed behind her. Light from twenty-four candles in the ornate candelabra suspended from the sixteen-foot ceiling was reflected in all directions by Harriet's diamonds. Gilded floor-to-ceiling mirrors flanking the ten-foot wide passage between the double parlors accented the effect by multiplying the light. Dark-haired Heart, as close relatives and friends called Harriet, moved through the adoring throng like a queen.

Bianca watched Heart's triumphant entry in silent awe from her perch beside a plant on the front wall almost as tall as she. "Dese folk are richer dan I thought. How dey git so much when most peoples haves so lil'?"

* * *

Circling the main party areas thrice meant Bianca served and looked after drinks of guests in the two large adjoining parlors, the first-level piazza, dining room, and library. The dining room table had been extended to a length of more than twenty feet and covered with white linen. For the two hundred twenty guests, the table bore five hams, six turkeys, thirty ducks, grilled catfish, twelve quarts of shrimp, trays of deviled eggs, piles of fruit, bonbons, pies, and numerous cakes. There was no chicken in sight.

Bianca passed young women in long colorful dresses gossiping about the goings-on at the French School for Young Ladies while they stayed in range of hearing range of the young men in gray officers' uniforms. The older women were talking about their daughters and how bright their favorite maids and butlers were. They also discussed their membership status in the exclusive St. Cecilia Society for the benefit of anyone within earshot. The young men talked of war, the execution of a deserter by firing squad earlier in the week at Washington Race Course, and whispered about which pretty young thing would make a good lay.

On her third pass, Bianca saw that the same older men were still talking to Governor Aiken in the dining room. She supposed Luke would want to know what was said since the group included General Beauregard, John Tiffany, and Charles Manigault. She noted their drinks and the level in each glass and restocked her serving tray accordingly with identical glasses. She stood between the men and the silver service in the front corner of the room. Her chance to demonstrate why she should serve in this space came when Governor Aiken's cigar ashes were ripe to fall. She grabbed a small bowl. Bianca crouched down and darted forth. An instant later, she was by his side holding the bowl under his cigar. He appeared momentarily startled, then smiled through his white beard, dusted his cigar, and continued talking. Bianca listened to the men gathered around the governor as she discreetly swapped glass after glass for a fresh one half-full.

General Beauregard raised his chin and took a long drag on his cigar. "Governor, I still believe pragmatic minds in Ohio could be persuaded to come to our side."

Governor Aiken looked pensive and pulled at his long beard.

Charles Manigault raised his glass toward General Beauregard. "Gen'l, pragmatism has its place. But, for your plan to work, it seems to me we need people in power in Ohio who are the opposite of the likes of Salmon Chase and that fella, Dennison, who replaced him."

Bianca almost lost her concentration on making herself inconspicuous when she heard John Tiffany's voice. "William, weren't you and Chase in Congress at the same time?"

Governor Aiken released his beard. "Yes, John. I knew Salmon Chase quite well before he became governor. He and his lovely bride attended several of our socials in Washington. And further, my assessment is that it would take strong political action in favor of the Confederacy to get Ohio to secede. I agree with Charles. You know, of course, Chase and Dennison are now in Lincoln's cabinet. Both are vehement abolitionists. This current governor up there is less so against our cause, but, mark my words, David Tod is no friend of the Confederacy."

Tiffany stirred his drink with a finger. "Gen'l, I suppose you have the same strategy in mind for bringing Indiana and Missouri to our side. Is that right?"

General Beauregard cleared his throat. "The plan would be essentially the same. But, remember, successful military action can make changes in today's political reality. Again, we will need to convince President Davis to, first, strengthen our western army. Second, we can then force Grant to reduce his forces surrounding Vicksburg to counter our moves into western Tennessee. Third, we destroy Grant's army and hold the Mississippi River. That success practically closes Union trade on the Ohio and Missouri Rivers; plus, it re-opens Texas and Arkansas for us. Then, and only then, are we prepared to persuade these states to come to our side."

Governor Aiken slowly shook his head, like he was in deep thought. "And where do we get the tens of thousands of soldiers needed to create a western army large enough to draw or drive Grant away from Vicksburg?"

"We must convince Davis to take them from the Army of the Potomac."

With a look of disdain on his face, Manigault raised both hands, almost spilling his drink. Bianca started to move, but Manigault turned a palm toward her. "Who do you think can convince Davis to *take* troops from Lee? Forget the political pragmatism that would follow your suggested military action. Let me tell you, no soldiers, then, no large western army. Therefore, there will be no defeat of Grant. We're back to where we started. Ohio and the rest remain in the Union."

The debate went on for almost another hour with no resolution. Dancing began. The group broke up when Margret Tiffany appeared and put a hand on John's arm. John patted her gloved hand. "My dear, may I have this dance?"

Bianca was sad. She believed General Beauregard could carry out his plan. After all, he had dealt the Union significant defeats over the past two years. If the Confederacy could force the Union to give up the fight....

Her thought was interrupted by a bright flash of blue-white light followed immediately by crashing thunder. Her mood turned as dark as the weather. Heavy rain fell for the rest of the night.

Chapter 3: Rachel

"Gal, I don't wanna hear no mo' 'bout no damned snakes. You let the monkey git one o' these plow hands and I'll tan yore hide. Now you git on down to that spring and fetch some water up here by the time I git back from the house or else!" Griffin Bender was shaking the rolled whip in his hand at Rachel as he sat his horse in the freshly plowed field.

Rachel moved her eyes from her toes to Bender's toes. "Yessuh."

She loaded her yoke onto her shoulders with a wooden bucket dangling from each end. Rachel hurried over the uneven ground with her buckets swinging to and fro. Her braids hanging beneath her bonnet bounced on her shoulders. She knew Bender would make good on his promise to beat her – or have Wash do it. Rachel had disliked Bender the first time she saw him at the auction the year before. She disliked him even more today. Bender had been mustered out of the Confederate army because he was too old. He and his valet, Wash, were passing through Raleigh, the county seat of Smith County, Mississippi, when Bender stopped and bought Rachel, her sister, Rebecca, her father, John, Miss Mabel, a mule, and a wagon. Bender had John drive his daughters and Miss Mabel in the wagon and follow him east to his plantation, just west of Montrose in Jasper County.

The five-foot one–hundred-pound Rachel struggled. Her shoulders ached from carrying the yoke and buckets of water all day. Rachel imagined painting scenes to avoid the boredom of her mindless work. Her imaginary paintings made her dark brown face smile and her dimples show. Some of the paintings in her mind were detailed enough to show the vivid textures and patterns of the bark on trees.

Approaching the spring, Rachel was startled by the call of a bobwhite. The bird was under a plum bush between the big cottonwood trees that stood about ten paces from the creek. Somewhere in the distance, more softly, another bobwhite called. One by one, Rachel released the two buckets from her yoke and gently set them on the ground, hoping not to disturb the bird. She had never been so close to a bobwhite. She wanted to hear it make its call again while she was nearby. She took a deep breath as she let her wooden yoke slide from her shoulders to the ground without a sound. Rachel surveyed the spring and the clear water flowing from it at the head of the small nameless creek. The timber rattlesnake she saw more than an hour ago on her last visit to the spring was nowhere to be found. She was afraid the viper would bite her bare feet. The bobwhite under the plum bush called again. Except for the call of the bobwhites, chirping of wrens, and the sound of water spilling over the stones surrounding the spring, all was quiet.

Rachel glanced up toward the big house; no one was stirring – especially Bender. She decided to take a minute and enjoy a look at the bright green leaves on the thin line of cottonwood and poplar trees that were left along both banks of the creek when the fields of the six-hundred acre Bender Plantation were cleared for crops. It was late afternoon and the midday breeze had stopped. The small puffy white clouds overhead hung motionless in the bright blue sky. Leaves on the trees around her were not yet full size and their youthful green was her favorite color. She picked a black-eyed susan and stuck it in her bonnet. Her brown eyes followed the tree line to the west, toward Otak Creek. She thought of Otak Creek as a river and always wondered why it was called a creek.

From where Rachel stood, the furrows curved around the rolling hills where her father was plowing. At her vantage point, John and his two-mule team were walking on the horizon. The land sloped gently down toward Otak Creek, which was beyond a marsh – hidden behind a grove of trees. High over the marsh, a lone vulture tipped its wings and made a wide, graceful turn toward her. She thought this would be a great scene to capture on canvas if she could paint as well as Isabelle Taylor painted. She would have to remember the scent of freshly plowed soil and the sound of the birds that went with the scene.

Only Rebecca and John knew Rachel's secret, one that had to be kept as long as they labored at the Bender Plantation. It was illegal for enslaved people to be taught to read and write in Mississippi. In their youth, Isabelle Taylor and Rachel had broken that taboo when the two little girls played school together in the shade of a sprawling oak in front of the big house. The consummate teacher, young Isabelle had also let Rachel use her art supplies in their outdoor school.

Budding wildflowers and singing birds reminded Rachel of springs past when, as a little girl, she would follow her mother to the fields. She recalled that her mother never seemed to tire of answering her questions about the names of wildflowers, grasses, herbs, and trees they passed.

"Ma, where are you?" Rachel asked aloud and began dipping water from the spring with a green and yellow gourd to fill her buckets. She had asked the same question hundreds of times since the spring of '58. Now, five years later at age sixteen, she could still clearly picture the Taylor Plantation in Smith County on the Leaf River Valley where she last saw Edna, her mother.

* * *

In 1858, the planting of cotton seeds at Taylor Plantation had begun in April on the first day the sign was in the foot. That was the day the speculator came to the Taylor Plantation. He had arrived with a ragtag shuffle of slaves chained together by the neck – three women, seven men, and two boys about Rachel's age at the time. The men's hands were chained, but the hands of the women and boys were not. They all wore a crude iron collar with two loops, one in front and one in back, for the purpose of attaching the chains of two other slaves. A chain about four feet long connected each person's collar to the next person. The first woman in the shuffle walked behind the speculator's wagon. Everyone else followed in a line behind her.

The speculator, Bernard Moss, was a burly man, almost six feet tall. His blond and gray hair stuck out from under his derby. Every day, he wore a black suit with his pant legs tucked in the top of his black boots, and carried a pipe that always hung from the right corner of his mouth – sometimes lit, most times not. Rachel thought Moss looked like the Taylors' undertaker.

Moss had his charges set up camp under the white oak trees next to the plantation cemetery. The camp was little more than a place to have a fire at night and morning to cook the three small chunks of salty bacon and half-dozen sweet potatoes he gave them from a locked box in the wagon twice a day. This was divided among twelve people. They slept close together in a circle of uncovered bodies around the fire each night trying to keep warm against the chill of the April night air. Moss slept in the Taylor's guest cottage.

On the Saturday afternoon Moss and his shuffle arrived, Rachel was cutting chunks of lye soap, made the previous fall, into bars on an old weather-beaten table in the yard just outside the back window of their cabin, when she overheard Miss Mabel through the window. The shutters on the glassless window were open to let in light and fresh air. Miss Mabel, who worked in the kitchen at the big house, told her mother, "Since old Marster Taylor passed on, the bank done sent mail askin' Missus Lillian to pay up their debts. I heard her myself say to lil' Miss Isabelle that young Marster George sent that speculator, Mister Moss, here."

Rachel's mother asked, "Do you 'spects Missus Lillian might auctions off some of us?"

Miss Mabel took a deep breath and let go with a long sigh before she said, "Edna, I's mighty 'fraid that's zackly what gone happen."

Edna gasped. When Rachel heard her mother gasp, she suddenly felt a cold shiver, though it was a warm spring day. Edna lowered her voice to a loud whisper, "Lawd, Mabel, you don't mean to tell me, I could lose my John or my babies?"

"Could be me, or you, or anybody. That young Marster George is pushin' Missus Lillian, tellin' her and Miss Isabelle that sellin' some of us is the only way to keep the place."

Rachel could not bear to hear more. She ran to the spot she always went when she was troubled. Rachel could not discuss this new trouble with her mother. Edna would want to know why she was eavesdropping on grownups' talk. Rachel sat at the base of her favorite tree, a giant walnut with limbs as large as a good size tree. The huge lower branches reminded her of massive arms, arms she imagined that could sweep her up and protect her. Here, Rachel sat as

41

the afternoon shadows turned slowly into dusk, pondering the incomprehensible thought of being sold and separated from everyone on the plantation where she had lived all her life. She started for home thinking, Missus Lillian just can't sell anyone away. It just wouldn't be right. How could any of us get along widout each other?

It was first dark on that Saturday, the third day of Moss's visit, with just barely any light of day left, when Rachel met Miss Lucille and the people she was chained with at the cemetery campsite. On Rachel's way home from her walnut tree retreat, she decided to stop and visit the people in the shuffle. While Miss Lucille was eating her small piece of bacon and half a sweet potato, she answered Rachel's questions about where they came from and where they were going. No one else said anything to Rachel. They kept their eyes cast downward.

Lucille said, "Mister Moss bought me from my marster over in Columbus. He bought others of us here and there along the way from Columbus. He sold a passel of us near Philadelphia. There was jes five of us left when he finished up selling back in Philadelphia. Now he's buying up more to take with us to Natchez and on to New Orleans."

Rachel had heard enough. She ran home to the cabin she shared with her older sister, Rebecca, her mother, and her father, John. "Mama, did you see those poor people out by the graveyard? They walked here from far away, being bought and sold all along the way. And they ain't got hardly nothing to eat!" Rachel was still panting from running to report what she had observed at the cemetery campsite. "Can we give 'em some of our food?"

"Rai, is you done loss yo' mind? We can't give away no food. We ain't hardly got enough to feed ourselves," Rebecca snapped before her mother could respond.

Rachel felt the warmth in her mother's smile as Edna extended her arms to embrace her. Rachel did not want to say what she was really worried about – a family member being sold. She could not speak the unthinkable. Rachel ran the three steps between them and into Edna's outstretched arms. Edna held two wooden spoons in one hand and, in her other hand, a rag to grab a hot iron skillet from the fireplace. Rachel felt the knuckles of Edna's fingers gently stroking the back of her head.

"Rai, honey, we don't have enough for us and them. I wish we did. I sho' do."

"Mama, isn't there something we can do to help them?"

"Child, you sho' 'nough got your heart in the right place," Edna told her daughter in a soft voice.

"They already look weak and puny from walkin' here from who knows where and on nothin' much to eat," said Rachel.

Rebecca demanded, "Rai, gal, can't you hear? We ain't got no food for them. You already knows Griffin Bender only gives us barely 'nough every Saturday to last us 'til the next Saturday."

Rachel let her arms fall from Edna's waist. She turned to her sister, and, with hands akimbo, said, "I ain't talking to you."
Edna used the wooden spoons to turn the bacon in the skillet while she said, "Now, now, girls."

"Mama, can we give'm one piece of cornbread each day? If we...."

Rebecca cut her off. "What good is one piece of cornbread going to do? Which *one* of'em you gonna give it to?"

"Hush! Let me finish. Mama, do you think your friends, Miss Eva and Miss Mabel, could help?"

Edna put one hand to her chin and thought about Rachel's question. "Rai, that's a good idea. I'll ask Eva, Mabel, and each neighbor for a piece. If each house can give one piece.... Let's get our supper et. Call your pa."

"Thank you, Mama." Rachel hugged her mother. "I'll find Pa." As she ran for the door, Rachel made a face and stuck her tongue out at Rebecca. Rebecca stared back at her little sister with a look of disbelief.

After supper, Rachel and Rebecca gathered pieces of cornbread from their neighbors in a small hand woven basket and slipped into the camp of the speculator to feed his captives. Though they had already eaten their bacon and potatoes, they grabbed the pieces of fried cornbread offered by the sisters. Lucille urged all to eat quickly, lest the speculator discover they had been given more food and cut their meager rations. Lucille and everyone in the shuffle said their thanks and watched as Rebecca led Rachel into the shadows and back toward the cabins.

When they were almost home, Rachel asked, "Ain't that Missus Lillian and that mean ol' Les Nelson in front of our cabin with Mama and Pa?"

Rachel hated Les for the time he beat her pa and made everybody watch. Les was hired as overseer when young George Taylor II went off to school at West Point. When George's father fell ill and they had an overseer who could not read or write, it became Rachel's task to record tools and supplies purchased and crops and livestock sold. Old man George would not allow Missus Lillian or Miss Isabelle into the fields and barns. George Taylor believed a gentleman planter's wife and daughter should live a life of leisure. He turned to Rachel when Isabelle revealed that she had played school and taught Rachel to read and figure. When his anger with Isabelle passed, Old Man Taylor had put Rachel to work with Les. Though Rachel disliked being with Les, even for an hour a day, they worked together each evening before supper to make the appropriate entries in a small journal as Marster George instructed. She returned the diary to Marster George each evening at the big house where he was spending more and more time in bed.

"It sho' is. At this time of night and it Sadday too. It can't mean anything good."

As they walked closer, they heard Edna say to Missus Lillian, "My girls are coming. Please don't mention anything to them. I will do it myself." Edna's voice sounded low and sad. Rachel saw that John had one arm around Edna's shoulders. It was not like their pa to hug Edna when the neighbors or the Taylors were around. Rachel and Rebecca exchanged glances.

* * *

Sunday morning was bright and sunny. Rachel had cried all night and the beautiful day did not lift her spirit. She sat on the rough wood floor of their cabin in front of Rebecca and watched their mother carefully fold two dresses and place them in a cloth sack that had a shoulder cord attached to each end. Rebecca hugged Rachel and stared out the window into the brilliant sunlight. The only sounds in the cabin were Rachel's sobs and sniffing noises from John and Rebecca. Rachel watched as Edna prepared for a journey with no return.

The night before, John had called Rachel and Rebecca to come and sit with him and their ma. Rachel sensed a new tone of foreboding and despair. By the dim light from the small candle in the center of the cabin, they could see that Edna had been crying. Rachel and Rebecca held hands as they sat close together waiting for John to speak. He stood beside Edna and held her hand with his head completely bowed.

When he spoke, all he said was, "Lawd, give us strength."

Rachel knew for certain at that moment, that Edna had been sold. But she was unable to put words around her feelings, much less speak the awful truth. Slowly, her throat constricted and her palms became sweaty.

Edna moved from John and knelt in front of Rachel and Rebecca and put an arm around each of them. Rachel could feel the warmth of her mother's familiar hug, but she sensed cold along her spine and felt the muscles across her stomach tighten.

With her voice cracking, Edna whispered, "Missus Lillian done sold me to that speculator."

Rachel and Rebecca screamed. "No!" They sprang from their seats to their knees and held on to Edna as if they wanted to merge with her spirit.

Rachel denied what she knew to be true. She cried, "No, Mama, no! You must be mistaken."

Edna tried to answer and console her daughters, but Rachel could not hear her. Both continued to scream and shout, "No!" They held on tighter.

John came over, knelt with them, and put his arms around all of them. Rachel wished his strong arms could change things, and that his great physical strength could keep her mother in the cabin and on Taylor Plantation. But since she had seen Les beat him so badly last year that he was in bed for four days before he could walk again, she knew he could not change anything. Rachel felt the searing pain of knowing her mother was leaving and the utter helplessness of not being able to help her. She felt deeper despair realizing John could do no more than she or Rebecca could.

Anger and sorrow swept over Rachel in waves. Her head felt as if it would burst. The pain was especially intense at her temples, just before her ears. When there were no more tears, she still cried and screamed. Suddenly, she wiggled free of the embrace of her family and tried to run to the open window. She fell and vomited on the floor and on her dress before she could take three steps. Rachel lay there panting and making a strange sound that resembled a frog's croak. She felt her stomach churn again and tried to crawl to the window. This time she made it before the bitter yellow bile passed through her mouth and nose. Though the sound seemed far away, she could hear Edna calling, "My baby! My baby!"

* * *

The cool wet cloth on her head made Rachel sit up with a start. Miss Mabel put a gentle hand on her back to support her. Rachel was embarrassed at first, but when she looked down; she discovered she was on her pallet and wearing a clean dress that was not hers. She heard Miss Eva singing softly beside her mother's pallet.

Miss Eva's singing was interrupted by Edna, "Rai, baby, you feelin' better? Are you all right?"

Rachel wanted to reply, "Yes." She thought this would make her mother less concerned. Instead new tears rolled down her cheeks and she said, "I ain't ever gone be all right again." Now Edna and Rebecca began crying again. By the light of one tiny candle on the table where they ate their meals, Rachel saw John sitting on the floor, his shoulders slumped, staring out the door into the dark night. Miss Eva and Rebecca were massaging Edna's shoulders and arms. Miss Mabel and Miss Eva stayed with them until the first light of dawn. Miss Mabel had to leave and start breakfast at the big house. She heard Miss Eva say more than once, "Lawd, I'm so glad dis is not a field day."

An hour after dawn, Les called out, "Edna, you come on out here, gal. Don't you keep Mister Moss waiting. You hear me?"

"Yessuh."

Edna turned to John and her daughters and said, "Ya'll stay inside. I'll say my good-byes here and be on my way. I don't want y'all to 'member me all chained up."

Edna put the cord and cloth sack containing her two dresses over her left arm, then over her head and let it rest on her right shoulder. She adjusted it so the sack hung on her left hip, just below her waist. With silent tears streaming down her face, Edna hugged and kissed each of them.

Edna dried her tears on her sleeves. In a shaky, but clear voice, she said, "Bec, you and Rai do your best and look after your pa. See that he gets his rest and that he eats right. You look after yourselves and grow up to be good women. Life done dealt us a mighty heavy blow here today. But be strong and pray every day. We gits through this...." Edna's voice trailed off. She cried no more, turned, and walked out the door and across the bare dirt of the front yard of their cabin that Rachel had swept the day before.

Rachel thought Edna meant to say, "We gits through this together." Her reaction was to sob louder. Her breathing now came in spastic gulps. Her chest heaved with each breath and her tears and mucus wet the top of her dress. She watched Edna walk out the door and into the sunlight. Rachel's legs felt weak and she sank to her knees. When she could no longer see Edna through the doorway, her crying and wailing grew even louder.

Before John or Rebecca could move to catch her, Rachel struggled to her feet and summoned the strength to bounce out the door calling, "Mama! Mama!" None of them had slept or had any breakfast. Rachel ran and stumbled along the path toward the cemetery as fast as her legs could carry her. Through her tears, she couldn't see the cemetery very clearly, but realized Moss's wagon was not there. Her panic grew as she glanced about. She was determined to see her mother one more time. From the corner of her eye, she noticed the wagon moving toward the big house. She held the front of her ankle-length dress up to her knees and ran in that direction. With a burst of energy,, she felt a bit stronger and was able to run faster.

The shuffle was chained and walking behind Moss's wagon. With her blurred vision, Rachel could not see her mother's face but did recognize her dress and the bandanna she wore over her hair. She noticed that the shuffle was larger by several men and women the speculator had purchased at Taylor Plantation. Rachel ran on as fast as her legs could carry her toward her mother. John and Rebecca were still in pursuit. From the front of the big house, Miss Mabel, Les Nelson, and Isabelle Taylor were calling out to Rachel. Even if she had heard them, she would not have stopped running. By now, the wagon had turned onto the avenue in front of the big house and was headed for the main road.

Rachel decided to run through the garden of the big house and intercept the wagon and shuffle. She was leaping over the last rows of freshly planted turnips when she tripped and fell face first into the brown dirt, landing on her nose, mouth, and chest with a thud. Rachel screamed in agony. She ignored her pain, rolled over, and struggled to get to her feet, spitting grit and trying to catch her breath. Dirt clung to her face and the wet top of her dress. With her right foot, she stepped on the hem of her dress. It ripped at the waist and Rachel fell again. She crawled into the grass at the edge of the garden. With her braids and face already covered with dirt and blood dripping from her nose and bruised lips, she sank flat on her face again. She felt weak now, her hands and legs trembled, but still she tried to rise. Rachel raised her head slowly and looked again toward the shuffle. She could no longer make out individuals. The people in the shuffle appeared to be one mass of moving colors. Everything in her sight was spinning to the left and down. She was dizzy and nauseous. John and Rebecca caught up with , but she could barely hear them calling her name. The sound of their voices grew weaker and the bright sunlight grew dimmer as Rachel fainted and lay motionless at the side of the garden.

* * *

Jerome called out to Rachel's father. It was Jerome's voice that brought Rachel back from her memories of '58. She was on her knees, filling her second bucket with water from the spring. Jerome was carrying a set of leather traces in one hand and walking briskly over the newly plowed rows while looking back over his shoulder toward the big house.

The lengthening afternoon shadows were not long enough for Rachel. She judged that soon Griffin Bender would again ride his horse out to where the plowing was being done. That would give him time before dusk to inspect the progress made today and make plans for Saturday morning's work assignments. She knew she had to hurry with the water. Bender acted as overseer because most of the able-bodied white men in Jasper County were away serving in the Confederate army. By the time he would finish his inspection, it would be first dark and Rachel and all the hands could start for the barn with the mules and their tools.

It was only the last Friday in April 1863, but it felt more like mid-June to Rachel. She stood, pushed her bonnet back, and wiped her brow on the long sleeve of her dress. When she turned her back to the sun and hooked a heavy bucket of water onto each side of her yoke, Jerome had almost reached her father. Rachel could not remember seeing Jerome bring traces to the field before. Rachel bent her knees and placed the yoke across her shoulders. She stood again and the two buckets lifted smoothly from the ground without sloshing.

No matter what Jerome was doing, Rachel stopped paying attention to him and listened to the birds for any change in their singing while she glanced about for some snake that might be passing by. She stepped from the line of cottonwoods and poplars and onto the freshly plowed cotton field. The dirt was damp from yesterday's rain and felt pleasant and cool to her bare feet. She stepped from row to row with rhythm and a slight dip in her step to avoid spilling water from the buckets. Spilling water meant she would have to make more trips to the spring for the thirsty plow crews and other field hands. The drinking gourd hung from her yoke near her right shoulder. It swung back and forth in time with her steps as she made her way toward the crew.

Jerome was pretending to examine the traces on John's mules. But, clearly, he was there to tell John some hot news. Rachel was still twenty paces away when she heard John repeat the word, "Yankees."

Chapter 4: **Bianca and Isaac**

"Yoo, hoo. Mister Luke, I need help." Bianca called out from the community garden across the street from the livery.

It was Saturday morning, a week since the big ball hosted by the Aikens in Charleston. After her return to Tiffany Plantation on Monday, Bianca had spent much of her time scheming and planning how to be alone with Isaac. Because Isaac had not responded or given her any sign since she had spoken to him the night of his father's funeral, Bianca was apprehensive.

Luke crossed the street and found that Bianca had gathered four baskets of mustard greens for the kitchen at the big house. "G'mornin', Miss Bianca. Looks like oonah got 'e self a load here."

"Yessuh. G'mornin'. I need to get'em to the kitchen house 'fore the sun wilts 'em. I think I picked 'nough greens for the Fosters and the chillum's house dinner on Monday. Please help me carry dem in one trip." Without looking back, she lifted two baskets and set out. Walking slowly, she rehearsed again what she would say to Luke when he caught up.

"Okay. I'll bring dese two baskets for oonah. Maybe next time, don't pick so much when de sun so hot lak t'day. If oonah need mo', come back."

"Yessuh. Next time, I do lak oonah say." Bianca's throat began to constrict and her voice tightened. She cleared her throat in an effort to overcome her tremor. "Mister Luke, will oonah give a message to Isaac fuh me, please, suh?" She hurried on before Luke could answer. "Oonah know I can't write, and I 'spects Isaac can't read. So I can't send a note. I will trust oonah wid my secret. I respects you – a settled family man. I can't think of a woman to ask for help without makin' myself into juicy gossip. You already know I have 'onorable intentions toward Isaac. But he so young, and I don't wanna scare'im and make 'im run from me. So, oonah see why I need help? Jes to carry dis one message, please, suh?"

* * *

At first dark, Bianca poured hot water on the yellow jasmine blossoms she had tossed into the bottom of her wooden laundry tub. She had gathered the fragrant vine flower from the edge of the woods and also used the plants to decorate her cabin. She emerged from her bath humming bars from Robert Schumann's Piano Quintet in Concert in E flat major and donned her one Sunday go-to-meeting dress. She paused and admired the off-white hand-embroidered lace sewn around the collar and cuffs of the ankle-length white dress. Bianca tilted her head as she remembered the first day she wore it her mother told her, "Oonah de purttiest gal in Colleton Districk." For the first time since the loss of Andrew, Bianca felt beautiful.

Curfew sounded at ten. Bianca opened a shutter on her front window and looked about. The street was quiet. She saw no one. The only movement she saw was that of broken clouds and two calico cats.

Bianca's palms became sweaty and she began to pace. She tried to sing, but stopped when she realized she could not think of a song that fit her mood. Lost in thought, she absently twirled a braid of her hair between the fingers of her left hand. If Isaac received her message, he should arrive at any minute. What if Luke told Isaac after midnight instead of after curfew? What if the Fosters caught Isaac out after curfew? What if I cause him to be flogged? What if he decided to stay away?

With that, Bianca dropped wearily onto a chair and held her chin cupped with both hands, elbows on her knees. In a minute, she was standing again and determined to keep her spirits up. Bianca carved several shavings off a sassafras root and made tea. When she had taken one sip, there were three taps on a rear window shutter. She smiled; delighted that Luke had delivered her message down to the last detail. Bianca swallowed tea into her windpipe. She had a coughing spasm on her way to extinguish her one candle and open the shutter.

Isaac deftly climbed through the window and whispered, "Here I is."

Bianca coughed again while securing the shutter. "Let me light a candle and see who oonah is." She tried to laugh, but coughed again and again.

Isaac laughed. Then they laughed together and their laughter broke the tension.

With the candle relit from her fireplace, Bianca turned and reached for Isaac's hand. "Welcome to my home. I'm so glad oonah here." She coughed and pulled him toward a chair. She felt his sweaty palm tremble.

"Bianca, I'm happy to call on you. Thanks for invitin' me." Isaac stopped speaking for a moment and cast his eyes down. When he looked up again, his smile was gone. "Bianca. Bianca, yo' name is reel purtty – like music. Please forgive me if I say the wrong thing. I don't know much 'bout callin' on a 'oman."

Bianca thought that he looked ready to bolt. She saw fear in his searching eyes and. She smiled. "Thanks. Why, that's the most beautiful ting anyone done eber said 'bout my name." She gave his hand a little squeeze. Isaac's smile showed his teeth.

In a few minutes, they were quietly laughing and talking like old friends. They ate the fried chicken legs and pear preserve biscuits Bianca had prepared at the kitchen house and kept warm in a covered iron skillet at the edge of her fireplace. They drank sassafras tea from tin cups.

Isaac set his cup down and was suddenly quiet. Bianca thought, *am I scaring him?* Isaac formed a pyramid with his fingertips in front of his lips, elbows on his knees. "Bianca, I likes oonah jes fine. But I'ma hafta tell oonah somethin'."

Bianca shuddered and inhaled deeply. She drew her elbows to her sides and thought, *is this it? Is this where he up and leaves?*

"I don't want to tell oonah dis, but I feel bein' as we likes each other, you need to know. I'm sure oonah keep my secret."

Bianca's eyes were wide and she held her breath.

"Bianca, I'ma run t'night."

Bianca exhaled and turned away to blink back the tears welling in her eyes. She thought of General Beauregard's victories over the Yankees and his new plan to split the Union. After the ball, she had told Luke that she believed the Confederacy would win the war. If the Yankees were forced to quit the fight, who knows what would happen to the coloreds who volunteered and joined their ranks. Immediately, Bianca realized that she may never see Isaac again. Then she decided now was not the time to talk of war.

Momentarily, she turned back to Isaac. Again, she thought she saw fear rise in his eyes. She reached out and held one of his hands in both of hers. She caressed the back of his hand, turned it over, and traced the prominent lines in his palm with a fingertip. Neither spoke.

Presently, Isaac broke their silence. He fingered the lace at her cuff for a time and said, "This is almost as purtty as oonah."

Bianca felt beautiful, beamed, and landed a playful slap on Isaac's wrist. "Sweet mout! Sound lak oonah know jes what ta say ta his 'oman."

Upon hearing the words, "his 'oman," Isaac thought, *uh-oh, what do I do nigh?* His heart rate quickened and his body felt warmer. Now, with wide eyes, he was speechless again.

With a playful sideways glance, Bianca continued, "Oonah sho' dis heah yo' fus call?'

They laughed together as she moved from her chair and sat on his lap, one arm around his waist. Slowly, he embraced her. Bianca rested her head on his shoulder. They sat wordless for a time. And then she held his face, kissed his cheeks, and then pecked his lips with hers. Bianca stood, took his hand, and led Isaac across the one-room cabin to her pallet.

Chapter 5: Escape

"Nigger! What the hell is you doin'?"

Isaac's head snapped up from his work on his hands and knees in the dark. He had not heard Jeb Foster approach. He was so engrossed in gathering food and reliving his loss of virginity with Bianca that he forgot to be watchful. Startled, Isaac dropped the sweet potato and the pine straw that came with it from out of the potato hill. He castigated himself for allowing Jeb within a few feet undetected.

Jeb took a step closer and kicked Isaac in the ribs, rolling him over onto his gunnysack. Isaac let out a loud grunt and grabbed his side as he opened his mouth to breathe again. The pain was excruciating and hurt worse with a sharp intake of air. Isaac glanced up at Jeb, who was removing a two-foot-long wooden club from his belt. Jeb's body blocked Isaac's view of the rustler's moon just above the tree line. With the light of a quarter-moon behind Jeb, the white man's face appeared as black as Isaac's.

"Stealin' taters, is you?"

Isaac made no reply. He rolled over and grabbed the hoe lying beside him on the potato hill. Still on his back, Isaac swung the hoe with all his strength at Jeb's legs. The metal head of the iron hoe hit a shinbone. Jeb let out a yelp and fell beside Isaac onto his hands and knees. Isaac dropped the hoe and grabbed his gunnysack, while scrambling to his feet.

"Damn you, nigger. Yo' ass is gonna get it now!"

With no thought of Jeb, Isaac said, "Damn! Only three taters."

Isaac ran, leaning toward his sore left ribs. Still running, he slipped the cloth strap of his gunnysack over his head and right arm. The three yams, cornbread, and bacon in the gunnysack bounced against his right hip, assuring him that he had at least a small amount of food for his journey. He ran toward the winnowing house. When he looked back, Jeb was hobbling along in chase.

Crossing the wagon road to the winnowing house, Isaac glanced toward the banks of the bush-lined canal where he had hidden his canoe. The canal led east to Ashe Creek and into the Pon Pon River.

Instead of heading for the canoe, Isaac ran in the opposite direction. He led Jeb behind the first row of slave cabins. Passing the second cabin, Isaac ducked a clothesline laden with several shirts that someone had washed that evening. Isaac stopped behind the third cabin and grabbed the coarse grass-rope clothesline from the top of the post that held it aloft. This clothesline was empty. He wrapped the rope twice around his right hand, knelt in the shadow of the cabin, and waited. Seconds later, Jeb arrived, running as fast as he could with a sore shin. Isaac leapt from his hiding place when Jeb was one step from the rope. Isaac pulled it tight against the opposite post. The rope caught Jeb just below his Adam's apple. Isaac held the rope taunt and watched Jeb's feet fly forward and up as he landed on his back with a thud. A violent rush of air left Jeb's lungs. He thrashed about on the ground, holding his throat with both hands and gasping, trying to get his breath.

After standing stupefied for a few seconds watching Jeb's agony, Isaac finally had the presence of mind to drop the rope and run. He ducked between two cabins, crossed the sandy street, then ran between more cabins, and passed vegetable gardens teeming with tiny new plants. On the next street, Isaac turned west again and checked over his shoulder for Jeb. He slowed to a trot. He pushed on westward pass the smithy, his place of work with Big Gus. He was passing the carriage garage when a neigh went up from a horse in the stable just ahead. Isaac quickened his pace to a run and darted past the stable and the cattle barn. He looked back over his shoulder and, seeing no sign of Jeb, slowed again to a trot.

It was after midnight when Isaac reached the canal that led to the west rice fields. He was following his escape plan. Getting caught while raiding the sweet potato hill was a major blunder and presented a new challenge to his escape from Tiffany Plantation. He slowly made his way down the bank, thrashing the grass and vines with a stick. He had both bare feet in the water when the bell near the commissary began to toll – Jeb had sounded the alarm. His father, the head overseer, and his brothers would join the hunt.

Mud from the bottom of the canal oozed between Isaac's toes. The mud and water made a squishing sound as he turned and climbed out of the water. He removed his bandana, damp with sweat, and dropped it in the weeds. He ran from the canal to the east, along the same route he had traveled in the opposite direction minutes before. Isaac could hear the hounds in their kennel. The dogs knew what the bell meant. He ran as fast as he could, for by now every man, woman, child, and animal at Tiffany was awake. The pain in his side had lessened. His attention was on getting past the barnyard, stable, and smithy before the Fosters arrived. "The Fosters will run the dogs west," Isaac spoke aloud to himself as he ran and panted. "They must. Dear God, please send them west."

A small cloud hid the moon as he reached the barnyard. Cows and sheep made their noises. The horses were quiet. Isaac's steps were slower and his legs a bit unsteady, but he ran on. His throat felt parched and he was very thirsty. Sweat ran down his face and into his eyes. He drew a sleeve across his brow. Though the moon was hidden by a cloud, Isaac could follow the wagon road that led back past the stable, garage, and smithy. At the smithy, he turned and ran though the yard where he and Big Gus shod horses less than twelve hours before.

A hundred painful yards further, Isaac slowed to a trot. He had passed the point where he entered the wagon road when he ran from Jeb. He walked past more vegetable gardens and could hear the voices of the white men looking for him. He knew that his neighbors were awake and praying that whoever was out after curfew would be able to sneak back into his cabin without being caught. He had hoped no one would miss him until morning – especially his mother.

Isaac shrugged his shoulders, "Well, right now, Ma is worrying and Bianca is praying for me to have better luck."

Excited yelping and barking came from the direction of the cabin where Isaac had ambushed Jeb with the clothesline. The dogs had his scent. Isaac froze. He scarcely breathed, squatted, and waited. He strained to hear the direction the dogs would take. The dogs ran west, between the cabins, and continued west to the smithy. In front of the smithy, the dogs paused, sniffing and milling about in separate circles. Isaac was near the east canal, but still frozen in his tracks. He heard the dogs yelping excitedly.

"I told you he was on the run. He's headed west, toward Snuggedy Swamp. That's the direction all niggers run." It was Jeb.

Jeb's teenage brother wanted to know, "Why are the dogs movin' in circles?"

"Get these damned dogs moving from this smithy. They don't know he works here. We need to catch that nigger before he reaches the Ashepoo." Tom Foster was sounding impatient with the dogs and his sons. Without waiting for the dogs, Tom shifted his shotgun from his left shoulder to his right and started walking again toward Snuggedy Swamp.

Still, Isaac waited. The cloud passed. There was moonlight again. He looked toward the end of the wagon road, where it met the east canal. He hoped he would not need to run the entire distance to reach his canoe. This part of his plan must not be discovered. Yet he did not move.

"Com'on, boys! Get'em over here. Head'em this way." Jeb was talking to his two brothers.

When the dogs started to run again, the barking and yelping were receding. Isaac let out a sigh and sat down heavily in the dirt road. He sat, staring to the west, picturing the dogs leading the Fosters to the west canal. Isaac dragged his gunnysack onto his lap. Through the burlap, he used a hand to assess the size of his three potatoes. Satisfied, he absentmindedly dropped the gunnysack by his side. He looked wistfully at the nearby vegetable garden, wishing something was large enough to harvest. The sound of the barking dogs was fainter.

"Well, I best get goin'. Else, sunup will cotch me 'fore I can get myself to Jehossee." Isaac spoke aloud. He stood, lifting the gunnysack as he did so. He adjusted the gunnysack strap on his left shoulder and bag on his right hip. It was almost one o'clock when Isaac reached the point where the wagon road ended near the winnowing house and where the east canal began. He walked past the flatboats, tied to wharves at the head of the canal. Each flatboat was the size of four horse drawn wagons. Flatboats were used to haul laborers and tools to the rice fields; harvested rice stalks were also transported from the fields in these ungainly boats. When loaded, each flatboat required four men using long poles to control its passage through the narrow canals.

Isaac walked along the dike beside the canal. He could still hear the dogs baying afar off in the west. Minutes later, he started down the canal bank to retrieve his canoe. He looked under the bushes halfway down the bank and could not find the canoe. His eyes widened. Isaac turned and searched under the bushes behind him. Panic started to well up in his chest. He crawled back to the top of the dike, he was sure this was the spot where he and Caleb had concealed his canoe. He walked a few paces back toward the winnowing house. Here, Isaac turned and crawled on all fours, with his gunnysack dragging over the dirt and patches of grass. He was looking for the yellow pine splinter that Caleb had driven into the ground to mark the point where he was to descend from the dike. Within minutes, he found the splinter. The splinter was as they left it – with only the length of the tip of his little finger showing above ground. This was the point where he had descended from the dike a few minutes before. Though he had laughed when Caleb pounded the splinter into the ground with a rock, he was grateful, now in the semidarkness, that he was able to verify that this indeed was the spot where the canoe was concealed.

Isaac pulled the splinter from the ground, broke it into half, and put it in his gunnysack. Then he repeated his search of the bank. He remembered that the canoe would be three feet above the water, secured to the base of a bush. Again, he failed to find it. He started to crawl up the bank. Had the Fosters discovered the canoe? "Arrgh!" The thought caused Isaac to cry out. As was his habit, he wanted to lash out at something for his plight. He struck the ground again and again with his fist. He knew that, without the canoe, his escape plan was useless. The Fosters were searching the west side of the plantation. The east side was bounded by the twelve-hundred- foot wide Pon Pon River and alligators. Jeb Foster had discovered him with a gunnysack and knew he was running. The consequences were too terrible to contemplate.

Tears blurred Isaac's vision. He felt weak. He attempted to stand when he was within two paces of the top of the dike. A mosquito's wings sang in his right ear. He tried to hit the mosquito with a vicious swing, borne of his frustration. Isaac missed the mosquito and slipped on the dew-moistened grass. He fell and slid, feet first, on his back down the bank. Small bushes bruised his arms and face. The branches of the few small bushes he grabbed broke and the last one came out of the ground by its roots. He expected to slide into the canal, but came to rest when his feet hit a log. Isaac cursed, rolled over, and yanked the gunnysack closer to his side. He noticed that his feet were in the water, pressed against a log. When he pushed against the log to stand, it moved.

Isaac blinked away his tears to look at the log. It was not a log – he had found his canoe. Isaac laughed aloud, but quickly covered his mouth. The dirt from his hand stung in the small cuts made on his face by the bushes. Because he was so grateful to see the canoe, the cuts and mosquitoes seemed like minor annoyances. He glanced over his shoulder up the bank and looked back at the water. "Oh, stupid me! The water rose! I measured the hidin' place up from the water level at low tide. I shoulda measured it from the top of the dike. If a jaybird had my brains, it would fly backwards." Isaac laughed again.

His provisions were all in the canoe, just the way he left them the night before. Atop the oilcloth package was another bandana and a piece of rope. Inside the oilcloth were two pieces of rawhide the size of a man's hand, a tinderbox, fish hook, a cotter pin, and line. Underneath this package lay two oars and the machete he had made at the smithy. After checking each item and tossing in his straw hat and gunnysack, Isaac swung himself into the canoe.

The canoe floated away from the bank for the length of its tether to a bush. He used an oar to push it close to the bank, where he reached into the shallow water and retrieved a handful of soft gray-brown mud. He smeared the mud on his hands, wrists, face, and neck. He even dabbed mud on his ears. With his mosquito protection in place, Isaac untied his canoe. After a few strokes, he was in the middle of the canal gliding toward Ashe Creek. As the minutes passed, Isaac began to notice the night sounds. While he was busy trying to outmaneuver the Fosters and their dogs and find his canoe, he had not heard the frogs, insects, and night birds. Now they were a loud chorus, noisier than Isaac could ever remember.

The familiar whistle-like call of a chuck-will's-widow came from the tree line. The pigeon-sized bird made seven calls in as many seconds. Shortly, another chuck-will's-widow answered somewhere in the distance. Isaac smiled at the sound, for the chuck-will's-widow's call was his favorite fall-asleep music. In front of his canoe, a chuck-will's-widow darted left, then dove and flew up and to the right and out of sight. Isaac shook his head, assuming that the bird caught a beetle or a moth with each sudden midair turn.

Presently, another cloud hid the moon. It was pitch dark on the canal, which was surrounded by banks covered with bushes, grass, small cypress trees, and skinny pines. Isaac followed the flat, black, glassy path before him; it served as a guide in the darkness. Without the moon, the canal, sky, and trees became variations in blackness. The sky was black. Clouds were mostly charcoal gray around the cloud hiding the small rustler's moon. That cloud had a thin silver border nearest the point where it first passed between Isaac and the moon. The water was black with odd flickers of silver here and there as the light from the hidden moon and a few stars reflected off the canal's surface. The trees and bushes formed an uneven outline of a black border between the water and the clouds.

After many minutes of the concert presented by the night creatures and the tranquil lighting, Isaac reached the point where the canal widened into a natural inlet. Instinctively, he remained in the center to avoid the mud flats in the corners of the inlet where it met Ashe Creek. He relaxed as he remembered Uncle Jacob's prediction of a high tide at about half past midnight. The inlet formed the headwaters of the canal, dug during the last century by Isaac's great-grandfather and his neighbors. The inlet took him left, right, and left again. Moonlight returned. Ahead lay Ashe Creek. Ripples in its surface glowed ghostly shimmering silver in the moonlight. Isaac lifted his oar to take in the sight. He heard the singing of a mosquito's wings passing his head.

Across the hundred-foot wide Ashe Creek, the west bank of Oakhurst Island loomed as a black border for the silvery water of the creek. Isaac thought about how his mother worked nearly all her life from dawn to dusk in the rice fields on Oakhurst Island. Passing Oakhurst, he sang softly, changing the words of a familiar song as he paddled, making slow, but steady strokes with his oar.

Steal away, steal away,
Steal away to Jesus!
Mama steal away home, to freedom,
Bianca, you ain't got long to stay here.
My Lord calls me;
He calls me....

Isaac rounded the bend in Ashe Creek and stopped singing in midsentence. He heard thrashing. There was enough moonlight for him to see white foam in the water ahead of his canoe, near where Ashe Creek flowed into the Pon Pon River. He recognized the commotion as a sign of alligators feeding. They were along his route of travel, near the south bank of the Ashe.

Isaac pulled his oar from the water. The canoe's momentum, created by Isaac's previous paddling and the current, caused it to glide swiftly through the creek toward the alligators. Isaac glanced down for a piece of rawhide. It was too dark to see. Quickly, he put the paddle into the water on the left side of the canoe and heard the water ripple as he braked that side. The bow swung left, away from the alligators. He wasted no time bringing the oar back to the starboard side. In his panic, he gripped the oar too tightly with his left hand, but paddled furiously. The oar made a noisy, splashing sound. The canoe was headed away from the alligators, but moved no faster.

Isaac spoke aloud. "Got to get better strokes. Fast strokes ain't gone matter none if dey ain't good."

Isaac dug his oar deeper into the water and covered the blade. He gave a mighty pull on the oar. The canoe surged forward, passing the point where he first saw signs of the alligators. Gone was the sound of the oar splashing into the water. The water rippled gently after each firm stroke. Glancing over his shoulder, he noticed two alligators not far behind his canoe.

He spoke again. "Don't hold your breath. Stroke. Breathe. Stroke. Breathe."

A sudden gust of wind blew the bow to starboard. He was near mid-channel, but less than fifty feet from the south bank. Isaac paddled faster on the starboard side. The bow steadied but was still pushed by the wind off course. Isaac knew he needed to remain in mid-channel to get help from the current and keep away from more alligators on or near the bank ahead. He also knew that there were mud flats where the south bank of Ashe Creek turned to become the west bank of the great Pon Pon River. The river was only two to three minutes ahead.

Isaac felt a sharp pain between his thumb and index finger on his left hand at the knob of the oar. He took a quick glance and in the moonlight saw crumpled skin and blood oozing from the web between the two fingers. He missed one stroke and the bow swung more starboard. He held his breath and paddled hard and fast again. After several strokes and on the next breath, he spoke aloud and reminded himself to breathe between strokes. The south bank was twenty feet away and the alligators were making bellowing calls and thrashing the water behind the canoe. Despite his best effort, Isaac felt his strokes wobble and the oar turn in his hands ever so slightly with each stroke, losing power and speed. Sweat rolled down his face and the salt stung his eyes. He blinked repeatedly and rowed on.

Ashe Creek turns almost thirty degrees to the south as it enters the river. This put the wind at his back. Isaac now gained speed and left Ashe Creek and the alligators. He entered the Pon Pon River, paddling slowly to get a feel for the river's current. He remained close to the west bank. According to Luke, there was a Confederate artillery battery on the east bank, on the bluff above the river. Though he entered the river about a thousand feet southwest of Willtown Bluff, he hoped that his movement would not be spotted by a Confederate sentry. Soon, the current and falling tide carried him out of harm's reach. The sweat on Isaac's skin had dried and evaporated. He was wearing a damp shirt and, in the night air, felt cold. He also was starting to feel sleepy. He fought drowsiness by keeping his oar in motion. It had been eighteen hours since Isaac last slept.

A large eddy gently changed his direction near the entrance to a creek on the west bank. Isaac was tired and did not notice the change in direction until he ran aground in the mud flats and shallow water at the south edge of the waterway. The jolt from running aground rendered Isaac completely awake and alert. He was even more alert and paddling furiously after hearing the bellow of more nearby alligators. He paddled in reverse to free the canoe, with his oar sometimes hitting the soft muddy bottom. Each time he struck the mud, in less than a foot of water, more mud stuck to his oar. The oar felt noticeably heavier to his tired arms.

The sound of thrashing water came from the direction of the bellowing over his right shoulder. Glancing back, Isaac saw sliver geysers and water splash from the surface of the river and gently descend again. Isaac began to rock the canoe from side to side between strokes. In less than another minute he was afloat. With a heavy oar, Isaac rowed with dispatch to the middle of the channel. He glanced back again to check the progress of the alligators. They were still trashing the water in about the same spot.

Perplexed, Isaac slowed his rowing. Then, he laughed. He decided several alligators were probably trying to eat the same catfish. Perhaps, the alligators back in Ashe Creek were merely chasing fish or turtles, and not him. Perhaps, only his panic caused him to injure his hand in a desperate attempt to escape from the alligators. He stopped laughing and rowing, deep in thought, he looked into the dark water, without seeing. On the other hand, maybe they wanted me for supper. A shudder ran down his spine. He wiped the mud from his oar and replaced the mud on his sweaty hands and wrists. He began rowing again. This time he had no problem with drowsiness. His mind was, again, on Bianca.

Faint light was beginning to show above the trees on the eastern horizon. Isaac guessed the time to be about four o'clock in the morning. The small moon was high in the sky as he paddled past a peninsula on his right and made the turn with the river to the northeast. The narrow peninsula pointed directly into the mouth of the Dawho River, which joined the larger Pon Pon River in a horseshoe bend. The mouth of the Dawho was over three hundred feet wide. The small gurgling sound made where the rivers met was barely audible above the sound of frogs, owls, and crickets. A half-mile further, Isaac saw Fishing Creek on the left bank. Isaac rowed across the Pon Pon to the east bank and toward a point of land on the south of Fishing Creek. At last, he could see Jehossee Island. His first thoughts were of food and a warm place to sleep. By now, the beginning of daylight was encroaching on the darkness. He had hoped to arrive on Jehossee Island before first call and avoid being seen.

Because of the need to transport large crops of rice by flatboats to steamers tied up along the river, the winnowing house and storage barns at Governor Aiken's plantation on Jehossee Island were located on high ground near the head of a large canal. Since it was the season to plant rice, not harvest it, Isaac looked forward to hiding in the winnowing house for several days. He wanted to arrive and depart in darkness. His plan was to steer clear of contact with anyone – enslaved or overseer.

Isaac avoided the main canal from the river and entered Jehossee from a smaller canal that connected to Fishing Creek. He dragged his canoe into the woods at the edge of the marshes along Fishing Creek and hid it among thick bushes and vines in almost complete darkness. Taking care to leave no trace of food in the canoe, he slung his gunnysack over his head and wore his straw hat hanging on his back. Isaac set out for the dike that would lead him into the plantation. On the dike beside the canal, with no trees to hold back the faint light of the coming dawn, he was able to see the winnowing house in the distance. Whitewashed and built on stilts, the one-room winnowing house was as tall as a two-story building.

* * *

In the quiet of the early morning, the sound of the horn for first call startled Isaac. Startled, he sat upright, looking about and trying to remember where he was. He had slept almost an hour. The winnowing house was shuttered and almost dark inside, though it was quite light outside at six o'clock. He took a breath and let his shoulders sag. His next breath was a sigh. He lay down again on the hard, crude floorboards of the winnowing house. His head hurt. So did his ribs. His hand was sore. His arms and shoulders ached. Even so, he was soon asleep again among the cobwebs with his hat over his face. At the sound of second call, Isaac barely stirred.

Isaac dreamed that he was looking for Bianca and opened a door on rusty hinges. There was a slow creaking sound in his head when the light penetrated his straw hat. He pushed the hat from his face and sat up slowly. His eyes went wide when he realized that the door to the winnowing house had been opened by someone else and he was not dreaming.

A small black boy stood in the doorway. The boy's mouth was open and formed an O. Isaac frowned in exasperation. The surprised look on the boy's face turned to fear. Isaac tried to smile, but realized that his face did not feel as if it showed a smile. Isaac put a finger to his lips and made a "sh-h-h" sound. The little boy's face changed into the smile of a co-conspirator.

Isaac whispered, "Close the door and come over here."

"But my friend Roy is on the ladder."

"David, who oonah talkin' to?"

"Tell him to come on up."

"Yessuh. Roy, com'ere. Got sumptin' to show you."

"K. I'm a comin'."

"Roy is a-scared on ladders."

"Is not!"

"Is too!"

"Who you talkin' to?"

Again, Isaac put his finger to his lips. "Sh-h-h."

David and Roy stood before Isaac with the door closed. They appeared to be five or six years old. Remembering his little sisters, Isaac knew that secrets are short-lived among children of this age. He knew that he could not keep them for the day any more than they could keep his secret until nightfall. His attention was turning to the need to escape from Jehossee in broad daylight.

"Who knows oonah playin' in the winnowing house?"

David and Roy looked at each other. David became the spokesman. "Nobody."

Isaac guessed. "Weren't y'all told not to play on the ladder?"

David and Roy simultaneously dropped their heads. David answered, "Yessuh."

"Should I tell the overseer?"

The whites of their eyes shone large and brightly as Roy found his tongue. With arched eyebrows, they answered in unison, "Oh, no, suh! We won't do it no mo'! Please don't tell!"

Isaac suppressed a grin. "All right. On one condition. David, you go get me a hoe and tell me which fields the hands are working in today. Speak to no one."

"Yessuh! I gits you a hoe! And I ain't talkin' tuh nobody neither!"

While David was gone, Isaac learned from Roy where the overseers' quarters were located, the fact that they rode horses along the dikes instead of traveling by canoe, and the location of the kennels. Isaac ate Bianca's bacon and cornbread. He removed his shirt and tied his gunnysack so it would not show. When he donned his shirt again, Isaac rearranged the bulges created by the sack by sliding its contents to fit more or less under one arm.

Isaac waited until he spotted David approaching before descending from the winnowing house. Isaac and Roy were sitting on the ground at the base of the house when David arrived. David was grinning from ear to ear and holding a hoe by its head in both of his small hands. He dragged the handle behind him, through the dusty yard of the winnowing house. Isaac wanted to laugh aloud, thought better of it, smiled, and reminded them about not playing in the winnowing house again.

David wanted to know and couldn't wait any longer to ask. "Is oonah runnin?"

Roy wanted to know too. He emphatically nodded, "Yes." Roy joined David in wide-eyed anticipation.

Isaac considered his words. He looked at his small admirers and told them, "I'm a free Negro, jus passin' through this part of the country." His words sounded to him as if someone else spoke in his voice. Isaac felt exhilaration as this was his first opportunity to reflect on being free. He was deciding what to do, which direction to travel, and beginning to dare think of having a family not dominated by overseers. His feelings surprised him. He imagined Bianca's smile.

David and Roy looked disappointed. This was less exciting news than discovering a runaway. He told them good-bye without once asking that they keep their discovery of him a secret. He knew they would relay the news as soon as they found an adult. Isaac thought that would take, at most, ten minutes. He figured the overseers would know in thirty minutes. That gave him twenty minutes to walk to his canoe and launch it.

Isaac pulled his straw hat down to his eyebrows, put the business end of the hoe into the air with the handle resting on his shoulder, and took off. He marched from the winnowing house toward the fields David had pointed out. It was half past seven and all the workers were at their field tasks, running errands, or at work in shops and the big house. Isaac wondered where, among Governor Aiken's nine hundred or so enslaved workers on Jehossee Island, might Uncle's Jacob's nephew be today. He hoped that by keeping his distance, walking with purpose, and carrying a hoe, he could get to Fishing Creek without anyone realizing there was a stranger in their midst. He saw large gangs of hands in field after field, using hoes to make neat rows of small holes, followed by groups performing the second seeding of rice that spring. They were in turn followed by another detail closing the holes. He marched swiftly along the top of a dike beside a canal that connected to Fishing Creek, suppressing the urge to break into a trot. No one paid any attention; he saw no overseers.

When he was about fifty feet from the tree line bordering Fishing Creek, he heard shouts, dogs, and horses from behind. The sounds came from the direction of the winnowing house. Isaac broke into a sweat, but did not quicken his pace. The voices were white males and growing more emphatic. In the background, there was the sound of children crying. He heard a woman in the last field he passed say, "Oh, Lawd! What is dis heah agin dis mornin'?"

At the sound of barking dogs, Isaac dropped the hoe. He turned and glanced back for the first time. The people in the fields were all looking toward the winnowing house – it was being circled the horsemen and dogs. Isaac knew that in a few minutes the dogs would separate his scent from David's and Roy's. Isaac retrieved the hoe and used it like a machete to make his way to his canoe.

He saw the canoe in the thicket near the water's edge and headed directly for it. He was nearly ten feet away when he was stopped suddenly in his tracks. There, between Isaac and the canoe, was a cottonmouth, about half as long as Isaac was tall. The snake had been alerted by Isaac's noisy approach and was coiled and ready to strike. Its mouth was open and its fangs bared. The white inside the snake's mouth glistened and stood out from the background of green foliage, fallen tree branches, twigs, and the thick carpet of brown dry leaves and pine needles. Cottonmouths were common in the canals, creeks, and rivers around rice plantations. Isaac knew that people died from their bite. The sound of hoofbeats and barking dogs signaled that the chase was on. Isaac's heart beat increased yet again as he slowly backed away from the snake.

Isaac decided the better of his bad choices was to sacrifice precious minutes of his slim lead and avoid the cottonmouth. He used the hoe to make a new path to the canoe to his left and away from the coiled snake. Each step took seconds more, for he continued to scan the area for another cottonmouth, adding to the minutes he was losing by his detour. The horsemen were following the dogs at a smart canter.

With a quick poke and pull of the oilcloth with the hoe, Isaac assured himself that no snake was waiting inside his canoe. He was sweating as he dragged it through the mud at low tide. His sweat-soaked shirt and gunnysack clung to his body. As he struggled, he could hear the dogs approaching on the dike. Finally, with mud between his toes and green algae on his legs, he pushed the canoe into the water and scrambled inside. He started to toss the hoe into the water, but, on impulse, decided to keep it. Fishing Creek was lined by cypress trees on both banks. There were pines and the odd live oak here and there between the cypress trees and the dike at the edge of the last field. Isaac used this natural cover and immediately crossed to the north bank, almost two hundred feet away, before heading west for the Pon Pon River.

Isaac was still shaking from his encounter with the cottonmouth as he rowed toward the river. He could hear the overseers calling to each other above the din of the barking dogs. They had reached the north end of the dike where it joined an east-west dike at the wood's edge on Fishing Creek. They followed his trail along the dike in single file to the east. Isaac rowed west along the creek's north bank. Within five minutes, he was at the mouth of the river. Once upon the Pon Pon, he turned and rowed back toward Tiffany in case the horsemen tried to cut him off along the river. He remained as close as he dared to the river's east bank, turning right again into the mouth of the Dawho River in the middle of the channel.

The canoe glided silently into the Dawho. The tide was low. Ahead, between two cypress trees, a buck stood in the mud near a log and was drinking at the water's edge. Isaac cupped his hand, dipped into the river, and also drank. The deer raised its head to look at Isaac. Water dropped from its lips back into the river. Though the sound was faint, Isaac could hear the dogs half a mile behind him. The death scream was sharp and blood-chilling. It sounded not unlike the way Isaac imagined a human child would sound if grabbed by the jaws of a savage beast. Isaac froze. The Dawho's current brought his upstream progress to a halt. He pulled his oar into the canoe and sat petrified, watching the deer struggle against the largest alligator he had ever seen. The alligator was several feet longer than twice Big Gus's six–and-a-half foot height. The alligator had locked its massive jaws about the deer's midsection and was dragging the deer into the water at amazing speed, despite its flaying hooves. The water splashed and churned as the deer's scream became weaker and was silenced under the water.

Isaac blinked in disbelief. He completely forgot about the dogs and horsemen. He forgot about the current of the Dawho and the Pon Pon behind him. He sat transfixed, his eyes still on the now peaceful spot of calm water at the river's edge. The alligator, which appeared at first glance to be a log in the mud, was wider and much longer than his canoe. It had moved with a swiftness that Isaac had not thought possible and demonstrated tremendous strength by dragging a full-grown buck into and under the water. Isaac easily pictured a man in place of the buck in the alligator's jaws. He threw up his breakfast into the Dawho. Isaac sat slumped, chilled, and shaking in his canoe as it drifted backward into the Pon Pon. The current was carrying him back toward Jehossee Island.

Isaac was still facing upriver and traveling backward when the canoe stopped suddenly as it ran aground on the tidal mud flats near the middle of the river. Because of his canoe's momentum, it slid almost a foot onto the mud before coming to a halt. The mild jolt of the stop brought Isaac out of his daze. At once, he experienced hunger pains, felt chilled in his sweat-drenched shirt, heard the dogs at Jehossee, and saw the horsemen moving to and fro on the dike between Fishing Creek and the wide canal entering Jehossee. Isaac judged the distance to be less than a quarter-mile between his canoe and the horsemen.

The first bullet made a plunk sound in the water, short of the mud and well short of Isaac. The next shot was also short. He was a couple of hundred feet beyond the range of the 1853 Enfields the overseers used, but the shots served to motivate Isaac into action. He lifted his oar from the deck of the canoe and began paddling forward to escape from the mud. He glanced at the overseers and saw that one had dismounted. The dismounted rifleman took aim, then gently raised the elevation of his muzzle and fired. Isaac saw the smoke from the rifle, and then heard the sounds of its fire and the thwack of the bullet landing several feet behind him. With new urgency, he rocked the canoe from side to side as he used his oar to push against the soft mud. Several overseers were laughing at his frantic paddling while the dismounted rifleman rammed another charge and ball into his single-shot muzzle loader. Isaac paddled only on the right side to turn the bow to the west and his back to the rifleman. If he succeeded, the canoe would present a smaller target. He reasoned that if the canoe took a hit he would likely die almost as surely as he would if the bullet struck his body. He needed to keep his craft out of harm's way.

Isaac felt weak and lightheaded. The next shot landed in nearly the same place in the mud. He caught his breath while grabbing a piece of rawhide from the deck. He placed it in the web of his injured left hand. Isaac rocked the canoe more violently and paddled as fast as he could in his weakened condition. The bow slowly turned to the west. A shot splashed into the water where the bow had been. The oar was heavy with soft mud caked on the blade. Isaac struggled with all his strength to not drop the oar and move forward with each stroke.

On the next stroke, he broke free. Immediately, he had to balance paddling on both sides of the canoe and not allow the current to push him sidewise back onto the mud. He moved rapidly toward the west bank. With the bullets landing behind him at midchannel, he turned the bow to the south. Traveling with the current, the canoe picked up speed. He glanced one last time at the overseers. They stood or sat their horses, brandishing their rifles aloft. They appeared quite small from Isaac's vantage point. After several minutes, Isaac was on the west side of an island that sat in the middle of the Pon Pon. At low tide, the island was about two thousand feet long and four hundred feet wide. Behind the unnamed island, Isaac was finally out of sight.

At about mid-island, the mud receded to the bank. Near the southwestern tip of the canoe-shaped island, Isaac landed to rest and eat. He leaned the bow gently against a small indentation. To check for salinity, he looked for and found no black needle rush, a plant that would thrive in freshwater areas. He cupped his hand and tasted the river water, found it brackish, and spat it out. Isaac removed his gunnysack and saw that Bianca's cornbread was a dissolved mess of wet crumbs. He put the potatoes on the deck. Then, slowly turning the gunnysack wrong side out like a sock, Isaac ate the wet cornbread crumbs, salted by his sweat. He devoured the last piece of bacon and took a long look at the two potatoes he had left. Isaac noticed the abundance of fiddler crabs scurrying to and fro on the bank beside him. He decided that he was not hungry enough to find out how they tasted yet. He moved the stern so he could reach the bank with his hands. Because there were so many, it was easy to grab a crab at low tide. During high tide, this area of the bank would have been under water. He put one squirming female fiddler crab on his hook. The hook was attached to a line weighted by a small washer made in the smithy. Isaac tied the end of the line to his seat. He grabbed more fiddler crabs and secured them in his bandana on the deck.

At midmorning, Isaac cast off. He felt that his next priority was to find food and shelter instead of making significant progress toward his destination. He cleared the tip of the island and traveled south along the river's west bank. At this location, the river was almost sixteen hundred feet wide. He looked for the Jehossee overseers, but they were not to be seen. Warily, Isaac remained close to the west bank as the river narrowed to nine hundred feet, within rifle range, in a bend at the top of Jehossee Island's fishtail shape on its western end.

Isaac dropped the fishing line behind his stern. He remained outside the clearly visible slime line and in the current, which was slow due to the rising tide. For several miles down river from Jehossee and Sampson islands, there were swamp lands between the river's edge and high ground with trees suitable for a campsite. After Sampson Island, the river grew more and more brackish. He saw no more rice fields and was relieved that there would be no more encounters with overseers or patrollers.

This mid-May day was warm and uncomfortable. Isaac donned his straw hat to shield his eyes and face from the sun. The tide ebbed at noon. He was able to travel faster without expending more energy. Large cumulus clouds began to gather in the early afternoon – huge white puffs in a brilliant blue sky. He caught a catfish as long as his two hands, along with a spotted tail bass that was a tad shorter. Catching the bass, a saltwater fish, reminded Isaac that he was thirsty and could no longer use the river as a source of fresh water. He had traveled about eight miles since his encounter with the overseers at Jehossee. From his position, looking south, he could see down river for about three miles. Where the river made a bend and disappeared to the west, Isaac noticed a stand of trees close to the river's edge. By now, much of the sky in the west and south was covered with ominous looking, dark gray clouds blocking the afternoon sun. Isaac judged that he was rowing into a collision with a thunderstorm. He paddled with deliberate speed toward his new destination – Raccoon Island.

Isaac's shirt was dry, but the wind that was beginning from the west felt damp and cool. The water was choppy. Thunder rumbled in the distance. Ahead, lightning darted from cloud to cloud and from clouds to the ground. Isaac fought to keep the bow pointed to the south of the stand of trees near the river's east bank on Raccoon Island. His canoe was bobbing on the waves, and the wind was pushing it directly toward the marsh lands. Isaac kicked his two fish and hoe toward the center of the canoe and spread his feet apart. He leaned left, then right, to rock the canoe back and forth as needed for balance against the wind and waves. He rowed with the same vigor as he had when he thought he was being pursued by alligators.

Isaac felt his heart pounding and knew it was not because of his rowing. He thought again about how the safety of his canoe was one and the same as keeping his body safe. The wind grew stronger and the thunder rumbled within a few seconds after each flash of lightning. According to Uncle Jacob, each five seconds between a flash of lightning and the sound of thunder meant a mile in distance from the strike. Isaac was more frightened of the waves than lightning. But he had no time to focus on fear. All of his energy was invested in reaching Raccoon Island and stepping on land. He prayed, rowed, and rocked the canoe. The only sound he heard between claps of thunder was the wind. Suddenly, the wind ceased and settled into a gentle breeze. Isaac made a dash for the stand of trees that was his target at the edge of the island.

As Isaac approached the river's east bank, he could see heavy rain falling on the tree line about a mile down river. The treetops swayed violently back and forth in the wind. The waves ahead were high and crashing into the marsh lands below Raccoon Island. Isaac's eyes were fixed on the growing darkness and sheets of rain advancing in his direction and his attention to landing the canoe came too late. He frantically tried to slow it down, but it crashed into the river bank. He wasted no time tying the stern to a cypress tree root at the water's edge and he scampered up the bank with the other rope and tied the bow to a small tree. Returning to the canoe, he untied the stern from the tree root and was hit by a few very large and cold drops of water. Each drop stung his skin. He grabbed the bow line and dragged the canoe from the water. The wind was up again and louder now, whistling through the marsh grasses. A powerful gust whipped his straw hat from his head. The hat bounced on his shoulder, pulling the cord taut about his neck. He paid no attention. Isaac untied the canoe from the small tree and dragged it uphill toward a large live oak. The rain was heavy and horizontal. Lightning struck in the river behind him. The thunderclap was instant and deafening. In spite of himself, he was startled and tripped and fell. He scrambled to his feet and moved the canoe to the leeward side of the massive trunk of a live oak. By now, his clothes were soaked. In the few minutes that passed since the rain started, all of the mud he had placed on himself to ward off mosquitoes had been washed away by the rain.

Isaac wrapped his fish and potatoes in his gunnysack and turned the canoe upside down. He positioned it between the oak's huge, gnarled roots and crawled underneath. Isaac lay on the wet grass and leaves with two giant roots on either side and listened to the sound of the rain beating against his roof. He glanced about in the growing gloom for snakes. When he was satisfied that he was alone, he let out a loud sigh and thought of Bianca.

"So, ol' Uncle Jacob was right." Isaac spoke aloud as the rain droned on against his roof. Slaves on Pon Pon River rice plantations had few choices. "If'n a nigger gonna run, he can run wes' to da Yankees. De patroll'rs knows dat. Dey ready wid dogs and hosses. Dey cotch'em 'fore dey'se outta Colleton District. Jes lak they cotched Bianca and Andrew and so many others. Or oonah can run norf true boff Carrylinas and Birginny. Dat a powerful long way. Only Gawd knows how many patroll'rs dey is b'twix here and freedom." Isaac now had a new understanding of the old man's warning about a river escape. He made an ironic chuckle as he recalled the old man's words. "Go souf and oonah find out dat de white man done hired ol' Mister No Shoulders and Mister and

Missus 'Gator to patrol de waterways and de swamps. Done promised dem plenty o'pay – dey can eat all dey cotch!" Isaac feared his remaining journey on rivers and St. Helena's Sound – actually including several miles of ocean-edge travel.

"Well, how much do I wanna be a soldier? To git to be a soldier, fus', I must be free." Isaac's thought was punctuated by the bright flash of a nearby lightning strike, followed by a crash of thunder. He clapped his hands together to imitate the thunder. "Come tuh think of it, I've been free ever since, I thought of myself as a free man back there at Jehossee. Busting loose is me actin' like I'se free!" His smile vanished. "But all this comes to nothing if I don't reach de Yankees."

The words of Mister Luke came back. "Boy, if'n oonah gonna run, ride. I wouldn't walk no where's. Much work as oonah done did on dis heah plantation, oonah done earned more'n a hoss or a canoe. Dese white folks ain't gone be no less mad if'n oonah walks. So ride, boy. De punishment's de same."

That night, Uncle Jacob was pragmatic. "Luke, oonah oughta stop fillin' dis heah boy's head wid all dat nonsense. Dem Yankees is a fur piece from here. B'twix here and dere, mark my words, dey's critters in the waters and the swamps that will getcha. Dat is, if 'n the weather don't get you 'fore dey does. Trab'lin' for days on big water with tides in a little ol' canoe is more'n a notion." Now Isaac agreed that Uncle Jacob had been right. The hail joined the cold rain and was pounding on the upside-down canoe. The last time he saw the river, it looked like surf at the beach, for the waves were high and he could not see the west bank.

One night last week, as the men left their nightly gathering around an outdoor community fire and headed for their cabins, Luke had pulled Isaac aside. "One time a'fore de war, we was fishin' St. Helena Sound, we stayed overnight on Otter Island, down near de point. On a clear day, from dere oonah can see de rivers out to de wes' pouring into de sound. In my trabels, drivin' Massa about his bitness, I done heared told since den dat one ob dem rivers, de second from de left, will lead about two miles to whar dem Yankees is camped on Port Royal Island." Isaac had followed Luke's advice to tell no one when he was leaving – not even his mother – until he visited Bianca. He tried to picture what Bianca, Eve, and his little sisters were doing. Maybe parents back at Tiffany were running home from the fields to gather the children into their cabins ahead of the storm. Isaac shook his head in an attempt to get the thought out of his mind.

The hail ceased and rain continued to fall softly. The temperature dropped. Isaac was cold. He raised the canoe enough to unfold the oilcloth and wrap it about his body. He lay down again under the canoe and dozed. He awoke with a start. At first, he did not remember where he was. The rain had stopped. He peeked out and saw vapor rising from the ground and grasses. The air was cold and damp. Water drops fell, here and there, from the leaves and Spanish moss of the live oak. His world was gray and green. The gray clouds, the mist, and rising vapor from the wet ground blended with the gray Spanish moss overhead to create a ghostly scene.

When he tried to move, every muscle hurt. His rib cage was especially sore. He struggled from underneath the canoe and stood and stretched. A bird called. Another answered. More birds called. Isaac wondered why he had not missed them before now.

Isaac picked up his gunnysack and crude machete. He left the canoe and followed rainwater flowing down from his hill to the east. He stopped in a grove of loblolly pines, looking for trees with high resin content. Isaac selected a small loblolly that had resin oozing through its bark. He wrapped both pieces of rawhide around the metal handle of his machete and began to hack at the base of the tree. When the tree fell, Isaac noticed that the groundwater runoff led to a small lake a short distance away. He dropped the tree and machete and ran for the water.

* * *

Back at camp, he opened his tinderbox. The tinderbox was actually a rusty, discarded tobacco tin with a single hole punched in both the lid and bottom. Inside was previously burned cotton, a piece of flint, and a small shard of steel. The steel and the tobacco tin were retrieved from the scrap heap at the smithy. He used the tinderbox to start a fire in a shallow depression he had dug in the soft gray dirt with the hoe from Jehossee. The machete was useful in splitting half of Caleb's splinter into needle-sized sticks and for chopping and splitting the resin-laden loblolly for his fire. Though not nearly as large as the fires he made for Big Gus at the smithy, his small fire of loblolly branches, Caleb's splinter, and dead sticks lifted his spirit, dried his clothes, and cooked two fish he had gutted and dressed for the fire using the machete. The loblolly also yielded the sticks that held the fish aloft over the fire, while one potato baked slowly in the ashes.

Darkness fell early. The sky was still overcast. Isaac finished his feast at the time fog began rolling in from the south. He laid more sticks on the fire and went to get another drink from the lake. As he returned, he realized that he would not have been able the find his camp and canoe had it not been for the light from his fire. With the fog, early darkness was now total. As Isaac sat by the fire munching his baked potato, he judged that it was about six o'clock and, according to Uncle Jacob's reckoning, the tide had ebbed.

* * *

The end of sounds from night critters, which Isaac did not hear, and the beginning of a chorus from songbirds signaled the coming of dawn on Raccoon Island. Isaac removed his oilcloth, stirred, and stretched. His body ached. Still yawning, he gave thanks for a peaceful night. He went through the fog to the lake for a final drink of water. Isaac found a Chinese plum tree and harvested a few ripe pieces. He retrieved his last potato from the cold ashes, loaded his empty gunnysack, tinderbox, and other accouterments into the canoe. He could not see the river through the fog as he started downhill to the west. The tracks he made the day before were gone and he followed a trail of weeds broken from dragging the canoe.

Isaac was pushing away from the tree roots at the river's edge at five o'clock. The tide was low and the water calm. He could not see more than fifty feet in any direction. The average width of the river between Raccoon Island and the ocean was half a mile. At Otter Island and Edisto Point, where the river met the Atlantic, it was more than three miles wide. He looked back at Raccoon Island, made sure his canoe was perpendicular to its edge, then rowed toward the west bank. When he could see the west bank, the uneasy feeling of being enveloped began to wane. In the fog, he had no hope of using Caleb's suggested shortcut to the Ashepoo. His new plan was to keep the west bank in sight so that if the fog had not lifted by the time he reached Otter Island, he would not inadvertently travel into St. Helena's Sound and become lost at sea. Isaac rinsed the ashes from the potato and nibbled as he used one hand to hold the oar in the current like a rudder.

* * *

Had it not been for the fog, Isaac would have seen the Atlantic from his position off Pine Island. It was about eight o'clock, or two hours after ebb tide, when he followed the curvature of the island and turned west. There was mud beneath the canoe. He glanced at the shore. He moved to a point he thought was roughly one hundred feet from the shore. The fog was less dense, but obscured his view of landmarks and the ocean. He could not see the sand on the shore, and did not recognize it as a barrier island. Isaac followed the shore of Pine Island for another hour. He was very confused when he left smooth water and felt tide rips, but also saw land to his front. Minutes later, he reached a hairpin point beside Pine Island and realized that he had entered the mouth of another river. He turned his back to Fish Creek and followed the new shore, keeping it on his starboard side. This time he saw the waves at the tide rips and increased his speed, hit them head on, and crossed into an area of mud less than a foot below the surface. He continued moving away from shore as he followed it, yet he clung to it for dear life. This island also had a sandy beach. But Isaac was too far away to see the sand.

By nine-thirty, Isaac knew for sure that he was on the ocean, for he was greeted by gentle waves and flying fish. When the first one splashed back into the water beside him, Isaac nearly leapt from the canoe. In his peripheral vision, he noticed a winged gray thing disappear into the water. He stopped paddling. His eyes were affixed to the spot where the flying fish disappeared. Another leapt from the water and Isaac sucked in a deep breath, ready to hit the creature with his oar. This time he got a good look and marveled at a fish with wings as it splashed down a few feet ahead. Isaac took a deep breath and let out an audible sigh.

The shore was out of sight in the fog and panic welled up in Isaac's chest. He turned right to what he thought was ninety degrees to his previous direction and paddled furiously for two minutes. He could not see mud beneath his canoe. Though he spent energy and time avoiding mud, it would be a welcome sight now. He calmed himself with the thought that turning right was the logical action. One minute later, among the flying fish, he celebrated sighting land as men have done for centuries with screams of "Land, ho!" He moved toward the shore, this time looking to avoid the mud instead of hoping to see it. He closed to within fifty feet and encountered a sandy beach. He turned left and followed the beach until he could see a sharp curve to the west. He had reached the Point of Otter Island where St. Helena's Sound meets the Atlantic Ocean.

Isaac decided to go ashore and look for water beyond the tree line behind the beach. Because of the fog, he was unable to see the fort beyond the trees. To reach the shore, he had to cross tide rips. Instead of rowing through the rips, he turned right and made for the beach above the point. On landing, he walked along the beach towing the canoe. He rounded the point and looked about; he was not sure which way was west. He believed he was standing where Luke had told him to look west over the sound at the rivers pouring into it. All Isaac could see were waves larger than he had ever seen before, and more fog.

In the quiet seconds after a giant wave crashed onto the beach, Isaac heard the indistinct voices of men in the tree line. Isaac could not see them and he assumed they were Confederates.

Immediately, he began a hasty escape from Otter Island. He knew that the people he heard were white, but had not heard him. He wanted to keep it that way. In his haste, Isaac pushed and pointed the canoe into the oncoming waves. As soon as he reached water that was about waist deep, a large wave caught the canoe when it turned parallel to the shore during Isaac's scramble to get aboard. The canoe rocked wildly and flipped upside down, dumping Isaac, his hoe, machete, and all else into the surf. Isaac surfaced sputtering and coughing. It was difficult to stand as the waves continued to push him toward the shore. When he established his footing, the water was up to his shoulders. He grabbed the rope on one end of the canoe, flipped it right-side up, and headed for shore. He beached the canoe and waded back into the surf and retrieved the floating oilcloth, both oars, straw hat, and his bandana. His handful of plums floated away and all else was lost in the surf. Dejected, he sat in the sand until he remembered the voices from the tree line.

On his next attempt, Isaac towed the canoe to his right along the beach. Though he could not see the landmarks Luke described, Isaac reasoned that he was moving west along the beach. This time, as soon as the canoe was pointed into the waves, Isaac released his fiddler crabs in his bandana and boarded. He wrapped the bandana about the end of the oar and sat, bobbing to and fro, waiting for smaller waves to challenge and make a run for open water. He watched over his shoulder for movement in the tree line and listened for voices. From his new position, he could not hear the soldiers, only the surf. While he waited, he became impatient, realizing that he had no food or water and no means to find any. He needed to be under way as quickly as possible to make it to Port Royal Island by nightfall.

The fog began to lift. He could notice the waves further out. When he spotted his opportunity of relatively smaller waves, he took a deep breath and was off in a dash. After resting on Otter Island, he was able to propel the canoe quickly beyond the surf. He turned right to get his bearings and one last look at Otter Island.

The morning was still cool and gray. With the fog lifting, Isaac could see several hundred feet in all directions. That was not nearly far enough for him to observe any of the rivers that flowed into St. Helena's Sound from the west and north. The tide was rising as he turned north to keep the shoreline in sight. One mile further north, Isaac spotted the mouth of the Ashepoo River and Hutchinson Island. It was noon and full flood tide when he crossed the mouths of Two Sisters Creek and Rock Creek. Both were several hundred feet wide.

At high tide, Isaac's canoe rode easily above the mud flats beneath him as he rowed past Ashe Island.

Light rain began shortly after noon. Now Isaac believed the fog would not lift completely before the next day. The steady drizzle dampened his spirits and optimism. He began to tire as he followed the shore of Ashe Island to the northwest. At the mouth of the New Chehaw River, a giant white-headed bird crossed within twenty feet of Isaac's bow with talons fore. The sight of a bald eagle caused Isaac to stop rowing and watch. The eagle's wing span was greater than Big Gus was tall. While in a swift glide, the bird seized a fish from the water with a splash. With the fish flapping, but secured by razor-sharp talons, the eagle's wide wings broke with grace from glide configuration into mighty strokes upon the air that propelled it and its catch up and away from the water. The bird turned inland, leaving Isaac to watch, his mouth agape. His hunger pains started.

Isaac looked about before rowing again. He saw nothing. The drizzle continued. He rowed another half-mile before he realized that he had entered the mouth of a large river, whose name he did not know. He had discovered the Combahee River. Its mouth was almost a mile across, with its shores obscured in the fog and drizzle. On a sunny day, Isaac would have realized that he was entering the mouths of the Combahee and New Chehaw rivers where they emptied into the Coosaw River. He would have also noticed that he had left St. Helena's Sound as he traveled past Ashe Island and entered the broad Coosaw.

Wet, cold, and dispirited, Isaac turned south out of the Combahee along its swampy western shore. He wanted to get out of the canoe and stretch his legs, but found more salt marshes and no place to land. He rounded the point of land on Buzzard Island and reentered the Coosaw, which he thought was the sound. Isaac rowed due west, following the south edge of Buzzard Island. By mid-afternoon, he discovered the mouth of another large river. He did not know this was the Bull River. The entrance flowed into the Coosaw from the northwest. Isaac sat with his oar across his lap, looking out over the salt marshes that stretched endless miles into the mist and fog. To the west and south, the broad Coosaw flowed as far as he could see. He reasoned that this might be Luke's river that would lead west into Port Royal Island and the Yankee army camp. Isaac was thirsty and hungry. He rowed past the mouth of the Bull River and followed the Coosaw west along the south shore of swampy Chisolm Island.

The rain stopped. The overcast remained. Soon it would be night. The tide was falling. His throat was dry and his lips parched; his thirst was more acute that his hunger. Isaac passed several small creeks flowing out of the salt marshes and into the Coosaw. Near the fourth creek after the mouth of the Bull, he stopped and tasted the water. It was brackish, but not as salty as the ocean water he tasted when his canoe capsized off Otter Island. Isaac gulped two handfuls before he could stop himself. After rowing for a few minutes, he felt even thirstier. He knew he had made a bad choice.

Isaac felt weak from hunger and thirst. As night fell, he could see the banks of the salt marshes. The tide had ebbed. The banks and vegetation looked similar to what he had observed on the Pon Pon River below Raccoon Island. This told him that he was traveling on a large river. He believed that he was headed west, but was only guessing since he had not seen the sun, or stars, in almost two days. He thought, *maybe this really is Uncle Luke's river.* Isaac was desperate to find a place to camp. He rowed on into the darkness. The only sounds he heard were the water lapping against the banks of the marshes and water moved by his oar. His ribs hurt and his shoulders ached. Still, he rowed upstream, making little progress against the current. Ahead, he saw trees. He found more energy and rowed faster. But the distance to the trees never closed. Soon he could no longer see the trees. The fog was dense again. After rowing for another half-hour, he was more tired that he could ever remember. Then he saw the ship. Isaac felt better as he turned toward open water and rowed to reach the tall ship, a man-of-war with a red and white striped banner hanging above her stern. He thought he was rowing faster. But when the marshes were out of sight, the tall ship disappeared. Isaac looked about and saw nothing but water and fog. He put his oar on the deck and tried to trace the blisters in his hands. When he could not, he put his face in his hands and his elbows on his knees. Isaac wept.

When his eyes were dry again, Isaac sat remembering why he left Tiffany Plantation. He sighed and said aloud, "Lawd, if I neber see another Yankee, thank you for lettin' me taste freedom 'fore I die."

Isaac lifted his head and glanced around. He could see less than he saw an hour before and became aware of the sound of water lapping against the side of his canoe. He closed his eyes and listened. There were no voices from a crew on board a would-be man-of-war. In the distance, he could hear the familiar sound that had followed him since ebb tide, the faint sound of water lapping against the banks of the marshes. Isaac smiled, lifted his oar, turned about, and rowed gently toward that sound. He reached the bank and turned left. He heard himself say, "Thank you, Lawd."

The night was quiet. Feeling weak and dizzy, he resumed rowing northwest on the Coosaw along the banks of Chisolm Island. After rowing for several minutes, Isaac stopped to rest. He closed his eyes to concentrate on sounds. The third time he stopped, he heard the voices of black men. He bolted upright. His shoulders no longer slumped; he was less dizzy, but felt no stronger. He was afraid to call out, for there might be white men about as well.

Isaac followed the shore slowly forward, prepared to stop his progress without being heard by rowing backward. When he was close enough to understand the voices, he halted and listened. Three men were camped less than twenty feet away, on the first high ground Isaac had seen since Otter Island. They spoke of loading and unloading ammunition from pack mules for the Confederates during the rain. Isaac smelled smoke from their small fire. Soon, the odor of fish cooking over an open fire wafted past his nose. Water, that Isaac did not know he had left, filled his mouth. Isaac asked himself: if they worked for the Confederates, would it be safe to make contact? Swallowing his saliva was followed by a loud growl from his stomach.

"What dat?"

A pause. The only sound came from the crackling fire. "I ain't yeddy nothin'."

"Well, I yeddy sumptin'! Told y'all dis placed is hainted! Now, I guess oonah b'lives me." Lowering his voice to a whisper, the same voice continued, "I'm a goin' and camp on the other side of the grove, closer to the soldiers."

"Aw. Don't be silly."

Footsteps receding, a voice said, "I'm a goin' now, a 'fore it's too late. Oonah comin'?"

"Naw, Eddie. I stayin' with Uncle Cephus."

Uncle Cephus stood and stretched as Eddie grabbed his bedroll and made a hasty retreat. "Timothy, com'on. Less see who's out dere."

Isaac heard the sound of the hammer on a musket being cocked. He tried to whisper to Uncle Cephus and Timothy. His voice was buried in his throat. He coughed. Isaac swallowed, to try again.

"Uncle Cephus, oonah yeddy? He's ober dat way!"

"Stay behind me. I'll put a ball tru'im."

Isaac's eyes widened. Trying to wet his throat, he swallowed again – hard. "Uncle Cephus, please don't shoot!"

"Show yourself."

"Yessuh."

Uncle Cephus lowered his musket.

Armed with only a stick of firewood, Timothy's jaw dropped. When he recovered, he challenged his partner. "Uncle Cephus!" he hissed, "Oonah don't know who's out dere yet."

"I know enough to know dere's a boy out there who's scared and in trouble. He's lost, cold, thirsty, and hungry. Ain't dat right, boy?"

The big grin on Isaac's face was heard in his reply, "Yessuh!"

"Well, com'on in and eat ol' Eddie's fish."

* * *

Timothy held one of Isaac's ropes while Isaac crawled from his canoe. On the bank, he wobbled as he tried to stand. His legs felt stiff and weak. Isaac tripped and fell.

"Hey, oonah don't look so good." Timothy offered his hand and helped Isaac stand. How long oonah been in dat canoe?"

"Never mind all dat. Get the boy over by the fire and give 'im some water. And both of y'all keep 'e voices down."

85

"Yessuh." With Isaac leaning on his arm, Timothy whispered, "What oonah name?"

"Oonah shore full o' questions dis night. Let dat boy sit down and drink dis water a'fore you 'terrigate'im." They chuckled.

Though it was ordinary creek water from the side of a road, it tasted sweet and pure to Isaac. Uncle Cephus held the gourd for Isaac, ensuring that he drank slowly and did not strangle or cough. When Uncle Cephus removed the gourd from his lips, Isaac wiped his mouth on his sleeve.

In a hoarse voice, he spoke. "My name is Isaac. Why are we keepin' our voices low?"

The old man smiled. "I see Timothy ain't the only young fella here wid questions."

Sitting in front of the fire pit, Isaac relaxed and flexed his legs back and forth.

"We keeps our voices down to keep from gettin' attention from the soldiers."

"What soldiers?"

Uncle Cephus held up a hand. "We's valets and laborers for a Confederate infantry patrol."

Isaac's jaw went slack. His mouth dropped opened. He managed to stammer, "Wh-what?" He closed his mouth and swallowed hard. "Suh?"

Uncle Cephus held up a hand again. "Now, I 'spects oonah a runaway from a riverfront plantation, likely left dis mornin' from someplace up de Combahee."

"Yessuh. No, suh. I mean...."

"Now, you seem like a youngun dat's respectful of his elders, even when oonah still in 'e canoe."

Timothy slapped his knee. "By Gawd, I get it now! Dat's why oonah didn't shoot."

Uncle Cephus shushed Timothy and turned back to Isaac. "So which is it? Yes or no?"

Isaac's first thought was that he traveled all this way, only to be captured by Secesh-lovers. Or, worse, they were as close as they could be to becoming Confederate soldiers. Isaac wanted to run for his canoe. Then, he thought, he would surely be shot.

Timothy removed the skillet from a rock by the fire and silently handed it to Isaac. Isaac took it, thoroughly perplexed. His looked at and smelled the warm fish. His mouth watered again.

Uncle Cephus was waiting. "Well?"

"Yessuh. I mean, yessuh. I'se a runaway. And I mean, no, suh, I ain't from no Combahee plantation. I ran from Tiffany up the Pon Pon."

For the first time, Uncle Cephus removed his unlit corncob pipe from his mouth. His eyebrows rose as he considered the distance from the Pon Pon. "Why, thunderation, boy! Oonah been trab'lin' not on ribbers – but going on mighty nigh three days — and on ocean waters too?"

Isaac was more confused. Was he a prisoner? Was he being praised, or called a fool? Barely audible, he responded. "Yessuh."

"Son, my hat's off to oonah. Oonah sho' a brave lad. G'on and eat Eddie's fish. Oonah look like oonah needs it."

Isaac used both hands to eat. He ate with relish, his stomach growling after each swallow. Soon the fish was gone. "Uncle Cephus, thank oonah for the water and de fish."

"Oonah most welcome, Isaac. Pleasure to have oonah in our camp."

Still confused, Isaac asked, "Suh, am I a prisoner?"

"Oh, Gawd, no!"

"Thank Gawd!"

"Me and Timothy will get oonah under way a'fore the soldiers know oonah here. That is, unless Eddie returns. You see, Timothy is my sister's grandson. We come from de White Hall Plantation, up dere at the head of the Cuckolds Creek, off the Combahee. These Confederates grabbed us off de plantation."

"Oonah welcome tuh come with me."

"Thanks, Isaac. But 'e canoe too small for both of us and oonah. Besides, we gits back to our family from time to time."

"Where is we?"

"Dis the banks of the Whale Branch that feeds the Coosaw."

"What is Coosaw?

Uncle Cephus laughed. "You mean, you don't know that Coosaw is de widest, biggest, shortest river feedin' into St. Helena Sound?"

Timothy broke in, "Remember the fog. I 'spects Isaac couldn't see much."

"Oh, dat right. Anyway, Isaac, I guess oonah headed for the Yankee camp."

"Yessuh. Where is it? How do I get dere?"

"Port Royal Island is d'rectly across the river. Rest. Sleep. We get you started shortly after midnight."

A big grin crossed Isaac's face. He had more questions, but he lay back in the spot that Eddie had prepared and fell fast asleep. He did not need the music of a chuck-will's-widow.

It was Isaac's intent to awake and steal away on his own. A hand gently shook his shoulder and Isaac opened his eyes. The starless night was pitch black. He smelled smoke from a corncob pipe, but could not remember where he was. The man with the pipe was speaking, though Isaac could not understand a word. He blinked and shook his head. Finally, he recognized Uncle Cephus's voice.

"Time to go. Git up."

Still groggy, Isaac rolled over onto his knees and used his hands to push his body up. Finally, on his feet, he stretched and yawned. He pumped his legs and repeatedly lifted his knees to his waist while Uncle Cephus gave him instructions.

"Point 'e canoe the way I shows oonah. I figure it's after midnight. The tide is fallin'. Paddle hard, so you won't be swept back into the Coosaw and miss Port Royal."

That got Isaac's attention. He was so close, yet so far from his destination. Being swept anywhere off-course was not what Isaac wanted to hear. With that revelation, he was wide-eyed and fully awake.

"Do as I say and oonah should hit one of two small islands just short of Port Royal. Don't go further 'till daybreak. You don' wanna to be greeted by a rifle ball."

Timothy appeared from his watch. "Guard's comin'."

Isaac whispered, "Thank y'all."

Uncle Cephus nodded, grabbed Isaac's elbow, and propelled him silently toward the canoe. Isaac had forgotten in which direction his canoe rested. In several long strides they reached the canoe and pushed it into the water. Uncle Cephus held it while Isaac boarded. He threw the rope in after Isaac and turned the canoe in the water so that the bow was pointed southwest. Without speaking, he pointed over Isaac's shoulder into the fog. Isaac nodded, picked up his oar and bandana, and pushed away from the bank.

As he rowed into the fog, Isaac heard the Confederate guard call out. "Cephus, where you at?"

Uncle Cephus's voice called back. "Latrine. Dat you, Mister Billy?"

"Yeah. Y'all get some rest. Got a long march tomorrow."

"Yessuh, Mister Billy."

Isaac used the cover of the voices to make strong oar strokes that caused the water to ripple. In ten minutes, he had his canoe nestled against the south bank of a small swampy island.

On a clear day, Isaac would have been within sight of Port Royal Island. Here, out of sight of Yankee sentries, he waited for daybreak.

Chapter 6: Grierson's Raid

Sergeant James Darby's horse suddenly reared and sent him tumbling into a puddle. A shrill blast from the whistle of a steam locomotive had startled his horse.

Sergeant Richard Surby and Corporal Sam Porter laughed as they struggled to maintain control of their equally startled mounts. Richard said, "James, I see you take any excuse to sit on your ass!"

James scrambled to his feet and clung to the reins as his frightened horse danced sideways away from him. Even so, he smiled. "Fuck y'all – and your horses too!"

Only minutes before, they had stopped at a house on the edge of Newton Station for information. Richard had told the old man on the front porch he wanted a drink of water for himself and his two friends. Richard had engaged the man in conversation and learned that there was no Confederate garrison in Newton Station, Mississippi, only a hospital with a few convalescing soldiers.

James had wanted to know more. "Sir, what time will the next train arrive?"

The old man had pulled a watch from a pocket of his frayed vest. "Why, that'un a be in heah in half an hour. She'll be a comin' in from Vicksburg and Jackson."

That was when the whistle sounded and James's horse threw him to the ground.

From his horse, still in the front yard of the house, Richard called back to the man, "What train is that?"

The old man leaned back, raising the front legs of his weather-beaten chair off the floor of the porch. He held a tin cup of water in his left hand. With his right, he slowly stroked his white whiskers. "Oh, why, that's an ol' freight a comin' in from the east. You got time fer the passenger train. Taint never early nor late. Jes' you watch and see."

James could not believe their good fortune. Not one train, but two targets. He told himself, this Friday, April 24, 1863, is getting better by the hour. Back on his horse now, James turned his face away from the man on the porch, for he could not suppress his smile. Though they had ridden more than six hours to arrive in Newton Station at quarter past eight this morning by his dad's big pocket watch, he felt fresh and ready for a fight.

As Richard and the men moved their horses toward the road, he turned in his saddle and said to the old man, "Much obliged, sir, for the water."

When they reached the road, James saw Corporal Sam Porter turn his horse north in anticipation of the order they both knew was coming.

Nudging his horse with his heels, Richard urged his horse closer to Sam, "Get back to Colonel Blackburn as fast as you can. Tell him he needs to bring the battalion into Newton Station at double-quick march in order to capture the freight train arriving minutes from now. Is that clear?"

Sam was spurring his horse and James heard him shout over his shoulder, "Got it! I'm gone."

As Sam galloped away on the red dirt road, the sound of his horse's hooves was somewhat muffled due to the rain that had fallen the day before. James turned and looked down the hill at Newton Station to the south of them. He reflected on how well the scouts worked together; James was proud to ride with them. He realized that to capture Newton Station and the approaching train without delay, he and Richard would need to move quickly. Though Richard Surby was the scout leader, James felt comfortable making suggestions. "Richard, do you think you and me can take the depot by ourselves?"

"Yeah, if we take it fast. You cover me. I'll go in and destroy the telegraph as our first business."

James held up his revolver, spun the cylinder, checked for spent cartridges, and, on the final click, holstered it. "Okay. Let's ride!"

James and Richard were part of an eight-man squad of scouts. Each scout was a volunteer from the Seventh Illinois Cavalry Regiment, which was riding with the Sixth Illinois on the Union army's first raid through Mississippi. General Grant assigned the mission of the raid to their leader and present brigade commander, Colonel Benjamin Grierson. Grant needed to divert the Confederates' attention while he crossed the Mississippi River to attack Vicksburg.

Grierson's seventeen-hundred-man brigade included the two Illinois regiments and the Second Iowa Cavalry Regiment. The scouts felt close kinship with Grierson and Lieutenant Colonel William Blackburn, their cheerful and dashing battalion commander. Grierson approved Blackburn's plan to organize the scouts.

Grierson created diversions of his own to keep the Confederates guessing his whereabouts and intentions. On the seventh day of the raid, Grierson sent the Second Iowa, commanded by Colonel Edward Hatch, back to Tennessee, and dispatched a company east on separate raids, while he moved south with the two Illinois regiments. The Iowans were to conduct raids and continue back to Union lines. Grierson ordered the detached company, under the command of Captain Henry Forbes, to cut telegraph lines, destroy a railroad bridge near Macon, and make its way back to the main column after its raid was over.

James felt the scouts had an important advantage in the disguise he helped design. Instead of their blue Union uniforms, they had worn gray slouch hats, gray shirts, and butternut brown jeans since the fifth day of the raid. They were armed with captured shotguns, rifles, pistols, revolvers, and sabers. The brigade's scouts achieved the look of Confederate irregulars. They were affectionately called the Butternut Guerillas by their comrades in the Sixth and Seventh.

The Butternut Guerillas rode at various times five to seven miles in front of the lead battalion, seeking information and verifying targets the main body would destroy. Their chief objective was to help the raiders avoid riding into an ambush. They performed this task with skill, daring, and relish.

They dressed like Confederate irregulars at their peril. Captured Union soldiers were treated as prisoners of war and those wearing Confederate garb would be immediately executed as spies. James and each scout were volunteers.

At half past ten Thursday night, the old man, as they called Grierson, gave the order to destroy as much of the rail and telegraph facilities as possible at Newton Station. Grierson's raiders resumed their march south, this time with about one thousand men. James had ridden with the seven scouts at the head of the column for five hours.

They passed through Decatur without incident. The Butternut Guerillas learned from a Decatur citizen, whom they had awakened in the middle of the night, that probably no more than an infantry company was garrisoned at Newton Station.

Blackburn's battalion was often the lead or point battalion when the Seventh was on the march. Again, his men took the lead and rode on through the night. This night ride was coming after a day when they captured a key bridge to allow the brigade to cross the rain-swollen Pearl River and overrun minor resistance in Philadelphia. Blackburn halted his battalion at a creek ford about six miles north of Newton Station to water their horses shortly after sunrise. From there, Blackburn had sent Richard, James, and Sam ahead to Newton Station to be his forward eyes and ears.

Now, James held onto his loose-fitting hat with his right hand and the reins with his left as they neared the depot at a gallop. The depot was a small two-room wooden building perched near the tracks. The shape of the A-line roof on the whitewashed, smoke-tinged building reminded James of his schoolhouse in Springfield. James let go of his hat and pointed to a man walking on the otherwise deserted street. Richard said, "I'll handle him. You secure the east end of the depot and cover the door."

"Okay."

At a couple hundred paces from the man, James and Richard slowed their mounts from a gallop to a smart canter, headed straight for the hitching rail in front of the depot. As they dismounted and tied their horses, several more men strolled out of a building about a hundred yards away. The first man met the strollers near the door. James surmised that these unarmed men were the convalescing Confederate soldiers mentioned in the information they obtained in Decatur the night before. The building fit the description they were given of the hospital.

Richard drew his revolver and shouted to the men, "Remain inside! Don't come out on peril of your lives."

James pulled his rifle from its boot, slung low on the right side of his saddle, and dismounted. He was tense and looking for a defensive position and an escape route at the same time. He knew the risk they were taking was necessary to ensure that the telegraph was not used to warn any nearby Confederate units of the presence of the raiders. He also hoped that Sam Porter and Colonel Blackburn's battalion would soon appear. If not, he and Richard may have to shoot their way out of Newton Station.

"Okay, Richard, I've got them." James stepped forward with his rifle at port arms and stood beside a wooden rain barrel at the corner of the tiny railroad depot. From his position, he could cover the hospital door as well as see the water tank and a woodshed beside the side track. A single track served the Southern Mississippi Railroad from Meridian west to Vicksburg, passing through Newton Station.

"Dammit! The door is locked." Richard moved from the railroad station door to look through a dingy window.

"See anyone?"

"No. Just as well. There's no telegraph that I can see. The door is padlocked from the outside."

For another long minute, James and Richard kept watch in all directions without speaking. The only sounds were occasional chirping from birds. There was no one on the streets. James thought it was too quiet, even for a small town. It made him edgy. The feeling was the same as he remembered from his first cavalry charge the year before with the Sixth under Grierson at Shiloh.

The locomotive whistled and broke the silence with a long, low mournful call, followed by two quick blasts. James was snapped from his memory of Shiloh and his full attention was back on the scene. Two Confederate soldiers stood motionless in the doorway of the hospital looking at James and his rifle. James glanced down the track to the east. The train was still not in sight. He thought he saw movement through a hospital window. James stepped behind the rain barrel and pointed his rifle toward the hospital. He surmised the longer they waited, the more likely it was the convalescing soldiers might try to overcome a party of two scouts. Richard had taken up a position at the opposite end of the platform, still in sight of James.

It was a clear day. James heard a sound like low rumbling thunder. He recognized it immediately as the sound of a battalion of horses in full gallop. Moments later, Blackburn's men surged into Newton

Station, down several streets; some of the men crossed the main track and the siding before bringing their mounts to a halt. James was now a bit more relaxed. He stood beside Richard with his rifle cradled in his left arm.

Blackburn had been out front leading the charge. He turned his horse and rode toward them, waving his hat and yelling at the top of his voice, "Yahoo! Yahoo!"

Blackburn wore his blue uniform smartly, with his shirt tucked in his trousers under his suspenders and blouse. His trousers appeared to grow out of his knee-length boots. Though his uniform and those of his men were caked with mud and covered with dust after seven days of raiding, he sat tall and proud in the saddle. James said to Richard, "I'm glad we know these guys. This scruffy bunch could be any gang of outlaws. But I sure am happy to see them."

Blackburn bounded from his horse and onto the platform with them. He shook Richard's hand and then James's furiously. "Great job, lads! Great job!"

James pointed to the east. They could see a stream of smoke above the pine trees. "Here she comes."

Blackburn called toward the troops, "Company commanders! Up here. Double-quick time!"

He ordered pickets out to block all streets and approaches to the depot. Next, he ordered company commanders to move their men out of sight from the track and siding. He kept James and Richard nearby in case he needed them to relay orders. The troops rode their horses behind buildings near the track and dismounted. They readied their weapons and concealed themselves. Everyone was excited about capturing a train.

This was the eighth day of the raid. The troops were beginning to understand more fully the mission they were on, deep in enemy territory, completely isolated from the rest of the Union army. They were to inflict as much damage as possible on Confederate supply lines and draw attention away from Grant's coming attack on Vicksburg. James felt the prospect of a victory at Newton Station would be a major boost for the morale of these troops and the nation.

He made a mental note to ask about press accounts of this day's action in his next letter home.

This was the eighth day of the raid. The troops were beginning to understand more fully the mission they were on, deep in enemy territory, completely isolated from the rest of the Union army. They were to inflict as much damage as possible on Confederate supply lines and draw attention away from Grant's coming attack on Vicksburg. James felt the prospect of a victory at Newton Station would be a major boost for the morale of these troops and the nation. He made a mental note to ask about press accounts of this day's action in his next letter home.

Sam Porter rejoined them beside the station. James guessed they looked like a man in a dark suit and three Confederate irregulars to the train engineer as he rounded the last curve and the station came into view. They were ready. The troops waited for Blackburn's signal. They were hidden behind buildings, the woodshed beside the track, and across the water-filled ditch on the far side of the tracks.

The brakes of the locomotive were squealing and screeching as the engineer slowed the twenty-five-car freight train. The cars rattled and rocked left, then right, but not in unison. James expected a larger locomotive because of all the noise, but it did have the largest cowcatcher he had ever seen. Steam was pouring from the top of the rusting boiler and mixing with smoke from the smokestack mounted above the firebox. Steam was leaking from pipes on its left side and from underneath her boiler. He thought the locomotive looked old and in serious disrepair. As it slowed to a crawl, a trainman dropped and jogged ahead to set the switch and allow the train to move onto the rusty tracks of the siding. The trainman did not see the pair of troopers in the tall grass near the switch or the other pair at the opposite end. The job of these four troopers was to ensure that the switches were not thrown to allow the train to escape from the siding. James and the Butternut Guerillas watched the train groan and creak onto the siding. The locomotive came to a halt next to the water tower. The trainman, waiting by the switch, reset and locked it. James tightened his grip on his rifle. He saw Richard and Sam draw their revolvers, as Blackburn raised his right hand to the brim of his hat. Because he was in plain sight of the engineer, James remained still until Blackburn dropped his hand.

James and the Butternut Guerillas watched the train groan and creak onto the siding. The locomotive came to a halt next to the water tower. The trainman, waiting by the switch, reset and locked it. James tightened his grip on his rifle. He saw Richard and Sam draw their revolvers, as Blackburn raised his right hand to the brim of his hat. Because he was in plain sight of the engineer, James remained still until Blackburn dropped his hand.

When the trainman locked the switch, Blackburn dropped his hand. The company commanders yelled, "Charge!" The Sixth's bugler sounded, "Charge!"

They leapt from their hiding places and ran shouting and cheering to the train. The surprised engineer and trainman immediately raised their hands and allowed themselves to be taken without a struggle. The troopers continued cheering and waving their carbines and hats. James observed to Sam with a chuckle, "With all this noise, you'd think we just won the war."

Richard reminded Blackburn that the passenger train from Vicksburg was due in any minute. Blackburn ordered his troops back into hiding. They took the freight train crew with them and kept them out of sight behind a warehouse. They heard the passenger train's whistle as the last of the troopers took their positions. Blackburn stood waiting with his three scouts. James looked at his dad's watch. Richard saw him pocket the watch. "Well...?"

Poker-faced, James leaned back and put his hand to the stubble on his chin, just as the old man had done. "Well, she ain't early and she ain't late."

While Richard and Sam broke into laughter, Blackburn looked from one of them to the other.

The battalion was almost quiet again by the time the passenger train rolled into view from the west. Her whistle sounded again as she slowed for Newton Station. James and Sam began walking to meet the lone passenger car, which was attached behind twelve freight cars. As the locomotive passed the station at low speed, Richard leapt onto its steps. He put his revolver under the engineer's nose. "Stop the train! If you reverse the engine, I'll put a ball through you."

With large eyes, the frightened engineer obeyed immediately bringing the train to an abrupt halt. The passengers were startled, first by the jarring stop, then by the appearance of James and Sam holding revolvers at opposite ends of the aisle. James spoke in a calm, firm voice: "I'm Sergeant Darby, Sixth Illinois Cavalry."

A woman gasped and in disgust spat out the word, "Yankees!"

The other passengers were wide-eyed and began murmuring.

James continued. "Remain where you are. You will be evacuated from the train in a few minutes."

Blackburn signaled the battalion. The troops charged from all directions, cheering and creating more noise than they did capturing the first train. Then James and Sam moved to the exits to let the troops know the passenger car had been secured. The troops shouted over and over, "The train is ours! The train is ours!"

Meanwhile, though no shots were fired, the passengers became alarmed at seeing and hearing hundreds of armed men in blue uniforms charge their train. A slow panic ensued. "There are so many of them!"

"How did that many Yankees get through our lines?"

"They're hell-bent to free our damned niggers!"

"Is there no place safe any more?"

While James and Sam were in the exits, several fearful passengers threw their revolvers and valuables out the windows on the opposite side of the car from the station. James and Sam reentered the car. James heard several soldiers scrambling between the cars, then on the other side of the passenger car. Richard and several enterprising soldiers were fishing wallets out of the rainwater-filled ditch where some of the discarded articles had fallen. When the passengers saw this, a new cry went up. "This is an outrage!"

One shouted, "Quiet! They'll kill us all!"

James held up a hand. "Remain calm. No harm will come to you."

"What of our valuables?"

"Well, you shouldn't have thrown them out."

A woman, wearing a fancy hat, and her husband pressed forward toward James. "What is to become of this train?"

"After we evacuate you, we will burn it."

She screamed and, as if repelled by James's words, fell back against her husband. Other passenger began murmuring. Her husband implored, "Please, Sergeant, spare us our furniture. It's in one of the cars. It's all we managed to save from our home at Vicksburg. Please."

"Sam, move the passengers to the west end of the station. You two, come with me to see Colonel Blackburn."

The troops were running about laughing and looking for personal booty. Blackburn called for his company commanders. James thought things were getting a little out of control and he told the distraught couple from Vicksburg to wait for him at the depot door. He went to Blackburn and reported the couple's concerns about their furniture and made himself available for new orders.

Blackburn ordered the companies into formation. He gave them orders to inventory the cars of both trains and report back for instructions. The commanders took charge. It was found that several cars on both trains contained artillery shells. The westbound train also carried other munitions, commissary and quartermaster items, railroad ties, bridge planking, and uniforms. Blackburn directed the cars carrying artillery shells be moved, with the assistance of the captured trainmen, a safe distance from town. His troops then set fire to the cars.

While the inventory was under way, several more families joined in begging that their household goods be spared. The families stood waiting near the station in the dust, smoke, steam, and noise. Blackburn assigned a squad to unload the furniture before the cars were burned. Several men were asking for the return of the wallets they tossed out the windows of the passenger car. Two were reported to contain $2,500 and $8,000 in Confederate currency. Of course, the wallets had not been seen, according to soldiers in the vicinity.

Shortly after the cars were set afire, the artillery shells began exploding. They exploded at various intervals, giving the effect of an artillery duel. James learned later that Grierson and the main column were nearing Newton Station and heard the exploding shells. Grierson feared Blackburn had walked into an ambush and quickly returned the Colton's map of Mississippi he was studying to his blouse pocket and ordered, "Trot, gallop, march!"

The main column slowed from a gallop as they crossed the rise in the road north of the station. A relieved Colonel Grierson removed his hat and wiped his brow. Blackburn reported the capture of the trains and the fires that had been set. Grierson was delighted. He immediately ordered the destruction of track, telegraph poles, telegraph wire, buildings with military content, trestles, and cross ties.

Major Matthew Starr lead two battalions of the Sixth, destroying track and ties and telegraph as far east as the trestle works over the Chunky River. James and Sam rode ahead of the detachment. Just short of the Chunky River trestle, they set to work prying out the spikes and iron plates that held the rails in place. They used tools taken from the depot. A company of soldiers worked alongside the scouts. The sun was high in the sky and the day was as warm as early summer. Sweat soon soaked the backs of their shirts. They kept their carbines strapped across their backs and revolvers on their hips. Major Starr placed guards in the mostly pine woods on both sides of the railroad.

Sam held the pointed wedge end of an iron bar against the iron plate holding spikes that were used to secure the rails on the wooden cross ties. James wore his gauntlets as he swung the ten pound hammer and struck the end of Sam's bar. "Hold it steady."

"This is steady. You be sure you hit the bar and not Mrs. Porter's handsome, bouncing baby boy!"

After another clank of metal meeting metal, James caught his breath. "If I miss, it will be because you moved and Mrs. Porter's ugly ass soldier boy will bounce into the river!"

"Yeah, and what a sorry time it will be for your butt when I return."

"If *I* hit a square-headed corporal, he won't be returning!"

On the next strike, the bar slid under the iron plate and raised the spikes an inch or so. Sam put his weight on the end of the bar. James dropped his hammer and together they pried out the spikes. A crew from the company leapfrogged them and began prying up the next plate. Another group gathered cross ties into several huge piles in the middle of the railroad bed and set them ablaze. Rails were piled on the burning ties and heated until red hot. The soldiers called it a necktie party. They twisted the hot rails into grotesque shapes, rendering them completely useless. In two hours, they were riding back toward Newton Station.

James said to Sam, "Not a bad morning's work."

"How long you reckon it'll take the Secesh to put it back together again?"

"The locomotives? Never. We exploded'em into too many pieces. The trestles, telegraph, and tracks? Take'em at least several weeks, I suppose. I guess in the meanwhile, they'll have to find another way to haul stuff to their soldiers in Vicksburg."

"Yep. Tough shit."

"Did you hear that passenger back there at Newton Station say we are 'hell-bent' to free their niggers?"

"Yep. Is that why we're here?"

"I've been hearing and reading for two years that we're trying to squash a rebellion and save the union."

"You believe that?"

"Nope. I think it is all about their wonderful institution of slavery."

"Well, I didn't sign up to free no niggers. I'm for squashing the rebellion and going home. Besides, I heard that freeing the niggers will wreck the economy and way of life down here."

"Whose economy? Whose way of life? As far as I can see, only the well-to-do own slaves. I didn't see any back home in Springfield. So all I know about slaves is what I have seen in Tennessee and Mississippi. They look like oppressed people to me. So if in the course of squashing the rebellion, the slaves are freed, it's okay by me. I don't give a rat's ass about wealthy southern gentlemen losing their investment in free labor."

Sam rubbed his chin. "Hmm. James, I'm gonna to have to think on that."

It was shortly after noon when they arrived again at Newton Station. The depot and storeroom were burning. James could see the storeroom's food and supplies had been removed and the hospital's surgeon and several walking patients were allowed carry some of it to the hospital. A warehouse near the depot containing rifles, uniforms, and saddles was also burning. The ties leading into Newton Station had been burned and the rails heated and twisted. They rejoined the main body near the center of town. The detachment sent west to destroy the railroad and telegraph for ten miles toward Jackson was the last to return to Newton Station.

The raiders sat about waiting for the order to march. James noticed their droopy eyelids. This morning's work had also taken its toll. They had not slept for almost forty hours. They smelled of horses, new and old sweat in uniforms covered first with mud and dust, and now soot. James detected new smells coming from the men – wood smoke and whiskey. Troops from the main body had discovered a barrel of whiskey in one of the cars of the passenger train. More troopers than James could count were at some stage of drunkenness.

Word was passed by Grierson that they should be overheard discussing plans to depart to the east. James and the scouts made inquiries of townspeople and the sick and wounded Confederate soldiers about conditions east of Newton Station. They knew Grierson would not allow a break for rest. Word would soon get to the Confederate forces in Jackson and Vicksburg that the raiders had struck again, this time with their closest and most destructive attack. Only their speed and deception would keep the Confederates off their trail until they were miles and many hours from any strike.

The bugler sounded "Boots and Saddles" and Grierson gave the order to march. James and Sam rejoined Richard and rode at the head of the column east out of Newton Station along the smoldering railroad. Several miles short of the Chunky River, they turned sharply southwest. They were headed again for the heartland of the Confederacy and the unknown. Their horses were tired and marched with empty nose bags. Their saddles had not been removed for almost two days.

James shook his head and took a second look through the trees. "Appears to be a north-south road," he said pointing into the afternoon sun.

They stopped. Richard looked at his watch. "We can't be more than ten minutes ahead of the lead battalion. Better find out quick if we can use it or if the Secesh are using it."

"If everybody is as tired as I am, this is not the time to find the Secesh on this road – or anyplace else."

Sam looked at his horse and sighed. "My horse is all wore down. Couldn't chase any rebs until tomorrow. Tell'em to come back then."

The three chuckled quietly while sitting their horses at the edge of the forest. With rifles in hand and using hand signals, they spread out and edged toward the road. Out of earshot, but still within sight of each other, they moved onto the road. James was flanked by Richard and Sam. He signaled them, and then dismounted to examine the fresh tracks. He knew they would keep watch while he was on the ground. After checking the opposite side of the road, Richard and Sam joined him. "Several wagons passed to the south a short time ago. I think civilians. A number of the party is on foot. At least two are children."

Richard ordered, "Sam, go back and let Colonel Blackburn know that we can use the road. Catch up to us. We're going south."

By mid-afternoon, the column overtook a band of citizens "fleeing the Yankees" in wagons and buggies. They carried household goods and valuables. As the troops passed them, they relieved the refugees of bacon and other foods they could put into their empty haversacks.

The exhausted troops were ready for the next plantation and a good night's sleep. Among Grierson's papers was a report from a Mississippi Unionist who identified for the Federals the state's largest plantations. He had the foresight to include directions and an estimate of livestock at most of the plantations in his report. Grierson's raiders used several plantations for bivouac, food for the troops, and forage for the horses. They also replaced worn horses with fresh ones or mules from plantation stocks. During these stops, the brigade farriers had time to attend to loose or missing horseshoes.

Riding three miles ahead of the column with Richard, James kept watch on both sides of the road for anything that would affect the brigade's passing. He also looked for signals from Sam and the two Butternut Guerillas reconnoitering the right flank. Richard watched for signals from another three man scout team on the left.

James demanded, "How far is it to this place where the ol' man said we could take a break?"

Richard glanced down at his hand-drawn sketch of Jasper County then at the southern horizon. "I think we're almost there. Maybe a mile more."

"Since Philadelphia and Decatur, this march has been tough on both the men and horses. But extra riding to divert attention is better than giving the Secesh a chance to catch up to us or, worse, cut us off with an ambush."

"I don't mind a forced march as much this afternoon. Can you imagine how pissed that Secesh General Pemberton is going to be when he gets word about what we did to his trains and main railroad?"

James laughed and took another long glance to the west looking for Sam. "Pennsylvania man or not, Pemberton may be madder than the bees were when I hit that nest the other day."

"I must say, you had the good sense to run like the very devil himself was after you."

"I agree, a forced march to avoid pissed-off Secesh or a head-long run from angry bees is nothing compared to letting either of 'em catch your ass!"

Richard laughed and again compared his sketch, made from Grierson's map, to the landscape unfolding before them. "That's our turn up ahead. Take Sam and his bunch on a wide sweep of the west side past the turn. When you're satisfied, return and post a guard of four to guide the column into the plantation."

"Okay. So, you're doing the east side with the left flank guys and riding ahead to the plantation?"

"Right. If I find anything amiss, I'll send word to you at this junction. You do the same."

"Got it!" James spurred his horse and turned her toward the afternoon sun. In two minutes, he was riding beside Sam and the right-flank scouts.

The brigade stopped at the plantation along the Bogue Falema and rested for three hours. James was convinced that Grierson would have preferred to continue the march. He also knew the "ol' man" was resting the brigade only to continue the march and put as much distance between them and Newton Station in as short a time as possible. Most of the troops slid from their saddles and fell fast asleep where they landed on the new spring grass. A few had to wait their turn while standing guard at various picket points.

By the time Grierson's officers had the brigade mounted and under way again, Richard, James, and the Butternut Guerillas were on the road south and could see the outskirts of Garlandville. The town appeared more prosperous than Philadelphia or Newton Station. The houses in the distance were white and glowing in the late afternoon sunlight. From the ridge where they stood, James could see that the road into town was blocked with overturned wagons, barrels, and boxes. Richard ordered his men to the flanks, telling them to stay out of sight.

Richard turned to James and handed him his field glasses. "You ready to see what we're up against?"

James took a look. "I detect movement, but can't see well enough to recognize weapons or count men. Let's get closer."

They moved forward together at first. Richard carried the field glasses on a strap over his head and left shoulder. Now they took turns advancing slowly, one at a time, while the other covered his movement with his rifle. James could see the barricade was manned by men too old to be in the Confederate army. There were more than twenty men behind the barricade, but not many more. They were armed with shotguns and a few rifles. They obviously were a volunteer home guard and wore civilian clothing.

Richard signaled. He had seen enough. They made their way back to the Butternut Guerillas. Leaving Richard and the scouts maintaining visual contact, James went back north at a gallop to meet the main column.

James reported their discovery to Blackburn. Blackburn took James with him to report to Grierson, who was riding near the middle of the column playing his Jew's harp. When he saw them approach, he stopped his music and put the harp into his pocket. After reflecting for a moment on their report, he ordered his officers to organize a charge.

Richard reported no change when they reached the position of the Butternut Guerillas. The Federals moved their charge line, two horsemen deep, into plain view of Garlandville's home guard. The locals' response was to take cover behind their makeshift barricade and point their weapons at the Federals.

James was mounted and on the right flank of the charge line. He was annoyed with himself because he was trembling. He thought these are just a few little old guys – this will be over in a minute. Yet he didn't feel any different than just before his first battle at Shiloh. The sun was almost down, but James noticed sweat inside his gauntlets and on his spine. He shifted in his saddle and held his saber at order arms. He turned his head to look down the charge line for Richard. He could not see him, but knew he was there on the left flank. His eye caught the glint of a shotgun barrel in the waning sunlight. He tried to relax, but instead his back stiffened.

James was mounted and on the right flank of the charge line. He was annoyed with himself because he was trembling. He thought these are just a few little old guys – this will be over in a minute. Yet he didn't feel any different than just before his first battle at Shiloh. The sun was almost down, but James noticed sweat inside his gauntlets and on his spine. He shifted in his saddle and held his saber at order arms. He turned his head to look down the charge line for Richard. He could not see him, but knew he was there on the left flank. His eye caught the glint of a shotgun barrel in the waning sunlight. He tried to relax, but instead his back stiffened.

Grierson gave the order and the bugler sounded, "Charge!"

The horses nickered as spurs hit their flanks. They leaped forward into a gallop. Most of the old men in the home guard fired too soon and were reloading their shotguns at the time the charging Federals were upon them with raised sabers. Several held their fire until the charging troops were in range.

James was yelling to his horse, urging her to go faster, when the second barrage of gunfire was leveled at them. Suddenly, the ground rushed up at his face. The center of the line sailed over the barricade. The second charge line was fast approaching the barricade when the home guard dropped their weapons and ran, trying to dodge the oncoming saber-bearing horsemen. The first charge line rode through them without striking the fleeing unarmed men. They wheeled their mounts about and the home guard stopped running and stood there, surrounded. They held hands above their heads while the second charge line was sharply drawing rein to avoid trampling them.

In his dream, James could hear a piano and see the wedding party smiling and waving as he and his bride left the church. The church was decorated with white ribbon and flowers. Leaving the doorway of the church, a Butternut Guerilla threw water in his face. He sat up, coughing and sputtering. His vision was blurred and his head was pounding. As his vision cleared, he realized he was sitting on the ground. Sam was kneeling beside him holding an open tin canteen with a worried look on his face. James felt the evening breeze on his bare chest. He looked down and found his shirt torn open to his waist. The shirt was a bloody mess. He frowned and tried to focus on Sam's face. Several soldiers in blue stood next to Sam. He tried to hear what Sam was saying.

At last, James spoke. "Did you ask, 'Am I all right?'"

Sam was still worried. "Yes. Are you all right? We couldn't find where you were hit."

"Hit?"

"Yes. It looked like you were shot."

James felt a rush and looked down at his chest and abdomen again. "I feel fine, except for my head."

"That must be your horse's blood on your shirt. You both took a tumble. When the tumblin' ended, her head was on your chest."

This new information made James's head hurt worse. He looked around. "Where is she?"

"She's dead. Killed outright. Shot in the head. We thought you too had gone on up."

James looked down at his boots to break eye contact. He reflected for a moment on the fact that the bullet taken by his horse had been aimed at the center of his body. He shuddered.

Grierson and Blackburn rode over and dismounted. Blackburn worriedly asked, "James, how are you?"

James struggled to his feet, stumbled, and started to fall, but Sam and the surgeon caught him.

"Okay, sir."

After a minute or so, he felt steadier. Sam and the surgeon explained that it was James's horse that was shot. Before Grierson and Blackburn headed off to the captured home guard, Grierson offered, "I am pleased to have you still with us."

"Thank you, sir."

Sam had removed James' bedroll, rifle, saddle, and saddlebags from the body of his horse. James pulled on a fresh shirt from his saddlebags and they walked to a nearby stable that belonged to a citizen of Garlandville. There, James "requisitioned" a fine black stallion.

On their way to the stable, they had walked past the home guard. James thought the Garlandville men looked more ill at ease now than he felt before the charge. Some of them were clearly frightened for their lives. Dust from the charge still swirled about the surrendered men of the home guard as they stood facing the brigade's officers. From the town beyond the circle of horsemen, women and children were crying. Horses snorted and nickered. The brigade soldiers were already storing their weapons and the captured arms of the home guard.

Soon, Grierson gave them a short but sincere talk about the foolish way they had endangered themselves. They acknowledged their mistake, but thought they had to defend their families and homes. Then Grierson released them. When they understood that the brigade's mission would not bring harm to them, they welcomed the Federals to Garlandville. One of their home guardsmen volunteered his services as a guide.

As a result of the charge, the brigade had one severely injured trooper from a gunshot wound and the loss of James's horse. James was now mounted on the tall, strong black horse; he knew this was a horse the army could not afford to buy. The Butternut Guerillas admired the new addition to their outfit.

It was dark by the time the brigade marched southwest out of Garlandville. The volunteer guide rode with the Butternut Guerillas at the head of the column. Grierson told the scouts to lead on through the night to the next designated plantation. James was not sure how effective he and the scouts would be. He was looking forward to a night's rest.

It was dark by the time the brigade marched southwest out of Garlandville. The volunteer guide rode with the Butternut Guerillas at the head of the column. Grierson told the scouts to lead on through the night to the next designated plantation. James was not sure how effective he and the scouts would be. He was looking forward to a night's rest.

Two hours later, James yawned for what he thought was the twentieth time. "Richard, I'm dog tired."

"Yeah. Me too. How're you feeling?"

"My head still hurts. My shoulder and back have joined the pain chorus."

There was no conversation in the hours that followed. Richard fell asleep in the saddle. Richard and many soldiers had tied themselves to their saddles. More of the command was asleep than awake.

It was almost midnight when they arrived at the Bender Plantation.

Chapter 7: Rachel's Secret

Just before midnight, the ground shook. Rachel was awake in an instant. The vibrations continued, growing stronger by the minute. Rachel had been asleep for less than an hour when she was awakened by the tremor. She lay back and listened while fidgeting with one of the one hundred forty-four tight rolls of colorful scrap cloth stitched together to make her six-foot long pallet. Each roll was an inch in diameter and almost three feet long, giving her pallet a comfortable width when sewn together.

* * *

Rachel and Rebecca had stayed awake with their pa discussing the day's big news that Yankees had reached Newton Station.

Yankees were all she and her neighbors had talked about on the way from the fields to the barns. They were careful not to be overheard by Griffin Bender. Some had been wild with joy at the thought that freedom could soon arrive. Others cautioned that because the Yankees were at Newton Station was no reason to believe they would come to Bender Plantation. Or, even if they came, that it would mean freedom. After all, they argued, in two years of war, the news brought back by Wash, Jerome, and Griffin Bender told the stories of many victories won by the armies of the Confederate States of America.

After supper, John, Jerome, Wash, and two other men had engaged in a heated argument about the news from Newton Station. Rachel sat on the step to their cabin eavesdropping. Wash was skeptical. "The Secesh hab strong d'fense set all 'round Jackson and Vicksburg. Same be true for Philadelphia and other towns. I jes don't see how dey could be dis close 'thout us hearin' 'bout it a'fore now."

John had pointed to Wash. He spoke evenly and without excitement. "Wash, we've heard your stories from the time you valet'd for Massa back when he was in the Secesh army. Now, you tell me, is it not possible that Jerome's friend *might* have seen Yankees up at Newton Station?"

Wash pushed his straw hat to the back of his head, revealing his receding hairline, and sighed. "Well, I s'pose it's possible. But a'fore Griffin Bender figured he was too ol' to be in the army, I saw how dey planned to stop the Yankees from invadin' Mississippi."

Jerome argued, "Well, I b'lieves dat carriage driver from up Garlandville way. I'se talked wid him when we's met up drivin' our marsters to the same places. He told me he seed dem Yankees wid his own eyes. He say dey storm'd into Newton Station on hosses and took ober de place."

Wash raised an eyebrow at this. "Well, sounds mighty convincin'.... But, I don't know."

John offered, "The real question is, what does all this mean for us on dis here plantation? Jerome tells us this Garlandville fellow goes back to his marster and spills the beans. Dem white folks up there in Garlandville are makin' preparations to defend against dem Yankees. I say again, whether the news is true or not, we don't tell Marster Bender nothin'."

Wash said, "John, you'se been a saying dat eber since you heard."

Jerome added, "Sho' is, John. I been tellin' eberbody, not to let on we heared nothin' a' tall."

"Good. Let's keep it dat way."

Rachel was sure the same talk was repeated in every group of family and friends around the supper fires that Friday night. She heard that everyone had agreed not to share their news with Griffin Bender. Rachel was more interested in what they would do after being freed. She felt that John's discussions with her and Rebecca were entertaining – the three of them had laughed about their visions of life after the war and the coming of freedom.

Rebecca had told them what she wanted. "Why, I would head straight for New Orleans. Dey ain't nothin' in Mississippi! I'll start me a lil' ol' inn, serving meals. I know one thing. I'll be outta dem cotton fields! Dat fo' shore! What about you, Rai?"

"Oh, I don't know. Maybe I stay here. Start a school, or somethin'. Everybody will need some education."

"Hmm. Maybe I stay long enough fo' you to teach me readin', writin', and figurin'. Sho' don't want nobody cheatin' me. Den, I'm gone!"

* * *

The gentle tremor continued. Awake now, but groggy, Rachel sensed those conversations had ended just minutes ago. A few hours before, she had thought there were many places the Yankees could go and not pass through the Bender Plantation. In her haze, she asked herself why would anyone – even the Yankees – go out their way to come here?

Rachel spoke urgently, just above a whisper. "Bec? Rebecca, you feel that?"

It was dark in the cabin and she could see only the outline of Rebecca's covered body. She thought about touching Rebecca, but instead called again softly, "Rebecca?"

Rebecca slowly awakened and answered her sister in a hoarse voice, "Huh? Wha-What? What's wrong?"

Rachel could feel her heart flutter with excitement. She could hear horses. She felt joy, but tried to suppress it in case it was all a dream. She did not want to hope for the impossible. She tried to whisper, but her voice was rising. "Rebecca, the ground is tremblin'! I think I hear them. I think they're here!"

"Gal, what you babblin' 'bout now? What you mean, the ground is trembling? Dem who's here?"

Rachel and Rebecca's pallets lay side by side on the ground that was the floor of their cabin. Their father slept on the other side of the one-room log cabin. Rachel had found and dragged home three leftover slabs of wood from the sawmill. Each slab was less than an inch thick, but together they were wide enough and served her purpose. Rachel used them to keep her pallet off the damp ground.

Rachel was wide awake and still on her pallet. She sat up and leaned back on her elbows. She had lived all her life, nearly seventeen years, in south central Mississippi – first on the Taylor Plantation and now the Bender Plantation – and this was the first time she had felt the ground tremble. She remembered their old cabin and its wooden floor at the Taylor Plantation on the Leaf River over in Smith County.

Unlike the cabin built of planks at the Taylor Plantation, this one was made of crude logs and chinked with mud to keep the wind out. The shutters were slabs with some of the bark still attached. The one table they used for preparing and eating meals and two log benches were also made from slabs that rested atop short sections of tree trunks. Rachel and Rebecca slept with their feet toward the fireplace at their end of the cabin. The ground inside the cabin near the fireplace remained drier than John's end of the cabin.

"Bec, I think they are here. Somethin' strange is goin' on...."

"You could a waited 'til mornin' to tell me dis nonsense. It's *you* that's strange! Now let me sleep. It's the middle of the night!"

Rebecca turned her back to Rachel and covered her head in a huff.

Rachel smiled at her older sister's retort in spite of herself. She lay down again and listened.

Rebecca suddenly sat up. "Rai, the ground is tremblin'. Somethin's goin' on."

Rachel smiled in the darkness and said nothing. She listened again to the sound of approaching horses – many horses. She could not imagine the size of the herd that could make that rumbling sound.

"Rai, you hear that?"

Rachel made no response. She put her hand over her mouth to stifle her giggles but couldn't. She didn't want to wake her father.

She laughed softly. "I don't hear nothin'."

The sound was closer. She heard her father stirring, fitfully, in his sleep.

By now, she was almost convinced that the night horsemen were the Yankees arriving at the Bender Plantation. Her father stirred again. Next to her, Rebecca sat up, spilling her covers to the side of her pallet.

"Okay, I deserved that," said Rebecca.

Rachel could hear a smile in Rebecca's voice.

Through a yawn without raising his head, John said, "Sounds like we got more comp'ny than we can feed."

Jumping up from her mattress, Rachel exclaimed, "Let's find out if it's the Yankees!"

They did not waste time lighting a candle. Rachel and Rebecca dressed in the dark faster than one could say Brer Rabbit and were out the door before John moved from his mattress. Once outside, they saw their neighbors also coming out to see what was happening.

From the top of the small hill in front of the smokehouse, Rachel notice the shadowy figures of men mounted on horses in a column of twos, moving at a walk toward the big house. They came from the direction of the road that ran east to Montrose. The first men had arrived at the big house, but still she could not see the end of the column, somewhere beyond the pecan tree-lined entrance to the plantation. Word was moving quickly through the crowd that the riders were Yankees. By now, all of the enslaved crowd of one hundred twenty-six adults and their fifty-two children were outside and buzzing with excitement.

Time and again, Rachel heard the same question asked by different voices. "Is freedom come?"

She edged away from the crowd. Rachel wanted to know more. She moved through the shadows, ever closer to the back of the big house where the head of the column of horsemen had stopped. She saw Griffin Bender come out of the rear door of the big house. He shouted something angrily to the men, but Rachel could not make out the words. She was determined to hear what was being said. She felt her heart beat faster and her temples throb as she crept forward. Her hands shook as she slowly raised them and placed both over her heart. Rachel thought again, could freedom really be here?

Rachel dried her sweaty palms on the coarse homespun cloth of her ankle-length dress. She grasped it with both hands, raised it to mid-calf, took a last look about, and ran, with her pigtails bouncing, across the street that led from the quarters to the big house. She paused at the edge of the kitchen house to catch her breath and try to let her heart beat slow. The kitchen house sat only a few yards from the back door of the big house – just far enough not to endanger the big house if there was a kitchen fire. Both the big house and the kitchen house faced east. They occupied the top of a hill that was shaped like the moon in its first quarter. The hilltop was the middle hill of three that together formed two saddles. Just east of the easternmost hill was a large pond where livestock drank when returning from grazing. It was from this direction the troopers continued to arrive.

Rachel made sure she stayed out of Bender's line of sight. She remained in the shadow of the kitchen house and took a few more cautious steps toward Bender in the open door and the men with whom he was still arguing. She could hear Bender clearly now.

"This is an outrage! You and your men have no right to be on my property! You are to leave forthwith."

A stern-faced man replied, "Sir, I am Colonel William Prince, Quartermaster of the Seventh Illinois Cavalry."

Rachel thought he had a strange accent. But, she could make out what he said, for he spoke in strong, measured tones. "Mister Bender, we require forage and fresh mounts. We will appropriate what we need from you. My commander, Colonel Grierson, has decided that we will bivouac here tonight. The matter is closed."

When Bender heard this, Rachel saw him turn on his heels and stalk back into the big house and slam the door. She looked again at the Yankee colonel. She thought Colonel Prince looked almost as tired as her father.

Rachel was startled by a voice behind her. She heard another man's voice in the same clipped accent as Colonel Prince's say, "You there in the shadows, come on out with your hands up." Rachel quickly raised her hands and slowly turned to face a man in a gray shirt and a gray floppy hat pointing a revolver at her. His shirt reminded her of Bender's Confederate uniform. She froze. Her mouth dropped open, but she could not speak. The man nudged his horse's flanks with his heels. His tall black horse moved toward Rachel. She thought, *oh my God. Maybe these people aren't Yankees after all.* Her hopes were fading. The horseman moved to cut off her retreat toward the quarters. Expecting to be beaten, Rachel closed her mouth and swallowed hard. She became aware that her knees were weak as she tried to move to obey his order. She stumbled over a clump of Johnson grass and into the light in front of his horse, struggling to maintain her balance.

Even in the dim light, Rachel could see that the white man's face and trousers were covered with dirt and grime. But somehow his shirt did not appear to be as dirty as the rest of him. He looked at her from head to foot over the long barrel of his .44. Then he holstered it.

She heard him say over his shoulder, "It's okay, Sam. It's only a slave girl."

He turned back to face Rachel. "You can put your hands down now. Don't go sneaking around in the shadows. You could get shot."

Rachel found her voice. "Yessuh."

"Come with me. You can help us remove rations from the kitchen and smokehouse."

"Yessuh."

Rachel felt less frightened now that she heard the man *almost* ask her to help instead of barking orders to her the way Bender always did. He had spoken in even tones to her as if giving advice, then asking for help. Rachel walked beside his horse the short distance to the smokehouse where Colonel Prince's quartermasters were already removing salted beef and pork.

"I'm James. What is your name?"

"Rachel."

"Well, Rachel, you go on and help my friends with the meat."

"First, please, suh, tell me if y'all are Yankees."

"We are."

Rachel's face broke into a toothy smile and she took a little leap into the air. "Oh, thank God!" She more skipped than walked to the smokehouse, her joy returning.

When Rachel came out with her arms loaded with meat, she heard James talking to Jerome, Bender's liveryman, and his friend Cicero near the smokehouse. He asked both to help. Jerome shuffled his feet, held his head down, and looked at the ground as he always did when a white man spoke to him. Cicero behaved much the same way. Rachel knew that Jerome, Cicero, and other black men did this to avoid conflict with whites, yet it still grated on her nerves – like putting salt into a fresh wound. She turned away and tried not to listen. They came over and worked beside Rachel. In spite of not wanting to show her disappointment in Jerome, Rachel shot him a cold glance. She could see his shoulders sag and she felt remorse for having made him feel worse. She realized she should have shown more respect to a man old enough to be her father.

Together, they helped the quartermasters load the meat into one of Bender's wagons – which Jerome had cheerfully provided along with two mules – for the short ride to what was rapidly becoming a campsite near Otak Creek. Rachel and Cicero sat on the board seat of the wagon with Jerome as he drove it slowly down the street between the cabins, following the quartermasters toward Otak Creek.

While passing near the cabins, Emma, Jerome's wife, came out and walked beside the slow-moving wagon. Emma demanded, "How you git yo'self mixed up wid dese Yankees?" You know ol' Massa gone be so mad he can't see straight 'bout dem takin' his stores! What you think he gone do to any nigger he finds out helped dese Yankees?"

Jerome replied, "Soon, we gone be free. We won't have no Massa to think 'bout den."

"Ain't a one of dese Yankees said a word 'bout freein' no nigger. Don't be so simple!"

Rachel noticed Jerome stiffen. His nostrils flared. Jerome's response was to slap his lines against the backs of his mules. "Com'on, git up dere!"

The mules picked up the pace, gradually pulling ahead of Emma. She called after them, "Jerome Bender, you gone git worse dan beat. Massa gone sell you off to New Orleans or Texas or Gawd knows where."

Rachel looked back and saw Emma put her hands over her face and heard her say through her tears, "Den what me and the chilluns gone do?"

Colonel Grierson's brigade camped by company, battalion, and regiment at the edge of a freshly plowed field. Some of the brigade was scattered in groups among pine trees and on unplowed ground that sloped gently down to the west and Otak Creek. A few men made fires, but most were already asleep. Though Rachel could not see them, there were sentries posted in the tree line and mounted scouts patrolled beyond the camp's perimeter. The troopers she could see appeared to have more interest in spreading their bedrolls than eating.

As the quartermasters and scouts built their fire, they reveled in the day's adventures in and around Newton Station. Rachel asked of no one in particular, "Does this mean that freedom has come?" She was surprised that her voice did not quiver or sound shaky. For a long moment, no one spoke. All of the men, black and white, stared at her. From the look they gave her, she began to have second thoughts about asking questions. Emma, Rebecca, and others had told her it was not proper to discuss certain topics with men – said it threatened their manhood.

James took a step toward her. "Good question. You're Rachel, aren't you?"

"Yessuh."

James turned to Jerome and Cicero, "And you?"

"I'm Jerome. Dis here is my friend, Cicero."

James turned again to face Rachel. "I don't think freedom has come for you all, Rachel. Not yet."

"Why not?" They stared at her again.

"Well, that's because the Secesh ain't been whupped in these parts. They're still carrying on the war. Our brigade is just passing through."

Stares or no, Rachel was determined to learn all she could from James while he was willing to respond. She asked, "Why ain't y'all goin' to whup the Secesh and stay?"

James took a deep breath and put a finger on his chin. Before he could speak, Jerome said, "Rachel, didn't you hear'em? They done already whup the Secesh up yonder at Newton Station."

Several of the quartermasters agreed that they had been successful at Newton Station. One concluded, "It looked to me like we gave them a pretty good kick in the ass at Newton Station today."

Snickers and agreement could be heard from the quartermasters.

"Now hold on." James put in, raising a hand as he spoke. "Yeah, Josh, we hit the rebs pretty hard today, that's true. Oh, this here is Josh, and over there is Davey and Sam."

Josh held up a hand in a small wave. Davey and Sam just stood there – trying to figure how to react when a white person is introduced to an enslaved person. James ignored them and turned to Rachel. "Like I was saying, we're down here now, but just passing through. Any slaves in and around Newton Station before we hit there are still slaves. Why? Because there aren't any Union troops up there now and that means Newton Station is still in Confederate territory. Rachel is right; we would have defeat the rebs here and stay in order for you to be free. But with just our Sixth and Seventh Illinois Cavalry Regiments, we're not nearly a large enough force to do that."

Reproved, all eyes were on Rachel again, more intense than before. Jerome's face and the faces of Cicero and the white men around them had fallen after hearing James's conclusion. Rachel felt her face flush against the chill of the midnight air. She almost smiled as she remembered that her face would not betray her and turn red like Isabelle Taylor's did when embarrassed or angered. Rachel decided to change the subject. "What happened at Newton Station?"

Though tired, they smiled again and launched into recounting their exploits. Davey started with, "Well, yesterday, Colonel Blackburn's battalion captured a bridge we needed to get to Newton. After all the rain the night before, we would've had to ride a lot of miles looking for a place to ford the Pearl River."

Sam spoke, warming to the subject. "The bottom lands were flooded with reddish brown water at least three hundred yards away from the bridge. Fording would have been out of the question."

Cicero hit Jerome's elbow with the back of his hand. "Did it rain here night a'fore last?"

Jerome answered without taking his eyes off Sam. "Jes a lil' light shower."

James laughed at his memory of the bridge capture. "If we hadn't grabbed that bridge in time, the two Confederate trains we captured this morning would have been long gone by the time we got to Newton Station."

Cicero inquired, "How many Secesh did y'all kill?"

James answered, "None."

"How cum?"

"There was no Confederate force at Newton Station to fight. There were a few convalescing rebs at the little makeshift hospital in town. We galloped in with such speed and total surprise they had no time to resist or run. We captured both trains without firing a shot."

"What is con-va-lescin?"

"Means sick or wounded, recovering from what ails them."

"Oh."

Jerome asked, "What did y'all do wid dem trains?"

The soldiers roared with laughter. Sam said, "That's when the fun really began! A group o'us ripped up rails and set fire to piles of cross ties. We used the cross tie fires to heat and make neckties of the rails. Meanwhile, others blew up both locomotives, burned the cars, and tore down telegraph lines."

Rachel thought there is that word again: telegraph. She wanted to ask about words sent by telegraph; she wondered how it worked. She had heard Bender talk about sending messages by telegraph. She decided not to express interest in anything related to messages, for it could lead to the discovery of her ability to read and write. If Bender ever learned she could read, there would be big trouble after the Yankees left.

"Neckties?" asked a skeptical Jerome.

"Yeah, we heated the rails and twisted them so the rebs can't use them anymore. We call the twisted rails neckties."

"Oh."

Jerome and Cicero clapped their hands in enthusiastic applause and shouted hurrah and hallelujah while Rachel smiled. Somewhere in the remuda and picket line, a horse nickered and two more answered. When the applause stopped, the night was quiet again, except for crickets and the crackling sounds from the dry pine limbs burning in the small campfire.

James stretched and yawned, with both hands above his head. "Okay, enough stories for tonight. I've gotta get some sleep."

Rachel turned with Jerome and Cicero toward Bender's wagon for the trip up the hill to the quarters. "Yessuh. Us too."

* * *

The sound of reveille from the brigade's bugler echoed through the pines soon after first light. Bender had already sounded the horn for first call for the field hands. Everyone in the quarters was up before that on this Saturday morning, though many had been awake late the previous night, talking among themselves or with the soldiers. At the dawning of the new day, the excitement caused by the arrival of the Yankees had not abated. Though up and about early, the enslaved at the Bender Plantation showed little interest in putting in their half-day of tasks in the fields. As was their custom, on Saturdays they returned to the quarters for the usual afternoon of work in their personal gardens. They wanted to spend more time talking about the arrival of the Yankees and what it meant.

Rachel draped the family's mattresses over a crude log rail at the edge of their garden to sun as she did every Saturday when it did not rain. She opened and hooked the shutters on their two windows and emptied and washed their chamber buckets. Then she sat in the doorway to wait for Rebecca to call her and John to breakfast.

Looking down toward Otak Creek from slave row, Rachel saw a light blue haze hanging over the valley. She smelled smoke from pine wood burning and bacon frying in the quarters and over the soldiers' campfires. Though they were in the middle of a war, she felt there was a happy, almost hopeful sound in the voices of the soldiers and her neighbors. It resembled the anticipation she had experienced in the days waiting for the annual harvest celebration. She saw James pass two cabins over on his way. As she watched him stride up the hill toward the big house, she tried to imagine how her life would be different when Yankee soldiers like James returned to Jasper County and put an end to slavery. Over the sound of human voices and birds singing, Rachel heard the hammers of the brigade's farriers, replacing lost horseshoe or tightening loose ones.

When John returned from harnessing his mule team at the barn, he joined Rebecca and Rachel for breakfast. They ate their bacon and fried cornbread hurriedly. This was their habit in order to be on time for second call. Rebecca gave John and Rachel some of the molasses she kept for special occasions to eat with their cornbread. During and after breakfast, their conversation shifted again and again from the day's expected tasks to the Union soldiers who spent the night camped near Otak Creek.

"Freedom may ride in most any day now. Jes like dis here group of Yankees rode in, another bigger bunch will follow someday." Rebecca and Rachel hung on to each word John spoke. They still had more questions this morning about how he imagined being free would change their lives and the lives of their neighbors. The threesome was ready for field tasks, but this morning they would wait for second call at their cabin before moving toward the barn and stables.

Rebecca said, "That can't happen soon enough for me."

Rachel thought of her mother and was somber. She asked John, "Pa, do you think it is possible, someday after freedom comes, that we could find Ma again?"

"Rai, child, anything is possible. I jes don't know. Five long years have passed since that awful day back in '58." John put his right hand over his eyes. He sighed and continued. "I know she is never far from your minds. I, too, think of her everyday. It was a long time ago that she was sold from us. She could be far away by now. I heard that speculator was headed for New Orleans. She could a been sold into Texas or Arkansas from that market in New Orleans...." John's voice trailed off and they were quiet.

Rachel put her head against Rebecca's shoulder. Rebecca hugged her gently. Rachel stood in the doorway, lost in thought about her mother. She could still feel the hurt. Only now, it felt like a dull ache.

Rachel remembered seeing Isabelle Taylor the evening after Edna was led away in chains and asked her friend how she could stand by and let her mother be sold. Isabelle's answer was incomprehensible. Rachel would never be satisfied with Isabelle's explanation of how the "property" had to be sold and the money used to save the place after old man George Taylor had died.

John was standing on the ground in front of their cabin. He turned to look into the faces of his daughters. "You know, when we lost your mother, we grieved because she was taken from us – like she died; it was like they killed her. It hurt then and it still hurts. But today it feels more like white people did a very mean thing to us – a thing much worse than me or y'all being forced to watch her being beaten."

Rachel exclaimed, "Pa, that's *just* how I feel!"

Rebecca's tears were flowing and she sniffed. "Hmm huh, me too!"

They were interrupted by Emma and Ruth running toward them. Emma was calling John's name. Emma was out of breath and panting, but still tried to talk. "J-j-john, y-y-you got to help me," she stammered. "Massa gone beat'em to deaf or sell 'em! You gotta talk to Massa fo 'em!"

Rachel had long wondered why fellow workers continued asking John to speak to Bender for them. Could they not see that Bender almost never changed his mind after John spoke and, many times, would not let him speak at all? It seemed to Rachel that Bender listened more to Wash. Yet neighbors would seek John's help when they saw trouble coming.

John caught Emma by one elbow and said, "Emma, slow down. Take it easy. Sit down here on the step and catch your breath."

Emma hesitated and then sat down hard, still stammering, "Y-y-you gotta help!"

Ruth was speaking at the same time. "Dat lil' Fred done told Massa 'bout Jerome helpin' the Yankees haul his stores last night!"

Rebecca frowned and her eyes bored in on Ruth. She asked sharply, "Did he mention Rai?"

"No. But he sho' told 'bout Cicero helpin'. Massa lookin' for both of'em!"

Rachel embraced Ruth, her best friend, as Ruth continued. "He got the biggest mouf to be sich a lil' boy."

John said to no one in particular, "Aw, he jes a lil' youngun. He didn't know any better. Fred was jes totin' big news and bustin' to tell it. Well, no matter now. What's done's done."

John frowned. "Massa ain't gone listen to nobody on dis."

Rachel took a deep breath. "Pa, maybe Sergeant Darby and the Yankees can take Jerome and Cicero with'em when they pull out of here."

No one spoke as John rubbed his chin. Finally, he responded. "Good thought, daughter." John smiled broadly at Rachel. "I'm proud of you."

Emma, who had caught her breath, let out a wailing sound as she leapt up from her seat on the step and tried to grab Rachel by the throat. But Rachel was too quick for Emma and side-stepped Emma's clumsy charge. Ruth and Rebecca caught Emma and hugged her while trying to console her. Rachel understood Emma's reaction.

John explained, "Emma, Rai's idea is much better than waitin' to find out what Massa will do when he gets his hands on Jerome and Cicero. It's not like being sold away and having no way to get back. If the Yankees will take Jerome and Cicero wid'em, dey will be the first of all of us on dis plantation to be free."

John held out both hands toward Emma. "Think of it. Jerome will be free! I'm sure he'll find a way to return for you and your lil' ones."

Emma was not struggling anymore, but was not speaking either. She just stood there with nostrils flaring and her chest heaving inside her disheveled dress. She let Rebecca and Ruth hug her while she continued staring at John through her tears. Rachel thought Emma looked like a perplexed child trying to accept loss.

While Rebecca and Ruth walked Emma back to her cabin, John and Rachel discussed how to convince the Yankees to take Jerome and Cicero. The execution of the plan fell to Rachel. Second call sounded. John left to meet Bender and his plow crew. When he saw Bender, he asked a lot of detailed questions about where it was best to plow today and about planting planned for the following week to delay Bender.

* * *

Rachel donned her bonnet and filled her water buckets at the pump behind the kitchen house. When she saw James Darby from her doorway, he was headed in the same direction. With the extra weight on her shoulders, she walked carefully on bare feet to avoid stepping on stones and horse dung that lay along the path to the rear door of the kitchen house. Her shoulders were stooped with the weight of two buckets of water hanging from her yoke. Today her pigtails were tucked under her bonnet.

Miss Mabel met her at the door with a big smile. "My, my. You shore are lookin nice dis mornin'. Dat's a pretty frock. Come on in and set yo' load down."

She set the buckets gently on the floor without spilling water. "G'mornin', Miss Mabel. I can't linger. Please tell me where the Yankee bosses are."

Miss Mabel's smile vanished and her arms flew akimbo. "Whatcha want wid dem? Dis here sounds like trouble to me."

"Miss Mabel, I needs to hurry on my way. My pa sent me."

At the mention of John, Miss Mabel raised an eyebrow and took a deep breath. "Now, chile, you know I promised yo' ma that I would look out for you and yo' sister. Are you mixed up in somethin' dangerous?"

"No'm." Rachel wondered if she had lied. She pushed the thought away. Now she had to focus on the task John had entrusted to her.

Miss Mabel glanced toward the front door of the kitchen house, which led to the rear of the big house. She looked at Rachel out of the corner of her eye and continued speaking in a whisper. "I 'spect dis, in some way, is connected to dis Jerome and Cicero bitness. A jaybud would fly back'ards on no mo' brains dan the two o'dem got put t'gether."

Rachel smiled. "Miss Mabel, please."

"Okay, child. I 'spect dat water is for dem Yankee mens you huntin' and not dis here kitchen."

"Yes'm."

"I served'em coffee. Dey's on the front veranda havin' a meetin'. Whatcha gone do now dat you know where dey is?"

"I met Sergeant Darby last night. We need him to help us."

"You mean you knows one o' dem?"

"Yes'm."

"Oh, my, my!"

Miss Mabel dropped her head and fidgeted with her apron. Soon her eyes brightened. "I know! I'll go wid you. I'll carry cups fo' de water."

Before Rachel could protest, Miss Mabel turned her ample frame and bounced over to a cupboard and was loading cups onto a tray. Rachel smiled and shook her head.

The men stopped talking when Rachel and Miss Mabel walked onto the veranda. Miss Mabel headed straight for the wiry man with long dark whiskers sitting at one end of the veranda, announcing in her most pleasant voice that she had fetched cool water for everyone. Colonel Grierson smiled, took a cup, and said, "Thank you."

From Miss Mabel's lead, and the deference shown by the men, Rachel knew that the slim, bearded man was the Yankee boss. She edged closer with a bucket of water to serve Grierson first. While she carefully moved about the veranda among the sea of dirty blue uniforms, she scanned the unfamiliar faces for James Darby. She saw a man seated next to Grierson turn his attention to a Colton's map of Mississippi. He looked like the man who identified himself the night before as Colonel Prince. Colonel Grierson resumed his staff meeting, discussing the merits of advancing west. Rachel heard talk of linking up with General Grant when Grant crossed the Mississippi River to attack Vicksburg. They did not seem to know when this crossing would happen, or if it had already occurred. This news was exciting and disappointing. Attacking Vicksburg was good news. She was disappointed that they seemed to know so little about what the other Yankees were doing. She feared this would lead to yet another defeat at the hands of the Confederates and jeopardize her chance to realize her dreams.

Rachel was working her way toward the steps to leave the veranda when she heard Richard Surby speaking to Colonel

Blackburn and Colonel Grierson about the need to find a place to ford the Leaf River. Rachel realized they would pass near the Taylor Plantation. She looked back at the man who spoke and found James standing beside Richard. Her heart pounded. She thought she would make her plea to James for Jerome and Cicero without anyone else hearing. She felt she could not ask James, a white man and a stranger, to speak with her alone.

Rachel glanced about. There was not a member of the Bender family in sight. She decided not to let this moment pass. "Sergeant Darby, I know where you can ford the Leaf."

Startled, James turned to her. He failed to recognize Rachel wearing a bonnet with her braids tucked underneath. "Your voice is familiar. Are you Rachel?"

"Yessuh."

Richard asked, "Did you say you know where we can ford the Leaf?"

"Yessuh. My pa used the ford in Smith County between the Taylor and Henry Plantations. It's less than a day's ride west of here."

Colonel Blackburn picked up the map and offered it to Rachel. "Here, show us on the map."

Rachel's jaw dropped and her face went ashen. She felt weak. She stopped and set her bucket on the floor. Looking into the bucket, Rachel closed her mouth and swallowed hard.

Blackburn waited. James asked, "Rachel, are you okay?"

Slowly, she nodded her head, yes. She felt as if her feet were rooted to the floor.

Blackburn asked again. "Please show us."

James offered, "Sir, maybe she can't read."

Blackburn dropped his hand holding out the map. "Oh, yes. Sorry. You're quite right, Sergeant."

This time it was Miss Mabel who glanced about for members of the Bender household. Miss Mabel stepped toward James. She lowered her voice and whispered in a proud conspiratorial tone, "Oh, *yes* she can too read! Now I sho' do hope and trust y'all won't let

Massa Bender find out. It ain't lawful for us to know how to read. She's the onliest one of us who can."

Rachel's jaw dropped again. She looked at Miss Mabel as though she thought the old woman had taken leave of her senses. Then she pictured the secret classes she held for Rebecca and John in their cabin. If Massa Bender only knew.... Rachel shook her head to help clear her mind. She had considered taking the risk to reveal that she could read, but made no decision about taking this risk with strange white men. Miss Mabel had spoken. So there was nothing left to consider except being seen or heard by the Benders.

She made a hesitant step toward Colonel Blackburn and took the map in her hands. Rachel turned the map, found Smith County, and pointed to a bend in the Leaf River. She suggested a route through the piney country and places to ford the Tallahala, Leaf, and Strong rivers. She handed the map back to Colonel Blackburn and looked up at James. "Sir, we need your help. Do you remember Jerome and Cicero, the two men who helped you load stores last night?"

"Yes. I remember."

"Well, Massa Bender found out the two of them helped you. They're in big trouble. Massa is out lookin' for them now. He will beat them, or, worse, sell them away from their families. Please, sir, take them with you when you leave."

James looked at Richard and Colonel Blackburn. "Colonel, one of these men is Bender's liveryman. He could help us with the horse and mule herd."

Colonel Grierson had listened quietly. He leaned forward in his seat and cleared his throat. His saber scabbard made a scraping sound as it rubbed against the side of his chair. All eyes shifted to him. "Rachel, it took courage for you to help us. We're beholden to you. Your secret is safe with us."

With a twinkle in his eyes, Grierson added, "Colonel Prince will see that Bender's two men and all of his horses and mules are well employed."

Chapter 8: **Return to Tiffany Plantation**

Sweat streamed down Isaac's face. It dripped steadily from the tip of his nose and chin. Isaac's coarse long-sleeved shirt was soaked; so was the bandanna tied loosely around his head to divert sweat from his eyes. Thursday, the ninth day of July, was as hot a day as was seen on the coast of South Carolina during the summer of 1863. It was hotter in the boiler room aboard the *John Adams*. It was even hotter after Isaac opened the firebox. Heat from the flames felt warmer on his face than the sun. Isaac was convinced that loading coal onto the *John Adams* was an easier task than his new job as a stoker, keeping the boiler hot. His broad shoulders and back ached from shoveling coal. Coal dust covered his clothes and clung in the crevices of his ever-present straw hat, now resting on his back, secured by the cord about his neck.

Though the afternoon sun shone brightly out on the decks, the boiler room was dark enough that the red-yellow glow from the open firebox brightened the dingy walls. As Isaac tossed two more shovel-loads of coal into the firebox, he sang along with his fellow stokers:

Jordan River, I'm bound to go,
Bound to go, bound to go,
Jordan River, I'm bound to go,
And bid'em fare ye well.

"Son, dat firebox gone need mo' dan dat two lil' shovelfuls. Rat now, we's just gittin' under way." Theodore was leaning on his stoker's pole with one hand and holding his corncob pipe in the other. He held the fire end like a knob. He used the unlit pipe to point first to the shovel, then to the firebox. Theodore finished speaking and his tenor voice broke smoothly into the second verse of "Jordan River."

Oh, Brudder Robert, I'm bound to go...
"Yessuh."

Isaac rejoined the singing as he shoveled more coal from the bin behind him.

Theodore was one of four stokers onboard for this voyage. He was older than all the men working in the camp at Port Royal and aboard Union army steamers. Like Isaac, he wanted to be a soldier. He was fifty seven years old, and had a great deal of white hair at the temples. Though he still did as much work as men half his age, Theodore was deemed too old to be a soldier in the Union Army. He was proud of his service aboard the *John Adams*. He was a stoker on the ship two months prior for the raid on plantations along the Combahee River with Harriet Tubman and Colonel Montgomery's all black Second Infantry Regiment of South Carolina Volunteers.

Isaac, still singing, was always watching their progress. He looked out at a wide body of water beyond the bow. The stokers were joined in their singing by several of the soldiers near them, as the two side paddle wheels propelled the former Boston ferry out of Brickyard Creek, past Jack Island and the wreck of the steam gunboat, the *George Washington*, on the port side, and east into the broad Coosaw River. At this point, near flood tide, the Coosaw was almost a mile wide. The *John Adams* was now a US Army troop transport embarking, along with the US Army Steamer *Enoch Dean* and US Army Tug *Governor Milton*, on a riverborne raid against Confederate forces and plantations along the Pon Pon.

Colonel Thomas Wentworth Higginson commanded the raiders and their flotilla, which carried nearly two hundred fifty men – white artillerymen of the First Connecticut Battery and soldiers of African descent from the First Regiment of Infantry, South Carolina Volunteers. The First Connecticut Battery manned the guns mounted on each of the vessels. Each gun crew was assisted by a squad of infantrymen from the First South Carolina Volunteers. The infantrymen, former slaves from the South Carolina low country, proudly wore their distinctive blue tunics with brass buttons and red trousers.

Isaac knew these units and every regiment stationed at Port Royal and Beaufort. Upon his visit to each, the officers told him that he was too young to be a soldier.

More soldiers joined the singing. Uncle Theodore's mellifluous voice raised the third verse above the den of the steam engine and the sound of the paddle wheels moving water.

Oh, Sister Lucy, I'm bound to go...

On this verse, the stokers and infantrymen on the *John Adams* were a single voice, joined by a handful of artillerymen. Isaac smiled as it occurred to him that they sounded more like a Jacksonboro camp meeting than a Union force enroute to raid Confederate positions and collect enslaved people.

"T'doe, how ol' is dat boy, anyway?"

Isaac's smile vanished. He looked at Theodore, the elder he called uncle out of respect. It was Archie again. Archie had harassed Isaac since he boarded the *John Adams* near Beaufort shortly after lunch.

Uncle Theodore sighed and turned to Isaac.

"Son, do you know how old you is?"

"Yessuh. I's sixteen. But they won't let me be a soldier."

Archie exclaimed in mock surprise, "A soldier? What kind of army sends a boy? He ain't even half a stoker."

Anger rose in Isaac like the fire under the boiler. In spite of trying to suppress them, tears welled up in Isaac's eyes and threatened to spill into the coal dust on his sweaty cheeks. He dropped his head and turned from Archie to shield his face as he fought to hold back the tears. He was determined that these men would not see him cry.

Uncle Theodore held up his pipe with his palm toward Archie. "It seems to me dat dis here boy done shoveled more coal dan you dis aternoon. Now Archie, why don't you jes leave him be?"

"Dat's not what I saw. I see a triflin' youngun. You mark my words. Gone double our work, if we don't watch."

"Son, did oonah say your name is Isaac?"

"Yessuh."

"Well now, Isaac, don't listen to Archie. He jes a tare-down kind of fellow. Jes do your work lak oonah doing and hold yore head up."

"Yessuh."

Isaac lifted his head and glanced toward Archie. Archie turned abruptly and limped away muttering, "That no 'count youngun will neber 'mount to a hill of beans."

Anxious to change the subject, but not ready to thank Theodore, Isaac asked, "Uncle Theodore, where's we bound?"

"I hear tell we's gone do some raidin' on plantations up one of the rivers between here and Charleston."

The water disappeared from Isaac's eyes as they grew wide. With this news, his jaw went slack and his mouth opened. But he said nothing. Maybe it was too soon to hope he would see Bianca and his family.

The *Dean* was a river steamboat and the *Milton* was a rather small tug. The three former peacetime vessels were now armed with Parrot and Armstrong guns ranging from ten to twenty pounders. The *John Adams* also had a couple of howitzers. Gunners from the First Connecticut Battery expertly mounted and maintained Higginson's long-range weapons.

From his station near the starboard boiler, Isaac looked back to the west at his new home, Port Royal Island, now receding in the distance. He could scarcely believe he was on the Coosaw again so soon after his waterborne escape from Tiffany Plantation. This time, he was a part of a team of Union army and navy men headed back toward the rice plantations of the Ashepoo, Combahee, and Pon Pon rivers. Too young to join the First South Carolina Volunteers at sixteen, Isaac had been put to work with other boys his age cutting wood and loading coal on army steamboats. His excitement rose when he was told he would replace one of the stokers on the *John Adams* who had been injured by a falling tree the day before. The other three stokers were men too old to serve in the army. Isaac felt a tingle in his spine, but was not sure if his excitement came from a chance that he might see Bianca, from being close to soldiers on a raid, or from anticipation of his first trip into harm's way.

By the time the sun was almost set, Isaac had mastered his new job. The western sky was fading from red to purple against a few long and thin clouds. The high, wispy clouds had a texture like the first grainy strokes of whitewash on rough boards. The hue of the clouds deepened ahead of the darkening sky. The little flotilla followed the Coosaw into St. Helena Sound, at the edge of the Atlantic, on a falling tide. Taking a peek past the port boiler, Isaac saw the wide mouth of the Ashepoo. His muscles tensed as memory returned of the ache in his shoulders and arms from rowing against the tide across the mouth of the Ashepoo during his escape in May. The three steamers swung toward the northeast as they passed the horn of Otter Island and headed for the broad mouth of the South Edisto River.

Dead ahead lay Edisto Point. Its green trees formed an uneven line of black against the darkening sky.

"Uncle Theo, why we stoppin'?"

"Well, Isaac, I don't rightly know. I 'spects it could be dat de kunnel may want to find out what de folks on dat man-o'-war anchored ober dere off to starboard may know 'bout de latest news up dat river yon."

"Dat be the Edisto. Some call it the Pon Pon River."

"The Edisto, eh?"

"Yessuh. Well, lookit. There is a bateau rowing toward us."

"Never you mind dem. Let's eat while we's got a chance. Never know when you git to eat again."

"Oh, good idée. I was making myself hungrier by thinkin' 'bout fishin' in the sound and eatin' by the campfires yonder on Edisto Point."

"Oh. You know dis place? You been here before?"

"Yessuh. My father brought me on fishing trips down the Edisto with men from Jehossee and Prospect Hill plantations. We have not been down here in two years because of the war."

An infantry corporal put his head in for a look at the boiler room. He stepped inside for a better view of the coal bins and fireboxes. He greeted them and continued his observations.

"How cum you didn't jes eat river fish?"

"We blacks did. We came to the sound for saltwater fish and shrimp. Our ol' massas were high society like and sont us down here 'fore they held big shindigs. The massa of Jehossee was once de gobernor of South Carolina."

"Well, I do say! How many canoes did you need to carry fish for a shindig?"

"We carried fish back to home in hoop barrels of saltwater loaded on flatboats bigger than four wagons."

"I'll bet everybody ate well after one of those trips."

"Yessuh. White folks and black folks."

"Well now, did oonah come from one o'dem plantations?"

"Yes, sir. I ran from Tiffany Plantation back in May. Where did oonah come from, suh?"

The corporal took his leave and waved good-bye.

"I lived on a plantation 'long the St. John River near Jacksonville down in Florida. I 'scaped durin' a raid just like dis here one we're on now. Fact is, I 'scaped on dis very steamer."

Isaac retrieved his gunnysack from the nail where it hung on the boiler-room wall. He walked a few steps with Uncle Theodore onto the main deck. There, they gazed into the coming darkness across the black waters of the North Atlantic, wordless, each deep in his own thoughts. The evening sea breeze felt refreshing to Isaac. The sound of steps across the upper deck and down the gangway behind them interrupted their solitude. Colonel Higginson and several of his officers made their way to the main deck and toward the bow to meet the small rowboat approaching the *Adams.*

A hush fell over the soldiers as they listened intently to learn who was coming aboard and any news that was to be had. Two officers climbed abroad and the two sailors who accompanied them rowed the small boat back toward the man-of-war. One wore a navy uniform and reported to Colonel Higginson as a river pilot, sent to guide the flotilla's ascent of the Edisto. The other wore a uniform bearing the emblem of an army surgeon.

Uncle Theodore cleared his throat and chuckled. "De kunnel didn't need tuh stop f'dat pilot fella. He ain't knowed he got you."

They both laughed. Not once did it occur to Isaac to report his South Edisto River experiences to Colonel Higginson and be involved, uninvited, in white folks business.

At two hours before midnight, the moon was up and the *John Adams* weighed anchor. Isaac and Uncle Theodore returned to their station and added several shovelfuls of coal to the starboard firebox. Shortly, the *Adams'* paddle wheels began to turn. When they were under way, the bow swung more sharply to the north.

Off the starboard side, the whitecaps of waves in the moonlight broke gently against the sands of Edisto Point. Instead of reminiscing more about his previous campfires on the point, Isaac looked for any signs of Confederate fires or light. The tree line was completely black by now. Isaac laughed to himself, "Of course, it is much too soon to see signs of the Secesh. Dere's a man-o'-war and other gunboats just off de point."

When the *John Adams* was beyond sight of Edisto Point, Isaac went to the rail to gaze into the dark mouth of Big Bay Creek, which flowed into the South Edisto River from the southeast. Above the sound of the steam engines and the water churned by her paddle wheels, a dog barked in the distance. He doubted anyone aboard the *John Adams* could arrive at a Confederate camp and surprise the occupants. In the quiet of the night, small sounds traveled great distances. He peered into the darkness at the north shore of the creek scanning again for light or movement. Here, the mouth of the creek was about a quarter-mile wide.

The vertical beam engine of the *John Adams* pulsated with its own rhythms, carrying her cargo of raiders beyond Big Bay Creek and toward the first curve in the Edisto. Isaac returned to the boiler room, retrieved his shovel, and slid it along the floor of the coal bin. It made the sharp sound of metal scrapping on rocks. He lifted a shovelful and, without stopping, turned in a continuous fluid motion and deftly flung the coal into the middle of the firebox. Without a word from Isaac or a break in his humming, Uncle Theodore had used his stoker's pole to open the steel door on the firebox as Isaac's shovel slid under the coal. He closed it after a second shovelful, still humming his song. They were a team now.

"Uncle Theo, we's comin' up to a turn in the river. Seems a mighty good place for a Secesh ambush."

"Could be, boy."

"Did the Secesh fire on the *Adams* when you were riding her in Florida, or on the Combahee?"

"'Course, dey did. Neber did hit us."

"Sometimes dey could get lucky and make a hit. Story is the Secesh blew up the *George Washington* with a single shot. How did that happen?"

"Cap'n o' dat *George Washington* gunboat stretched his luck. He was still at anchor in the north side of the Coosaw, exposed to territory infested with Secesh guerillas after daybreak. Ask me, he wuz askin' for it. That single 'Cesh shot got lucky and hit a boiler. Most ob the dead were scalded to def."

Isaac shuddered at the thought of scalding water on his skin. His voice quavered. "You reckon dat could happen to us?"

"Maybe, maybe not."

Archie chimed in. "Dat boy is a scared!"

Theodore ignored Archie. "How far are we from dat bend in de river?"

Isaac followed Theodore's lead and ignored Archie. "'Bout five minutes."

"When we's likely to be fired on, stay close to de coal bin. When any firing starts, fus', I open de box, oonah gib it two quick shovelfuls, and jump in de coal bin. I'll close de box and follow you."

"Why we gib her more coal den?"

"Dat so's the Cap'n will have steam power enuf to git us quick out of range ob de Secesh guns. Cap'n done tole me dat when we set out for the Combahee. He wants hot boilers, 'specially in time o' trouble."

The flotilla slowed for several ninety-degree-plus bends in the river. Each time, the infantrymen and artillerymen prepared to return incoming fire. None came. The river narrowed for a sharp bend to the right around the finger of Jehossee Island. The pilot on the *John Adams* had expertly chosen to stay close to the right bank, close to Jehossee, where the deepest part of the channel lay. Isaac whistled.

"Uncle Theo, dis pilot sho' knows dis river. He's stayin in the deepest part of de channel wid only moonlight to see his way."

The *Adams* rounded a second right turn and followed the finger of Jehossee. This time, Isaac watched the bank to see if the pilot followed the Jehossee bank. The *Adams* gradually slipped to middle of the river and led the *Dean* and the *Milton* into the next turn to the northeast, hugging the west shore close to Fenwick Island, across the river from Jehossee. Isaac whistled again.

"I see you likes dis pilot."

"He is as experienced as any man on dis river. Next we pass an island in the middle of the channel. Dat island is shaped like a big boat. Den we got us a big clothes pin turn to the west up ahead with two separate rivers coming into Edisto from the outside bank of the bend."

"kunnel say our first stop is Willtown Bluff. How far is dat?"

"After dat clothespin turn, Willtown Bluff will be a bit over two miles. It's direc'ly across the river from Tiffany Plantation. There's a Confederate artillery outfit up dere, on Willtown Bluff, high above de river."

"I 'spect dere are interestin' possibilities ahead. Let's eat a bite and fire de boilers before we hit the Secesh. Keep your body and the boilers ready for anythin'."

"Yessuh."

Isaac nibbled his hardtack and bacon while leaning on the starboard rail. The reflection of the full moon hanging above the tree line of Jehossee Island shimmered on the surface of the Edisto. In the moonlight, the bleached white trunk of a river-edge tree, long since dead, was visible, leaning almost horizontally over the water, pointing west. It looked like a marker placed there to guide night-traveling plantation raiders.

The pointing tree trunk reminded Isaac of the short, dead cypress tree on the west bank that looked like a man with outstretched arms. It was complete with Spanish moss in the top and its branches had been bleached white by the sun. The tree glowed silvery in the moonlight. As they approached, Isaac pointed it out to Uncle Theodore. Then he called out. "A ghost on the port side!"

Archie stuttered. "Wh-wh-where?"

Theodore answered. "Port side at ten o'clock!"

Archie spotted the "ghost." He dropped his shovel with a clatter and ran for the coal bin. "Lawd, save me! Save me!"

Theodore and Isaac doubled over laughing. They laughed even harder when Archie said, "Quiet! Ghosts ain't nothin' to trifle wid!"

Back on deck, Isaac heard the croak of a frog on the east bank. He closed his eyes to remember the night sounds of insects, whooshing bats, leaping fish, frogs croaking together, and owls in the tree-lined banks. He imagined the creatures hushed to hear the sound of the flotilla – listening from their hiding places, just as the Confederates could.

The *John Adams* cleared the mouth of the Dawho River and the clothespin turn less than a mile from the south most rice squares of Tiffany Plantation on the west bank. There was movement on deck. Soldiers were packing away their food and water. They busied themselves now with checks of the big guns mounted on deck, repositioning ammunition, and individual weapons. Isaac's stomach fluttered when he recognized the flat rice fields of Tiffany on the port side. He stowed his gunnysack and returned to his station shortly before ten to four o'clock.

"Uncle Theo, off to port is the plantation where I came from. Best get ready."

" I'm allus ready. I allus pray. Did you pray?"

"Yessuh. I prayed dat my ma and sisters and girlfriend make it to freedom."

"Don't forget to pray for 'e self. How far are we from Willtown Bluff?"

"Ten to fifteen minutes. Oonah see Willtown Bluff forward on de starboard side when we make de next turn. Willtown stands above the river in a grove of live oaks."

"Okay. Fire de boiler, boy!"

When the flotilla made the last turn before Willtown, all hands were at their stations. In the moonlight, Willtown loomed above the water on the east bank and looked like the top of a large head emerging from the water. Live oaks covered the head like a black hat. Though he could not see it from this distance, Isaac thought of the Spanish moss hanging in the oaks as gray hair under the hat. He imagined the Confederate artillerymen observing them in the moonlight and waiting for them to draw nearer.

138

"If de Confederates see us fus, dey could shoot us like fish in a barrel."

"Dey ain't nothin' you and me kin do 'bout dat. Now let's fire de boiler!"

"Yessuh!" Isaac opened the firebox with his stoker's pole as Uncle Theodore lifted a shovelful of coal from the bin and turned in midair to fling the coal through the open firebox door. After several shovelfuls and with the firebox closed, Isaac listened on deck for the sound of human activity on the shore. What he heard instead was the wail of the reed birds and the croaking of frogs.

Isaac felt the hair on his neck move when he heard the boom of a howitzer firing on the main deck, less than twenty feet away. The first shell was fired from the *John Adams* at four o'clock when she was at mid-channel opposite the mouth of Ashe Creek where it entered the west bank of the Edisto. Isaac felt the ferry shudder under his feet. In the seconds after shot, the birds and frogs were silent. So was the infantry. All eyes were on the hat on the bluff. The only sounds Isaac heard now were the engine of the *John Adams* and the gun crew preparing to fire another round. The smell of gunpowder filled the air as the fumes and smoke drifted back over the decks from the howitzer.

Uncle Theodore joined Isaac on deck. They did not venture more than a few feet from the door to the boiler room. Infantrymen were preparing to launch small boats for a landing. A second shell was fired from the *Adams*. This time Isaac was not startled by of the howitzer, but jumped nonetheless. He heard a boom from the direction of the hat before the whump sound of First Connecticut's second shell landing on Willtown Bluff.

The boom was followed by a whistling sound, high above the bluff, then over the water.

"In comin'!" shouted Uncle Theodore and experienced hands.

Isaac stood flat-footed and dumbfounded. As he was marveling at the new sound of a whistle moving through the air, Uncle Theodore grabbed him by the nape of his neck and pulled him into the boiler room. Above the din of scrambling boots on deck came the sound of an exploding Confederate shell in the river between the *Adams* and the *Milton*. Uncle Theodore was in the coal bin by the time Isaac understood that they were under fire from enemy artillery. From the coal bin, Isaac heard the Parrots and Armstrongs on the *Adams, Dean*, and *Milton* joined the howitzers firing into the live oaks on the bluff. Even in the boiler room, the smell of gunpowder was heavy.

There were a few more explosions in the water and the Confederate guns fell silent. The First Connecticut battery continued firing. When they ceased four minutes later, Isaac ventured from the coal bin in time to see the infantry rowing their boats through the haze and smoke toward the shore beneath the bluff. The First Connecticut gun crews were busy moving more shells into position to fire and cover the infantry's advance.

In the first rays of daylight, Isaac saw the uniform green of the flat rice fields below the bluff. Through the port doorway, he noticed the familiar rectangular dikes of named rice field squares. The sound of crows and wrens started. People appeared on the dikes, but none carried the hoes he expected to see. Men, women, and children ran to and fro along the dikes, not remaining in one spot for long.

"Yessuh. Dat boy wid de stoker's pole. He's de one."

Isaac turned toward the voice that described him. The curious corporal from the First South Carolina Volunteers was speaking to his white leader, Captain Trowbridge.

"What's your name, boy?"

Isaac hesitated, trying to recognize the words within a strange northeastern accent and assess a potential threat from being pointed out by a little known black man to a completely unknown white man.

Trowbridge crossed his arms impatiently. "Well?"

"Suh. Er, Isaac. Suh, my name is Isaac."

"Corporal Jenkins here tells me you came from that plantation there on the west bank. When did you take your leave from there?"

Isaac hesitated again. His mind fled to a familiar scene. Isaac remembered that scarcely two years prior, a young black slave driver stood beside Tom Foster and pointed out his mother as one who was chopping weeds too slowly in a rice field. He glanced at Uncle Theodore and Corporal Jenkins and back to Trowbridge's gaze. Since Uncle Theodore and Corporal Jenkins didn't fidget or look away, he sensed that he was not being accused of anything, but wanted to be sure.

"I 'scaped last month."

"How many escaped with you? How did your group arrive in Port Royal?"

"Suh, nobody 'scaped with me. I rowed a canoe to Port Royal."

Trowbridge took a deep breath, raised an eyebrow, and glanced at Corporal Jenkins. "Isaac, how many slaves live on this plantation?"

"'Tween three and four hundred, suh."

"How many overseers?"

"Three, suh."

"I want you to go with Corporal Jenkins and his squad to bring the most skilled slaves on the plantation to the riverbank. We can't take everyone. We'll take as many as we can back to Port Royal."

Isaac's eyes went wide. His first thought was of Bianca and his family.

Trowbridge continued. "I want the ones without whose knowledge and work the plantation will be crippled. We are doing the same at the east bank plantation. Can you help us do this on the west bank?"

"Yessuh!" Isaac could scarcely believe his good fortune. A plan was already taking shape in his mind to rescue his loved ones as well as Caleb's family. He was so excited that he dropped his stoker's pole. It fell against the wall, knocking down two shovels leaning there in a great clatter.

Everyone laughed.

A smiling Captain Trowbridge was not finished. "By the way, Isaac, for my report, what are the names of these two plantations?"

"Suh, Tiffany on the west bank and Prospect Hill on the east."

Colonel Higginson went ashore with the infantry to oversee the capture of the Confederate artillery outpost. Captain Trowbridge and the pilot took the *John Adams* out to remove the pile barriers the Confederates had set in place to prevent steam gunboats from sailing upstream and attacking the railroad bridge. Once the piles were removed, the *Dean* and *Milton* would go upstream and attempt to destroy the railroad bridge near Jacksonboro.

An hour later, Corporal Jenkins and Isaac set out for Tiffany in two small rowboats carrying five men each. Corporal Jenkins and Isaac agreed on a plan to capture or cause the overseers to flee. Once the overseers were subdued, they would set about removing men and women and their children from the plantation. Isaac kept to himself his plan to move Bianca and his family and as many of his former neighbors as quickly as he could to the *John Adams* before more space could be taken by people fleeing Prospect Hill Plantation. A few blacks from Prospect Hill had already begun making their way onto the *John Adams* while she was close to the landing at Willtown Bluff. None would attempt to reach her now that she was at midstream removing piles from the riverbed.

The first sniper bullets made a plunking sound as they struck the water on both sides of Isaac's rowboat. Corporal Jenkins's boat was only the length of three oars off his starboard side. They were leaving the *John Adams* when she was some six hundred feet from either shore. Isaac removed his straw hat with his left hand and used it to point out a tiny island southwest of their position near the mouth of Ashe Creek.

"We need to pass on the land side of that little island."

The next bullet ripped through Isaac's sleeve and the fleshy part of his upper arm as he withdrew his hat from pointing. He cried out with surprise at what felt like a bee sting followed by the sensation of a hot ember being placed on his flesh. His hat fell into the water and floated. Isaac grabbed his wound with his right hand and sank further into his seat.

An infantryman in Isaac's boat called out to Corporal Jenkins. "Let's get back to the gunboat!"

Isaac spoke before the corporal could respond. "Row to the island!"

Jenkins repeated Isaac's words. Both boats picked up speed as they changed direction from west to southwest and used the advantage of the river's current to help them get beyond the sniper's range. Quickly, the infantrymen learned to row together like experienced river men. The bullets plunking into the water were falling short. Isaac looked past the *John Adams* at a spot in the trees some four hundred yards south of Willtown where he thought the sniper was perched. The sound of the South Carolina Volunteers firing on the east bank ended further mischief from the sniper.

With the sniper quiet and a tourniquet on Isaac's arm above his flesh wound, they rowed past the small humpback island that had been their objective. The island was less than one hundred feet long and covered with reeds and marsh grasses up to four feet tall. It made an excellent shield. The two rowboats were within fifty feet from the edge of Tiffany's rice fields on Oakhurst Island. It was almost six o'clock.

The people on the dike, who had disappeared while the sniper was firing, reappeared at the edge of an emerald rice field. Cheering fieldworkers and children greeted them as they ran along the top of the dike that surrounded the rice field. Isaac guided Corporal Jenkins and his men into the mouth of Ashe Creek. The cheering throng followed along, a few feet from the edge of the creek. Isaac heard them through the trees while they were out of sight of the crowd making a clothespin turn in the creek, which was more than a hundred feet wide at high tide. The crowd was larger and the cheering louder by the time the boats reached the point where the levee came again to the water's edge. The infantrymen changed oarsmen as they passed flatboats tied up in a small inlet near the middle of Oakhurst Island.

Since Corporal Jenkins came from a James Island rice plantation, Isaac merely pointed to the wide flatboats that were used to truck workers, tools, seeds, and crops to and from the rice squares.

Corporal Jenkins acknowledged. "We'll use dese."

People were joining the cheering from the west bank of the creek. They put ashore with help from men and boys in the west bank throng.

A man who was friends with Isaac's father recognized him. "Why, breast de Lawd! It's Eve and Mark's boy, Isaac!"

Another cried, "We all thought 'e drowned or de 'gators got'im!"

A gasp went up from the crowd. Though Isaac was not wearing a uniform or carrying a weapon, word spread along the dikes that Eve and Mark's boy had returned as a soldier.

Isaac smiled and waved his greeting, but never stopped his preparation with Corporal Jenkins to evacuate as many people as possible. The squad of infantrymen encircled Isaac and Corporal Jenkins, listening intently, as they discussed their final plans.

"Just ahead, this dike turns inland and follows a main canal toward the center of the plantation and quarters. There is a wagon road on both sides of the canal. The overseers may fire on us. Let's leave the boats here on the bank of this levee and walk to the point where the canal narrows."

"Okay. I'll send tree men wid oonah and take tree with me on de north side levee."

"No. It will be better for me to run ahead alone and send back to oonah first dose who Captain Trowbridge asked us to bring out."

Corporal Jenkins's eyes narrowed as he considered Isaac's idea. "Oonah know de overseers will want to shoot oonah more dan any soldier. By now, dey probably know oonah back wid all dat shoutin' and shootin'. Dey hate examples like oonah and me. Dey may try to grab 'e ma or 'e sisters."

From the direction of the center of Tiffany came the sound of the first call horn.

Isaac's eyebrows rose, then lowered. "I know de people we need to get out and cripple dis place."

"And I don't." Jenkins completed the thought with a sigh.

"Okay. I'm off."

"Hold on. Not so fast."

Jenkins caught Isaac's good arm and lowered his voice. "I won't know who oonah sendin'. Have dem meet me at de narrows. Give dem a password, so I can know oonah sent dem. Tell dem: John Adams."

"I will. Thanks. Thanks for not lettin' me go off half-cocked." Isaac grinned and offered his hand.

Jenkins shook it. "Four of my men will follow you along de main canal. De others will round up flatboats on dis side of de creek. Good luck."

Without another word, Isaac turned and made his way through his former neighbors, shaking hands with adults and patting children on the head. Once out of the throng, Isaac started in a trot west along the levee toward the center of Tiffany. Four soldiers with rifles at port arms followed, two on each side of the canal.

When the first row of slave cabins came into view, the two soldiers on Isaac's right flank slowed their advance. From their position, they could cover Isaac and the soldiers with him. Isaac and his team waited in prone positions behind the bushes and grass that lined the dike and canal. They could see the top of the thirty-foot-tall winnowing house, less than a hundred yards ahead. With a loud report, Isaac smacked and killed a sand fly biting his neck. Both soldiers turned to him with a frown and a finger over their lips. No one spoke. They were sure the overseers expected soldiers after hearing the firing on the river.

When Isaac's team made their next advance, to the end of the canal, they heard shots. The bullets kicked up dirt around their feet. The threesome dove for cover behind the last remaining bushes.

A voice called out, "Isaac, you and your monkey-suit friends throw out your guns and nobody will get hurt."

"Thunderation!" Isaac pounded his fist into the gray sandy soil several times.

"Who dat?"

"Dat's Tom Foster, the head overseer."

"Keep yo' temper. Calm down and use yo' head. Answer him and tell 'im we'll do as dey say. Our boys hab us covered."

Still smoldering, Isaac could only nod, "Yes." He took two deep breaths. "Don't shot. We's throwin' out the guns."

"Smart boy, Isaac. We want to give you a special welcome home down at the corral."

One by one, they tossed the two rifles out.

"Now, you and your new friends stand up so we can see you. Hands up high!"

Isaac and the team slowly did as they were told.

Foster called to his sons. "Come on, boys. Let's make a proper example out of these uppity niggers!" Foster and his sons walked from behind opposite ends of the rice storage barn. They held their weapons waist high and advanced quickly on the threesome standing with their hands up.

When they were too far from the barn to return for cover, the command came from a strong voice: "Halt!"

Confused, Tom Foster and his sons froze, looking about for the man behind the voice.

A different voice spoke. "Drap 'e weapons 'n' clasp 'e hands 'hind 'e heads."

Angered, Foster turned again toward Isaac and raised his rifle. A shot rang out and Foster fell backward. His sons still could not see the riflemen and threw down their weapons as if the metal had scorched their hands. Foster was bleeding profusely and remained completely still. His sons did not move from where they stood. They kept their hands clasped behind their heads.

When Isaac's teammates had retrieved their own muskets, along with the Fosters' weapons, Isaac ordered the sons to carry their father to the stable where he had tied so many blacks to the rails of the corral fence and beaten them to within an inch of their lives. Foster's sons recognized Isaac's motivation and glared at him, their eyes brimming with tears.

They walked to the stable along a wagon path that separated a row of slave cabins from vegetable gardens and the blacksmith's shop. The soldiers continued practicing maneuver and cover as they advanced. Curious blacks peered from behind cabins and the smithy, the only brick structure on the plantation. A little girl ran to Isaac and hugged his leg. He patted her head.

Isaac knelt beside her. "Please get Aunt Ella. Ask her to come to the stable. Tell her we have a man who was shot."

"Isaac? Isaac, is that you?" It was Big Gus moving briskly through the doorway of the smithy. His long strides caused the leather apron about his waist to flap against his thighs.

Isaac stood. The little girl ran to Aunt Ella's cabin as fast as her bare feet could take her. "Yessuh, it's me." He took a couple of steps to meet Big Gus and was swept off his feet. Though Isaac was the size of an average man, Big Gus lifted him off the ground in a bear hug to a height where they were face-to-face.

"Well now, oonah a sight for sore eyes! Allus prayed for oonah make it to freedom. Thanks be to God, oonah did." Big Gus returned Isaac to his feet.

"I see dey are feedin' oonah well. Done growed too since oonah gone."

"Yessuh. It's good to see oonah, too. We's here to take as many as we can fit on the steamboat to Port Royal. I want to be sure oonah are among the number." He turned to the soldiers. "Fellows, dis here's Big Gus. I was proud to apprentice under him."

Big Gus put a hand to his beard. He stared at Isaac, then the soldiers. "I git my wife. We go wid oonah."

Isaac hugged the big man about his waist. "I am so glad oonah goin'." He stepped back and looked up at the big man. "Meet the soldiers at the narrows by Oakhurst. When the soldiers ask you for a password, say John Adams."

"Thanks, Isaac." Big Gus was off toward his cabin.

The soldiers were tying the Foster brothers to the rails of the corral when a breathless Aunt Ella arrived with her medical bag on her shoulder. As she walked briskly, her long gray braids swung to and fro and she had a blue bandana tied around her head. "Lawd, Isaac, I thought dat lil' gal told me oonah was shot! Son, it's so good to see oonah. Mmm huh!" She gave a Isaac a quick hug and turned to her patient, lying on his back.

Isaac said, "Good to see oonah, too."

"Is he going to make it?" It was Jeb, who was tied closest to his father.

Aunt Ella mumbled. "Neber should a moved him. All y'all too young to know." She did not look away from her work. "Maybe he makes it, maybe not. Now, shut up. I got to stop the bleeding."

A small crowd of onlookers was assembling in front of the stable. Isaac spoke quietly to Aunt Ella. "We's going now to round up folks and take them to freedom. We come back d'rectly to fetch you too."

"Bress you, son."

"What are you goin' to do with us?" Jeb's voice wavered with fear.

Before Isaac or the soldiers could speak, Aunt Ella snapped, "Ain't nothin' gone happen to you. Now, hesh. All of you."

Isaac and the soldiers looked at each other and realized that the matter of the Fosters had been removed from their hands. They left Foster's sons tied to the corral fence and continued their mission.

Isaac's sisters, Deborah and Mary ran to greet their brother in the street that led from the stable toward their cabin. They called out in unison: "You're alive! You're alive!" Isaac ran to meet them. He lifted them off the ground, laughing. He turned them around and around while holding them aloft. He sang the song he sang years before when Mary was a baby.

Um-m-m, baa baa.

Um-m-m, baa baa.

Um-m-m, baa baa, baby!

He returned them to their feet and knelt with them in the street. The threesome laughed together.

Mary, age six, wanted to know. "Isaac, oonah cryin'?"

Deborah, age ten, who was also crying, turned to her little sister. "Isaac can cry if 'e wants to cry. Oonah should be happy that 'e so happy to see us."

"I am. I am." Mary could reach his neck while he knelt. She put both her small arms around his neck and kissed his cheek.

Deborah used her fingers to wipe the tears from her brother's cheeks. Isaac did the same to her tears. Deborah grinned like she had just remembered a secret. "Let's go see Ma."

* * *

The squad arrived with Isaac and his sisters at his mother's cabin.

The girls ran up the steps and bounded through the door. "Mama! Mama! Isaac's home!"

A sound of clanging bells came from within the cabin. The sound was louder and faster as Eve moved to the doorway. Isaac stood on the ground for a moment, stopped by the sound of bells, looking up at his mother in the doorway. Then he too bounded up the steps and hugged his mother. They held each other in a fierce embrace. There was silence as the soldiers and little girls looked on.

They relaxed their embrace and spoke excitedly at the same time.

"Thank God oonah safe!"

"Ma, we's come to take you and the girls to freedom!"

"I thought I would never see oonah again!"

"We can all be free today."

Eve released her son and stepped back. Bells rang softly with each step she took. "Boy, what are you talking 'bout? Oonah know dese children's too young to run from here."

Isaac looked down at his mother's ankle. There, resting on a bandana tied around her right ankle was a rusty metal band of bells that sounded with each step. His anger rose. "Why Tom Foster do dis to oonah? I's the one who ran."

"Tom Foster thought I might light out after oonah."

"I'll get him fuh dis!"

"Son, now control 'e self. Oonah know better'n to go flyin' off de handle. I'm well. I'm not hurt."

"But still...."

Eve held up a hand. "Whoa! Back up. What wuz dat you say 'bout freedom? Don't let Tom Foster hear oonah talkin' lak dat."

Deborah ran to her mother's side. "Don't worry, Ma. Isaac can't get into trouble with Mister Tom. He's shot!"

"What?" Eve's question bounced off the cabin walls and out the door. The soldiers turned toward the door.

"Ma, calm down. Sit here and let me tell oonah what's what." Isaac reached for Eve's hand.

She pulled her hands back to akimbo. Eve was anything but calm. "Boy, what troubles hab oonah come here and made with dese white folks for all of us?"

"Ma, look out here at dese soldiers."

Eve looked past her son and, for the first time, saw the soldiers clad in blue and red uniforms. She put a hand over her mouth. "Black soldiers...." She could say no more. Tears spilled down her cheeks and she sank to sit on the door sill with Isaac holding her hand to let her down gently.

The soldiers greeted Eve in unison. "G'mornin', ma'am."

"Ma, oonah ain't seein' no ghosts. Dey's real enough. Dey shot Tom Foster." Isaac recounted the morning's events.

Eve wiped her tears on her sleeve. She stood and hugged Isaac again. "Your pa would be so proud of you."

"I 'most forgot. I made our last name Rice. Is dat okay?"

"Son, dat's fine."

Then Isaac whispered. "Have oonah seen Bianca?"

Eve leaned her head to one side and looked into his face, searching his eyes. Then, she smiled. "No, I don't see her often. Ask Caleb's mother or Luke. So what she told me is true."

Isaac flushed and grinned. "Yessum, we likes each other." He still held his head down.

"Son, it's fine. Hold 'e head up. Look at me. Oonah has done well to git her attention. Makes me happy."

Isaac grinned and changed the subject. "Okay. We got things to do. I'll send Deb to get Big Gus. He'll git dem bells off oonah." He took a few steps and rejoined the soldiers. Over his shoulder, he said, "Pack a few things, Ma. We'll be back d'rectly to take oonah to the steamboat."

*　*　*

Isaac found his best friend, Caleb, on the street near the commissary. After a gleeful reunion, Caleb joined Isaac and the soldiers in their mission. They walked together to the big house to find Luke.

As they passed the kitchen house behind the mansion, Caleb ran inside to get his mother. Isaac and the soldiers turned the corner onto the avenue leading from the big house to the main gate. There they came face-to-face with John and Margaret Tiffany on the mansion's front steps. Caleb caught up. Luke was in front of the mansion, preparing the Tiffany's finest coach for travel.

Margaret greeted them as she always did. "Good morning, boys."

Isaac and Caleb responded as they would have on any other day. "G'mornin' Missus."

John Tiffany appeared very pale. He stepped in front of his wife as if to protect her and he looked the soldiers up and down. "Did you come to kill us all?"

Isaac took a step forward and met John's gaze. "Naw, suh. We came to get Mister Luke and take him to freedom."

With fear showing in his eyes, John continued. "And what are you going to do with us? We heard all the shooting."

Isaac remembered Aunt Ella's declaration that nothing would happen to the Fosters. "Suh, you's free to go. We mean you no harm."

John took a deep breath. "Boy, I don't think we ever spoke. But I want you to know that my grandfather came here from Barbados and established this place back in the last century. He and my father made it a home for all of us." John made a circular gesture with his right hand to include all present. "We did all we could to make y'all comfortable here. Wasn't that enough?"

Isaac thought the man before him looked defeated; it reminded Isaac of the feeling he had when he was lost in the fog and thought he would die. "No, suh. Oonah right. We neber spoke. My great-grandpa and grandpa and pa holp build and meck dis place what it is. What do we want? What we want is freedom. Suh, that's all – nothing more."

Isaac walked away from the Tiffanys and left them staring after him. "Mister Luke. We come to let oonah know dat oonah and family is welcome to join us on de steamboat to Port Royal."

Luke stepped down from the driver's seat, high on the coach. He greeted Isaac with a handshake and a hug. "Isaac, son, I go way back takin' care of Massa Tiffany and his family. I done agreed to try and get'em safely back to Charleston. I got to stand by my promise."

"Mister Luke, I allus said I wanted to handle a team and drive like oonah some day. I also wanna be a man lak oonah who keeps ma promises."

"I'm much obliged to oonah for saying dat, son."

"Mister Luke, you might wanna take dem to Jacksonboro right soon. Dere may be trouble later near de railroad bridge over de Edisto. If me, I'd stay in Jacksonboro tonight."

Margaret put her hand to her mouth and stifled a small cry. John put an arm about her shoulders.

Luke continued nodding his head. "Son, many tanks to oonah. I hope y'all will have a safe trip."

"Er, Mister Luke, kin we hab a word in private?"

"Why, sho'." Luke followed Isaac.

As Isaac and Luke walked past the Tiffanys, Margaret reached out and touched Isaac's sleeve. "Thank you so much for…."

John cut Margaret off by waving his hand back and forth, palm facing her. He pulled her a step back. "That's enough, Margaret."

Isaac was stunned by her touch and surprised by what sounded like sincere thanks. He glanced down as the white hand slipped from his sleeve and nodded. He said evenly, "Yes, m'am."

On the opposite side of the coach, Luke spoke first. "Son, I know what oonah ask. It was jes yisditty dat I took Bianca to Missus Harriet in Charleston. Poor ting cried all the way to de city. De Aiken family is on dey way dis berry mornin' by train and coach to dey mountain home at Chimley Rock, Norf Carrylina."

Isaac's face was a mask of confusion and incredulousness. "Wh-wh-what?"

Luke cast his eyes down and stirred the dirt with his boot. Isaac was holding the sides of his head with both hands. Momentarily, Luke looked up. "Missus Harriet is takin' Bianca to Chimley Rock fuh de summer. Isaac, from de bottom o' my heart, I's as sorry as I can be. Miss Henrietta done took sich a likin' to Bianca dat Missus Harriet say she might buy Bianca."

By less than a second, a fierce primeval growl preceded the crunching sound made when Isaac's fist cracked the exquisitely carved wooden coat of arms mounted on the door of the Tiffanys' grand coach.

Chapter 9: Billy at Vicksburg

William Edward Duke's bullet entered the skull of a blue-clad Federal officer, just above the right eye socket.

It was midafternoon, Thursday, June 25, 1863, and the sun was on the officer's face when Billy Duke fired an Enfield Pattern 1853 rifle-musket from his sniper's nest, about a hundred yards from his target. Still looking through his rifle's aperture ladder sight, Billy saw the Yankee officer's head snap back and his binoculars drop from his face. Billy watched his victim's body fall from view behind the parapet built into the Union lines.

"Great shot, Billy!" It was Thomas Jennings, his boyhood friend from Copiah County.

A satisfied smile crept across Billy Duke's face. His smile turned into a surprised contortion as he dropped his rifle and was tossed upside down against the earthen wall of their sharpshooter's site. The ground beneath his feet erupted upward. His head hurt from the strong shock waves created by the blast. Loose dirt sprayed about and stung his face. Ears ringing, Billy landed on his back, gasping for air and inadvertently sucking dirt into his mouth and nose. It was the loudest and largest explosion he had ever heard. But now he was frantically clawing at the loose dirt that covered him, trying to get air into his lungs. After the blast, though Billy could not hear it, there was only the sound of dirt particles falling like rain. The few birds and cicadas were quiet, for the forests and farms east of Vicksburg had been practically denuded of trees.

When Billy was able to raise his face above the dirt and breathe again, he sputtered and spat for a time. Hearing began to return in his ringing ears. Shouts for help from the wounded and cries of confusion abounded. The dust settled and Billy looked out in disbelief at the sight of a huge crater in place of where a part of the Third Louisiana Infantry Regiment's redan once stood. The logs and earthworks that were stacked to build the sniper's nest he shared with Thomas Jennings were scattered here and yonder.

"Hey, Tommy. Lookit!" Billy had not thought of Tommy until he wanted to share the sight before him. Tommy didn't answer.

Billy looked around for his friend and sniper teammate. He began to claw at the dirt where he thought Tommy last stood. First, he found Tommy's booted right foot and leg. A log from the front of their nest lay across Tommy's chest. When Billy uncovered Tommy's face, he could see that Tommy was dead, his nostrils and mouth filled with dirt.

Billy let out a wailing sound as he placed Tommy's hat over his face. Billy cut his mourning short when he heard Union infantry charging into the crater and gaping hole in the Confederate line. Billy could not find his rifle, so he grabbed Tommy's and snatched the cartridge box from Tommy's belt. He shoved the extra box into his pocket and ran south from the right edge of the crater, then across the rear of the 6th Missouri's line position to rejoin his unit – Company F, Thirty-eighth Mississippi Infantry Regiment.

It was the thirty-ninth day of Major General Ulysses S. Grant's siege of Vicksburg, Mississippi. Grant was using large naval guns aboard gunboats and land-based artillery to rain cannon fire from all directions on Vicksburg and her Confederate defenders twenty-four hours a day. As he ran, Billy changed his mind and wished he could tell Tommy that he now agreed: Grant's siege had rendered Vicksburg and Lieutenant General John C. Pemberton into a position of severely limited choices – all of them bad.

* * *

The previous night, sitting around their cook fire among the flies on the filthy litter-strewn ground behind the seventeen-foot earthen wall of Third Louisiana's redan blocking the Union advance along the Jackson Road to Vicksburg, Tommy had argued for what he called the best bad option left.

Billy had been incredulous. "So what the hell do you want?"

Tommy was unruffled by Billy's raised voice. "Like I said, not only can we get no more bullets or men, the Yanks have seen to it that all we have left to eat once a day is this slosh shit." He raised his skillet. "We need to save our little army 'fore we all perish from hunger. I'm tired o' listenin' ta my ribs a scrappin' agin and a cussin' my backbone."

The Louisianans sitting with them laughed.

Billy was unmoved. "Well, I ain't 'bout ta let a little hunger make me do something stupid."

Tommy pulled a spoon from his pocket and stirred as he added weevil-infested cornmeal to the grease and mystery meat frying in the skillet. "The way I see it is first we gotta eat. Most ever'body I see is in bad shape. Lookit. We got more folks down with dysentery than we had men at Corinth – even a general! That damned Grant knows what the fuck he's doing. Ever time we lose a man 'cause he's too weak ta hold a rifle, the Yanks save a bullet."

The Louisianans chimed in, "Hear, hear! Bloody right!"

"Speaking of bloody, the last o' our boys ta die o' dysentery was poor Andy, just yesterday. The po' boy bled to death outta his ass.

"Look at the rest of us. We're all gettin' hollow 'round the eyes and we so skinny, our stinkin' rotten clothes flap ever time there's a breeze. Which one 'o us is next?"

They were interrupted by Yankee soldiers yelling across the trenches. One shouted, "Hey, Reb, I hear tell you's gotcha yourselves a new general – General Starvation!" Great hearty laughter wafted over the trenches to the assembled Louisianans and Mississippians who sat glum, staring into the fire.

Bill fired a shot into the darkness toward the Yankees. "Die o' lead poisoning, ya lousy bluebelly!"

After a pause, Tommy continued as if nothing had occurred. "Billy, look at this damned meat. Do you know what the hell it is? I sho' as shit don't. Do ya know what I was doin' over there 'fore I chopped it up ta put in dis heah skillet? I wuz shakin' and scrappin' fuckin' maggots off our supper!"

"Tommy, dat's exactly how cum we gotta bust out a 'fore we all too weak."

"Fuck dat! We already too damn weak to walk anywheres. We's doin' well jes to stand in dese stinkin' piss and shit-fouled trenches and hold a rifle."

Billy thought for a long moment. A Louisianan who agreed with Tommy slowly added scarce water from a clay canteen to the mixture of meat, grease, and cornmeal while Tommy continued stirring. Billy threw up both hands. "So I guess you wanna surrender?"

"We gotta make a move 'fore we hafta eat maggots, or, worse, each other."

A chorus went up from the dozen or so men waiting to eat Tommy's slosh. "Ughhh!"

Tommy continued. "I figure Gen'l Pemberton oughta go on and n'gotiate parole for his soldiers and allow us ostensibly to return home."

"What the hell good will that do?"

Tommy ignored Billy again. "But actually we would make our way ind'rectly to Jackson and join Gen'l Joe Johnston's army."

Many of the Louisianans responded "Hear, hear" and raised their tin cups of what they called coffee made from peanuts and rye.

* * *

Billy ran on in the extreme afternoon heat feeling impending doom. He felt weak, for he had not eaten since last evening. His hunger burned. Though the sun shone brightly, he saw moving stars and felt dizziness overtaking him. His condition, coupled with the Union's ability to create a single large blast and collapse a redan, blew away the argument he had made to mount a successful two-pronged breakout along the Southern Mississippi Railroad and further south along Hall's Ferry Road. He had argued that his idea would succeed if Pemberton employed similar subterfuge to that used by General Beauregard in their escape from Corinth the year before. In his weakened state, he now believed the unthinkable could happen any day now – surrender.

Billy slumped against the forward wall near the middle of the 38th Mississippi's trench. Everything was a blur. He blinked and then closed his eyes, but that only made the stars brighter. Panting, he said aloud to no one in particular, "What in blazes is wrong with me? I only ran a few yards."

Sergeant Grady Stith from Billy's hometown, Carpenter in Copiah County, stepped forward and put his canteen to Billy's lips.

"Lack of water and food is what's wrong with you and all da rest of us. Heah, drink, 'fore you monkey."

Billy took three gulps before Grady pulled his canteen away. He panted and leaned on Tommy's rifle. He told Grady and the company about Tommy's fate. Then he looked around at their depleted company, once a hundred strong – and all from Copiah County. He counted fourteen men, including himself and Grady. The company called themselves the Johnston Avengers. After losing thirty-five dead and thirty-nine wounded in the siege, the entire Thirty-eighth Mississippi Infantry Regiment had less than two hundred men left – little more than a tenth of what the ten-company regiment started with at Jackson thirteen months earlier.

Little wonder that General Hebert, the brigade commander, had moved the Sixth Missouri into the line between them and the Third Louisiana just this morning. The Twenty-first Louisiana was still on their right. Billy listened as the Sixth Missouri counterattacked and stopped the advance of the Yankee infantry, mainly the Forty-fifth Illinois, in the crater, but failed to evict them. As he rested, leaning against the earthworks, a new idea started to take shape.

Calling from the top of the earthworks, Grady interrupted the formation of his idea. "Com'on, Billy. Get your ass up here and help us give some cover for the Sixth!"

When the Union was repulsed, Billy, Grady, the Thirty-eighth Mississippi, Sixth Missouri, and the two Louisiana regiments worked past suppertime in the waning sunlight of a long June evening to build their earthworks higher. Billy did not mention his hunger and thirst. He focused on his new idea. He worked beside Grady. "Hey, Grady. How cum we don't copy the Injuns' style o' fightin'?"

Grady threw another spade of dirt high onto the earthworks. "Huh? What? Injuns?"

"Yeah, I said Injuns. I never heared tell o' them diggin' the first damned trench. You?"

"Naw. Can't say that I have. What're you gettin' at?"

Billy's eyes lit up. "Just this. Why don't a few o' us bust outta heah and fight the Yankees lak the Injuns do? You know, use surprise, bushwhacks, and the like."

Grady leaned on his spade. Like the rest of the company, his rifle was strapped across his back while he worked. "Hmm." He scratched his chin. "So how do we eat and get supplies?"

"We raid and take what we need from the Yankees and the countryside."

Grady smiled. "Hmm. Why, Corporal Duke, given our present circumstances, I do believe you're onto something."

* * *

The battle, which was sometimes hand-to-hand in and around the crater, raged for several days. Not until late Sunday afternoon were the Confederate forces of General Hebert's brigade able to force the Forty-fifth Illinois to withdraw. The next evening, Billy and several soldiers made slosh from the usual cornmeal and a stray cat he had shot from his new sniper's position. Billy chopped the cat into small pieces and fried it for a few minutes before adding cornmeal and water.

"Com'on boys. Get ready. We got fresh meat tonight."

Sergeant William Tunnard of the Third Louisiana was walking by. "Say, that smells and looks like rabbit. I didn't think there was a rabbit left within ten miles of here!"

With a big grin, Billy waved Tunnard over. "Com'on by and have a bite of fresh meat for a change. Now I won't be a'tall surprised if you meowed insteada hopped atter you eat."

The soldiers waiting about the cook fire laughed.

Sergeant Tunnard held his nose and made a long, "Me-o-o-ow!"

All assembled guffawed and slapped their knees or the backs of their comrades.

Presently, Billy turned serious. "Say, Sergeant Tunnard, I remember listenin' to you tell a bunch o' us one night last month about damned speculators in Vicksburg who wouldn't sell meat, or anything else, to soldiers."

"Yeah, the bloodsuckers!" Grinning, Tunnard continued. "They got what they deserved in that nice big fat bonfire downtown 'round the first of the month."

Grady joined. "That oughta teach'em!"

The soldiers laughed.

Billy did not laugh or smile. "Did the fire get'em all?"

When Tunnard stopped laughing, he continued. "Naw. I heard there're a couple of'em left."

Billy's eyes were riveted on Tunnard. "Where?" Billy sounded more like he was making a demand than a person expressing curiosity.

Tunnard paused and looked at Billy's hard dirty face. His smile vanished. "Well, I heard there're at least two on Cherry Street, south of Jackson Road."

Billy grinned. "Thanks. Okay, com'on boys. Gitcha a lil' taste! Real catsup for supper!"

* * *

When Billy finished his meal, he wiped his mouth on his dirty frayed sleeve and stared gloomily at the faltering fire. He sat on a two-foot-tall tree log, sweating and slapping at mosquitoes. His mood darkened each time he missed a mosquito biting his neck. Finally, he spoke. "Boys, y'all know ol' Tommy and me played marbles and stuff together when we wuz youngun. Already, it feels like he died a long time ago, though I know only three, maybe four, days done passed. It took us all this time and the loss of o' a lotta good boys to drive them blue-bellied devils outta that accursed crater. Why, I'm still miffed 'bout day 'fore yesterday when one o' their snipers got General Green. Like Tommy, he wuz standing near me. I still kick myself for not warning him about stickin' his head up and looking over the parapet. A bullet in the head..." Billy's voice trailed off.

Grady reached over and put a hand on Billy's shoulder. "Yeah, Homey. Losing Tommy was a hard hit – losing General Green too. All o' our losses make me wonder how we gonna make our farms work back in Copiah when this war is over."

"Grady, at the rate we're goin', being rid of the Yanks is a mighty long ways off."

"Yeah, you're right. But, even now, our homefolks can't make ends meet. In the last letter I got 'fore this damnable siege started, my Ann Ruth told me there ain't enough menfolks and animals left to plant more'n gardens this spring."

Billy turned on his log stool to face Grady. "We can fix that with nigger labor."

"How? We don't have money to buy niggers. Besides, who's gonna oversee'em?"

"One problem etta time. I'll tell you how we git 'em. We raid!"

"What?"

Billy grinned. Grady's question had gotten the attention of Louisiana and Mississippi soldiers rolling dirty wooden dice by the waning light of the cook fire. "When I went down to the quartermaster this evenin' for cornmeal, I heard talk of a raid that's gonna happen sometime this week at Goodrich's Landing. Y'all Louisiana boys oughta know whar that's at. One o' our colonels by the name o' William Parsons is gonna lead the raid and take back niggers stolen by the Yankees. When we bust outta here, we can do the same thing on this side o' the river for Copiah! When we raid, we can take niggers and animals too!"

"Whoa!" Grady leaned back and scratched his overgrown whiskers. "Not a bad idea. Say, that oughta help us get our farms back up and running in no time."

A Third Louisiana sergeant with red hair and matching beard pushed his campaign cap from over his eyes and spat. "Don't you fellas see what the hand done writ on the wall?"

Billy spun around on his log stool. "Jean Pierre, don't start. Like Gen'l Lee said, we have a duty to our country. And, by God, I'ma see it through."

Grady shifted the rifle on his back. "Jean Pierre, I can't read. What did the hand write?"

Some laughed so hard that they rolled on the ground. Billy realized as he laughed that all of them were waiting for something to laugh about. Even Jean Pierre laughed.

When several men had imitated Jean Pierre and Grady, repeating their exchange several times, and the laughter finally died, Jean Pierre responded. "Why, Grady, it's as plain as that big-ass mole on your nose."

More laughter.

Jean Pierre ignored the laughter. "Here, lemme read the writin' to you. It says, 'It's all over, you dumb shits. The cause is loss. Go home.'"

Billy was incredulous. "Why, that's the sorriest drivel I ever heard. It ain't over 'til we drive the stinkin' bluebellies from our land."

Jean Pierre sat up and removed his cap. "Me and none o' my kin ain't got no land. So, if the Yankees will stop shootin' et us, I'll lay my rifle down. They're welcome to be my neighbor."

Billy was on his feet. "You talk like a traitor! What in blazes is wrong with you? Ain't you wantin' to go on defendin' the South's way o' life?"

Jean Pierre remained seated and calmly folded his arms. "I guess I more or less see things Tommy's way – with one exception. Right etta Gen'l Pemberton surrenders and gits us paroled, instead o' walkin' to Jackson and joinin' Gen'l Johnston, I say we go on home to our kin and pick up the pieces and try to live our lives as best we can."

"And let the Yankee abolitionists take away our niggers?"

"Well now, I can't rightly say I ever owned one. For that matter, I don't know nobody that did."

Grady cleared his throat. "Oh, but you do. They ain't got no big plantation, but Billy and his pa owns a farm and five niggers."

"Well, I do declare." Jean Pierre stood, waved his cap, and made an exaggerated bow. "I stand corrected." He stood upright again and wagged a finger as he spoke. "But that don't change one word writ on the wall. 'It's all over.' It's taken'em two years to get on with it, but the Feds have the wherewithal to wear us down. They've done that right here in front of us. The comin' loss o' Vicksburg is just the beginnin' o' the end."

* * *

The cook fire died. Billy, Grady, Jean Pierre, and their comrades argued in the semidarkness of the humid and uncomfortably hot evening until shortly before midnight. They scratched intermittently at their lice and succeeded in stomping to death two large rats that had been sniffing for dead soldiers in shallow graves or for scarce scraps. The rats would mean extra rations for the skillet come morning, for usually, of late, there was no morning meal. As was the case every night, rain or no, Grant's shells fell randomly over the city and their position. They only paused in their deliberations when exploding shells came so close that it momentarily impaired hearing.

The next day, Wednesday, July 1, the Union army exploded another more powerful mine beneath the same Third Louisiana redan. This explosion caused greater damage to the Confederate fortifications than the blast of the previous Wednesday, only this time, the Union army did not follow the exploding mine with an infantry assault. Nonetheless, the blast caused death for a dozen or so Confederates and over one hundred wounded.

That evening, Billy and Jean Pierre used dull bayonets to hack apart a large bird that Billy had shot out of the sky. His leg was grazed by a Federal sharpshooter as he bravely exposed himself for a few seconds while retrieving his prize from atop the parapet. Blood had soaked through Billy's dirty bandana tied around his left calf. The flesh wound smarted, but he did his best to ignore the pain.

Billy was sullen and somber. Nonetheless, the suffering of fellow soldiers did not escape his notice. "Jean Pierre, why don't you take half o' the carcass over to your wounded boys in the Third Louisiana?"

"Yeah, I will. They ain't gonna feel much like cookin' tonight."

"By the way, just wanna let you know. I think you're right about the fact that the hand done wrote. I differ a bit on the meanin'."

"Oh? You've come a ways, eh?"

Grady stopped to inspect the evening meal. "Good Lawd, have mercy! Where and how did you get a turkey?"

Billy did not look up from his butchering. "Call it turkey for the boys. But, between you and me, this heah's a fuckin' vulture."

"Oh, no! Those damn things eat anything. Are we gonna eat *it*?"

Jean Pierre laughed. "He who eats pigs and had rat for breakfast is now particular?" He did not let Grady reply.

"Billy was telling me he has second thoughts about what the hand wrote. Go ahead, Daniel, give me your new insight on the meanin'."

Billy took a deep breath. "The meanin' is clearer today. It's no longer 'if we surrender.' The hand is right. It's over for Vicksburg, or it will be in a matter of hours – not days."

"Okay. We finally agree on something."

Grady clapped Billy's back. "Now, that's really somethin'!"

Jean Pierre continued. "Of course, Dan, I suppose you know that I continue to hold to the meanin' that the whole damn cause is lost."

Grady put one hand on his hip. "JP, why are you callin' my homey, Daniel and Dan?"

Billy spoke first. "Grady, you heathen, JP's jestin' me with the prophet's name."

"Oh."

Billy wiped his bloody hands on his only trousers. "Since we only have a few hours until the end, tonight I'ma put it to the boys straight and simple. I'm slippin' through the lines Friday night at first dark. I ain't waitin' 'round heah to be paroled – or, worse, sent off to that Cairo POW camp. Anyone goin' wid me best be ready to march soons we eat Friday night."

Billy searched their faces, his eyes darting from one comrade to the other. Grady blinked. Jean Pierre did not hesitate. "Count me out."

Grady swallowed and recovered. "I'm wid cha, homey."

* * *

As the sun set on Friday, Billy, Grady, and four others from Copiah County's Company F, Thirty-eighth Mississippi Infantry collected ammunition from fellow soldiers waiting for their hoped-for parole. Fresh rumors had it that Pemberton would surely negotiate from Grant a parole for each man and they would all go home. Grant's shelling had ceased. New excitement stirred over the prospect of leaving the trenches for food and a bath. They happily handed over their ammunition.

They ate at first dark. Even Sergeant Tunnard and Jean Pierre from Third Louisiana were there to send them off with more ammunition and well wishes.

Grady lined the men up for the usual patrol equipment check, though they had not patrolled since April. He turned to Billy. "From now on, you're the sergeant. I'll be your corporal."

Billy looked dazed. He blinked and stared at Tunnard and Jean Pierre. Both smiled and nodded. Finally Billy exhaled. "Okay."

The little patrol let out a cheer. "Hip, hip, hurray. Hip, hip, hurray!"

Billy stepped in front of Grady. He turned toward Jackson Road and Vicksburg. With a forward motion of his hand toward the west, he said, "Let's move."

Jean Pierre called after them. "What shall we call you in our diaries?"

Billy did not miss a beat. He shouted over his shoulder, "The Avengers!"

* * *

The Avengers marched on rutted and muddy Jackson Road when they could. At times, it was necessary to walk in the grasses that had grown up where woodlands stood before the siege. The road followed the ridgeline formed by joined hills north and east of downtown. As they passed, Billy thought it was curious that lanterns were ablaze at General Bowens's division headquarters. It was still odd to have no harassing fire coming from the Federals. Their brigade commander, General Hebert, and his staff were just emerging. In the dim light, Billy thought they looked as glum as he felt. They moved in a ragged column of twos, each man chatting with the soldier next to him.

"Hey, Billy. Is that you?"

Billy turned toward the familiar voice. "Yes, sir. It's me." He issued no commands by the book. Instead, Billy said, "Hold up, guys."

He saluted the figure approaching in the darkness. "Fellows, this here is the famous Captain Henry Carter II from Jackson. Captain

164

Carter is a member of our state legislature and a Mexican War veteran. He and my pa sometimes argue over matters 'fore the legislature."

The Avengers snapped to attention.

"At ease, boys." Captain Carter spoke in the same deep drawl they heard back home. "I may live near Jackson now, but I was born and raised right down there in Utica, not five miles as the crows flies from y'all's town.

"Billy, I guess you're doing what you told me you'd do and bustin' out."

"Yes, sir. It's the only way I see to drive out the blue-bellies."

"You're probably right. But, as you see, the brass is still mixing politics with their military decisions. Whereabouts y'all headed?"

"Oh, we'll head home and regroup down there. You're still welcome to join and lead us, if you want."

"Depending on the events of the next day or so, I'll decide."

"Be mighty proud to have ya, sir."

Captain Carter's sword scabbard slapped his high top boot as he turned to leave. "It would be my honor. In the meantime, keep yore powder dry."

For the first time in several days, Billy smiled. "Yes, sir!"

* * *

Billy and the Avengers arrived downtown at Main Street. They followed Main west for two blocks before turning south on Cherry Street. In the west block, bound on two sides by Cherry and Clay Streets, Billy found one of the remaining speculators identified by Tunnard. A sign in the window read: "Flour five dollars a pound and molasses ten dollars a gallon." An evil grin and snarl curled Billy's upper lip as he pointed out the sign and read it to Grady. The handpainted black and white sign above the door declared, "George Wheatley and Company, General Merchandise."

Billy's grin grew broader. "Okay, boys. In the absence of Grant's shells, let's make some noise." With the butt of his rifle, Billy broke two panes of the multi-paned storefront's window, reached in, and unlatched the door, only to find it chained and padlocked from the inside. Without a command, his squad formed a defensive perimeter. One shot from his musket undid the lock.

"Now boys, use whatever you can lay hands on to shape and make a cone. Go out several blocks toward the dwelling caves and use your cones and announce 'free supplies at Wheatley's while they last.' Be back in fifteen minutes. Meanwhile, me and Grady will collect supplies for our lil' trip to Carpenter and the folks back home." A cheer went up as Grady lit a glass kerosene lamp.

The good cave-dwelling citizens of Vicksburg responded, including George Wheatley. Wheatley sputtered and cussed while the parade of his fellow citizens relieved his store of goods. He cried out several times, "Why that lil' ol' sign there in the window was jes' a temporary trial thing. I was fixin' to replace it first thing come mornin'." The only response was laughter. Billy and Grady ignored Wheatley.

Thirty minutes later, all that stood were the walls and empty shelves. Billy tossed the lit lamp toward the rear door of the store and exited through the front as the wood-frame building became engulfed in flames. Wheatley stomped away in a huff, still cussing the Confederate army.

The Avengers, with ammunition and full haversacks weighting them down, arrived at the place about a mile south of downtown on Cherry Street where the brigades of Cumming and Reynolds met to form Pemberton's southeast flank. Here they were advised by friendlies not to try a breakout through the Union's finest sharpshooters in this corridor, much less steal Union horses. Reluctantly, Billy turned back. Near General Stevenson's division headquarters, they turned south again and followed Stout's Bayou.

It was around midnight when they arrived at General Barton's far south perimeter defenses. Word had been passed down the defense line ahead of them that General Pemberton had signed a surrender document about a half-hour earlier. The siege of Vicksburg was over. Billy led the Avengers past General Barton's lines, still following Stout's Bayou's every twist and change of direction. Through the woods on the hills above the bayou, Billy could hear soldiers from both armies celebrating the end of the siege. Quietly, they passed the southern end of the Union's blockade.

The bray of a mule caused Billy to halt mid-step. They followed their noses and found an unguarded remuda of sixteen mules. Each mule wore a halter with reins and was hitched to two rope lines attached to trees. Adjacent was a near perfect row of empty Union army wagons. Billy and Grady signaled for each man to untie and lead one mule to the road above the bayou. He could not believe the ease with which they stole the mules. After a few minutes, they were a mounted force, riding bareback.

Before they were comfortably settled on their mules' backs, an alarm went up followed by the heavy sound of hoofbeats from horses bearing a load.

Billy called out. "It's the cavalry! Hightail it! Split at the east-west road and meet up at Hamer Bayou."

Grady yelled back. "Okay!"

The mules crossed shallow Hatcher Bayou in full stride and made the long climb up the ridge on the south side. Billy knew the mules were no match for the cavalry horses. The pursuing hoofbeats were louder before they reached the top of the hill south of Hatcher Bayou. About a mile later, Billy heard the first shot fired over their heads. He searched for the east-west road. The winding route did not allow one to see more than a quarter-mile ahead – even in daylight. More shots rang out as the junction came into view. Billy's heart beat even faster as he realized the Union cavalry was using the new Spencer repeating rifles that could fire seven shots before reloading. A few hundred feet after the junction, the east-west road split; Grady and two men took the right branch. Billy and two more rode on together.

"Dammed!" Billy had hoped the Union cavalry would follow him into the ambush he planned at the next junction. But now he realized the cavalry was in hot pursuit of Grady. This was confirmed by gunfire echoing up from Redbone Creek. Billy could think of nothing to do but continue through the semidarkness of the quarter moon clear night to Hamer Bayou and set an ambush there on Fisher's Ferry Road.

With the mules tied to trees behind them, Billy and his two comrades lay in wait. Faint hoofbeats became louder. Billy sighed when three mules appeared. His sense of anxiety rose again when it became clear that one mule was riderless. Billy called to his team, "I'll hit the leader; you guys get the number two and three riders. That oughta hold'em for awhile. Then we hightail it again."

They let the three mules gallop through.

In sight now, the Union cavalry bore down in numbers larger than Billy could believe.

Chapter 10: **Ortega**

Ortega shivered. He was cold and hungry. He was always hungry. He had been hungry for three years. There was never enough to eat – either from failed crops or army rations.

It was two hours before midnight. He wondered if the cold November night caused his body to shake, or was it his excitement over participating in his closest activity to a raid. Kneeling, he blew on his fingers and put his hands inside his high-top buckskin moccasins that covered his calves.

His wiry five-foot-six frame was shielded from the cold only by a cast-off gray shirt and brown vest shipped west to the reservation by Quakers. He wore a dark blue headband to keep his shoulder-length black hair away from his face. Over his gray trousers, Ortega wore the traditional breechclout, secured at the waist with a cracked and aged black leather belt. The belt also held his only weapon – a small knife.

As was his habit, Ortega repeated the sentence he wanted to memorize, making note of this important night. Like many of his kinsmen, he spoke Apache and Spanish. His lips moved, but he made no sound. He thought, *some day I will share this great event with my children.* He recalled the quick smile that lit up Jacali's face when her mother's attention was elsewhere. He smiled. Three more times, Ortega said, "Dunna'idziidashi ąąshdlai hiiskągu, tai´shu nuúka', guusts´ iidi tł´ eéńa' aí -keé naagundzù' -gii pindah lickoyee. *(Friday, November 3, seven moons after war between the White Eyes.)*"

Ortega marveled at the wisdom of the shaman who calculated and suggested to their chief this night as the time to take action. First dark was obliterated by the rise of a full moon on the eastern horizon at dusk. Now the moon was high in the sky, like a noon-day sun. From where he knelt beside an army corral, made of split logs from the sparse cottonwood trees in the vicinity of the Pecos River he alternately scanned the horizon in the direction of the barracks of Fort Sumner and then looked toward the camps of the hated Navajo on the opposite end the Bosque Redondo Reservation. No movement. He was commonly called on for sentinel duty because of his unusually keen sight.

Ortega stood and opened the corral gate. His grandfather coaxed two horses toward it. Both horses nibbled dry corn leaves collected as fodder from the previous season's crop two moons before. Without a word, Ortega slipped a rope bridle over the head of each horse, led them outside the corral, and tied them to the log fence. His hands no longer trembled. To keep the horses quiet, he gave each another dried corn leaf. He repeated the process two minutes later as he received two more horses, this time from his best friend, Jorge. Silently, the threesome repeated the practice until they had a dozen horses outside the corral.

Ortega's grandfather, Nantahe-totel, made a chuck-will's-widow call to signal the unseen warriors standing guard on a perimeter beyond the corral that they were coming out with the horses. Nantahe-totel led the way back to the Mescalero camp. Fifteen-summers-old Ortega and Jorge followed in silence, holding the reins of two horses in each of their hands. They did not ride for fear that their weight would increase the sound of the horses' hooves.

Along their way back to camp, Ortega violated his grandfather's teaching about mental discipline. He had been instructed during his ongoing warrior training to remain alert and focused on the mission. Ortega's mind drifted back to a council held the previous week. Chief Zhee-ah-nat-tsa, who was also called Cadete, led the council. All the Mescaleros living at Bosque Redondo were present. For the purpose of having the people memorize their history, Cadete recounted the misery inflicted on them since the arrival of the Spaniards in their lands. Reciting history he had heard and memorized from his father, Chief Barranquito, Cadete reminded his listeners that Mescalero, Jicarilla, Chihenne, and Chokonen Apaches had made many treaties with the Spaniards and now with the White Eyes who called themselves Americans. Cadete was joined in the recitation by elders and clan leaders. Ortega smiled with pride as he recalled the rendition of the fight put up by Chief Cochise's Chokonen warriors and those of Chief Mangas Coloradas's Chihenne band against the hated White Eye General James H. Carleton's California Volunteers at Apache Pass three summers before. He involuntarily tightened his grip on the reins of the horses as he remembered hearing of the murder of old Chief Mangas Colorado by White Eye soldiers who took him prisoner when he accepted an invitation to talk at their camp. Mutilation of the chief's body disgusted Ortega, for the White Eyes removed and carried away the great chief's head. While still leading the horses, Ortega was further angered remembering the description of the attack by White Eyes on Chief Manuelito's band of Mescaleros in their camp, killing men, women, and children. Manuelito, another old chief, was murdered while he held up a hand attempting to sue for peace. Ortega did not need the recitations at the council to teach him the history of soldiers' attack on his own camp less than one moon after Manuelito was killed. The band to which Ortega belonged was camped on their homelands in the Sacramento Mountains where he was born. It was during this surprise attack in 1862 by Carleton's soldiers that both of Ortega's parents were murdered before his eyes. He was twelve summers old that year. With this memory, he felt rage build within. Ortega intensely loathed the accompanying feeling of helplessness. He spat.

Ortega thought for a moment of the screams of the women and children fleeing the camp. In his head, he could still hear the gunfire and smell the gunsmoke. He relived running and trying to tie a tourniquet above the gunshot wound in his grandfather's left arm as they sought a hiding place among the junipers. Days later, he and his grandfather, along with other survivors, had arrived at Fort Stanton where Cadete sought the protection of Colonel Kit Carson and his New Mexico militia. It was then that they learned Carleton had ordered his soldiers to kill, on the spot, every Apache man they saw. Instead, Carson took them in and sent Cadete and Lorenzo Labadie, the Indian Bureau agent for the Mescaleros, with a military escort to Santa Fe to plead for peace before the governor – which General Carleton ignored. Carleton ordered Carson to campaign against any Mescaleros not confined on the Bosque reservation.

Cadete repeated to the council his Santa Fe speech for what felt, to Ortega, like the hundredth time. He was still embarrassed by it. He kicked a clump of black grama grass. He despised the speech. Cadete had said, "You are stronger than we. We have fought you so long as we had rifles and powder, but your weapons are better than ours. Give us weapons and turn us loose, and we will fight you again; but we are worn out; we have no provisions, no means to live; your troops are everywhere; our springs and waterholes are either occupied or overlooked by your young men. You have driven us from our last and best stronghold, and we have no more heart. Do with us as may seem good to you, but do not forget we are men and braves."

Cadete had returned from Santa Fe and walked with the tribe, surrounded by soldiers, into captivity at Bosque Redondo – more than one hundred miles from their beloved Sierra Blanca and Sacramento mountains. Some hundred or so tribe members refused captivity and had fled west to join the Mimbres across the Gila River. Band after band made the winter trek north to Bosque Redondo. By March 1863, over four hundred Mescaleros had arrived at the reservation. Ortega was thinking how he and the young warriors who advocated for a fight could take revenge on the evil White Eye Carleton when suddenly the reins in his hands went taut. Ortega looked up and his face met the swish of the tail of one of Jorge's halted horses. It stung. While he had not, the horses Ortega led had paid attention and stopped. His reminiscing abruptly stopped. He spat.

They had reached the edge of their camp. Ahead, Nantahe-totel was talking and gesturing toward the horses with Chief Cadete. Everyone was speaking in low voices. Ortega made his way to Jorge's side. "I wish we would have left two summers ago when the first light-fingered Navajos arrived."

Jorge took a deep breath. "Yes. Me too. We would not have suffered through two summers of crop failures and losing the little we made to Navajo thieves. I'm sick and tired of being hungry."

"Constant hunger is no way for any people to live. Plus, we're surrounded by enemies." Ortega pointed first toward the Navajo camps and then Fort Sumner.

"Yes. Between the White Eyes and the Navajos, we would starve here."

"I told you from the start, that's exactly what the White Eye Carleton wants."

"No doubt. He is one evil man. While we are weak from lack of food, many new sicknesses have killed our people. But, still, this is the happiest night of my life."

Ortega shook his head and put a hand on Jorge's shoulder. "I fear for our people. The White Eye Carleton will send his soldiers to kill us. Four moons ago, you saw that he used his soldiers to prevent two Navajo chiefs and their people from leaving."

"But will Chief Cadete's new strategy work for us to escape?"

Ortega dropped his hand and his head. "I hope so. Even if we get away safely, with few losses, the day will come when Carleton's soldiers will find us."

"Why can't they just leave us be? First, they want us here, then there. Now they drive us to this Ussen-forsaken place – like cattle."

"It has been clear to me since Grandfather explained that the White Eyes want our lands. And they want us gone."

"I have never understood why."

"I don't fully understand it either. But I have heard from Grandfather that the White Eyes have an insatiable want for the yellow and white metals found in our lands."

"Oh, and they bring large herds to graze in our lands."

"Yes. And more and more White Eyes appear every year. They even kill each other for possession of our lands. They killed their great Nantan Lincoln. They are a ruthless and savage people."

"But Ussen made them as he made us.... This is very confusing."

"I do not understand, yet, why the White Eyes have such strong greed in their hearts that they will kill to possess that of another."

"How is that different from our raiding the Mexican and American sheep herders?"

"I do not know. But, remember, they brought their sheep and cattle to graze on our lands and drive us away. I say, since they brought their animals to our lands...."

Nantahe-totel called. "Ortega. Jorge. Bring the horses this way. We must hurry and help load the remaining packs on these new animals."

* * *

Several old horses and two ancient mules taken from army and Navajo corrals early in the evening stood hobbled at the edge of their camp nearest the reservation boundary. When all of the packs were loaded, Nantahe-totel called Ortega. "It is time to feed the people."

"But, Grandfather, everyone packed the small rations we saved this week. There is no food left."

Nantahe-totel gestured toward the first hobbled horse. Ortega gulped. Jorge took a step back, but did not leave. Nantahe-totel pulled a long knife from the buckskin scabbard on his belt and handed it to Ortega, handle first. The threesome walked to the first horse. Ortega heard footsteps behind him. He turned and saw the faces of several women about the age of his grandfather. Each carried a long knife. Behind them, a line of families began to form.

Nantahe-totel placed one palm on the horse's head and gave thanks to Ussen for providing the animal. His face lifted, Nantahe-totel extended his free hand toward the stars as he prayed. After a few sentences, he stepped away from the horse and nodded to Ortega. Ortega looked pleadingly toward Jorge.

Together, in silence, Ortega and Jorge approached the horse. First, Ortega rubbed the horse's muzzle with a trembling hand. Jorge watched and then did the same. Ortega turned the knife over in his hand twice as he nodded to Jorge. While Jorge patted the horse, Ortega used all his strength and, in one swift motion, slit the horse's jugular. Immediately, he smelled the horse's blood as it gushed and flowed down its breast. With its severed blood-filled windpipe making a gurgling sound, the animal's legs buckled and it lay on its side. Ortega was frozen in his tracks until the women pushed him aside and began their work removing the entrails and the hide, and slicing the buttocks, loins, breast, shoulders, and brisket into small pieces to be eaten immediately – raw, while it was warm. They followed the plan. No fires. No cooking, for surely the smell of cooking meat, when food was short for them, the Navajos, and the soldiers, would attract the attention of even sleeping hungry people.

Nantahe-totel beckoned Ortega and Jorge to the next horse. The same scene unfolded until more than three hundred Mescaleros were fed.

At last, when the young mothers finished breast-feeding their infants, the Mescaleros vanished from Bosque Redondo.

Though they knew well Carleton's oft-repeated order to kill any Mescalero or Navajo male found off the reservation for any reason, that night every Mescalero man, woman, and child who could travel walked south out of the Bosque Redondo Reservation. At a point where the Pecos made a large horseshoe turn, creating a wide peninsula that pointed east, they separated. About half crossed to the west bank. Two mounted hunting parties, armed with bows and arrows, departed ahead of the people. One headed west for the Capitan Mountains. The other followed the Alamosa Creek, a tributary of the Pecos, to the east.

From the river, the women topped off water jugs woven from grass and sealed with piñon pitch. They filled the intestines saved from the slain horses with water and loaded the make-shift bladders atop the cargo borne by their pack animals. When the people and their animals had satisfied their thirst, they said their farewells and set out. With the packhorses in tow, they formed a line, walking side by side like a cavalry charge; they spread and swept, like a fan, across the desolate, almost barren landscape in every direction except north. Ordinarily, dogs would drag small packs on litters made of sticks and rope. But not this time. Dogs were left behind with the infirm, lest their barking betray the movement and location of the people.

Ortega and Jorge were proud to be the only teenagers to travel with the rear-guard warriors who were armed with an odd assortment of firearms they had been able to hide from Carleton's soldiers. The warriors employed Ortega's keen sight. Jorge was permitted to assist by holding the horses for the warriors – the only saddled horses in the exodus.

When they reached the place where some of the main body forded the river, Ortega felt less nervous about the escape plan. "The soldiers will track us to this point and turn back."

"Yes. Chief Cadete reasoned that there would be too many tracks in all directions for them to follow. So they will follow none – I hope."

"Our chief is wise. I wish we were going east with him to hunt buffalo with the Comanche people."

"Me too, for I have never seen a buffalo or a Comanche."

They laughed together.

The rearguard waited as Ortega climbed a cottonwood tree on the east bank of the river. After ten minutes or so in the tree, Ortega climbed down. "I saw no movement about the fort."

The rearguard leader was Klo-sen, whose exploits in battle were legend. He beckoned for Ortega to follow. "Thanks, Ortega. Let us separate and follow the people."

Following Cadete's and the council's plan, the thirty-two-man rearguard became four units of eight warriors each. They bade farewell to each other and rode to gain sight of the four groups that should have already formed after the main body split. Ortega held the reins of a large bay horse. Riding double, Jorge sat behind Ortega on an antelope skin thrown across the animal's back. They rode between the warriors.

Nantahe-totel led a band of about eighty people on a zig-zag course to the southwest across the almost flat Staked Plain of New Mexico Territory. After each ten-minute stop, Ortega and Jorge mounted their large horse and Ortega would nudge the animal with the heels of his moccasins. The patient horse would then walk in pace with the mounts of the rearguard. All was quiet. No one talked. Sound from the horses' hooves was muffled by the soft soil of the Staked Plain over which they traveled. When they stopped before dawn, the sleeping Jorge fell to ground and startled their horse. The alarmed animal leapt forward and was quickly in full gallop. Ortega grabbed the mane with one hand, leaned forward, and held on. He spoke soothingly to the frightened horse and rubbed its neck. He gently pulled back on the reins. After a romp of nearly half a mile, the horse slowed and Ortega turned back. He was met by two warriors. When they rejoined the others, all were laughing. Jorge looked embarrassed. Ortega slid down from the horse and sat on the ground beside Jorge amid the laughter.

Mounted again after a few minutes, Ortega scanned the horizon behind them. Nothing. A short time later, the first signs of dawn appeared to his left. Spotting a small knoll to the east, Ortega turned their horse and used the knoll for an observation post. Still nothing. Though it appeared that their escape plan was working, he expected at any time to see Carleton's soldiers in pursuit. They rejoined the rearguard.

They rode on without stopping after the sun rose. Before them, the flat plain stretched for miles in all directions and was covered by patchy brown grasses with sparse spots of green. There was not a tree or a bush in sight.

Jorge demanded, "Where are we going?"

"Grandfather told me that he knows a canyon east of the Sacramentos where there is game, wood, and a small river."

"Oh, my aching back."

"What? Did the fall hurt your back?"

"No. The thought of carrying water for farm plants makes my back hurt."

Ortega grabbed his mouth to cover his laughter. "Would you rather dig a canal?"

"That thought is no less painful!"

"Agreed. Growing plants is no life for a warrior."

"But your grandfather made sure everyone packed and brought all the hoes and shovels the army issued to us. I guess you know what that means."

"Grandfather was once a warrior. I don't know.... Maybe warriors grow soft when they are old. He thinks we need to stay in one place and be farmers."

"Why do you think he changed?"

"I'm not sure. But, I think he believes the White Eyes are too many for us to defeat."

Silence. Ortega loathed the thought that the Mescaleros would become farmers before he became a warrior. The thought made him shiver on the antelope skin upon which he sat.

At length, Jorge spoke. "What do you believe?"

Ortega chuckled. "I believe I will marry Jacali!"

"Dreamer! Dream on."

"Oh, but I will. You just watch!"

"That will never happen! Think about it. Next summer, Jacali will have her puberty ceremony. Most likely, her mother will have her wait the usual two years after the ceremony to marry, and then the race will begin. Within two years, the young warriors will fall all over themselves trying to lure such a prize as Jacali. You will be only eighteen summers old and have no horses to offer her father. You won't even be a warrior by then."

"Jacali will wait for me."

"Ha! You *are* a dreamer. What makes you think such a beauty as her would even notice the likes of you. She never even looks my way. And Ussen knows I've tried to catch her eye."

"Of course, she would never notice you. What are you thinking? You have the face of an elk!"

They laughed together.

"I suppose you think she would like your jackrabbit face?"

More laughter.

"When her mother is not looking, Jacali flashes me a quick and secret smile."

"Really? Jacali?"

"Yes. Jacali. And, when I smile back, she seems to glow with happiness and drops her head to hide her blush."

"No shit!?"

"No shit."

"Well, I'm happy for you, my friend. I hope you're right about her waiting."

"Uh-huh."

They rode in silence. Jorge pointed to the skeleton of a horse, half-buried in the sandy soil. Ortega nodded. Jorge reminded Ortega, "You didn't answer my question. Can we defeat the White Eyes?"

Ortega let out a big sigh. "No matter that I want to fight, I fear that Grandfather is right. He usually is. He is a wise...."

The rearguard leader, Klo-sen, was Jacali's father. He called to Ortega. "Ride ahead to that knoll yonder and let me know if you see anyone behind us."

"Yes, sir."

Barely above the horizon in the northeast, Ortega spotted a cloud of dust. He watched and said nothing. Jorge was silent, apparently seeing nothing unusual. Shortly, it became clear to Ortega that the dust cloud was moving south. Still, he watched, motionless. At length, he was able to see men on horseback riding at a smart canter. Ortega pointed and announced, "Soldiers." He spat.

Chapter 11: **Walk to Davis Bend**

Rachel bolted upright on her pallet.

The singing was barely audible, but she heard it again – a baritone: "Steal away, steal away, steal away to Jesus." Rachel knew then that this was no dream. She looked around in near total darkness at the shapes formed by the sleeping bodies of Rebecca and John. Neither moved. Now she heard the sound of sand thrown softly against the shudder on the rear glassless window of their cabin. Her eyes went wide. It was the signal used by the enslaved at Bender Plantation to raise the alarm that a runaway needed help.

She cupped her hands about her mouth and called just above a whisper toward John. "Pa."

John opened one shutter. A man's voice whispered urgently, "John, let me in!"

John kept his voice down. "Rome? Boy, is that you?"

Jerome whispered, pushing aside the open shutter. "Yeah, John. It's me."

John opened the second shutter and Jerome climbed through the window.

Rachel clasped her hands together in excitement. "Oh, it's so good to see you! Well, almost see you in the dark." They laughed and Rebecca stirred. On her pallet, Rachel was bouncing on her butt and firing questions: "Where is Cicero? Is Emma with you? Where are the children?"

Rebecca sat up, rubbing her eyes. "Who's there?"

"Becky, Jerome is back. Rai, slow down. One question at a time. First, let him tell his story. Maybe when he's finished you won't have any questions."

"Yeah, windmill mouth. Let Jerome say something."

Though she knew Rebecca couldn't see her, Rachel rolled her eyes and made a face at her sister.

"Rai, Becky. It's almost good to be back. I can't believe I've been gone from dis sorry place for eighteen months. Time went very quickly for me. To answer your question, Rai, Emma and the chillun don't know I'm here."

"Why not?" Rachel was climbing out of her covers.

"'Cause, they make too much noise. Next thing you know, ol' man Bender and Wash will be at the cabin door. Besides, I didn't come for a visit. I came to fetch you and my family."

John, Rachel, and Rebecca talked at the same time, sometimes asking the same question. "Where're we going? When are we going? Have you thought this thing through? How far is it? What of the lil' ones?"

Jerome laughed softly, holding up both hands. "Whoa! Hold up. One at a time."

John shook his head. "I can't believe I'm askin' questions the same way my daughters are."

Jerome sat backward on a ladderback chair in the dark, his hands on the top rung supporting his chin. "Well, it's okay. The place I want to take my family is called Davis Bend. It's right on the east bank of the mighty Missisip herself! Great bottom land for farming. The Bend is right over in Warren County, a little ways south o' Vicksburg."

Rachel held up a hand. "*Davis* Bend? Well, I, for one, want nothing to do with *your* president."

"Wait Rai. It ain't like you think. True. The place was owned by ol' man Joe Davis. But that Gen'l Grant and the Feds done took it over and he put dis John Eaton in to 'stablish a Freedman's Department on the place. The farmland is given over to us coloreds to rent. Dey even got a bank for us. And, best of all for you, dey need teachers. John and Bec, here's your chance at usin' y'all's heads for bitness!"

John put a finger to his lips. "Now there you go gettin' excited too. Sounds excitin'. Sounds too good to be true. Have you seen this place?"

"John, I jes came from Davis Bend directly here. You ain't heard nothin' yet. Ol' Joe Davis ain't nothing like his younger brother – *your* president. Why, ol' Joe had a colored man by the name o' Ben Montgomery running his store and the whole plantation!" Jerome pointed to Rachel.

John let out a low whistle. Rachel noticed that Rebecca had covered her mouth with both hands. Almost immediately, Rachel realized that she too had covered her mouth in an effort to contain her excitement, lest she scream. She could see Jerome's head move from side to side. She guessed he was waiting for a reaction.

At length, John spoke. "Rome, we have nothing here but Bender's work. If you have a workable plan that does not bring too much jeopardy to my family, we'll accept your judgment about how we could fit in at this Davis Bend place."

Rachel jumped up and danced a little jig. Rebecca grabbed her sister and they hugged fiercely. Rachel whispered, "Thanks, Pa. Thanks, Jerome. Hallelujah!" Rebecca repeated the same words.

"Aw, no thanks necessary. Y'all be a nat'ral fit for the Bend.

"But, right now, we gotta git goin'. John, here's my plan. I need you to let me send your girls to fetch Emma and my chillun while you hep me with some preparations." Jerome waited for John to nod his head. Then he turned to Rebecca and Rachel. "Tell Emma to meet us in the cottonwood grove behind the big garden in one hour. Y'all wear overalls. Pack two changes of clothes tied up in a shirt. Roll your pallets inside your oilcloth. Wear work shoes. Bring one cook pot, a cup, a jar for water, a fork, and a knife – nothing else. Same goes for my family. My guess is it's 'round two in the mornin'. I need y'all to move quickly and quietly. Time's a wastin'. Any questions?"

Rachel and Rebecca shook their braids.

John was tying his shoes. "Sounds to me like some o' the Union army done rubbed off on you."

Jerome laughed and shook a finger at Rachel and Rebecca. "Then be gone!"

* * *

In the low light of a quarter-moon at the edge of the grove, Rachel watched Emma hold her son, Aaron, ten, and daughter, Zipporah, six, by their hands. When John and Jerome approached, Aaron dropped Emma's cook pot and ran into his father's embrace. Zipporah followed. Jerome was on his knees for a long silent hug with a child in each arm. Rachel smiled as she heard Emma sniffing when she finally embraced her husband.

"Wait a minute. Who're you?" Jerome was pointing to the young woman standing next to Rachel.

Rachel put on her sweetest smile and voice. "Uncle Romey, don't you recognize Ruth? She's my best friend."

"Oh, yeah. I 'member." Jerome held his head with both hands and looked at John. John stared at Rachel, who shrugged and said, "Ruth spotted us as she stepped from the women's outhouse. I knew then we had to bring her. She can wear my clothes. I know she will be a big help."

Ruth stood looking down at her ankle-length dress and the toes of her shoes.

John put his hands on Rachel's shoulders. "What will her mother say at daybreak when she finds her daughter is missing?"

Rachel smiled big again. "Pa, we went through that. Ruth doesn't think it'll be a problem. Her mother will be happy for her once she figures out that she's with us. Besides, I'll need an assistant teacher at the Bend school."

John turned to Ruth. "Is that so? You gonna learn to read real fast?"

"Yessuh, Mister John. Besides, Ma won't be unhappy for more'n a few hours."

Jerome was fidgeting. "Looks like we're all in this thing together. We's gotta move – now!" They picked up their belongings and walked as quietly as they could along the edge of the grove toward the path to Otak Creek. Ruth carried little Zipporah. Presently, Jerome held up a hand and signaled a halt.

"Now, don't be embarrassed. Is one of you womens on yo' menses?"

The four women looked at each other. Rachel gave Jerome a harsh glare but, before she could scold Jerome, Ruth replied, "Me."

Rebecca dropped her bundle. Her hands flew akimbo. "Now why, pray tell, is that any of your bitness?"

Jerome looked at Emma, then Rebecca. "Every time something comes up, I may not have the chance explain my every move. But this time I will. Listen carefully, 'cause there ain't no time to repeat. Ol' man Bender, as usual, has his dogs staked out 'round the place as sentinels. He got ol' Buster tied down there by the path to the creek. John, I'ma overpower ol' Buster's senses when me 'n' Ruth feed 'im the bacon I got for'im in my pocket. You take our little group to that tallest tree yonder and then turn to the creek. This way ol' Buster won't smell the group and set off an alarm. We'll meet'cha at the creek. Ruth, put Zipporah down and come with me."

Rachel let out a sigh. "I never woulda thought of that. I'da had that dog barking his fool head off and we'd a been caught before we set foot off the plantation."

They waited at the creek. In the moonlight, Rachel surveyed the plainly visible cotton still on stalks that were over waist high. She smiled, realizing that they would not pick cotton come daylight on Thursday morning. She strained to hear ol' Buster make a sound. The next noise Rachel heard was Ruth and Jerome's footsteps.

The going was slow as they picked their way along the edge where the woods sloped to the bank of the marsh by the creek. Rachel had seen the Mississippi River on Isabella Taylor's and Colonel Grierson's maps and had a good idea of how far they were from the river. She shook her head as she calculated that, at their present rate, they would probably arrive in the middle of November – some six weeks hence. They followed Jerome and Aaron. John remained some distance behind. They used twine John had fetched from Bender's barn to tie their bundles. Ruth carried a cook pot in her hand and Zipporah on her back most of the time.

They remained on the east side of the creek headed south. Just before Rachel made up her mind to pass Emma and confront Jerome about not turning west, he did. The place was south of Bender's cultivated land and showed signs of a well-worn trail that she had not known. They followed the trail and forded the creek at a surprisingly shallow point. They traveled, without talking, in single file due west for half a mile and crossed Tallahala Creek where it was joined by a tiny stream. In a wooded area above the Tallahala, Jerome called a halt. He disappeared into the tree line. He re-emerged five minutes later leading a mule with a large crop basket on each of its sides, strapped over its back. Aaron and Zipporah would have easily fit into one. Emma exclaimed, "Oh, Romey! Thank you so much."

Jerome grinned. "Dis here is Maude. She's an old mule, but 'pendable."

Emma and the other women unburdened themselves of their bundles, pallets, and cook pots. Everything fit in the two baskets alongside the shovel and two wooden rabbit guns already in one basket. They moved on. Rachel noticed the North Star just to the front of her right shoulder most of the time they waded up the small stream with their shoes hanging about their necks by their laces. She figured their direction to be northwest. Three miles on, they turned due west and Rachel decided Jerome must know his way. After all, he followed Colonel Grierson's brigade to who knows where and found his way back to Bender's plantation. So she put her mind to work trying to imagine actually teaching students to read and write.

At the top of a small rise in the rolling hills they traversed, Jerome halted the marchers and secured Maude a ways apart where she could graze and drink. It was about an hour before sunrise. They had traveled only six miles and that made Rachel nervous. Bender and patrollers on horseback working with dogs could cover that distance in a short time. She felt less nervous when she remembered wading in the stream, beginning where it joined a larger stream. Bender and his dogs would have had miles of streams to check in three directions before finding where they climbed out of the creek. And, of course, she would hear the dogs coming.

Jerome dug a latrine for the women behind low-growing bushes. Rachel used the pots to fetch water from upstream. John and Aaron set out the rabbit guns with small strips from Jerome's handful of collards leaves inside each gun. They raised the doors and tested the triggers. Once inside, a rabbit could only eat the bait in front of it. The critter would trip the trigger and the door would fall behind it. There was not enough space for the rabbit to turn around, much less attempt to raise the door. There, the rabbit would have to await its fate.

Rachel and Emma drew first watch. Jerome assigned their positions and fields of view. He gave them a bird call to imitate and raise an alarm without losing sight of a potential enemy. Rachel knew the call well. It was that of a bobwhite. The only weapon they had was the Colt .44 Jerome had acquired following the army. He showed them the rusting revolver, hidden in the waistband of his trousers, behind the bib of his overalls. Rachel knew the best contact with a potential enemy was no contact.

They took turns sleeping through the daylight hours of Thursday, a warm early October day. Using a butcher knife, Rachel helped Ruth cut a strip of cloth from the hem all the way around her dress. Ruth carefully removed the folded rag she had used as a pad in her underwear, wrapped it in leaves, and dropped it into the women's latrine pit. Ruth rubbed away traces of blood on her hands with dirt. Rachel poured a slow stream of their precious water for Ruth as she washed the dirt from her hands. Ruth carefully folded a new pad made from her dress and put it into place. Rachel dreaded the thought that her menses was due in two weeks. She had not thought to pack cloth or rags. To herself, she said, "Oh well, I guess my pallet will be smaller by the time we reach the big river."

After a meal of rabbit cooked in a pit at first dark, they were ready to set out again to the west. Before departing, Jerome and John refilled the latrines and fire pit with the original dirt and covered it with leaves and pine needles.

Thursday night was clear and the stars appeared very bright. Two miles west of their first campsite, they used a road for the first time. Their pace quickened. Rachel and Ruth walked side by side, talking as they went. Soon they caught up with Jerome leading Maude. Zipporah rode on Maude much of the night. Rachel saw Jerome glance over his shoulder at them and then set an even faster pace. "Com'on, Maude. Let's go. We can't have these gals pushing us." Emma and Rebecca walked with Aaron, who declared as they set out, "Don't worry, Ma. I'll look out for you and Miss Becky." John remained in his usual rearguard position, two to three hundred feet behind.

The road was quiet. They did not meet or pass anyone – even a critter. By sunrise on Friday, they had covered twenty miles and arrived at Strong River.

"I know y'alls tired. But com'on wid me a lil' further."

"Aw, Romey, my feets are real tired. Honey, why can't we stay here by the river?"

"'Cause this is too close to the only bridge for miles. There's bound to be folks traveling this way during the day."

"Oh, all right." Emma reluctantly picked herself up from the mossy spot she had settled onto and fell in beside Aaron. "Ma, I'll help you up the hill."

They walked by the riverbank for five minutes before Jerome had them wading in a small tributary of the Strong. They went another mile to the northeast before emerging from the creek bed. Their campsite was set up the same as Thursday's. After Maude's cargo baskets were off-loaded, Jerome secured her by rope to a tree over the next ridge. They ate cold bacon and again slept in shifts.

Shortly after three o'clock Friday afternoon, John and Aaron brought back two rabbits. John showed Aaron how to slit and pull the rabbit's hide off in one piece.

Aaron ran to Jerome. "Pa, look. Mr. John showed me how and I it did right on my first try!"

"Son, that's a mighty fine job."

"What do I do with it now?"

"Son, spread it on that bush over yonder. Let the sun dry'em. Tonight, we'll spread the hides on one o' Maude's baskets. There they can dry some mo' tomorrow."

Rachel and Ruth cleared leaves and pine straw from a space on the ground by the fire pit. Rachel called, "Aaron and Zip, com'on over here. We're going to have school until your ma and Rebecca come off watch."

"Aw, Pa. Do I have ta?"

"Boy, you better git yo' self on over there wid Miss Rachel and Miss Ruth and learn everything you can. Gettin' educated is the most important thing you can do for yo' self, me, yo' ma, and all colored peoples."

"Yessuh." Aaron's shoulders sank.

Aaron slumped down beside Zipporah, who was already copying capital letters Rachel had made in her dirt blackboard. Rachel smiled to herself when she saw Jerome position himself behind Aaron ostensibly to whittle a walking stick but all the while carefully studying the letters in the dirt.

Jerome had the fire going before Emma and Rebecca came off watch. At first dark, they had boiled rabbit from one cast iron pot and fried cornbread from the other.

When they reached the road and the bridge over the Strong River, light rain began to fall. The oilcloths that usually served to keep ground moisture from their pallets were now used like ponchos. They walked on dirt roads all night again without meeting anyone. They camped on Saturday morning above a little tributary of Richland Creek. On Thursday and Friday nights, they had crossed Smith County. Rachel said to Ruth, "I know we are well pass the Taylor Plantation. I can feel it in my bones. My mind was on my ma most of this past night."

"I feel for you."

On Saturday afternoon, the rain stopped. Jerome announced. "We're near Brandon. Dat be Richland Creek over the rise. That'll lead us to the rai'road and on into Jackson on Sunday."

Rachel observed. "Oh, we've made more progress than I thought. That means we've walked forty to fifty miles."

"Dat's 'bout right."

Emma announced, "My feets coulda told y'all dat. Next time, jes' ask."

Laughter.

Jerome ignored Emma. "We stay here Saturday night and walk in the daytime on Sunday. The bridges and rai'road around Jackson be guarded by colored soldiers. Dey be sharp in dem blue uniforms."

Rebecca cleared her throat. "I'ma see if I can find one o'dem soldier boys interested in settin' up a lil ol' inn and eatery wid me in New Orleans and making babies."

More laughter.

John smiled and shook his head. "Lawd, where did go wrong with this child?"

Jerome gave up trying to be heard. "I'll tell y'all the rest later."

Rachel did not think anyone heard Jerome but her.

On Saturday night, Jerome was back from a trek into Brandon with collards and carrots for the group and potential rabbits. By the fire, he continued his announcement from the afternoon. "We gonna meet all kinds o' peoples 'round a city like Jackson. No matter dat some are colored. Some o' dem ain't up to any good. So I'm askin' y'all not to trust nobody. Tellin' our bitness could lead to trouble."

* * *

On Sunday morning, they joined the main east-west road near Brandon that connected Meridian, Jackson, and Vicksburg. They met and passed many travelers walking in both directions. A few had valises; others carried their goods in burlap sacks, while some had single-axle ox-drawn carts – even one drawn by a milk cow. Rebecca exclaimed, "I never saw so many colored people at one time in my life!"

Emma wondered, "Where can they all be going? Can't be nobody left on a plantation."

Rachel observed. "And in equal numbers they're headed both east and west."

John chucked. "Well, I guess them in the east ain't told the ones from the west that it ain't no better where they left and vice a versa."

Jerome let out a guffaw. "That's the funniest thing I heard this month." They all laughed. He recovered, holding his side. "But if you think this is something, wait'll you see Jackson."

* * *

Passing Jackson, Jerome did not break his stride. When Emma and Rebecca tried to persuade him to find a place to camp there, Jerome said, "I heard in Brandon that there're problems in Jackson. Among them are dysentery and cholera. We don't need a mess o' neither. Let's git on to the hills and find clean water for us and the chillun." They did not ask again.

They left the main road and camped near a spring about six miles northwest of Jackson. A family, the Fullers, that included two sons and two daughters, arrived and also camped near the spring. Emma made fast friends with Mrs. Fuller. Jerome and John spoke briefly with the father, who had heard the same bad news about Jackson's diseases. The teenagers from both groups mingled. Taking Jerome's advice, both groups remained at the spring until first dark on Monday.

Following the main road and railroad, around daybreak on Tuesday they arrived at Champion Hill and went up a dirt track beyond the village into the hills. Once atop the first hill, the Fullers decided to encamp. Jerome convinced John and Emma, to press on southward and they ascended an even higher hill above the headwaters of a small tributary to Bakers Creek. There, Rachel discovered a sharp incline between their camp and a spring on the far side that reminded her of canyons she had read about. She tried to imagine boulders and desert in place of the trees and vines in front of her. She thought of painting both scenes and tried to memorize them. Maude's bray from across the next stream and ridge brought her back to her task: fetch water for the group.

At noon, Rachel heard something. She signaled her watch partner, Ruth, to remain quiet while she made the bobwhite call. Presently, Jerome, bleary-eyed, appeared beside her. "What?"

"I heard horsemen coming from over toward Champion Hill."

"I don't hear anything but the Fullers. How do you know they're horsemen?"

Ruth crawled over on all fours. "The Fullers is all I hear too."

"From the sound and vibration, I know the horses are carrying weight, traveling fast, and aren't pulling a wagon."

"Girl, you're amazin'. Becky told me you were first to hear the Yankees comin'."

Fully awake now, Jerome appeared to be in deep thought. "I hear'em now. Keep close watch. I'ma get everybody up."

Ruth returned to her watch position. Rachel found she had to sharply focus on the approaching horsemen while trying to ignore the Fuller teenagers engaged in lively conversation and the sounds of Jerome rousing everybody in their two families. Rachel's eyes went wide as she heard the first shots. There were screams and sounds of pandemonium from the Fuller camp. Rachel tightly gripped a branch of the bush she hid.

Rachel made the bobwhite call again. Jerome and John appeared and she pointed down the hill to the north. "Two of the horsemen crossed the creek and are headed this way!"

Both men looked in the direction Rachel pointed, saw nothing, and then looked at each other. John spoke. "Rome, trust her hearing."

"Okay. We got to move – now! Can't wait until we can see'em."

"But, we can't run with women and chillun."

"You're right. But we…"

Rachel grabbed Jerome's sleeve and whispered. "We can restore our campsite and hide among the bushes and vines in the steep gulley where I found water."

"Okay. No time for argument. You get everybody hid. I'ma take care o' de camp."

Rachel, John, and Ruth had everyone hidden in two clusters by the time Jerome discovered them. Rachel said, "The two horsemen are taking their time coming up the hill – like they're looking for tracks."

Jerome held up his Colt .44. "All right, quiet everybody."

Rachel watched Jerome crawl slowly through the vines back toward the top of the gulley. There he stopped and waited. Rachel heard Emma trying to calm Zipporah, who was dripping tears and sniffing quietly.

Rachel whispered. "They're coming."

Ruth clutched Rachel's hand. They waited. Rachel watched Jerome and prayed that the rider's horses would not smell them. Then she saw a horseman at the top of the gulley stop and look about. The man was tall and blond and cradled a rifle in the crook of his left arm. He was also armed with a revolver and wore two ammunition belts over each shoulder that crossed in the middle of his chest and back. His face was dirty and unshaven. The man's clothing was made from butternut-colored denim. Rachel could hear the leather of his saddle squeak as he turned to and fro and looked about. Then she noticed that he wore a Confederate campaign hat and that his shirt bore CSA buttons. In her hiding place, Rachel inhaled.

The rider turned his horse away. "Dey ain't nobody up here. Let's git on back and hep round up dem niggers we done already cotched."

"Yeah, not a bad haul for half a day's work."

"Yep, that bunch'll fetch a good price."

They lay in the vines for a time after the riders departed. Rachel wiped her brow on her sleeve. She rose and pulled Ruth to her feet. She whispered, "That was too close for comfort."

Ruth gasped. "Whew! I thought I would give us away 'cause my heart was beatin' so loud!"

"I couldn't hear yours 'cause mine was thumpin' even louder!"

"So, what'll we do now?"

"I don't know. But here comes Jerome and Pa." Rachel paused. "Where're we going next? It's only shortly past noon."

Jerome threw up one hand and shrugged. "I don't know."

John put one foot on a fallen and rotting pine tree. "Well, I think the safest place is our present camp."

Rachel smiled. "Pa, I like it! They aren't likely to search again where they just searched."

"That's right, baby girl."

"Yep, my windmill-mouth sister is as right as rain." Rebecca made a face. Ruth and Emma laughed, but Rachel ignored them.

Jerome looked up. The clouds were low and dark. Light rain fell. "Okay. We stay."

Not until dark did Jerome start a fire with his tinderbox. John and Aaron brought in empty rabbit guns. They ate stew made from collards, carrots, and leftover rabbit legs. The rain was a steady drizzle. John offered a prayer of thanksgiving for their food and safekeeping. He prayed for the safety of the Fuller family.

The drizzle became steady rain. They ate in silence until Emma wept for Mrs. Fuller. "That poor sweet woman didn't deserve what happened to herself and her family."

Jerome put a hand on his wife's wet shoulder. "Emma, you's right. None of us coloreds deserved to be treated the way white folks treat us."

"Who is dose mens? What'd that one mean, 'they'll bring a good price'?"

"Baby, dems Confederate guerillas. Dey was soldiers 'til Gen'l Grant and Gen'l Sherman beat their armies 'round Vicksburg 'n' Jackson. Dey capture and sell us to plantations south and west o' here where they ain't no Yankee soldiers – white or colored. That's why we have to be so careful every day."

"Thank you. You're a good man. Rome, is we got to walk tonight?"

"We need to. But … John, what do you think?"

"I think walking in a downpour at night in pitch darkness is asking for trouble. You know, like a mishap lookin' for a place to happen."

Though Rachel was soaked to her skin as well as cold, she managed to chuckle with everyone. Jerome and John trenched an area around the fire pit large enough for all to lie down and covered it with a deep layer of pine needles and leaves. They burned the needles and leaves with a few twigs to warm the ground. Next, in the light of the fire, they built a brush arbor as a sort of windbreaker. With the trenching, water flowed away from the fire pit. Wrapped in their oilcloths, the two men, four women, and two children slept huddled together for warmth, their feet toward the fire pit. The two persons on watch sat among the bodies of their sleeping comrades. Rachel tried, but could not remember spending a more miserable night.

As Wednesday dawned, it was colder than the night. The rain continued. They took a risk and kept the fire going, believing no one would pass by. Rebecca remarked, "No need to worry 'bout the fire. Ain't nobody desperate or stupid enough to be out in this kinda weather."

The rain stopped shortly before sunset. The western sky displayed a progression of art with light and the remaining broken clouds. From white to yellow, to orange, to red, to purple, and finally to black, making Rachel wish for canvas and paint. She almost forgot her wet clothes or that she was cold. The approaching harvest moon was growing larger, promising an easy walk.

As they set out, Rachel noted, "This night is the eighth night into our journey."

Emma was quick to chime in. "Dat sho' ain't no news to my feets!"

They walked briskly through the night, in part to generate body heat. Early on, they crossed Bakers Creek. Hours later, which to Rachel seemed like an eternity, they reached the wide Big Black River, its level raised by the recent rain. The temporary bridge built by Union army engineers stood welcoming the travelers in the moonlight. Rachel smiled; she knew from maps that they had journeyed more than halfway to Davis Bend.

"Halt! Who goes there?"

"Whoa, Maude. Whoa." Jerome kept his voice calm.

Rachel's smile vanished and her heart beat quicker. She thought, *what now?*

Jerome answered the sentry. "A friend with two families."

"Advance and be recognized!"

Jerome left Aaron holding Maude's reins and walked to the colored sentry, who had been joined by another. They inspected Maude's baskets, wished the travelers well, and allowed the families to pass. Bone weary from trudging the last five miles through thick woods, the group arrived after the sun was halfway to noon on another steep hilltop Jerome had selected. This one was about four miles southeast of Vicksburg and sat above the Hatcher Bayou.

At first dark on Thursday, they started and Jerome announced, "We almost dere. We walk tonight and then just one more."

Emma exclaimed, "Hallelujah!"

"Not so loud, honey. What night is dis anyway?"

Rachel replied, "Thursday. We've traveled a week."

Rebecca hit Emma with her elbow. Whatcha dogs got to say 'bout dat? Huh?"

"Didn't you hear'em? Hallelujah, honey chile!"

They laughed while Jerome shushed them.

Rachel scratched among her braids. "Jerome, the closer we get, the more nervous you seem. Am I right?"

"You're right. De guerillas be real active in dese parts o' Warren County. Dey snatchin' coloreds lef' and right."

Emma covered her mouth with both hands and whispered, "You shoulda said somethin'. I know how ta keep my big mouth shut."

Rebecca whispered. "I ain't got nothin' else ta say till we reach the Bend."

Climbing a long hilly rutted road on the south side of Redbone Creek, John imitated the call of an owl. Rachel had told Jerome when they left Bender Plantation, "No bobwhite worth her feathers would be up all hours of the night." They gathered in the edge of the woods by the road. Rachel looked at the expectant faces waiting for John to speak.

"I think we're being followed. Twice, I heard a horse snort. Each time, it was on the road behind me, but not in sight."

They waited in the woods for almost an hour. No one passed. No horses were heard, even by Rachel.

Jerome took Maude's reins from Aaron and waved his hand forward over his head. "Let's go. We need to make it to the next camp 'fore sunrise."

Rachel said to no one in particular. "Friday."

After walking along rough roads for another five miles south of Redbone Creek, Jerome called a halt and handed Maude's reins to Rachel. "John, dis here is danger country. Last month, I marked a tree wid a twine tied up higher than a man's head. Y'all follow me while I 'xamine these trees on the right-hand side o' the road for my twine tree. Dat tree is at the head of a ridge leading to our last camp."

Jerome started first, moving slowly, looking for his tree. Suddenly, he returned. "We real close to the road that leads to the Bend. If some evil befalls me, let me tell you how to find it."

Rachel heard Emma gulp.

When he had told them, Jerome set out again. They followed. After a mile of slow walking and with the first light of Friday starting to show over her left shoulder, Rachel figured that they had traveled less than fifteen miles during the night. The road was heavily wooded on both sides, mostly pine trees. She wondered how Jerome could expect to find a tree with a string tied on it in this light. When she concluded that it was a silly idea, Jerome happily announced that he had located his tree – a sycamore, one of the lesser seen trees in this forest of mainly pines.

Rachel smiled. Her estimate of Jerome went up again. She kept Maude's reins and followed as Jerome picked his way along a trail that led to the top of a hill. From around a bend where Jerome had disappeared came the sound of a thud. Rachel paused. She shushed Ruth and Aaron. Hearing only birds, she pulled Maude forward. The mule would not move. She sent Aaron for John, whom she thought an expert on the ways of mules.

John took the reins, tugged gently, stroked Maude's muzzle and whispered quietly, "Com'on Maude, gitup there."

Maude moved four steps and stopped. A few minutes passed before she would move again, and then ever so slowly.

Rachel made the turn, following the bend in the trail. In the improving light, she saw Jerome's feet and legs protruding from underneath a bush. She gasped, and then shouted, "Pa, stop! Turn back!"

She heard John respond, "Gee, Maude, gee! Everybody get back!"

Rachel ran to Jerome's side and, down on all fours, found that he was unconscious, lying face down. She felt for his revolver and pretended to give aid to Jerome while she slipped the .44, barrel first, into her high-top work shoe and covered the grip with her trousers. She crawled into the forest.

A man waving a revolver stepped from the bushes. "Okay, boy. You hold that mule right there. This is the end o' the line for you and yo' little band o' niggers."

Derisive laughter came from both sides of the trail.

Rachel did not move. Emma, Ruth, and Rebecca surrounded the children. Aaron's eyes were wide and Zipporah whimpered. John stood, stuck in his tracks a few feet away holding Maude's reins.

A second voice spoke. "Hey, Floyd, yo' moonlight eyes work real good. That'n in the middle's real purtty."

Floyd answered, "Well, speak for yo' self. I like the one next to her."

The leader who had spoken first spoke again. "Will y'all stop yo' yammering? We ain't got time to fool with the merchandise. One of you go find dat other gal."

Rachel had moved behind the trunk of an old pine. She could not see Ruth or Rebecca, but knew who they meant. She crawled deeper into the forest, taking care to avoid twigs. She counted three men and kept track of them by their voices when she did not have them in sight. As they searched for Rachel, she moved in a semicircle away from Jerome and toward where the men had hidden in ambush, using John's logic that they would not look for her where they had hidden.

Floyd and his partner reported back. "The nigger boy is still out cold. That gal done got clean away. A scared as she was, she could be in Claiborne County by now."

"Dammit! Now her value is coming outta yo' share o' the profit. That's what happens when yo' mind's on yo' lil' peckerhead 'stead o' bitness!"

Floyd raised his chin and hitched up his gunbelt. "Well, now, if it's gonna be like that, I might as well go on and shove my lil' peckerhead in som' brown sugar. Sounds like I jes paid for it. Ain't dat right, George?"

"Yep. Sounds fair to me. Besides, why're you in sich an all-fired hurry. Ain't no rush to git these niggers over to Copiah County. We got all day. Let Floyd have a lil' fun. I might join'im."

"Oh, aw right. Go ahead. But make it fast. I wanna collect my money today."

Rachel singled out Floyd and kept him in sight, still paying attention to every sound made by the other two. She watched Floyd grab Rebecca by her arm and then Rebecca snatch it away. John lunged and hit the back of Floyd's head with his fist. George smashed the barrel of his revolver against the side of John's head and John fell in a heap. Rachel winced and put a hand over her mouth.

Rebecca screamed. "Pa!"

Floyd pulled his revolver from its holster and pointed it at John's head where he lay. "Shut yo' noise, bitch! So that the relation. He's yo' pa, huh? Now you come along quietly and have some fun with me or Georgie here is gonna make a hole in Pa's head. Ain't that right, George?"

George pulled his revolver. "Dat's right!"

Rebecca shot a fist into the side of Floyd's face. He immediate applied the back of his hand to her face and grabbed her arm and dragged her screaming into the bushes. Both children, along with Emma and Ruth, were crying loudly. Rachel ignored their cries and crawled to keep her eyes on Floyd.

From Rachel's new position, she saw that Floyd had Rebecca on her back and was making slow progress pulling off her overalls. When he succeeded in getting the trousers over one of Rebecca's shoes, he used his knees to force himself between her thighs as he removed his gunbelt. Although pelted by Rebecca's fists, Floyd kept her penned down. Next, he opened his other belt and trousers. With both hands on the grip, from thirty feet away, Rachel took aim along with a deep breath – and held it. Floyd had his penis in his hand when Rachel's bullet hit the back of his skull.

The loud report of Jerome's old Colt .44 startled Rachel. As her hearing cleared, she heard more screams from Ruth, Emma, and the children. She moved away from her shooting position to wait for George.

"Go get that fool Floyd. I may shoot him, if he's damaged that gal's worth."

Gun in hand, George burst through the bushes and was stopped in his tracks by his discovery. Rachel thought his face registered total surprise. In front of George was the partially nude Rebecca, struggling to hide her vagina, and Floyd flat on his face with his legs across Rebecca's left thigh. Rachel shot George through his right temple.

Then she wept.

Chapter 12: **The Hurricane**

The first shot startled Isaac. He looked at Caleb, who shrugged. They continued poling their flatboat toward the square where they would load some of the season's rice still on the stalks, scythed, in sheaves, and laying in the field. Minutes later, there were more shots, fired in rapid succession.

Isaac raised his pole from the water of the canal and turned in the direction of the gunfire. "Look! There's lots of smoke coming from close to our cabins."

Caleb turned. "I see it. What do you think it is?"

More shots. This time, sporadic.

Now Isaac was worried, and it showed in his face. "I don't know. But I have a feeling it's trouble come for a visit. Let's go find out."

They turned about in their positions, standing at diagonally opposite ends of the flatboat. There was no need to turn the flatboat about in the narrow canal nor could they. It was shaped the same at either end. Isaac and Caleb began poling toward the settlement as fast as they could. But their speed in the lumbering flatboat was less than half the speed of two men rowing in a canoe.

They passed fields of rice stubble on squares they had just harvested; the 1864 crop marked the end of a better than expected year for their freedmen's community of home farms. The debate raged between the War Department and Treasury over control, mission, name, and function of a new Federal agency proposed by President Lincoln to assist the newly freed people in supporting their families beginning at the end of the war. The president had countermanded General Sherman's General Number 15, designed to give forty acres and a mule to each family. The War Department in South Carolina, under General Saxton at Port Royal, did not wait for the end of the war to provide assistance. To be rid of "refugees" clustered around military camps, the army immediately assisted newly freed men by overseeing work contracts with land owners and other various means, including settling families on confiscated and abandoned lands.

Since the previous summer, Isaac and Caleb had been among the War Department's employees as stokers on army steamers, plying South Carolina's coastal rivers. As such, they were among the first to move with their families in the fall to Best Plantation on the Combahee River, not far from the prominent White Hall Plantation. The little community of eight families occupied the plantation's former slave cabins and agreed to pool their labor and together work all the tracks of land allocated to them by the War Department – and split the profit. They worked through the winter removing straw from the fields for livestock and burning the stubble from the previous rice crop. By spring, they were ready for the planting season.

Blue and black smoke billowed above the yellowing leaves of tulip poplar and clusters of pines. Isaac could hear screams and braying. The crackling and popping sound of the fire soon reached him. Neither Isaac nor Caleb spoke. Sweat poured from Isaac's head and stung his eyes. He blinked, but did not lose a single stroke with his pole.

When he should have been able to see the roof of the two-story winnowing house, he could only notice smoke above where it would have been. In an instant, Isaac knew. "Caleb, before we see who's alive or what's left, oonah know dat dem damned go-rillas done got 'round to us."

"I'm sure oonah right. I just pray that it ain't as bad as it sounds from here."

They crashed the flatboat into the wharf and Isaac made her fast with a quick square knot. They ran side by side toward the cabins. It was clear at that point that the harvest was lost. In addition to the winnowing house, two storage barns containing most of their crop lay smoldering and four cabins were ablaze. A frightened mule cut them off as it raced for the woods. Regaining his footing, Isaac slowed and then stopped. There on the ground before him was Eve with Aunt Ella bending over her. Isaac screamed, "Ma!"

Aunt Ella used Eve's apron to cover her face. Aunt Ella struggled to stand in her ankle-length dress, using both hands to press down against her right knee. Slowly, she straightened her back and stood to her full height of fifty-five inches. "Isaac, son, com'on over here and let me hug you. You, too, Caleb.

"We's all dat's left – 'ceptin' ol' Jacob, Luke, and Caleb, yo' pa. Dey down yonder in dat far square making and stacking sheaves."

Hot tears covered Isaac's cheeks. Deep sorrow and bitterness made his head hurt – front and back. His heart pounded. His teeth were clenched. His body trembled.

Aunt Ella removed her hug from Isaac and Caleb, and stood back, looking up into Isaac's face. She put a finger to his jugular. With a stern voice, Aunt Ella spoke. "Boy, sit yo'self down over there 'fore you pop. Isaac, if you don't 'member nothing else I ever said, 'member dis: 'Vengeance is mine, saith the Lawd God.'"

* * *

On the first day of November, Aunt Ella, Uncle Jacob, Luke, and Caleb's pa went to Port Royal. They stood on the wharf at Brickyard Creek and waved good-bye to Isaac and Caleb. Aunt Ella continued waving up at the ship while she dabbed her eyes with a handkerchief and Uncle Jacob patted her shoulder. Isaac called out a cheerful response. "Good-bye and good luck. God bless y'all everyone and fare thee well."

Thus began Isaac and Caleb's first ocean voyage. They had signed on as experienced stokers aboard the Union navy's Agawam-class side paddle wheel gunboat, the *Benjamin Franklin*. She was built at Portland, Maine, and commissioned in April. The *Franklin's* usual duty was blocking Charleston harbor. Now it was on special assignment to New Orleans and was laden down with artillery and small-arms ammunition headed for General Grant's Department of The Mississippi. She was resting low in the water – her bins were piled high with coal for the voyage.

The *Franklin's* large paddle wheels began to turn slowly, backing her away from the wharf.

Caleb followed Isaac toward the bow. He squinted and tapped Isaac's elbow. "Who's that ol' codger behind our folks a wavin' like he knows us."

"Well, bless me! It's Uncle Theodore! I sailed with him on my first voyage. He taught me all I know about stoking."

"Hey, Uncle Theo! Thanks for coming. Fare thee well!"

The old man beamed, held up his corncob pipe in salute, and said not a word. Isaac saw Uncle Jacob turn and offer his hand to Uncle Theodore. He could no longer hear the little group as the *Franklin* slipped further away, her engine noise increasing. The *Franklin* turned to leave port. Isaac and Caleb ran to the stern, over two hundred feet away. They waved until the ship headed toward Jack Island and they could no longer see their loved ones.

Isaac slumped to the deck and sat cross-legged with his back against a bulkhead. He held his face in his hands. Caleb slid his butt down the bulkhead and joined him. "Isaac, oonah okay, man?"

Isaac sighed and answered on the next exhaled breath. "Yeah."

"Man, oonah look like you carrying the whole world on yo' shoulders. We'll be back 'fore Christmas."

"Maybe not. Maybe, I'll just find someplace else to go. Now, mind, oonah don't hafta follow me. To be sure, I'm mighty glad oonah agreed to come wid me on this voyage. But I don't want oonah to feel stuck wid me."

"Well, I was hoping I could help you look at the bright side o' things. Oonah know – see what's in front o' oonah. I know losin' 'e ma and sisters weighin' reel heavy. I know you been through some stuff, man. But, count yo' blessin's, too. Oonah got a good friend and I know you gonna meet another good woman like Bianca."

At the mention of Bianca's name, a slight smile played briefly across Isaac's lips. "Yeah, man. She was the best."

"Partna, I'm here ta tell ya, there's another good woman like Bianca out there waiting for a good soldier like you."

"I ain't no soldier yet."

"You can be in another year."

"War'll be over by then."

"I think the Union gonna hafta to keep an army. Lak you always say, 'you can be mindin' yo' own bitness, and trouble will still invite his ol' ugly ass to join you.' Same's gonna go for the Union. I know this to be true jes as sho' there's white folks and 'gators shit in de river."

Isaac laughed.

"Good. That's why I'm here. Keep yo' ass laughin' and in line. And not go jumpin' overboard 'cause o' yo' troubles."

"Thanks."

* * *

Captain William Saddler, US Navy, an experienced ferryboat captain from New York, was on his first voyage in southern waters. He had replaced the *Franklin's* previous ailing captain in Port Royal. He set a course directly to Florida's Jupiter Inlet, putting the *Franklin* out of sight of land for several days. The Atlantic Ocean was rolling swells of only a few feet under an almost cloudless sky. Isaac remarked to Caleb, "Maybe I wanna be a sailor, not a soldier."

"How cum, man?"

"Don't you see? These navy folks have the life. I could get use to dis gettin' time outta dat coal dust for six hours. On an army boat, we ate and slept in the coal bin. But folks like you don't know nothin' 'bout a lil' hardship."

Caleb showed a toothy grin. "What kind o' ship?"

"You heard me, asshole. Hardship!"

"Tell you what, turd. I'ma play my harmonica and enjoy dis November sun. I don't need to know no mo' 'bout yo' *hardships* or any other ships on dem army boats."

Uproarious, back-slapping laughter followed.

Caleb played several jigs that Uncle Jacob had taught him for Tiffany Plantation balls and harvest celebrations. Isaac listened with his eyes fixed on the morning sky, day-dreaming about Bianca. When Caleb followed the lively tunes with a melancholy Irish piece, Isaac's mood turned blue as he tried to imagine an unhappy Bianca somewhere in the mountains of western North Carolina.

The sound of panting brought Isaac back to reality and the hard deck on which he sat. They stoked for six hours, two shifts per day. Still covered with coal dust that clung to his sweat, Isaac felt weary to the bone. Only when he heard the panting did he notice that

Captain Saddler's black Labrador retriever, Eight Ball, was sitting beside him. Caleb hit a long high note and Eight Ball threw his head back and howled. Laughter came from the officers and crew members relaxing under the canvas-shaded fore deck. Caleb finished the piece and applause was led by several black crew members who sat grouped to themselves against the forecastle mending a sail. Caleb gave them a little nod and held up his harmonica in salute.

Eight Ball leapt over Isaac's legs and licked Caleb's face. Then he barked twice, sat, and pranced with his front paws.

Isaac stroked the dog's shoulders. "Partna, it looks like you gonna hafta play another number."

The crew members sitting nearest Isaac laughed.

"Yep. I reckon." Caleb leaned back and began "Swing Low, Sweet Chariot."

* * *

Captain Saddler took the *Franklin* close to Jupiter Inlet and changed course to follow the coast, staying within sight of land most of the time. He followed the windward side of the Keys to the island known as Long Key. About three-quarters of a mile beyond Long Key, Captain Saddler ordered a course heading of three-two-two and the *Franklin's* bow pointed northwest, passing east of Conch Key. Most of the crew was on deck under a cloudless sky for the change of course and the passage through the Keys.

On the leeward side of the Keys in the Gulf of Mexico, they met a schooner on schedule, November 9, 1864, and took on more coal. With the coaling stop completed, Captain Saddler headed the *Franklin* straight on course for the mouth of the Mississippi River, about nine hundred nautical miles away.

A day later, the waters of the gulf were calmer than the Atlantic. They were making good time at about eight knots per hour when the sky was red at sunrise. Isaac overheard the boiler-room petty officer say, "I knew we've had it too good for too long. Now we got us a red sunrise."

Isaac looked at Caleb and saw recognition in his face. "What dat mean?"

Caleb put his shovel on his shoulder and took a deep breath. "Well, it could mean storm trouble or it could mean nothing a'tall."

"What does a red sunrise have to do with a storm?"

"I don't know, zakly. But Uncle Jacob said that a red sunset means good weather ahead; red sunrise means bad weather's coming."

Petty Officer Brownlee overheard Caleb and joined them. He was a coal miner from Pennsylvania. "Would your Uncle Jacob agree that, most of the time, this ol' saw is true?"

Caleb nodded. "Yessuh. He would say mostly true."

"What else did this Uncle Jacob tell you?"

"He say look around fer anythin' unusual in nature and add it up."

"Okay. It's 'bout time for your shift to knock off. But I want you two to report anything you see that's unusual." Petty Officer Brownlee pointed to both Caleb and Isaac.

They responded in unison. "Yessuh."

After breakfast, Isaac sat on the deck with Caleb in their usual spot. Caleb played Eight Ball's favorite howling tunes. But Eight Ball did not appear. The gulf's waters had more chop than previous days and Caleb stopped playing.

Isaac nudged Caleb with his foot. "Play some more. Everybody enjoys your morning concerts."

"Me too. But I can't play my best when I'm nauseous."

Isaac let go with a guffaw. "Landlubba ain't got no sea legs!"

Before Caleb could answer Isaac's taunt, two officers passing by greeted Captain Saddler as he approached. "Good morning, sir!"

One asked, "Where is your trusty canine friend this fine morning?"

"It is a fine morning, indeed. Why, it's the strangest thing. Eight Ball is hiding under my desk. He won't even come out for food."

Caleb hit Isaac and rolled his eyes toward Captain Saddler. Isaac nodded. "I got it. And, you know I watch the sky. Ain't seen the first bird today."

"Oh, shit!"

"What, man?"

Caleb scrambled to his feet looking around at the horizon. "Com'on! Time's awastin.'"

"What?" Isaac ran behind Caleb as he raced astern.

Once astern, Caleb turned about. "We gotta find Brownlee. Quick!"

"Will you slow down and tell me how you got ants in yo' britches on a ship?"

"Listen while I tell Brownlee."

They found Petty Officer Brownlee stepping onto the deck from the boiler room. Caleb blurted, "Suh, me and Isaac here, we wanna report on unusual matters."

Petty Officer Brownlee smiled and folded his arms. "Okay, I'm listening."

Caleb took two deep breaths. "Okay. Well, here goes. First, Isaac hasn't seen any birds today. Second, I'm nauseous."

Brownlee laughed. "That ain't unusual. Even seasoned sailors puke sometimes. Don't waste my time."

Isaac thought Caleb's breathing was out of whack. He cleared his throat. "Suh, there may be something to this if we follow Uncle Jacob's teachin' and add these things up." Isaac did not pause for Brownlee to speak. "No birds and ol' Eight Ball hiding under the captain's desk is what Uncle Jacob would call 'de animals is runnin' for de cover.'"

Brownlee's smile vanished. He rubbed his fingers over his stubble and drummed his fingertips against his chin. "I see. Just who is this Uncle Jacob, anyway?"

"Uncle Jacob was the trunk and weather minder for the Tiffany Plantation."

Isaac thought Brownlee looked puzzled. Brownlee removed his hand from his face. "What does a weather minder do?"

"He's the one who oversee's protectin' the massa's rice crop, which is worth more money than I can count. He protects the crop from storms and de ribber. He knows when there's a storm coming. Caleb here was Uncle Jacob's apprentice."

Brownlee turned to Caleb. "What would Uncle Jacob say if he was here right now?"

Without hesitating, Caleb said, "He'd say, 'Batten down the property and crops. Git yo'self away. There's a storm acomin'. Follow de birds.' Dat's what he'd say."

At midmorning, Isaac, with Caleb in tow, watched Brownlee approach Captain Saddler, still having morning coffee under the canvas shading the fore deck. They could not hear the words spoken, but heard the guffaw from the officers and Captain Saddler. They saw Brownlee turn crimson and stalk away. Brownlee marched briskly past them without looking their way.

Isaac looked at Caleb, who appeared near panic-stricken. Isaac realized that nothing would be done to get the ship out of harm's way. "Oh shit!"

"Yeah, partna. That pretty much sums it up."

* * *

They were finishing their lunch when Isaac tapped Caleb on the shoulder. "Don't look now, but I think we're being followed."

"What?"

Isaac pointed astern.

Caleb shaded his eyes with his hands and squinted in the bright sunlight. "I don't see nothing. But you always could see better'n me. I'm guessin' you've spotted trouble on his way for a visit."

"You're damned right. What I see is a tiny, but a solid wall of white thunderheads, barely above the horizon, down there to the south and east. Trouble is here to take our butts to hell if we can't get dese northern white folks to listen."

"Are you outta yo' weak ass mind? They didn't listen to Brownlee, so you know they sho' as shit ain't gonna listen to two coal-dust-blackened niggers."

"Hey! I've thought of a way to appeal directly to the captain."

"Yeah, right, Brer Rabbit. Ain't no time for foolishness out here."

Isaac ignored Caleb. "Com'on! Quick – Before we're late for our shift."

Isaac talked the mess steward out of a piece of bacon for Eight Ball. He headed straight for Captain Saddler's quarters with Caleb in close pursuit. He knocked and waited. Presently, the Captain opened the door and asked, "Are you the two who made a fool of Petty Officer Brownlee?"

Isaac stood tall and looked Captain Saddler in the eye. "Suh, we're here to let you know that there's a big storm on the horizon behind us and that's why Eight Ball will not move from under your desk – not even for this heah piece o' bacon."

Isaac thought Captain Saddler looked amused, then annoyed. "Look boys, there are clouds – it rains at sea. Now run along. I have my work to do."

Isaac felt pain in his forehead. He let out a sigh. "Yessuh. Well, here's a piece o' bacon for ol' Eight Ball."

Captain Saddler called Eight Ball. He made not a sound. Captain Saddler took the bacon and closed his door.

* * *

Late afternoon in the boiler room, Caleb asked, "Did I imagine it, or did the captain turn a bit pink when Eight Ball wouldn't come out for the bacon?"

"You didn't imagine it."

"Fire the boilers! Pour on the coal! Look alive down there!" It was Brownlee, Isaac decided, in his stern I-mean-business face.

The engine's frequency and vibrations increased. They could not see outside from the boiler room. But Isaac knew the ship rolled more now than in any previous shift. They took turns scooping and flinging shovelfuls of coal into the open door of the furnace. They never missed. Isaac told Caleb, "Somebody up there has finally come to his senses. Question is, is it in time for us to haul ass outta here?"

"Guess we gone find out soon enough."

"You two. Come with me." Brownlee beckoned for them to follow him.

Out on deck the wind had picked up. The sea was rough. It was dark earlier than usual. Rain had not started, but one could smell it.

In the captain's quarters, Isaac raised an eyebrow when he saw all the officers standing around Captain Saddler's desk. Isaac could just make out Eight Ball's left front paw under the desk.

The captain looked grim. "Well, boys. I'll get right to it. What do we have here?"

Isaac and Caleb looked at each other, then Brownlee, who stood behind them.

"Com'on. Speak up. There's no time to waste."

Caleb took a step closer. "My friend 'scribed the clouds on de horizon behind us for me."

"What? Can't you see?"

"Yessuh, but not for great long distances."

"Go on."

"Well, de shape o' de clouds, time it took to catch up to us, and the effec' on ol' Eight Ball tells me we've been caught by a good-size cyclone."

Isaac watched the officers, one by one, shift on their feet. One breathed, "Cyclone?"

Captain Saddler ignored him. "What else you know about cyclones?"

"Done lived through three. Isaac too. Dese storms're big and shaped lak a doughnut. De middle be calm and peaceful wid no wind."

"Can we use the wind to increase our speed?"

"De wind will come from all directions. 'Round and 'round dat doughnut, lak a clock goin' backward. De winds be fierce. 'Fraid it'll rip your sails or capsize the ship."

Another officer huffed and puffed. "Why, that's preposterous! With the cargo, we displace nearly twelve hundred tons."

Captain Saddler turned to the officer. "Sam, even now, we're tossed about like a cork."

Isaac thought Saddler should sit before he falls. Suddenly, Saddler pointed at him. Isaac looked about for clues. Had he missed something? The room was silent. He could hear the *Franklin* creaking as she rose and fell with the waves.

"I'm told you're Isaac. So what do you think?"

"Suh, I think you should mind everything Caleb told you."

"What can we do to save the ship?"

"Suh, I have worked on a few ships, but know nothin' about how to drive one."

Snickers. Saddler shushed them. "Go on, lad."

"Suh, first, I would run from it for as long as the waves aren't too big. I mean run for land. Then, second, when the waves are too big, I would just try to maneuver and stay pointed into the wind to stay afloat. Third and last, I will pray. Suh, I hope you will too."

"I surely will. Thank you both. We need the steam – so off you go."

"Yessuh."

The night was pitch black and violent. There were no shift breaks in the evening or at midnight. Brownlee kept the stoker crews in motion, rotating two men off to rest for fifteen minutes every thirty minutes. The *Franklin's* engine was fully engaged but their speed did not increase. Isaac was throwing coal when he felt a sudden yaw motion, heard canvas tearing, along with curses from the deck above his head. Captain Saddler had ordered a sail deployed. Now the sail was lost and two men were overboard. They were not able to rescue either man.

By midnight, the wind had driven the rain horizontal and the seas were high. Isaac guessed that Captain Saddler had given up trying to run from the storm and was simply trying to stay afloat. The canvas that covered the fore deck had been ripped away. Caleb vomited again and again. The last time, even with Isaac helping to steady him, he didn't make it to the rail before yellow bile rushed up through his mouth and nostrils. They returned to the boiler room soaked to their skin. A few minutes later, steam rose from Isaac's clothes as he shoveled more coal into the open furnace. The temperature in the boiler room was, as usual, well over one hundred twenty degrees Fahrenheit. His clothes were soon dry, then wet again with sweat. Caleb rested in the coal bin. Isaac shoveled fast and took no breaks, except for water. He almost made up for the loss of Caleb's work.

At dawn, no one stopped to eat. Caleb still lay in the coal bin. Except for stokers, the crew wore oilcloth rain gear. Isaac put his head out long enough to see a huge wave wash over the bow. He prayed again. He remained in the boiler room, even during breaks, determined to do his part to keep the *Franklin* afloat. Then there was a loud crash on deck. The front mast had fallen and was moving to and fro in a trough it had gouged out of the port rail. With one end hanging over the ocean, the opposite end was ripping away the port side of the pilothouse. Isaac looked out again. The crew members, black and white, were working together feverishly to free the mast from the remaining cables that once secured it.

Isaac saw the wave coming. It was a wall of water higher than the *Franklin's* remaining mast. He ducked inside and grabbed two cork-filled life jackets off the boiler room's bulkhead. He unfastened Caleb's belt and refastened it through a strap attached to the life jacket. The wave was upon them before he could get Caleb to the door or secure his own life jacket. The *Franklin* was swamped and momentarily submerged. Isaac held on to Caleb with one arm. Both crashed into the ceiling with the sudden downward motion of the ship under the weight of the wave. All the while, Isaac never stopped clawing his way toward the open door. Cold water poured into the boiler room. They coughed and sputtered and spat seawater. Crew mates were scrambling behind him, trying to get to the door.

As suddenly as the ship went down, it rose. But the water in the boiler room also continued to rise. Once Isaac had Caleb on deck, with fellow stokers stepping over them; the boiler exploded, sending scalding water and steam throughout. There were screams from two stokers who did not get out. The cylindrical boiler went up through the deck and veered over the port side into the sea. Isaac still held on to Caleb. He looked up – the pilothouse was gone. The smokestack was crumpled like a wet cigar onto the rear deck. The rear mast still stood, but listed further to port, further than did the *Franklin*. From down in the hold, there came a rumble from wooden crates crashing against each other. The *Franklin* listed more to port. She was taking in water and could not be righted. Meanwhile, the wind continued, unabated.

Captain Saddler's voice was not among the two giving direction to the crew. Then the order came to man the life boats and abandon the ship. The *Franklin* carried four lifeboats. Two had already been swept away with the pilothouse. The remaining boats were lowered and immediately took on water. Above the boats, the ship lurched further to port.

Isaac struggled and pushed Caleb onto the rail on the starboard side. Together, they jumped into the surf. Once in the water, Isaac pulled his life jacket over his head and put his arms through it. Then he did the same for Caleb. Isaac moved Caleb slowly away from the ship. After almost fifteen minutes, her stern rose slowly from the water with a sound that Isaac thought of as a groan. The stern was perched, fleetingly, high above the water. She looked as if she was balanced on her paddle wheels. And then, bow first, the *Franklin* slipped from sight beneath the waves.

Isaac and Caleb were joined by Eight Ball, who immediately licked Caleb's face. They were pulled from the water by crew members already in a lifeboat. All took turns bailing.

Shortly after midday, the rains ceased and the sun returned. Warmth from the sun was welcome. In spite of all the water that had fallen, they had caught precious little to drink. The sea still churned beneath them. Caleb pulled his harmonica from his pocket and pounded it against his palm to rid it of water. He cheered the men seated in both boats with his music.

The two boats, containing twenty-two injured, hungry, sick, and dehydrated survivors of the *Franklin's* original crew of eighty-seven, arrived five days later, November 16, 1864, at Fort Massachusetts on Mississippi's sandy Ship Island, a barrier island. Captain Saddler was lost when the pilothouse was washed away. Eight Ball stayed with Caleb.

After three weeks at Fort Massachusetts, Brownlee got Isaac and Caleb onto a US Navy vessel as stokers headed for Vicksburg and Memphis. Eight Ball went with them.

Chapter 13: **Alejandra**

Alejandra screamed, *"Correr, Papa, Corre!"*

The horsemen came at a gallop from the road. They crossed the cultivated field in which Alejandra stood watching the horses' hooves rip away the strings she had tied to stakes as guides for the straight rows of maize she and Manuel were planting. She cringed and her horror grew as two of the men whirled lariats like vaqueros as they closed in on her running father. Both lariats found their mark and Manuel stopped running and held onto a rope with each hand.

The leader of the recruiters from the Mexican Army dismounted and secured Manuel's hands. He laughed as he went about his work. "Tsk, tsk. Senor, you should have already volunteered. Of course, I am sure a farmer of your intelligence must know how much Benito Juarez needs you to help drive the accursed French from our Motherland."

The recruiters guffawed at their leader's ridicule of the new recruit.

Alejandra dropped her hoe and ran after the horsemen.

The remaining six recruiters were still mounted and had encircled Manuel, who made no protest.

Tears flowed down Alejandra's cheeks. She pleaded with the leader. "Please don't take my papa away. We'll starve without him."

The man looked hard into Alejandra's eyes. He said nothing. Finally, he turned away and carried on with his work. She knew then that there was no chance he would release her father. She sobbed and sank to her knees as they led Manuel away at the end of a rope. Her shoulders shook. Through her tears, she could see several yellow seeds unearthed by the horses' hooves on the freshly plowed ground. She became angrier still. Her head throbbed; Alejandra felt it would burst at the temples.

Manuel called back over his shoulder, *"Allie, Te amo. Dile a Rocío, Ernesto y Rafael que me encantan. Ser fuerte para Rocío."*

Alejandra could make no reply. She had not yet thought of her mother. Rocío and Ernesto were at work in the Rodriquez hacienda. When she realized it would fall to her to tell Rocío, her sobbing turned to wailing. With her sombrero askew, Alejandra sank further and sat upon the cool earth in her nearly ankle-length calico skirt.

* * *

After supper, sixteen-year-old Alejandra wrote in her diary:

Monday, April 18, 1864. Dear Diary, Today, the army snatched Papa. Mama is still crying. Damned Juarez and Maximilian!

Ernesto, Alejandra's older brother by two years, rapped softly on her open door and walked into her room, one of four in their square adobe house. "Allie, here it is straight out."

Alejandra turned to him in her seat and thought, *what now?*

"Early in the morning, I'm leaving Carrizal to find work in the mines to the south."

Alejandra leapt to her feet. Keeping her voice down, she hissed, "Fool, you can't do that! Mama and I need you here. How can just I, Mama, and little Rafael make enough crops to satisfy the hacienda? Besides, we need that scrawny ol' horse."

Ernesto held up a hand. "Hold on, Sis. I'm not taking ol' Dan. Before you ask, I'll walk when I can't earn a ride with some farmer or freighter. Allie, you know we need the money. Forget the hacienda. At the end of every year, we're still under a mountain of debt to them. It won't be any different if I stay. Don't you know that?"

Alejandra's shoulders sagged and she sat down heavily on her bed. She nodded. "Yes. You speak the truth. I think I must try and keep you here because...." Her voice trailed off as she stared at the floor.

"Allie. Because of what?"

"Oh, I don't know. Maybe I was feeling I'm losing you too. You know your leaving is gonna hit Mama hard." She pointed with a thumb over her shoulder toward their mother's room.

Ernesto ran his fingers through his hair and nodded. "I know. Look, I'll leave before anyone is awake. Don't tell Ma and Rafael until I'm gone."

Alejandra sighed and looked up at Ernesto. "Okay." She paused. "What do we tell the hacienda?"

"Oh, I don't know...." He tapped his chin. "I've got it! Tell'em the army kidnapped me too. Hey. Unscrunch your nose. That ain't any bigger lie than they tell us."

Alejandra smiled for the first time since her father was led away. She walked over and hugged her brother. "May God go with you."

"And with you."

* * *

Alejandra leaned across the breakfast dishes and put a hand on Rocío's shoulder. "Mama, it's the best we can do. Ernesto saw what needed to be done and he did it."

Rocío sniffed and wiped her tears on her sleeve. "But what can we three do?"

Rafael took his mother's hand. "Don't cry, Ma. I may be only ten years old, but I'll be a big help. You'll see."

Alejandra smiled. "Okay. It's getting light outside. The sun will be up soon. Let's get our animals fed and we can have an early start in the fields. Raffy, herd all the hoofers down to the stream and bring back water for the chickens."

"Righto, Sis. Hey, that's a great way to say pigs, goats, cow, and horse."

"What?"

"You just said it. Hoofers."

"Oh, so I did."

Alejandra saw Rocío's smile. She smiled back.

* * *

Wearing the same clothes she wore on Monday, her loose-fitting skirt and yellow blouse that hung to her hips, Alejandra led ol' Dan to the plow her father had left in the field. By midmorning she was pleased, for she had plowed almost as much ground as her father had

215

by the same time on Monday. Across the field, she saw Rafael pulling a rope tied to the axle of their wooden wheelbarrow loaded with barnyard dung while Rocío pushed its handles. They were making good progress with the planting. After Alejandra and ol' Dan drank from the crystal clear creek near their field, she donned her sombrero and hitched ol' Dan to a drag harrow made from wooden rails and iron spikes. She stood on the drag harrow holding ol' Dan's lines as he pulled it and her across the ground they had plowed earlier.

The land was almost flat, with no trees to provide shade, except near the stream where many guajillo bushes grew and a few short mesquite trees. In the northwest, less than ten miles away, there stood a brown, mostly barren, mountain whose peak rose above six thousand feet – Sierra Santa Maria. In and around the village of Carrizal, Alejandra saw more brown landscape than green.

* * *

After supper and baths, Alejandra sat on a log bench in front of their house with Rocio and Rafael under a clear and bright night sky. The quarter-moon was high overhead. In the west, Venus shone brightly.

Rafael pointed to Venus. "Ma, what is that bright star called?"

Rocio turned and squinted at the sky. "I don't know which one you mean."

While Alejandra sat quietly and observed, Rafael tried again and again to tell Rocio which star he was pointing to. Presently, she said, "Mama, Raffy is pointing to Venus."

"Oh, that one. You see, Raffy, that star is also called the evening star."

"Why?"

"I think because it is so bright that it is the first one we can see after sunset."

Alejandra was concerned. "Mama, can you see that star? Years before Raffy was born, we sat right here and it was you who pointed out Venus and the North Star to me."

Rocio looked at her hands and fumbled with her thumbs as Alejandra remembered she always did before answering a difficult question. "Mama, are you okay?"

Rocio took a deep breath and let out a long sigh. "No. I'm not completely okay."

Before Alejandra could ask, Rafael spoke. "Ma, what's wrong?"

Rocio glanced from one child to the other and then focused on her hands. "My eyes are failing."

Alejandra gasped. Rafael jumped in front of his mother. "Ma, can you see me?"

Rocio reached out and pulled Rafael to her and hugged him. "Of course, I see you, naughty boy. How can I miss you?"

Rafael and Rocio laughed.

Alejandra smiled. Her concern ran deep. What of the future? Would Rocio become blind? She moved closer to Rocio who hugged her children to her sides. Rafael rested his head on Rocio's shoulder.

Rocio looked up again. "The few stars I can still see look fuzzy, like they have a white halo about them. That blocks my view of less bright stars. The same is true of the light in the window of that house yonder."

Alejandra was worried. "Mama, we'll have to find a way to buy a pair of those newfangled eyeglasses for you."

"What? And not eat?"

"What would Orestes do? I'll bet he wouldn't give in and he would find a way to eat, too!"

Rafael sat up and faced his mother. "Ma, tell us the story of Orestes again. Please."

"Aren't you tired of that story? I know Allie must be by now."

"No, Mama."

"No, Ma. Not me, either."

Rocio took a deep breath. "Oh, all right. Well, back in the seventeenth century the Spaniards brought another group of Africans to work in the mines of Zacatecas. Why did the Spaniards bring Africans?"

Rafael said in a singsong voice, "'Cause they thought it would be difficult for the Africans to run away and hide."

"In this new group was a young African named Orestes. He was big and strong, a prince among his people. The overseers in the copper mine where he worked beat him and his comrades. So, after a few years, he gathered strong and trustworthy friends and made an escape plan. One night at first dark, in about 1650, they overpowered the guards at the armory and, unlike other escapees, they went away into the night with weapons, headed north....

"Along their way, they fought and won many battles against the Spaniards. After losing a number of their men in combat, they arrived in the land of the Raramuri people, who, along with other Indian tribes, were also at war with the Spaniards. The Raramuri welcomed the new African warriors."

"Ma, why are the Raramuri now called Tarahumara?"

"I think the Spaniards must've written it down wrong. Anyway, these wars were on and off for many years until Orestes was a very old man. He was a brilliant and skilled fighter....

"When the Spaniards finally defeated the Indians in about 1698, Orestes and his Raramuri wife migrated with the tribe to new lands high in the Sierra Madre. Two of Orestes' great-great-granddaughters married mestizos. From the line of the eldest, my grandmother was born in 1790. She gave birth to my mother, your Grandma Maria, in 1809. The rest you know."

Alejandra and Rafael applauded and repeated the words they always said when they heard the story of Orestes. "Bravo! Bravo! Long live the memory of the warrior Orestes!"

* * *

On Saturday afternoon, Alejandra and Rocio were quiet as they raced to finish the hem in each of the new skirts they would wear in the evening to the spring festival. Alejandra knew all eight hundred or so souls of Carrizal would be there. She remembered each of her friends from long ago school days. By age ten, she and her classmates reached the end of their studies at the church and were put to work with their parents in one or the other of Carrizal's haciendas. She thought, it will be good to see them.

Outside, Rafael's voice and the bleating of the goats he drove home interrupted Alejandra's daydreams about the festival.

Alejandra glanced through the open door at shadows to judge the time. "Mama, I know you want to attend to your campechanos. I'll finish your skirt."

Rocio laughed. "Thanks. It's okay, I have time. I think I know why you want me to finish the campechanos early."

Alejandra joined the laughter. She put her tongue out and moved it from side to side. "Hmm! Your compechanos are the best in Carrizal."

"And, you want a taste before I take them to the festival. Nothing doing."

Rafael walked in. "Yeah, you tell 'er, Ma."

Alejandra pretended to pout. "Oh, Raffy, close your face."

"Do you know why the whole village loves Ma's compechanos?"

"Okay, genius. Why?"

"'Cause, Ma uses *my* great goat cheese!"

As they laughed together, Alejandra pricked her finger with her needle.

* * *

The village square was decorated in green, white, and red. Alejandra wore the same colors. She had small ribbons in her hair, wore a beaded necklace, and short strings hung from her quarter-moon-shaped earrings – all green, white, and red. She felt beautiful with her bare shoulders in the new white puffed-sleeved blouse Rocio had made for her. As with all the blouses created by Rocio, this one fit over her skirt and reached the top of her buttocks.

Two mariachi bands played music that relaxed the people milling about, chatting with neighbors and friends. Alejandra felt her spirit soar. She and her girlfriends danced in the streets around the square. She was surprised when a boy named Carlos from her school days asked her to dance. As Alejandra touched his hand to begin their dance, she glanced at Rocio. She thought, *yes, Mama is watching, just like all the other mothers watch their girls of my age.*

When Alejandra finished the third dance with Carlos, she felt sure he liked her, but was unsure if she liked him. She thought: *nice boy, not special.* Her reverie was interrupted by her friend Laylita, who giggled, took her hand, and led her aside. Laylita whispered, "Don't look now. That man over there by the church wearing the red shirt with ruffles has been watching you ever since your first dance with Carlos."

"How do you know? He could be watching any one of us."

"First, I hoped he was watching me. When I realized he was not, I tried to get his attention. Second, I'd like very much to have his attention. But he glances past me and the others and his eyes follow you."

"Is he looking now?"

Laylita was facing the church. "Yes. He's looking at your back."

"Let's hold hands and switch places twice to the music so I end up with my back to him again."

Alejandra saw the man. She felt the hair on her neck rise and a shudder go down her spine. She guessed the man was in his early twenties. In one hand, he held a beverage. The other hand raised a skinny cigar to his lips. His hat and clothes were expensive and his boots were the finest she had seen. His ruffled shirt was open halfway to his navel. The man's black chest hair shone in contrast against his red shirt. Alejandra felt revulsion and she thought she felt something else.... What? Was it his eyes? Yes. That was it, for she felt undressed before him. When she and Laylita stopped turning, she realized the other feeling was fear.

"Lay, who is he?"

"Why, he's Don Jose Rodriquez's nephew, Torres. My, aren't you the lucky one!"

"I don't feel lucky. If you want 'im, you can have 'im."

Laylita grabbed Alejandra's arm. "Girl, don't be a fool. This could be your ticket to a good life. He's handsome *and* he's rich. Where else do you see that combination in Carrizal?"

"It's a feeling I got when I saw his eyes just now. I already know. He's not the man for me."

"Do you want to spend your life cropping for a hacienda or would you rather have servants?"

"Okay, Lay. I'll tell you directly. He doesn't want me. He wants my body."

Laylita's hands went up. "*So?*"

"Lay, I-I-I gotta go."

Staring at the ground all the way, Alejandra headed straight for her mother. After another song, a mariachi band stopped in front of Alejandra and Rocio and sang a beautiful love song. She wondered how to avoid this man. What could make him turn his attention away?

The song ended and the bandleader whispered to Alejandra, "Senorita, this song was compliments of Torres Rodriquez." The musician gestured toward the man in the red shirt. She turned to look. He smiled and tipped his hat.

Quickly, Alejandra turned away, mouth agape, and hugged Rocio. Her fear had turned to panic. She wished with all her being that she was not beautiful. She wanted to make herself small and unnoticed. Her pretty clothes felt like a trap in which she was caught. Why couldn't it have been little Carlos? Of course, it would not have been possible, for Carlos would have no money to pay a band to serenade me. Still, I prefer Carlos. "Mama, let's go home." She looked anxiously into Rocio's face. Rocio was still looking back at Torres Rodriquez. Alejandra pulled her mother's hand to her side and pleaded, "Mama, I need you to take me home."

Slowly, Rocio nodded. "Okay. I'll get my things and we will leave." Rocio took three steps and began collecting her dishes and utensils.

The music started again. A young man wearing a red shirt appeared beside Alejandra, his eyes shifting back and forth from her breasts to her eyes. "Senorita, may I have this dance?"

Chapter 14: Lee Surrenders

At half past three on Palm Sunday morning, the Fifth Michigan Volunteer Cavalry Regiment's bugler sounded "Boots and Saddles." James Darby blinked and sat up. His head hurt. He put his hand on the scar above his right ear. It throbbed, and the pain in his old wound of two Aprils ago was intense. James had no idea what time it was. He felt like he had been asleep for only a few minutes. But, looking at the coals left from what had been their campfire, he knew he must have slept for two or more hours.

With the sound of dry twigs breaking, James glanced over his shoulder to find his friend, Sergeant Barry Dean, returning to their platoon. James yawned. "What's up?"

"The brass says the Secesh must have seen our campfires by now and know that we have captured their precious rations."

"And we're blocking their escape route to Lynchburg. Does General Sheridan think the Secesh will try to bust through?"

"Yep. At dawn."

James groaned, folded his arms, and rocked from side to side.

Like the men in his company, James had slept wrapped in his blanket and oilcloth on a bed of leaves and pine needles with his head on his saddle. Unlike some of his fellow troopers in Company A, he kept his boots. Boots on or off, they all slept with their feet toward the fire. He rolled and tied his blanket and then saddled his horse. There was no time for breakfast. They moved through the trees and to a point midway down the slope overlooking the small village of Appomattox Court House. There they began the task of digging in.

Digging was not difficult; it had rained several times during the week. Spring had come to Central Virginia and with it migrating birds and days-old tiny rabbits, squirrels, snakes, and other critters. Droppings and half-eaten fresh placenta confirmed that there was a new fawn not far away. The quiet in the woods was broken by the sounds of digging and the clanking of the accouterments of cavalry soldiers and their horses. James glanced back at the large moon hanging barely above the western horizon. He dug with his seven-shot Spencer carbine slung across his back. His mind darted from thoughts of home in Illinois to his Butternut Guerilla comrades of the Sixth Illinois Cavalry Regiment fighting somewhere in the Federal Military Department of Tennessee, and then to his capture by Confederate soldiers in Mississippi.

James slowly shook his head as he remembered being held at Richmond's Libby Prison instead of being paroled because the Confederates thought he was an officer. He smiled as he reminisced. In his mind's eye, he glimpsed Richard Surby again as he passed through Libby and was paroled in a matter of days. James imagined Richard would straightaway rejoin the Sixth. James had joined the Fifth because they were close to Washington when he was paroled from Libby and he did not want the war to end before he could get back into the fray.

"Do you think this will be our last fight?" It was Barry, a native of Detroit.

James started and his spade full of dirt fell back into the trench. He was digging in the dark, for the moon had set. The first light of dawn was breaking over the horizon in front of them and a curtain of fog began enveloping the hilltops. He wiped his brow on his sleeve. "I surely hope it is. I trust General Sheridan and George were completely right last night and that we've got the Gray Fox boxed this time."

Though George Armstrong Custer was his division commander, James thought of the boy general at age twenty-six, and just three years his senior, as a hard-riding kinsman of his Butternut Guerilla friends.

"Well, if you ask me, General Lee won't be boxed until the infantry gets here."

"So what are our odds if they get here by sunup?"

"With them here, it'll be a turkeyshoot."

James started to dig again. "Yeah, and without'em, our asses are done for. The Secesh are gonna fight like cornered animals."

With their horses removed over the ridge to their rear, James and the Fifth Michigan settled in trenches to wait for the assault they knew would come from the Confederate infantry. Aware that they would be outnumbered, James and his fellow troopers spaced themselves as best they could to defend against the expected onslaught. The Union cavalry had won the race the day before and taken the prize – Lee's rations and provisions on trains waiting at Appomattox Station. He knew the Confederates had only two options left – try to break through to the west or surrender. To James, if he faced their plight, it meant a desperate fight to break out. James checked his carbine for the third or fourth time he couldn't remember which. He dreaded fighting dismounted as infantry, for even with the Union infantry that arrived during the night James feared they had not nearly enough cavalry soldiers in place to defeat Confederate General Gordon's Corps.

When dawn came, the fog rolled in low over the valley and Appomattox Court House. James could hear Confederate infantry and cavalry, not two hundred yards below, preparing for an assault. Barry called out from his position, about twenty feet and three soldiers away. "Hey James, can you see 'em?"

"No. Not yet."

James blinked. He heard the same blood-curdling rebel yell he had heard at Shiloh in '62 and Wall's Bridge in '63. A shudder went down his spine. Marching toward him were Confederate soldiers on line, elbow to elbow, with bayonets fixed and their line disappearing into the fog on both flanks. James tried to steady his carbine and select a target. His body betrayed him. No matter how much he tried, he could not stop shaking. The firing started with a Confederate volley and was quickly followed by two more lines advancing past the first and firing into the blue-clad cavalrymen. James fired and missed as his target knelt to reload. Suddenly, with his first shot, his shaking stopped. He aimed and fired again, this time seeing his target fall, a Confederate infantryman in a tattered uniform wearing no shoes.

The two soldiers on either side of James were hit. James fired five more shots and hit four enemy soldiers. Though Confederates were falling, their ranks closed and they continued marching forward and firing deadly volley after volley into the cavalrymen. The Confederates were within a hundred feet of their breastworks and advancing rapidly. As James reloaded, he heard Barry above the din. "Back! Fall back!"

Realizing they were no match for the large number of bayonets rushing up the slope, the cavalrymen broke and ran for the ridge and trees beyond. The Confederate infantry swarmed over the cavalrymen's breastworks and pursued James and his comrades up the hill. James turned twice to fire into the ranks of the oncoming Confederates. The second time, he stumbled over a large rock. He was up quickly and rushed over the ridge.

With the Confederates behind him, James saw a large number of figures emerging from the woods and fog ahead of him at double-quick time. He exclaimed, "Oh shit!"

He looked to his right for an escape route and saw more infantrymen rushing toward him through the trees. Presently, James realized that the mounted officers leading the new infantrymen were pointing with their swords beyond him at the Confederates. As they rushed forward, James and his comrades cheered. They were close enough now to see through the fog and blue haze created by the smoke from cannon and gunfire. It was clear that the infantrymen in front of them wore blue uniforms.

When the Confederates reached the top of the ridge, their yelling and cheering ceased. The Union infantry was advancing toward them and the Confederates halted. James saw them look at each other and their leaders for a sign of what to do next. James and Barry ran between General Chamberlain's two brigades on their left and General Birney's Negro troops of the Second Division, XXV Corps on their right. James turned and followed Birney's troops back to the top of the ridge he had crossed. He watched Birney and Chamberlain's troops push the rebels from the ridge. The Confederates rallied and Birney's troops waivered under artillery fire, but recovered, firing volley after volley. Working on each other's flanks, Birney and Chamberlain's troops swept through the valley and up the next ridge. James followed. Now, for the first time, he looked down on the village of Appomattox Court House.

Though skirmishes in the village continued between scattered Confederates and mounted Union cavalry, Chamberlain's brigades stopped. Then Birney's troops stopped.

Barry joined James on the new ridge. It was midmorning and the fog was lifting. They looked out at the long lines of blue-clad soldiers surrounding the village on three sides.

James pointed to the XXV Corps. "Did you see the Negro troops advance?"

"I saw them."

James wore a toothy grin. "Well, is it true what they say about black soldiers that they can't or won't fight?"

"I believed that tale until I saw them today with my own eyes. How do you think they compare to our guys?"

"I've seen battles in the west and the east. I haven't seen any outfits do better."

For a time, they stood and watched the scene before them in silence, each man deep in his own thoughts.

At length, Barry sat on the grass. "Why do you think our guys stopped?"

"I suppose General Sheridan wants to get us back in the fight and finish the Secesh."

"Yeah. That's a good idea. Let's find our horses."

When James and Barry had taken a few steps toward their original position, they heard a bugler sound "Boots and Saddles" from the same direction.

Barry grinned and clapped James on the shoulder. "If George should fall, I'll hafta tell General Sheridan to put General Darby of Illinois in his place!"

"You're not as clever as I thought. Com'on. Let's go at double-quick time."

"Yes! On to the turkeyshoot."

They found their mounts and the regiment fell in. General Custer led his division and formed a line flanking Union infantry. Hours passed as they waited for the order to charge the Confederates in the village. James dismounted and sat with Barry on the ground between their horses. They ate hardtack from their haversacks. At about midafternoon, they heard cheering in the distance. The sound came closer and rolled across the hills. Several horsemen raced toward them, yelling as they rode. James stood. He heard them shout, "Lee surrendered! Lee surrendered!"

* * *

"James, what in thunderation are you doing?" Barry was laughing and shaking his head.

"What the hell does it look like, hardtack breath?" James's horse grazed in the lush tall grass beside the muddy road while James used his jackknife and carefully cut two Virginia spring beauty blossoms at the tip of their stems.

"Don't tell me you're going to put'em in a letter."

"And, why not, pray tell? This may help my girl take her mind off the assassination for a minute. She doesn't live far from the Lincoln home in Springfield."

"Oh, sorry. I forgot he was your homey. But sending a flower just looks to me like something a girl would send to her guy."

"Not that it's any of your business, but that usually works the other way around. Will I have to teach you everything about women?"

"Do you think women like flowers?"

Barry scratched his stubble. "Yeah. My ma sure does."

"Did a girl ever send you a flower?"

"Come to think of it, no."

"I rest my case."

On a leisurely march from Appomattox, they had returned to Cox Road on the western outskirts of Petersburg and bivouacked on a pleasant late April night. Around the cook fires, the dominant conversations were girls, why Joe Johnston had not surrendered, and John Wilkes Booth. Then, on April 24 word came that General Grant had ordered Sheridan to make an expedition to Danville.

"Boots and Saddles" was sounded shortly after an unhurried breakfast. On the first day, they marched only twenty-four miles. The second day out of Petersburg, General Custer's division took the lead for Sheridan's Sixth Corps. By the twenty-seventh, they reached the Dan River. The leisurely ride was over. This night, they learned of the death of John Wilkes Booth. Each of the divisions put out pickets, who kept a wary eye on the road to Greensboro. At this point, only a good day's ride separated them from Joe Johnston's army. The next day, they entered Danville and joined the infantry of the Sixth Corps.

On the twenty-eighth, word arrived from Grant that Johnston had surrendered to Sherman two days earlier.

Barry mounted his horse. "Now we can turn our asses around and march right back to Petersburg."

"I'd rather march to Washington." James kept his eyes on the road ahead. Cavalry horses and troopers of General Crook's division stretched as far as he could see down the tree-lined road.

"Ain't we gettin' muster out at Petersburg?"

"Where'd you hear that rumor?"

"Oh, around."

* * *

In the Grand Review celebrating the war's end on May 23-24, 1865, in Washington, nearly one hundred-fifty thousand men of the one-million-man Union army marched past the White House for six hours each day and were saluted by President Andrew Johnson and General-in-Chief, Ulysses S. Grant. James felt odd marching with General Meade's eastern troops on the first day. He missed his friends from Illinois and the west, led by General Sherman on the second day.

James and Barry watched from the side of Pennsylvania Avenue as Sherman's troops were followed by freed blacks, adventurers, and others who were in turn followed by cattle and horses captured in the march across Georgia and the Carolinas.

"Well, look at this menagerie." Barry made a sweeping gesture with his right hand.

"More important is what we didn't see – not one black soldier."

"Well, if you turn around, you'll see two."

James and Barry turned and came face to face with two tall broad-shouldered black men in infantry uniforms. One took a step forward and held out his hand. "How y'all doing? I'm Tim Lee,

Second Division, XXV Corps." Lee waved a hand toward his friend. "And dis one's my partner, Tom Blakely."

James pumped Lee's hand and then Tom's. "Thank you so much for saving our asses at Appomattox! I thought we were gone on up for sure! Y'all were great!"

Tom's grin displayed teeth. "Y'all did great, too. We wuz huffing and puffing at double-quick time trying to get there 'fore the rebs busted out. Y'all held'em 'til we got there."

Barry shook the hands of both men with a sly grin. "Next time, y'all don't hafta wait to see if we can hold'em. Come right on in!"

The four men and people around them laughed.

After small talk about hometowns, James asked, "How'd you feel about seeing no black units in the review?"

Lee sighed. "Man, that shows no respect for how we busted our asses and fought. True, we got our freedom. But allus got the union back."

James thought a fly might land in Barry's mouth if he did not soon regain control of his jaw. "We all have our thoughts about what the war was about. What say you?"

Tom put one hand on his hip. "I heard my white officers say time and agin it was all about savin' the union. The rebs say it was 'bout the rights o'dey states. I know better. Dis heah war wuz 'bout me. Nothin' else!" Sweat rose on Tom's nose.

Lee was quieter. "O'course, dey really meant their state's right to make it legal to own me lak a mule…."

James opened his mouth to speak. Lee held up a hand. "I been watchin' ol' Barry here. You gonna have a mighty dry throat from swallowin' all the dust bein' stirred up on dis street if'n you don't soon close yo' mouth."

James slapped Barry's back as he guffawed. Barry coughed, closed his mouth, and turned pink.

Lee started toward the capitol building and motioned for Barry, James, and Tom to follow. "Y'all com'on. Now that ol' Barry from Detroit has recovered, let me show you what y'all should expect from us coloreds, not tomorrow, but right now!"

Half a block later, Lee stopped and waited respectfully as three men wrapped up their conversation. Lee singled one out. "Sir, excuse me please, but I'd like to introduce you to my new friends."

The man turned. "Oh, hello, Lee. It's good to see you."

Barry's jaw dropped again. James felt surprise and great satisfaction; He then smiled, snapped to attention, and held his salute. Slowly, Barry came to attention and saluted.

Lee and Tom beamed. Lee gestured toward the man who returned their salutes. The man was black with a sharp handlebar moustache and wore a Union army officer's uniform with impeccable fit, adorned with the brass of a regimental surgeon. The officer said, "Good afternoon, gentlemen."

Lee turned to Barry. "I just wanted you to meet Major Alexander T. Augusta."

Chapter 15: **Davis Bend**

"Bec, who is that chap standing behind the sack?" Rachel pointed.

"Rai, I see three sacks on the field. There are guys close to each one. The sacks have numbers. Which one are you pointing to?"

Rachel thought Rebecca was being her usual ornery impatient self. She pointed again. "The first one, the closest one, right there."

"Rachel, the sacks are called bases. The one you're indicatin' is third base." Saul smiled and pointed to confirm they were talking about the same base, made of burlap sacks filled with dirt. Saul was Rebecca's new gentleman caller.

"Thanks, Saul. I remember now. Do you know him?"

"Oh, he's the new blacksmith. He works for Ben Montgomery."

Rebecca chided Saul and Rachel. "Doesn't everybody at the Bend work for the Montgomerys? Besides, why do you wanna know who he is? You ain't never asked about a guy before."

"Ain't seen nothing worth asking about – 'till now." Rachel laughed and made a little wave. She cleared her throat and with an impish smile added, "Of course, present company excluded."

Saul beamed. "Thank you, Rachel."

There was a sharp crack as bat met ball. The ground ball was hit toward third base, four feet inside the lime line. The third baseman moved to his right, bent to catch the ball, and came up empty. His teammates groaned as the ball skipped between his feet and bounced into left field.

Rebecca laughed. "Rai, I think you'd better pick another guy. This one's a loser. That's the fourth time he let the ball get past him."

Suddenly, Rachel felt confused. She caught herself before she told Rebecca to mind her man and leave hers be. My man? She thought, *why would I say that? I don't even know that boy. He is a boy, isn't he? He's big enough to be an average-size man – even has muscles. But he has a baby face with hair on it. Now here I am feeling defensive about this boy I haven't even met. I can't remember this feeling before. Do I like him already? Can I like him before we meet? Why do I think I like him? I feel....*

Saul interrupted Rachel's thoughts. "Becky, I wouldn't judge a man by his inability to play this newfangled game."

Rachel smiled. "Yeah, you tell'er, Saul."

The crowd cheered. The winning run was scored on the third baseman's error. As his teammates left the dusty field, the third baseman dropped wearily and sat on third base and held his face in his hands.

Rebecca reached past Saul and grabbed Rachel's arm. "Com'on. Let's go cheer the poor fellow up. You too, Saul. He looks like he needs some cheer."

Without waiting for an answer, Rebecca strode across the twenty paces that separated them from the player. She leaned down and offered her hand to the third baseman. "Hey, fellow. Let me introduce you to your new friends."

The player reached up and took her hand. Rebecca pulled him to his feet. Rachel and Saul were just arriving. Rebecca made a sweeping gesture. "First, my name is Rebecca. You can call me Becky. This is my little sister, Rachel, and my wonderful friend, Saul."

The player looked at his dirty hands and held them aside. "Er, well, my name is Isaac Rice. I would offer y'all my hand, but...."

Rachel overcame a feeling that was holding her back. She stepped forward, grabbed his right hand, and pumped it twice. "Isaac, as you heard, I'm Rachel. And, I want you to know, I'm not afraid of dirt."

Their eyes locked for a second, but it seemed longer to her. Rachel tried to perceive Isaac's essence as she stared up and deep into his eyes. She appreciated that he met her smile and did not blink.

Saul offered his hand, too. "Me neither." Rebecca followed.

"Thanks, y'all. Sorry, I messed up the game for...."

Two more people approached from different directions. Rachel turned to see who interrupted Isaac. She said, "Oh, Ruth, you're just in time. This is my best friend, Ruth. Ruth, this is Isaac Rice."

Isaac took her hand and introduced Caleb, the first baseman, to the group.

Rebecca put one hand on her hip. "Y'all sho' talk funny. Where y'all from anyhow?"

Rachel felt embarrassed and held her head down trying to think of something to say to save the day. Ruth ruined Rachel's concentration by poking an elbow into her ribs.

Isaac smiled at Rebecca. "Well, y'all sound pretty peculiar to me and ol' Caleb too. So where're y'all from?"

Saul said, "Well, Miss Mouth, I guess we can let that rest."

Rachel was happy to join the awkward laugher. She was especially glad Rebecca joined in.

Then there was a pause. Rebecca filled the void. "Well, let's go down to Montgomery's store for some treats. Maybe we can sit by the river after."

Isaac and Caleb exchanged glances. Isaac said, "We can meet you there in an hour. You know, after we wash up a bit."

Rachel spoke before her inhibitions held her back. "I think you're fine like you are."

Ruth spread her hands at her sides. "I agree. Let's all go now."

* * *

At first dark that warm Saturday evening, April 8, 1865, Rachel and Ruth said their good-byes to Isaac and Caleb. They left them at Hurricane Plantation. On their walk back to Brierfield Plantation, Rachel and Ruth walked ahead of Rebecca and Saul.

Ruth was euphoric. "Did you see the way Caleb kept admiring my girlfriends? Both of them felt warm because he noticed 'em so often!"

Rachel said, "Well, there's a word for that. I think it's ogling."

Rachel knew Saul was completely lost when he asked, "Ruth, I didn't see Caleb giving much notice to Becky and Rachel. Are you sure?"

Ruth burst into hysterical laughter. Rachel and Rebecca joined in with fits of giggles.

When she recovered, Rebecca said, "Saul, my dear, I'm going to let you in on a little secret. When a woman refers to her girlfriends, she's talking about her breasts – you know, titties."

Saul sounded embarrassed. "Oh."

More giggles.

Saul plunged ahead. "Well, what's ogling?"

Rebecca threw up her hands. "Now that I don't know. You'll have to ask our teacher."

Rachel felt herself flush. "Er, well, Bec, I'll tell you and Ruth when we get home."

Ruth caught Rachel's arm. "Oh, no. Tell us now. I know you. You want us to forget we asked."

Because Saul was present, she felt warm, as if she could break into a sweat, but Rachel took a deep breath and went ahead. "Oh, all right. It means he was staring at your girlfriends as if he wanted to lay his hands on them."

"Oh, that's a wonderful word! That's exactly what I thought – and wished. Oops! Saul, close your ears!"

It was Rebecca's turn for hysterical laughter.

Ruth waved a hand at Rebecca. "Oh, Bec, shut your face." She turned to Rachel. "So what did you learn about baby-faced Mr. Isaac while you two strolled by the river?"

Rachel knew the question was coming. But she was still perplexed about her feelings. She tried to suppress her thoughts. "Okay. I learned his baby face is thirteen months and a day older than me."

"What? Not possible."

"True. He wants to be a soldier, but the army won't believe his age. That's okay. I believe him. Oh, his birthday is Monday. He'll be eighteen."

Rachel looked back. Rebecca and Saul had stopped and stood in the middle of the rutted road talking as people walked by on either side. She smiled and imagined herself in the same scene with Isaac.

Ruth tugged at her arm. "Com'on. What else?"

"His whole family perished at one time or another in this awful war."

"How is he? I mean, do you like him?"

Rachel paused. She answered the question she had asked herself. Then she wondered if she was ready to tell Ruth. Rachel blinked.

"Yes. I do. I don't know why. But I do. Funny. I never saw him before today and now here I am thinking of nothing but him."

Ruth embraced her friend. "I'm glad for you."

* * *

Another week of toil in the planting season came and went. The next Saturday afternoon, one day before Easter, they were watching another baseball game on the field beside Long Lake. Late in the game when the score was tied, a horseman rode onto the field. His horse was sweating and snorting and prancing. Both the rider and the horse appeared excited. The players, umpire, and crowd were irate.

The rider called out in a loud voice, "Massa Lincoln's been shot dead!"

First, there was a second of stunned silence. The rider raced away toward Hurricane. Then the players and the fans erupted in a chorus of "Oh, my God!" and "Oh, no!" and "Lawd a mercy, what we gone do nigh?"

Immediately, the game was over. People gathered in groups around their loved ones, on and off the field.

Rachel's hot tears rolled down her cheeks in Ruth's embrace. She felt Ruth's tears as their faces touched. Rebecca joined them. Saul stood behind Rebecca, patting her shoulder. No one spoke. They held on to each other in a fierce grip, Rachel thought, as if they would surely be lost if they let go.

Presently, Isaac leaned down and rested his cheek atop Rachel's head. She wiped her eyes to see if it was really Isaac, as she hoped. When she knew it was him, she slipped free of the group and hugged his neck, standing on her toes. Slowly, arm in arm, they walked toward the river. Neither spoke. Rachel rested her head against Isaac's ribs as they walked.

They wandered near the three-year-old ashes of the Hurricane mansion. While they stood beside the remains of Joe Davis's former home, Rachel reflected on the modest plantation homes of the Taylors and the Benders. She thought, *this too will soon be my past, like those other places where I labored. Where is my mother? The surrender news came last week and now Mr. Lincoln is gone. When will the killing stop? Anyway, would Mr. Lincoln have been able to protect us from whites who kill us like animals? Even with Union soldiers here, white people continue killing and stealing us. Where can I be safe to teach or otherwise make a living? What should my dream be? Can I dare to dream of a future where I can live in peace together with this man walking beside me?*

Fresh silent tears flowed down Rachel's cheeks. Her body shook. Isaac held her closer. After a moment, he released her. But Rachel was slow to let go of him. When she did, Isaac broke a red rose from an overgrown bush in a garden that flanked the walk from the front of the former house to the landing at the river. Isaac gave the rose to Rachel and she produced even more tears.

They sat on the grass in the shade of a live oak. Rachel looked at the river with the late afternoon sun reflecting off it and wondered if, like the Montgomerys did for two years, she, too, could take a steamer to Cincinnati and have a better life. She blinked and wiped away her tears. *Perhaps, I could be happy and safe wherever this man wants to live.* She sniffed and smiled at Isaac.

Rachel traced his fingers in the grass with the tip of one of hers. "Thank you for being beside me and not interrupting while my mind rambled. You're kind."

Isaac chewed a long weed. "I'm jes happy to be in your comp'ny."

"What do you think will happen now with our people?"

He removed the weed from his mouth and leaned back on his elbows. "Oh, as my pa would say, it depen's. If we do nothin', nothin' will happ'n. I don't b'lieve we can depen' on white folks to treat us any diff'ant tomorrow dan dey treated us yesterday. I think the matter of what happ'ns next is more up to us dan to dem. If more of us – and it will neber be all of us – follow the zample of people like Mr. Ben Montgomery, matters may slowly git better. But I'm afraid that better time is a long way off."

Rachel sat up and stared into Isaac's eyes. When he finished speaking, they lapsed into silence again. Rachel thought, *I think I just heard the truth. But I don't like it.*

* * *

By September, General Grant's experiment at Davis Bend was described as another successful cotton season for the Negroes leasing Hurricane and Brierfield from the government. The number and severity of guerilla raids had been significantly reduced by the placement of the Sixty-fourth Regiment of Infantry, United States Colored Troops at the Bend. In spite of occasional friction between the colored refugees, like Rachel and her family who streamed into the Bend after hearing about the banner crop of 1864, and the original formerly enslaved Davis hands, they cooperated for the common good. Colonel Eaton and his Freedmen's Department basked in the glow of the accomplishments of colored farmers.

During the summer of 1865, Rachel felt her heart overflowing with love for Isaac. The more she learned about him, the more she knew he was the man to be her life partner. From his expression in words and deeds, she was assured of his love. Her waking thoughts were of Isaac except when she was fully engaged by the Freedmen's Department in teaching reading to young children by day and adults by night. She was never happier.

Chapter 16: The Avengers

Under a slither of rustler's moon at midnight, the two blue-clad sentries at the entrance to Davis Bend fell in the first volley. Hidden at the edge of a grove of willows that extended to the great river, Billy and the Avengers did not move or make a sound among the newly fallen leaves. Billy grinned when he heard commotion from the area of the cabins a quarter-mile away on the Ursino Plantation. He said to himself, the niggers are scared outta their damn wits 'fore we even get to'em. He sharpened his focus as Federal troops noisily scrambled through the trees from their bivouac toward their fallen comrades. Billy watched them halt at the tree line and advance cautiously. When he thought all the Federal guards were present, he shot the sergeant leading the guard detail.

"You blue-bellies are surrounded. Drop 'em and advance with your hands on top of your head!"

The Avengers collected the Enfields dropped by the guards and stripped them of their uniforms. When the guards were bound hand and foot, the Avengers had them lie face down like spokes of a wheel with their feet at the hub. Only one of the six Avengers remained to stand guard over their captives.

"Okay, let's get mounted. We ain't got all night." Billy and the Avengers moved at a trot and retrieved their horses from the woods on the neck of land that connected the Davis Bend peninsula to Mississippi.

Billy led them, firing as they rode, through the Ursino Plantation. Two of their number carried torches. They threw the resin and cloth torches onto the wooden shingled roof of every third cabin, driving the occupants out. Men, women, and children ran into the night screaming and praying. Able-bodied men and women were captured and bound. Those who were not fast enough to reach the woods or cotton fields were shot. Fire from the burning cabins soon spread to neighboring huts.

In less than ten minutes, several Avengers had their mounts galloping to the next plantation, Joe Davis's Brierfield. Billy heard the familiar sound of a bullet whiz past his head. He realized that the element of surprise was long since lost on people at Brierfield. Now he knew some would resist – not just run.

"Lasso those two bucks running into that cotton field and let's get back to Ursino." Billy pointed to his left.

Two Avengers wheeled and gave chase. Grady drew rein beside Billy. "Hey, Billy. Nice haul, huh?"

"Not until we're on the road outta here."

Another bullet hit a nearby tree. Grady turned his horse about twice, looking for a target. Billy raised his new stolen US Army Spencer carbine and fired twice at the nearest cabin. When no fire was returned, he called out. "Let's get outta here. Drag them niggers if they can't keep up with your horses at a trot. Let's go!"

Back at the guardhouse, they crowded ten men and three women onto a well-worn faded green wooden farm wagon with the sentries' weapons and uniforms. Billy glanced at the frightened faces of several of his captives. The women cried and sniffed. They avoided his eyes. He thought *this lot will work just fine.* Billy signaled the driver, a farmer from Copiah County, to start his two-mule team. The Avengers left the guards bound and shivering on the ground in the chilly October 1863 night.

* * *

Billy and Grady rode at the end of their column. They rode in silence for almost twenty miles of their forty-mile journey to Carpenter. Billy chose a little-used road to cross the Big Black River near Hamer Bayou, for the bridge on the Natchez-Vicksburg road was guarded by Federal troops that outnumbered the Avengers by at least five to one.

"Grady, why are you stoppin'?"

"I have a feelin' we're bein' followed."

Billy laughed. "What other fools would be out on this road at four o'clock in the mornin'? I heard a raccoon or a possum scale a tree back there. Is that what you heard?"

"I sho' hope the answer is nobody but your 'coon. But I got me a funny feelin' that thar's somebody back there."

"Well, why don't you wait for 'em here by the river?"

"Ain't you gonna stay with me?"

"You don't mean ta tell me you b'lieve in those haint stories 'bout the Big Black?"

Above the noise of hooves and the wagon's rattle, two alligators bellowed. Billy snickered.

Grady turned solemn. "Er, well, naw. But if you gonna ride on, I'll keep you comp'ny."

Billy laughed so hard that his sides hurt. Finally, he said, "Yeah, you do that and I'll be much obliged."

Grady lifted his chin and ignored Billy. "Yore welcome."

* * *

They arrived at the Duke farm near Carpenter at midmorning. They allowed their newly captured work hands to stretch their legs and gave them water. Billy, with his arms folded, stood between the driver, Mr. Dabney, and Grady, assessing the new hands.

"Billy, you reckon I could get an extra one, seeing as how we fetched two more'n we went for?"

"Sure. You and Mr. Dabney divide 'em up as you see fit. Just leave four here for my pa."

Mr. Dabney smiled broadly. "Why, thank you, Billy. That's mighty generous of ya. This will be a big help toward gettin' my cotton picked. But I guess all o' us are late gathering this year."

Grady pointed out two women and three men he wanted for his pa's farm. "Mr. Dabney, are you okay wid those over there?"

"Sure. That's fine. Well, let's get on down the road. I'll drop yours off for you and git on home. Need to get 'em fed and situated today and start 'em picking at first light tomorrow."

"Yes, sir, Mr. Dabney."

Billy waved. "See ya later. I'ma lock mine up at night. Y'all might wanna do the same. Since the damn Yankee invasion, more and more of 'em are up and runnin' off."

* * *

The twosome rode their horses through the woods to their favorite picnic spot under a large oak tree on the west hill of a saddle,

240

just shy of Scutchalo Creek, a tributary of Bayou Pierre. It was midmorning on a sunny and pleasant October day. They dismounted and put down an oilcloth and the patchwork quilt Mary Beth had brought.

Over her shoulder, Mary Beth cast her eyes upward at Billy and blinked her lashes twice. She pushed her blond bangs aside. In her silkiest voice she said, "Now Billy Duke. You shore you ganna marry me and make me a respectable lady soon's this ol' war is over?"

"Mary Beth, you ask me that same silly question every time we come up here. "O'cose, you know I'm gonna marry you. You've been my only gal for goin' on two years now."

Ten minutes later, they were making sounds of ecstasy. With Mary Beth on all fours and her ankle-length riding skirt resting on her back, Billy ejaculated in her vagina.

Billy watched as Mary Beth pulled her calf-length pantaloons over her buttocks and tied the drawstring that held the garment fast at her waist. While she rearranged and smoothed her skirt, he thought, *maybe someday I'll marry her. She's smart and pretty. Sex with her is really good. Maybe.... But right now, I want a nap.*

* * *

At noon, they dined on apples, fried chicken, and blackberry jelly biscuits. In the early afternoon, they were still in their hilltop retreat. Mary Beth sat facing the creek, which was out of sight down the slope. Billy rested his head on her lap, his hands clasped across his chest.

Mary Beth rubbed his stubble with the back of her hand. "Billy, why don't you quit the Avengers? Why don't we get married next month?"

"Now, May Beth, you know the service we provide to folks in this county. It woulda been mighty nigh impossible for some o' our farmers to gather what little crops they managed to plant without the hands we brought in. We can get married when the Avengers are no longer needed."

"Do you mean the hands you and the Avengers kidnapped to re-enslave?"

"Call it what you like. The farmers are grateful. They're happy to have replacements."

Mary Beth took a deep breath. "Billy, don't you know the war is already over? Sweetheart, after Vicksburg and Gettysburg, there's no doubt left. We've lost."

Billy sat up. "What? Do you know that blasted Jean Pierre?"

"Who?"

Billy lay down again. "Naw. I reckon you wouldn't. JP's a soldier from New Orleans. He was with us up at Vicksburg."

"Why did you ask?"

"He said the war is over and we oughta stop. I say nonsense."

"And I say your Jean Pierre has good judgment. Where is he now?"

"He went home."

"I rest my case."

Billy sat up again. His anger grew. "Mary Beth, don't start with your twaddle again about how we should quit and let all the niggers go. You talk crazy."

Mary Beth smiled. "Insulting me won't improve the lot of the Confederacy. When my Papa gambled and lost so much money that he had to sell our house and all of his slaves, I learned a powerful truth."

Billy cocked his head to one side. "And what was that?"

"When we were free of slaves, we became so much better off."

"What does that mean? That makes no sense a'tall!"

"In time, you'll see."

"In the meantime, me and the Avengers are goin' on our biggest operation yet. We leave tomorrow night. We won't be back for awhile."

"If you must go out raiding, why don't y'all join Captain Whitaker's scouts? I hear he has more'n seventy men. Won't that be safer than your little band?"

"No. With all the clatter of that many men and horses, we'd be caught for sure. Besides, when did Whitaker's Scouts ever help folks in Copiah?"

"From what I hear, it seems they're doing real well."

"Mary Beth, what're you gettin' at? What do you want?"

Mary Beth's gaze was steady. She did not blink. She spoke clearly and slowly. "What I want is for you to come to your senses, marry me, take me to New Orleans, and start a life together. Period. Nothing more. Nothing you can't do."

Billy stared at her in disbelief and shook his head. He stood and stretched. He thought, *it's times like this when I know I'll never marry her. She will surely make me crazy.*

Without looking back, Billy mounted his horse and rode north.

* * *

A short time later, Billy turned east and headed to the home of Captain Henry Carter's mother in Utica, arriving at sunset. Henry was waiting in a rocker on the porch. Billy hitched his horse and sat beside him. After they inquired about health and family matters, each of the other, Henry's mother called them in for supper.

Returning to the porch in the autumn evening, Henry drew on his pipe and leaned back. "Billy, I'm not ready to compete with Captain Whitaker. Actually, I don't believe there's time or space for a separate raider."

Billy swallowed hard. He thought, *is this the end?* "Are you suggestin' that we fold the Avengers?"

"Not at all. Y'all are helping poor people. I'm thinking I can do more in the legislature now that I have a military parole than I can riding over the countryside."

"I was still hoping you'd join us."

"Let me suggest how we can work together. Times are hard for our people – even for your family and mine. And we're the moderately well-off. We've folks in Hinds and Copiah who could starve this winter."

Billy nodded in acknowledgment. But he could not see how the Avengers could help matters. "So what can we do about it?"

"We can work together to requisition rations from the US Army for our people."

Billy stared at Henry, uncomprehending. "What?"

"Steal in plain sight and deliver goods down here like we ordered them." Pleased with himself, Henry chuckled.

He pulled on his pipe. "Billy, here's how this might work. The Avengers will need to wear the hated blue Yankee uniforms for this operation – which could take months. That will all depend on how long the fighting continues and how long our opportunity lasts.

"From time to time, I'll pose as a US Army quartermaster officer of commissary. Here's what happens next...."

* * *

In November, Billy led the Avengers to the US Army's Post Commissary of Subsistence warehouse at the corner of Crawford and Washington Streets in occupied Vicksburg, two and a half blocks uphill from the Mississippi River. The Avengers complained bitterly, but had their Union uniforms packed in their saddlebags. For a week, they scouted in civilian clothes from Levee to Cherry Streets and from South to Clay Streets. They made note of guard posts and the regular comings and goings of the parade of wagons entering and leaving the warehouse. Billy went across the street and persuaded the priest at St Paul's Catholic Church, dedicated in 1848, to allow him to take a look from its lofty gothic spire.

In the evenings, they camped along Hall's Ferry Road, just south of the former Union siege line. By their cook fire, the Avengers memorized their new identities as members of a special detail from the Eighty-first Missouri Regiment of Provisional Militia Infantry sent to haul stores in support of the occupation troops and the new Freedmen's Department created by General Grant.

After a week of scouting, one evening by their campfire Billy drew an envelope from his shirt. "Boys, we're ready for action tomorrow. These papers are requisitions made by the Eighty-first Missouri for three army wagons arriving by train at De Soto Point in the morning. We'll be there to take delivery and bring them across the river on the ferry. Being as we're supposed to be from Missouri,

Captain Carter says we oughta know the wagons were made in Missouri. I guess that's a point o' pride."

Grady asked, "Well, what comp'ny made'em?"

"Captain Carter says here in his note that it was the Hiram Young and Company of Jackson County, Missouri, and Fort Leavenworth, Kansas."

"I reckon I can 'member that."

"And, remember' to try and speak like them ol' boys from Sixth Missouri who helped us during the siege."

"You know, this is the damnest thing."

"What?"

"Missouri sent regiments to fight on both sides."

"Damn. It sure is. And Kentucky did, too."

Grady rubbed his stubble and lowered his voice. "Hey, Billy. I got me somethin' else on my mind. Suppose, now jes suppose, we're standin' amongst all them real Yankees tomorrow and Captain Henry's forgeries ain't up to snuff?"

Billy shrugged. "Well I guess, it'll be my honor to hang beside you."

* * *

Billy and the Avengers arrived early at the railhead wearing Union uniforms. Billy looked carefully about. Each Avenger carried a Spencer carbine and a Colt .44 revolver. The train arrived and Billy felt his heart rate increase. He waited and watched until several officers and noncommissioned officers presented their papers while the Avengers waited across the platform. Billy listened carefully to the quartermaster second lieutenant, who sat at a portable wooden field table, as he inspected each form presented. The lieutenant sounded to Billy like he may have come from New York or New Jersey – he couldn't be sure. Already, he disliked the officer. Billy took a deep breath and glanced about again at his escape route in case Henry Carter's forgeries were not good enough.

The bright-eyed lieutenant reached for Billy's forms. "Good morning, Sergeant."

Billy's hand trembled as he handed over his papers. He decided to hide his nerves with pleasantries. "Good mornin', sir. I hope my wagons arrived. I need to put my boys to work. You know what they say about idle boys."

"Yes, we hope not to create more workshops for the devil. Let's see…. Well, according to my bill of lading, your wagons are on the fourth car. Oh, I see you're from Missouri. You must be right proud to have such a distinguished Negro as Hiram Young in your state."

Billy's breathing stopped for seconds. When he recovered, he stammered, "I-I-I beg your pardon, sir."

"I said you must be proud of the Negro, Hiram Young. Say, sergeant, you look a bit peaked. Are you okay?"

Billy made a wave with his hand. "Oh, it's nothing, sir. It feels like my breakfast is disagreeing with my stomach."

"Should I send for help?"

"Oh, no, sir. Nothing serious. I'm sure it'll pass."

"Well, okay. I've signed your forms. Here you are. Wait by your car. Roustabouts will be there soon to help you move your wagons to the ferry. Maybe you should see the surgeon."

"Oh, no, sir. I'll be fine. Thank you for your kindness."

* * *

Billy was unaware of the lively conversation and banter Grady and the Avengers carried on during the ferry ride across the river to Vicksburg. He sat with his face in his hands, staring into space. His thoughts ran in circles. He thought, *how can this be? Apparently, a nigger owns a company that makes wagons I've seen everywhere. Good sturdy products. That Yankee officer sounds like a damn abolitionist. He must know. Stands to reason he would know. After all, he's a quartermaster. Oh, I'll bet this nigger's pa was white. That's it. That's got to be it. Isn't it? What if I'm wrong? And what if Pa and Mr. Alexander Stephens are wrong? What…?*

Grady shook Billy with a hand on his shoulder. "Hey, Billy. You asleep wid yore eyes open? What's wrong? Didn't ol' Captain Carter fool dem Yankees, but good?"

246

"Grady." There was a long pause. "Suppose I told you that Hiram Young is a nigger. Would you believe me?"

Grady hesitated and blinked. Then Billy watched as Grady's eyes narrowed before he spoke. "Why, hell no!"

* * *

Using more of Henry Carter's forgeries, they obtained six mules to pull each wagon and, with other papers, gathered loads of stores from the Union army's warehouse at Washington and Crawford Streets.

Grady declared. "This kinda raidin' is a hellava lot better 'n gettin' shot at! Three cheers for Captain Carter!"

They went south on Fisher's Ferry Road to Copiah County. Billy was at the head of the column as they headed down the slope beside Hamer Bayou in Warren County. He saw a lone rider sitting his horse in the middle of the road. Billy was immediately alarmed as he recognized that the Avengers were sitting ducks in the kill zone of the same ambush site he had used months before against the Union cavalry. He knew they could not run with the wagons. He glanced at the tree lines on both sides of the road. Nothing. He realized he would not see anyone in a well-prepared ambush and concluded that fighting would be suicide. Billy halted his column.

Now that he was closer, Billy saw the man was wearing the uniform of a Union army officer. Billy shifted in his saddle and subtly moved his reins to his left hand, leaving a clear path to his holstered revolver. He thought, *at least I'll kill the leader.* With the Avengers stopped, Billy nudged his horse and the animal walked forward toward the calm-looking cigar-smoking officer.

Without raising his hand in greeting, Billy stopped at ten paces and called out in his best imitation of a Missouri accent. "Good afternoon, sir."

"Good afternoon to you, too, Sergeant. I appreciate so much that y'all went to all the trouble to bring me them wagons. I sure kin use'em."

Billy recognized the local accent. His mind raced. What do I do now? He dropped his fake Missouri accent. "Sir, I'd be mighty obliged if you'd let us pass."

The rider removed his cigar from his mouth and sat taller in his saddle. "Say, are you the fellow workin' wid ol' Hank Carter, the lawyer?"

Billy grinned and he felt his shoulders relax. "And you, sir, are the famous Captain Isaac Whitaker, the doctor from Utica."

Whitaker smiled. "I am."

They nudged their horses closer, saluted, and shook hands. With a big smile, Billy said, "Sir, Sergeant William Duke, Company F, Thirty-eighth Mississippi Infantry, I'm at your service."

Captain Whitaker raised both arms and waved his men in. Billy watched in amazement as dozens of men emerged from the woods on all sides. The Avengers were completely enveloped. He thought, *we woulda died for sure.*

"So, we finally meet. I've heard good reports about you and the Avengers. Hank thinks quite highly of you. Y'all keep up the good work. The fine folks of Copiah need your help."

"Thank you, sir. We'll do our best."

"Billy, I'm sorry I can't stay and chat. We have some unfinished business with real Yankees and some uppity niggers."

"Yes, sir. As you always say, 'Surprise'em and give'em hell!'" Billy saluted.

At hearing his own words, Captain Whitaker's big grin showed teeth. He returned Billy's salute and spurred his horse.

Billy watched with the Avengers as the Whitaker Scouts disappeared toward Vicksburg in a cloud of dust.

* * *

Throughout 1864, the Avengers worked on their family farms and from time to time, when Billy and Henry declared a need, they donned their Eight-first Missouri disguises and sallied forth with freshly forged documents to requisition food and supplies from the Union army and the Freedmen's Department warehouses. In 1865, they made only one raid. They struck the plantation of a northern investor who hired Negro labor under contracts overseen by the Freedmen's Department. From that raid, they returned with seven hands mounted on as many mules along with an additional nine mules.

After Atlanta fell to General Sherman, Billy told Grady, "I guess ol' JP was a better prophet than me."

By the time Sherman burned his way across Georgia and occupied Savannah, Billy's thinking had evolved to concern about what essentials they would need to grab in the coming spring since the Confederacy appeared doomed. His mood was usually cranky. He was angry about the lost cause and disappointed about his puzzlement over whether Alexander Stephens's cornerstone premise was really true or just words to rally the Confederacy at the beginning of the war. Since the day he first heard of Hiram Young, he compared his image of the successful black businessman to the freedmen he observed in Mississippi's heartland. He thought he saw several who could match the image in his head. But, now that he had heard the tale of Ben Montgomery, a slave, of all people, successfully managing Joe Davis's Hurricane Plantation, he developed undirected anger about what was true or not, and his shattered understanding of the order of things between black and white. At times, his anger and bewilderment made his head hurt.

* * *

The Avengers took another requisition run three weeks after the death of President Lincoln. Lee had already surrendered and John Wilkes Booth was dead. By the end of May, Joe Johnston and Kirby Smith surrendered and Captain Whitaker called it quits.

"You know, it looks like we have a friend in the White House again." Henry sat on the Dukes' front porch with a cigar in one hand and a glass of tea in the other. It was the first Sunday in September.

The elder Duke agreed. "Yes, I agree. President Johnson has let it be known that our state governments will be recognized without a fuss. By the way, thanks for your help applying for my pardon. I'm a legitimate landowner again." He made a sardonic laugh.

"Oh, don't mention it."

Billy sat on the floor at the edge of the porch with his feet hanging down. He chewed a twig he had been using as a toothpick. "Folks around these parts are asking for some kinda order to control all the niggers overrunning the towns and cities. I heard Governor Humphreys is raising the same concern. Henry, when's the legislature gonna fix this."

Henry took a swig of tea. "Yes, I've heard the same question and seen the editorials too. I expect we'll have new laws in place before the end of the year."

Billy's pa pulled on his chin. "Now, Hank, what do you think these new controls oughta look like – given that niggers are free?"

"Oh, one thread I've followed and like is binding them to a job by January or they suffer penalties of the law; plus, they can't change jobs, and no employer could entice 'em away from a job. Moreover, Mississippi niggers won't be free to vote, own a gun, or to buy land. In other words, under our new state laws, they will be free in name only. Under President Johnson, we're back to the good ol' days."

Billy was impressed. "Oh, yeah. That'll keep'em in their place. I won't have to lock'em up at night."

Henry continued. "Just make sure you have'em here for contracting before the beginning of the year to make it stick under the new laws."

"I'll see to it. In fact, I think we oughta run one more raid before we call it quits. We can raid one o' them plantations run by that Freedmen's Department. What do you say, Pa?"

Henry interrupted. "By the way, it's probably becoming the Freedmen's Bureau before another year passes."

"So?"

"That will depend on which general is appointed to run it."

"Pa, do you think we kin use a few more hands?"

"Yes, I think another three or four would do it. And, while you're at it, drive a few mules on down here wid them niggers."

* * *

On a stormy night near the end of September 1865, Billy and the Avengers surprised the black soldiers assigned as sentries for the evening at the neck of land leading to Davis Bend. Without firing a shot, the Avengers rode in under the sound of a heavy downpour and captured the entire guard detail on duty. The guards were quickly bound and gagged. Their comrades, native Louisianans, in the garrison of the Sixty-fourth Infantry Regiment, United States Colored Troops did not hear the intruders arrive. Three of the Avengers went directly to Brierfield Plantation and rounded up eight hands at gunpoint to match the number of extra mules and horses they brought. In exactly nine minutes, the Avengers had collected their booty and left Davis Bend.

Chapter 17: A New Warrior

The rearguard dismounted and pulled their horses to the ground. The warriors held their horses' heads down. The horses lay on their sides, now and again attempting to stand. Ortega watched the soldiers ride past about a mile away on the flat plain and breathed a sigh of relief as they continued south toward Fort Stanton.

* * *

Ortega pulled back sharply on the reins. "Get down! Quickly."

"Okay." Jorge slid from his seat behind Ortega and off the left side of their moving horse. Jorge hit the ground and tumbled forward alongside the horse.

Ortega loosened the reins and frantically kicked the horse's flanks with his heels while shrieking, "Heeee – yi!" In four steps, the big bay was in full gallop. Ortega leaned forward. Her mane was flying in his face. Ortega gently massaged the horse's neck with one hand. He kept his eyes on the galloping packhorses ahead of him and his heels snug against the bay's flanks. He was sure his horse understood that he needed to catch the runaway packhorses.

The packhorses had been grazing unattended, still loaded with their cargo, when they were frightened by a rattlesnake. The people were very excited and had dropped the reins of the packhorses. They had scattered over Long Canyon, south of Panther Draw, to survey the place that was to be their new home.

Plants rushed by in a blur as Ortega and his mare raced out of the mouth of the canyon and onto the flats where three tributaries joined the east-west Rio Penasco. After about a half-mile of panicked galloping, the pack horses began to slow. Ortega and his horse narrowed the gap. They traveled along the east side of the creek that drained Long Canyon. At the place where the two creeks joined, Ortega drew rein beside one of the packhorses and grabbed its bridle. His horse and both packhorses stopped on his command.

On the ground and holding the reins of the three horses, Ortega set about ascertaining if any farm implements were lost during the runaway. He reckoned that at least two shovels were missing. With trepidation, he checked the second horse's pack and found that all of the seeds Nantahe-totel had carefully saved in sacks were still there.

Suddenly, the three animals began bucking and rearing. They pulled to run back in the direction of Long Canyon. Ortega tried to calm the horses with his voice. He tugged on their reins but failed to get them under control. Then Ortega noticed that his mare's eyes never left a tree on the north bank where the creeks joined. As the horses pulled him stumbling forward, he turned to see what had her attention. A mountain lion stood immobile in a tree near the bank. Not even its extended tail moved. Ortega's jaw dropped and, involuntarily, he loosened his grip on the reins. The horses jerked free and left him facing the mountain lion.

Though it was early December, most of Ortega's shirt was wet with sweat. The mountain lion slowly, almost imperceptibly, crouched on its perch. The large cat and Ortega locked eyes. Ortega then glanced about for a better place to stand. He knew he could not outrun the cat. Besides, he knew running would give the lion the advantage to attack him from behind. No better defensive position was closer to him than the mountain lion. He pulled the only weapon he had from the scabbard on his belt – the short knife with the palm-length blade his father had given him on his twelfth birthday. He moved his eyes to the animal's neck. Ortega tightened his grip on his knife, focused on where he thought the cat's jugular would be, widened his stance, slightly bent his knees, and braced for the anticipated impact. In a single bound, the cat leapt for Ortega's head. Ortega dodged right, but not far enough.

The one-hundred-sixty-five-pound weight and momentum of the airborne cat knocked the one-hundred-fifty-pound Ortega to the ground. Ortega never took his eyes from the cat's jugular – even as he was falling. Before his back hit the ground, Ortega stabbed the cat's neck twice. With his left arm around the cat, Ortega continued stabbing the mountain lion's neck, chest, and belly. The big cat clawed at Ortega. Ortega ducked and leaned his head toward his left shoulder to protect his own jugular. The lion's claw raked Ortega's blue headband off and opened four long gashes starting at the top of his head, then his left ear, his jaw, and down his shoulder. Blood streamed down his face. His shirt was soaked with blood and sweat. His trousers and thighs were shredded and blooded by the lion's trashing hind paws. Ortega continued stabbing the cat as fast as he could wield the knife.

Shortly, Ortega and the mountain lion relaxed their deadly embrace and lay panting near the bank of the creek. In rhythm with its heart, blood gushed from the lion's throat and jugular. Minutes later, the cat died, lying on Ortega's left arm. Ortega could not move. He was exhausted and feeling very sleepy.

* * *

Ortega heard faint voices in the distance. He thought he felt the weight of the mountain lion on his left arm. The voices came closer. He tried to open his eyes, but could not. Ortega wanted the owners of the voices to remove the lion. When he tried to speak, he heard his voice say, "M-m-m-gah."

The other voices stopped. There was a long pause. Then the bystanders became excited.

"Run quickly and bring Nantahe-totel!" It was the voice of a woman.

Ortega opened his eyes. It was day, but he only saw shapes. Two people were standing over him. He blinked repeatedly, trying to clear his vision. He attempted to sit up. Pain in his head, shoulder, and thighs caused him to abandon the thought. He let out a sharp groan.

The woman spoke to him for the first time. "No, Ortega. Do not move. You must rest."

Ortega closed his eyes. The light had caused more pain in his head. He moved his tongue over his teeth. His mouth tasted foul. Next, hunger pains hit him. And he was thirsty – thirstier than he could ever remember. His throat felt parched; his lips were dry and cracked. "Wah, wah."

Another female voice said. "All right, sip slowly when the spoon touches your lips."

He felt a hand raise his head. The cool clay spoon touched his lips. He tried to gulp the water. It ran down his face and neck. The two women laughed softly. The woman with the younger voice said again, "Slowly, there's plenty of water here."

When he finished drinking, he was tired. Ortega fell asleep.

He dreamed that Jacali and Nantahe-totel were sitting beside him and he could hear them speak of him. He felt a wet cloth on his brow. Then a hand smoothed his hair from left to right. The pain brought him fully awake; he opened his eyes.

Nantahe-totel spoke. "Ortega, we are grateful to see your eyes."

Squinting, Ortega tried to focus in the direction of the voice. "Grandfather?"

"Yes. It is me. Jorge is here. Jacali and her mother, Haozinne, have watched over you and kept vermin away."

At the mention of Jacali's name, Ortega's pulse quickened. The pain in his head grew more intense. He tried to smile. The crusted-over wounds on his scalp and face hurt. He winced. Jacali gently mopped his forehead with her wet cloth. He managed to say, "Thank you."

Nantahe-totel continued. "The shaman will return soon."

"Where is the lion?"

"Haozinne is making a fine cover from its hide for you."

Embarrassed, Ortega muttered, "Thank you." He tried to change the subject. "We must find the shovels that fell from the packhorse."

His grandfather laughed. "Jorge found the shovels day before yesterday. You have slept for three days. When the hunting party brought you in, I thought you were dead. You are a blessing from Ussen. Haozinne and Jorge helped me clean the blood from your body. The shaman came and made medicine. Since then, we have taken turns watching over you."

Haozinne laughed softly. "Ortega, your face looks puzzled. You must wonder why I help your grandfather when we are not related. It is because of Jacali."

Nantahe-totel interrupted. "Haozinne is wise. She has seen you and Jacali exchange glances. Haozinne and Jacali were among the excited people who gathered when the hunting party brought you and the lion to camp. Haozinne knew her daughter's heart when she ran to you. So she has accompanied Jacali to watch over you in our arbor."

Smiling shyly, Jacali's eyes were fixed on her moccasins; her chin rested on her collar bone.

Ortega suppressed his smile but could not hide the tears welling in his eyes.

* * *

By spring of 1866, the regular tasks of the new community were divided in council. Men and women volunteered or were assigned duties according to their expertise. The most dangerous was raiding and securing the approaches to their canyon. Klo-sen was designated to lead warriors on raids and trade pelts with White Eyes and Mexicans. Nantahe-totel led the tillers and planters. Others took the tasks of tanning, making mescal, hunting, and gathering wild fruit.

Ortega had regained his strength after his ordeal with the lion and rode with Jorge when they followed the warriors on patrols or raids. They cooked for the warriors, cleaned their weapons, and cared for their horses. But they ate only cold food as tradition required of apprentice warriors. Ortega and Jorge did not carry weapons, except small knives.

"Hey, Jorge. I've got news you've been waiting to hear!"

"Yeah. What?"

"Klo-sen told me Grandfather will borrow us. We are to join the tillers for three days and help with the canal."

"Oh, my aching back."

"Yeah, by the next night, more parts than your back will ache."

* * *

The canal led to a hole ten feet deep and twelve feet in diameter that the tillers had dug to store water. A rack loaded with logs and branches stood on four posts over the hole and shielded the diverted water in the hole from the sun while allowing in rain. A branch from the main canal led directly to the fields where maize, gourds, and vegetables were planted. The branch was used until the creek ran dry in the summer.

In the first year, the harvest was a success. Under the summer and fall sun, the women dried fruits, vegetables, mescal, and meats for the winter. Raiding, trading, and breeding increased their herds.

* * *

Jacali and two girls stepped from the specially constructed ceremonial lodge and faced the rising July sun. The three girls had reached the second year of their puberty. Ortega, standing in a crowd of onlookers with Jorge, gasped when he saw Jacali. His mouth remained agape as he took in the sight. For her puberty sunrise ceremony, Jacali wore dazzling white buckskin decorated with blue beads and tiny bells – even her moccasins were white buckskin with blue beads. Jacali's godmother and sponsor, her mother's best friend, stood behind her and wore matching blue beads on her white jumper.

Gazing as if in a trance, Ortega muttered, "She is more beautiful than in my dreams...."

Four days later when the ceremony was over, Jacali's two girl friends had removed their eyebrows, signaling readiness for marriage. Ortega made a long sigh of relief when he saw that Jacali still wore her eyebrows.

* * *

"Do we have enough twigs?"

Ortega and Jorge gathered dry juniper and pine twigs on the mountainsides above the new farmland. Ortega paused and looked at the bundle they had collected. "No, I don't think so."

"Looks like more than enough to me."

"I think we need to carry more. I heard we may journey as far as the Sierra Madre. Grandfather talks much of his adventures and raids near the homeland of Chief Juh's people. He said between the new White Eye-Mexican border and the Sierra Madre wood is scarce. Let's gather some dry wood from the top of this mountain."

"Okay. But hurry. Night will fall soon. Klo-sen warned me to beware of lions and snakes. If any are up here, I want to see them before they see me."

* * *

"Surely, we have enough now. Besides, we've picked this mountaintop clean."

Ortega looked up from his gathering. "Yeah, I think...." In the light of the setting sun, his peripheral vision caught movement on the flats to the north, near the Rio Penasco, half-mile away. He dropped his bundle and pointed. "Look!"

Jorge stood upright holding his bundle. "Where? What?"

"Look, there along the tree line by the river."

"I see nothing but trees."

"There under the trees must be twenty horsemen. They wear the hats of the White Eyes."

"Soldiers?"

Ortega caught the glint from the sun reflected by metal. "No. Ranchers! They're checking their rifles."

"I saw a reflection!" Jorge dropped his bundle.

"Run! We must sound the alarm!"

They ran with abandon down the side of the rocky mountain. Ortega called out, "Find my grandfather! He will be with the tillers. I'll find Klo-sen!"

"Okay." Jorge sprinted off toward the fields.

* * *

With the alarm sounded, women and children scrambled south up Long Canyon. When the ranchers fired their first shots, there was panic and pandemonium. Men rushed from the fields and grabbed weapons to block the way to their livestock. Klo-sen had no time to set a defensive perimeter. His warriors ran to preselected positions that were ineffective against the charging ranchers.

Klo-sen told Ortega to remain under cover. Ortega watched from junipers and rocks on the side of a small hill as the ranchers fired indiscriminately into the camp, hitting the slowest moving women and children. Ortega's anger seethed. He spat.

Not far in front of him, one of Klo-sen's warriors was shot in the head. The Spencer carbine fell from his hands and clattered, bouncing among the rocks. Immediately, Ortega lurched forward. He ran at top speed to the downed warrior. Falling beside him, Ortega retrieved the warrior's deerskin ammunition pouch. Bullets sang passed his head. He scrambled across the rocks, grabbed the carbine, and rolled behind a large rock.

Ortega caught his breath and concocted a plan to select as his first targets ranchers who were firing at the warriors. Three deep breaths later, he rolled over and focused on a White Eye taking aim at Klo-sen's back while Klo-sen was firing at another rancher. Ortega's first shot ever with a carbine knocked the target from his horse. He saw Klo-sen glance his way. Ortega did not pause. He selected another target and aimed as he always heard one should and fired a bullet into the middle of that man's chest.

Then half-dozen ranchers penetrated the camp, opened the corral, and stampeded the horses toward the river. Ortega reloaded and continued firing at their backs, hitting two, as the ranchers rode into first darkness at the head of a cloud of dust.

They had lost three of their best warriors and several other men were wounded. Three women and two children died. That night, the people slept on the mountaintop under the watchful eyes of their remaining warriors, new warriors, and former warriors.

* * *

At daybreak, while some rounded up strays that had wandered from the horse herd, Klo-sen and Nantahe-totel tracked the trail left by the ranchers. They led their raiding party north to the Rio Felix. There, the trail turned east and led more than one hundred miles into Texas. During the first night on the trail, Ortega sat between Klo-sen and Nantahe-totel.

Klo-sen gazed into the flames of a small cook fire. "Ortega, in the battle, you acquitted yourself well. You took the initiative and were effective. You killed four of the enemy."

The old warrior Nantahe-totel observed, "You have behaved as a true warrior, though you have not completed your training. My grandson, I am proud of you."

Klo-sen put a hand on Ortega's shoulder. "We have decided to make you a warrior upon return to camp."

Ortega glanced at Jorge cleaning weapons and suppressed a large grin. "Thank you."

* * *

A few minutes after four in the morning on the third day, they slipped into a ranch near Denver City, Texas, where the horse herd's trail had led. They had the last horse out of the corral before the first shot was fired and the ranch's bunkhouse and barn torched. Not a single warrior was wounded.

* * *

Raids and counterraids continued between Mescaleros, Mexicans, and Texans throughout 1867. They all lost more lives during the raids. The crop damage from raids and depleted livestock left the people unprepared for winter. By the next February, they were hungry.

Finally, as the first signs of spring appeared in the new year, Nantahe-totel stood before a council of the people. "We have worked hard since we left the accursed Bosque Redondo. We have proven that we can be successful farmers. The White Eye Texans and Mexicans have killed our people and stolen our livelihood. We are fewer since we arrived here more than two summers ago. Our warriors are tired and not many. We can no longer protect our women and children. Further, the evil Carleton has been removed by Washington. Therefore, I say let us go and farm in the shadows of Fort Stanton and the sacred Sierra Blanca within our homeland. I have spoken." Nantahe-totel sat.

After a debate that lasted two more evenings, the people decided. Nantahe-totel did not speak again. He sat with his arms folded. On the fourth morning after Nantahe-totel's speech, the people, cold and hungry, followed him sixty miles northwest to Fort Stanton.

Chapter 18: Striking the Avengers

As usual, under the watchful eye of John, three gentlemen callers took Sunday night supper on the twenty-fourth of September with his daughters Rachel and Rebecca, plus his adopted daughter Ruth. After hearing repeated thunderclaps sounding closer and closer, Isaac, Caleb, and Saul departed for their residences.

Isaac and Caleb headed west toward Hurricane, the opposite direction from Saul's destination at the other end of Brierfield. They had walked for two minutes when large cold rain drops beat on their heads. In seconds, the full fury of the storm was upon them.

Caleb looked over his shoulder. "Man, let's turn back."

Lightning struck nearby. Isaac was buttoning his collar when Caleb hit his arm and exclaimed, "Look!"

The lightning flash was gone and it was pitch black again. Loud thunder rumbled. Isaac turned and saw nothing. "What?"

"Three riders leading some horses just stopped Saul on the road. Wait for the next flash of lightnin'."

It came seconds later. "I see'em! Guerillas! They're puttin' 'im on a horse!"

"Let's tell the guards!"

They were shouting to be heard in the heavy downpour. "No! To get this far, they've already done in the guards. Get off the road 'fore they see us."

They crouched between the rows of waist-high cotton plants and watched. "We gotta do something."

"We will. Follow me after the next flash." The lightning struck again. Isaac looked for and located the Brierfield corral. "Okay, let's go!"

They ran for the corral. With both hands on the top rail, Isaac leapt the fence and landed with a large splash in the corral. With his blacksmith's voice, he calmed the closest horse. In seconds, he was mounted – bareback.

Caleb looked at Isaac, shaking his head. "You ain't doin' what I think you're... Man, those guys have guns! You ain't doin' it, right? Huh? Are you?"

"The hell, I ain't. We gotta see where they go. Are you coming?"

Caleb hesitated. Isaac yelled. "Open the gate. I gotta keep these guys in sight."

"Okay. Gate's open. You go. I'm gettin' me a horse. I'ma be right behind you."

Without another word, Isaac rode into the darkness. He waited thirty seconds for Caleb where cotton gave way to a cornfield. Caleb appeared. The lightning flashed. Isaac pointed south and rode between the straight rows of the two fields. He reached the levee, turned east, and followed it to the neck of the peninsular of Davis Bend. There he waited for the guerillas to gather enough hands to fill their empty saddles and for Caleb to catch up. Caleb arrived first. Minutes later, the guerillas rode past. He could not see them, but, from their hiding place in the trees, Isaac heard the raiders and victims' thirteen horses above the sound of the rain.

Isaac and Caleb followed without talking. Isaac slowed with the next lightning strike to study tracks left by the guerillas. He realized he would have to stay close because the heavy rain obliterated the tracks in a matter of minutes. He thought, *that'll increase the risk of being seen. All I can do, Lord, is ask you to stop the rain or maybe have less rain fall.*

Isaac and Caleb rode in single file to lessen the likelihood of being discovered if a guerilla glanced back when the lightning flashed. He held his horse at a trot. Without a bridle or bit, Isaac used his hands to squeeze, push, or pull his horse's mane or throat each time he gave a voice command. He was pleased that the horse learned his pattern of commands quickly.

When the guerillas stopped for a break, Isaac and Caleb waited in the trees at the edge of the road. After ten miles they encountered only light rain. Isaac let the guerillas slip out of sight and followed the road, watching for trails or ambush sites. At trails and road junctions, he would dismount to ascertain which direction the guerillas took.

They arrived at the Duke farm about ten o'clock on Monday morning. They used vines to hobble the front and back legs of each horse. Isaac and Caleb crawled to separate vantage points and waited.

They watched the goings and comings all day. They had neither food nor drink, but remained at their posts.

At first dark, they crawled back to their horses and departed for Davis Bend. They stopped at Hamer Bayou to allow their horses to drink. Then, one by one, they dismounted and drank. It was almost noon on Tuesday when they arrived at the Bend and slid from their horses and fell to the ground in front of the Sixty-fourth Regiment's headquarters.

Isaac and Caleb reported on their reconnaissance. The white officers called them fools for endangering their lives and displayed no further interest. Isaac was amazed to learn that the regiment had received orders to depart from Davis Bend in a few days at the beginning of October, leaving behind only half-dozen men as a guard detail. He also discovered that the regiment was not authorized to conduct a raid, even with knowledge of where the guerillas' trail led.

A sergeant saw that they were fed. After they rested, the sergeant called Isaac aside. "Son, are you sure you're eighteen?"

"Yessuh. I turned eighteen in April. Caleb is nineteen."

"Yes. I can see Caleb's age. But your face says you're fifteen or, at best, sixteen."

Isaac shrugged. "That's what all the army people say every time I try to join."

"All right. I believe you. It seems you already have some skills a good soldier needs."

"Thank you."

"So what're you going to do now?"

"I can't leave my friend, Saul, in the hands of dem damn guerillas. Besides, he's my girlfriend's sister's fiancé. But, I've made no plans. I was countin' on the Sixty-fourth."

The sergeant grimaced. "Well, I was hoping you'd want to rescue your friend. Listen, I need you to keep this quiet. Next month, after the regiment leaves, I'm staying on for a while. I need your word that no one, not even your girlfriend, will hear our plan – except, of course, Caleb. If word gets back to my commander, my goose is cooked. Agreed?"

Isaac looked into the man's eyes. "Agreed."

"Okay. Here's what we do. You draw a map of the route and a diagram of the farm with all of its buildings. Show especially, hills and streams around the farm. You can sit over there with Caleb and use his memory to enhance your drawing."

"Now?"

"Yes, now. I need you to get it on paper before you forget the details."

"But, I need to let Mr. Montgomery know where I am. I'm already a day and a half overdue."

"Son, I like your ethic. You leave Mr. Montgomery to me. I'll go see him while you draw your map. I'm going to borrow you from Mr. Montgomery for a special mission." The sergeant winked.

Isaac smiled. "Yessuh. I'm ready to start."

"Good." He slapped Isaac's knee. "You told me who you are. By the way, I'm Sergeant Charles DeFaux from Vidalia, Louisiana."

"Hey, that's where Saul is from!"

"Now you know we gotta go get my homey!"

* * *

By the time Isaac and Caleb finished their route map and diagram, Sergeant DeFaux had returned from his visit with Ben Montgomery. He looked at their rendition.

"Good job. Now we'll find a similar spot and buildings and starting training for our rescue mission."

Isaac and Caleb looked at each other. Isaac asked, "Now?"

"Yes. Now is the absolute best time. We can't wait for the prisoners to be moved or disappear. Besides, next week we'll have us a full moon. We need to go this week under a rustler's moon. We'll leave Friday morning, do the rescue that night, and be back here for the ball game on Saturday."

Isaac and Caleb looked at each other again. Caleb's jaw dropped and Isaac's eyes brightened. "Then, we won't have to explain Saul's absence to Rebecca. She only sees him on the weekend."

Sergeant DeFaux punched his palm with a fist. "That's real good. Okay. I know a farm down at Togo that may be just the place we need for training. You can ride government horses. Let's move."

264

They answered in unison. "Yessuh."

* * *

At the start of training, Sergeant DeFaux declared. "I brought along two o' my homies, who I can trust. With surprise on our side and spare horses, I figure we can pull this thing off with five focused guys."

On Tuesday afternoon, they walked through the approach and assault at the Togo farm. They learned each other's assignments and positions following the diagram of the target farm. Next came signals and weapons training on Wednesday for Isaac and Caleb. Wednesday and Thursday nights, they practiced the assault several times with Sergeant DeFaux introducing unexpected responses each time from the guerillas or changing the number of guerillas present.

They departed at dawn on Friday, all of them wearing black civilian clothes. By first dark, each man was in his assigned position in the woods north of Duke's farm and waiting for Sergeant DeFaux's signal. There was a ridge between them and their thirteen horses. Isaac waited and watched. The soldier he was paired with checked his carbine and thumbed its safety to the on position. Isaac did the same. He glanced at Caleb and the other soldier about forty yards to his right. They watched as Billy Duke and his brother, George, provided rations to the prisoners. Then they barred the door, locking the prisoners in the corn crib as Isaac and Caleb had observed on Monday night.

Finally, an hour later, Sergeant DeFaux raised and dropped a white bandanna. Each team acknowledged the gesture by waving a white bandana once. Caleb's team advanced toward the corn crib and stopped at a covering position. Isaac and his partner leapfrogged Caleb's team while they provided cover. Sergeant DeFaux repositioned himself and watched for the arrival of any third party. The teams maneuvered until, as planned, Isaac and his partner arrived at the corn crib. They waited in silence, listening to the prisoners inside. They awaited Sergeant DeFaux's diversion.

Sergeant DeFaux opened the corral and chased out mules and horses by hitting several on their romps with a tree branch. The animals stampeded.

Isaac and his partner sprang into action. Isaac whispered to Saul. "Be quiet. It's me, Isaac. Tell your comrades. When the door opens, follow me."

Saul sounded jubilant. He whispered back, "Sweet Jesus! Okay! Okay!"

Isaac and his partner lifted the four-by-eight beam barring the door. Six men ran out behind Saul. Isaac led them to the woods at double-quick time on a course that kept the corn crib between them and the Duke's house. His partner brought up the rear.

They passed Caleb's team who remained in place to cover their exit. Sergeant DeFaux sent the horses and mules south toward the road and past the house. Then DeFaux ran north past Caleb.

The rear door of the farmhouse was flung open. Billy and George frantically waved their arms, trying to stop the stampeding animals. An old man appeared in the doorway. The brothers succeeded in frightening the animals more. The horses and mules raced south down the road toward Carpenter, leaving the Dukes cursing and waving their fists.

They were all mounted when Caleb's team crossed the ridge to join the main body.

Sergeant DeFaux turned to Isaac. "Okay, you and Caleb take the point. Me and my homies will cover the rear...." DeFaux looked about. He hissed, "Wait a minute! Where the fuck is the other man?"

Isaac was stunned. He had not noticed that one horse was riderless. He muttered, "Oh no. Saul, where is he?"

"Willie said he was ascared he'd get shot. He stayed in the corn crib."

Sergeant DeFaux hissed again. "Dammit! You should have told Isaac that he wanted to stay behind – the Dukes will know who hit'em. They'll come looking for Isaac. "

Saul was wide-eyed. "How will they know?"

"You ever hear of torture?"

Saul stammered, "I-I-Is it too late to g-go back and get Willie?"

"You're damned right! We've been here far too long already. Let's ride!"

Chapter 19: The Avengers Strike Back

A soldier stood on the steps of their cabin. John called Rachel. She left her hot supper dish of bacon, collards, and cornbread. Standing in the door, she folded her arms under her breasts against the chill of the first Tuesday evening in December 1865.

"Good evening, I'm Rachel. How can I help you?"

The soldier thrust a folded handbill toward her. "Good evening, ma'm. I was instructed to give this to you."

Rachel took the handbill. "Thank you." She quickly closed the door and hurried back to her supper. She laid the handbill beside her plate.

Ruth spoke while chewing. "Rai, what does it say?"

Rebecca burped. "Yeah. What's it about?"

Rachel did not answer, but said, "Hmmm! Bec, your cooking is the best!" She pushed the handbill across the table to Ruth and lifted another forkful of collards to her mouth.

"Uh-oh!" Ruth put one hand on her chest and pushed the handbill back to Rachel.

Rebecca raced around the table to have a look at the paper. "Ruth, what is it?"

"I can't read very well. But I do know the word Caleb. His name is on that paper!"

Curious, Rachel picked it up. She screamed. "Oh, Lawd, no!"

> **Wanted: <u>Dead</u> or Live. Two Dangerous Thievin Agitatin Niggers at Davis Bend.**
>   **Isaac and Caleb**
>   **Reward: $100 United States Money**
>   **Attorney & Deputy Sheriff Henry Carter, Utica, Hinds County, Mississippi**
>   Dear Rachel, pleas let Isaac & Caleb kno soons you see this.
>   Your friend, Chas. DeFaux.

Twice, Rachel read the handbill aloud. John and the three women ate no more. They all talked at the same time. Standing, John tapped on the table with his fork.

John stared at the back of the handbill in Rachel's hand. "This Attorney Carter and his boys are smart, very smart. They just hired an army of poor people who will do whatever it takes to get that reward money. Legions will be after our boys." John paused. The quiet was palpable. He continued, "They'll have no chance. Unless...."

Rachel's fear was high. When she saw the look on her father's face, her mind went back to her memory of his face the day her mother was sold away. Now we're free to do, but not free *from* fear and terror. Oh, Lawd, my aching head....

John sat down hard. "Ladies, our first 'sponsibility is jes like DeFaux said. We must warn Isaac and Caleb. I think we'd best git that done before half an hour passes."

Rachel concluded that the whole matter meant Isaac was leaving her inside twenty-four hours. Her tears were silent and her voice trembled. She wanted to say it before John had to tell her. "Pa, Isaac and Caleb must run. They must run tonight, and run far. I'm assuming since DeFaux sent this handbill all the way from Natchez, they must have them spread far and wide."

Ruth began wailing. Rebecca positioned herself between Rachel and Ruth and hugged both of them.

John nodded solemnly. "Rai, you're right on all counts. We'd better get moving."

Rebecca wanted to know, "Pa, who's going to tell'em?"

John stood. "We all are. We can say our good-byes over there at Hurricane."

Ruth screamed. "No!"

Rachel sobbed. Though she knew better, she declared, "I'm goin' with'em!"

John pursed his lips and dropped his head. After a pause, he said, "Rai, I know you want to go." He paused again. "But Isaac will be in more danger trying to protect you. And, he won't be able to travel nearly as fast as I expect he'll need to. I'm sorry, Rai. I know you know this is true."

With tears streaming, Rachel nodded. She was glad he did not say he would not permit her to go unmarried. In that moment, she treasured John even more. She managed to say, "I do."

Rebecca brought them back. "Pa, I think you should tell them, you know, for clarity. It'll be all my sisters can do to bid them farewell."

On hearing that Rebecca regarded her as a sister, Ruth wailed louder. The three women clung closer, entwined in each other's arms.

John nodded. "Okay. I can't read the handbill, but I'll never forget what it said. All right, quickly gather anything you think they'll need while on the run."

In a quavering voice and with halting breath, Rachel pointed to the floor under the table. "Pa, please give Isaac my ol' Colt .44 revolver. I hid it under that board. Be careful. It's loaded."

"But it was a gift from Jerome...."

She shook her head. "I can't keep it when Isaac may need it more'n me."

* * *

Rachel and Ruth sometimes ran a few steps to keep pace with the taller John and Rebecca as they hurried to find Isaac and Caleb. Rachel carried the bacon and cornbread from their supper. When they arrived, Rachel waited on the road with her sisters while John entered a cabin at Hurricane occupied by single young men. Momentarily, John emerged with Isaac, Caleb, and Eight Ball. He gave them the handbill, which Rachel knew they could not read, especially in the dark.

Immediately, Isaac started toward Rachel. She held her breath. John caught Isaac's arm and pulled him back for more words. She saw Isaac nod. Then he ran to her and lifted her in his arms. Rachel was surprised by his tight squeeze. He held her aloft with her buttocks resting on his forearms. Now she was taller than he. She felt her heart beat accelerate and her hands tremble. They did not speak.

She gently cradled his head against her breasts. Rachel closed her eyes and savored his scent.

After several minutes, Isaac slowly lowered her. When her feet touched the ground, Rachel looked about for John. Not finding him, she stood on her toes and pulled Isaac's face to her. She planted a long and passionate kiss on his mouth, caressing his tongue with hers. She caught her breath and saw Ruth in a close embrace with Caleb. She laid her head against Isaac. Her tears flowed and wet his shirt in the middle of his chest.

Rachel saw John approaching with a young man in tow. She was alarmed that another person would know of Isaac and Caleb's flight.

John wasted no time. He cleared his throat and Caleb released Ruth. John announced, "I looked for Mr. Ben, but he is away. Fellows, I know you've met Mr. Ben's son, Isaiah. Ladies, this is Isaiah Montgomery. Yes, he's the same age as Isaac. Isaiah these are my daughters."

Rachel turned her attention from her father to Ruth. She saw Ruth's sad face brighten with a huge smile for a moment.

John continued. "On our way over here, I had an idea about how you fellows might git away from the Bend without witnesses. That's why I went to find Mr. Ben. Instead, I found Isaiah. He's okay with the basic idea, which is to git you off the Bend by steamboat tomorrow. Isaiah says a boat bound for St. Louis is due here around noon from Natchez. He's agreed to git his mother to pay your fare – and he's very happy to git Eight Ball."

A chorus of thanks went up, followed by hugs.

Then Rachel saw a problem. "Pa, if we don't want Bend people or passengers to witness their departure, we need some kind of disguise – like dresses and bonnets."

Isaac smiled and said, "Hmmm. Great idea. We surely don't want to create anymore Willie's. But where can we get dresses that will fit by tomorrow?"

Isaiah said, "I'll fetch a couple of my mother's dresses. She's taller than you ladies. But still, they won't exactly fit."

Rebecca was bouncing on her toes. "If you can get'em to me tonight, I can alter'em and make'em fit by morning. It may take all night, but I think I can do it."

"You'll have them within the hour."

Caleb wanted to know, "How will you know they'll fit?"

"Oh, I need to measure, don't I?"

Rachel looked from Isaac to Caleb to John. "No, you don't. We can fit'em to Pa. They're all about the same size."

Rebecca clasped her hands together. "Great! We have a plan! What do you think, Pa?"

"It sounds good to me."

Isaac waved a hand. "Hold up a minute. If Sergeant DeFaux was here, he'd add a diversion."

Rachel looked up at Isaac. The smile under her wet cheeks displayed her pride.

Isaac continued. "I think it would help us gain time if we send the guerillas off on a wild goose chase. So I suggest y'all spread the word early in the morning about the handbill. Then, add, 'You shoulda seed'em hightail it outta here last night on two hosses 'round midnight. They say they headed for Natchez.'"

Isaiah laughed. "That'll work for sure. Isaac, you and Caleb get your things and com'on and spend the night with me and my brother. Com'on Eight Ball."

They answered in unison. "Thank you."

John smiled and added, "I like it. Isaac, we'll spread the word. All right, you lovebirds. Rebecca and I will wait for you over there by that big tree for a few minutes and then walk you ladies home."

* * *

Wednesday at noon, five well-armed horsemen arrived in front of the Freedmen's School. For a time, they sat their horses. Rachel and two white teachers could not keep the children from the windows.

With swollen and red eyes, Rachel called the headmistress aside. "If those men are looking for me, tell'em I'm in the lady's outhouse." She did not wait for a response. She ran out the rear door.

Inside the outhouse, Rachel prayed that the riverboat would arrive on time. Minutes later, she heard the steam whistle announcing its arrival. She gave thanks. "Now, God, please let them leave soon, very soon...."

Her prayer was interrupted by a man's voice outside. "All right. Time for you come on outta there."

"Yes, sir."

She walked out and without looking at the men, washed her hands in the basin on the shelf on the exterior wall.

"Is your name Rachel?"

"Yes, sir."

"Look at me when I speak to you."

Rachel turned slowly to face the men. She thought, *these are the guerillas*. She said several times to herself, I will not let them see me cry. She held her chin up.

"Now, you're gonna to tell me what I wanna know."

"Yes, sir."

A second man spoke. "Hey Billy, I'm sho' glad you made her turn around. She sho' is a purtty lil' thang!"

Billy glanced at the man to his right. "Grady, shut up."

Grady laughed. "You know I speak the truth. My eyes are good – real good."

Billy ignored Grady. "So, Rachel, my friend Willie told me you're friends with a dangerous nigger outlaw we looking for."

Upon hearing the name Willie, Rachel flinched, and knew these were the guerillas. She stood frozen to her tracks and remained silent.

"Are you Isaac's woman?"

"Yes, sir."

"Well now, ol' Willie was right again. So, tell me, where is Isaac?"

Rachel decided to make Billy ask more questions and give the riverboat time to depart. "Isaac went away."

"Where did he go?"

She looked Billy straight in the eye and lied without blinking. "Natchez."

Grady said, "That matches what ol' Willie found out all right enough."

Billy slapped his saddle horn. "Dammit!"

"What, Billy?"

Billy ignored Grady. "When did he leave?"

"Last night."

"What time last night?"

"Oh, must've been a little before midnight."

Billy shifted in his saddle and pushed the brim of his hat back. A blond bang fell onto his brow. He turned to Grady and glanced at the other riders. He said to no one in particular, "There's no way in hell we can catch'im before he reaches Natchez. Once in the city, we'll never find him."

Rachel exhaled with this scrap of good news. She tried to control the motion of her chest to hide her reaction. Then she thought, *oh, good. They didn't notice.*

Billy turned back to Rachel. "Is this Caleb fella traveling with him?"

"Yes, sir."

Rachel thought Billy smiled when he asked, "So, Rachel, when's he coming back to see you?"

Rachel felt her heart beat faster. "He ain't comin' back."

Billy frowned and leaned down on his saddle horn. "Now why is that?"

"He saw a handbill that put a price on his head."

"Dammit!"

Grady appeared triumphant. "See. I told you to b'lieve in ol' Willie. We could a jes dragged ol' Willie 'long and made him find this Isaac fellow. We didn't need no stinkin' handbills. You and Captain Carter made a big mistake this time."

"Yeah. I guess we didn't count on niggers gettin' the handbill."

Rachel winced.

Grady spat. "So what we gonna do nigh?"

"Well, I don't rightly... Say, wait a minute. It stands to reason that sooner or later he's comin' back for his sweet thang. Ain't that right, Rachel?"

Rachel's eyes went wide. A shiver went down her spine and her hands began to perspire.

"Hey, Billy. I think you're on to somethin'."

"Yeah, I'ma take lil' Miss Rachel home wid me for a spell. We'll figure a way to use this lil' honey to draw in a fly named Isaac."

"Well, I don't wanna put you to any trouble. I'll be happy to keep her fer you." Grady laughed, showing brown teeth.

While they bantered, Rachel ran for the back door of the school as fast as her legs could take her. She skipped through the door and closed it. Then she realized there was no way to lock the front or rear doors from the inside.

Billy kicked the door open with a crash. The children screamed and ran to a far corner. The headmistress sputtered, "W-why, young m-man, w-what's the meaning of this outrage?"

Grady appeared in the front door, thumbs in his gunbelt.

Billy looked around the room. "We didn't come to burn down your fine nigger school – this time. We've only come for Rachel. We'll be gone in a few minutes and y'all can get on back to your lessons."

Rachel stood silent in the middle of the room. She thought, *I will not cry.*

Billy walked to her. "Comin'?"

Rachel kicked him in both shins and ran out the rear door. A horseman chased her down the path toward the corral and lassoed her. She fell backward and was dragged to the school.

Billy picked her up and slapped one cheek hard with the palm of his hand and the other cheek with the back of his hand. It hurt her face, but she thought it hurt more inside than outside to be powerless. "Now I want you to understand your place is to obey. Do you?"

Rachel was silent. Billy hit her jaw with his fist. She saw stars, felt dizzy, and fell in the yard where the children played. She spat blood. Rachel looked up and saw two Billys. She shook her head twice. Now she saw a single fuzzy Billy. In the distance, she heard three long blasts on a steam whistle. Rachel rolled over on her side, smiled, and whispered, "Thanks, God. Thank you. I will not cry. I will not cry."

The headmistress was yelling at Billy. "Stop it, you cad! Heathen! You stop it this instance!"

Billy ignored her and yanked Rachel upright. The lasso pinning her arms to her body fell to the ground. She immediately shoved her small fist into Billy's nose. Startled, Billy staggered a step back. Embarrassed in front of his men, Billy stepped forward to hit Rachel again.

Grady caught his arm. "Hey, Billy, this ain't a fair fight. You'll kill her. Besides, like you always say, 'Stay focused on business.'"

Billy took a deep breath. "Okay. I guess I lost my head. All right. Tie her hands and lash her to my saddle. I'll take a horse from the corral."

When they rode away with Rachel in tow, the headmistress was still protesting.

* * *

Thursday, Rachel went to work in a corn field pulling fodder with three men and two women, who, like her, had been re-enslaved. By noon, her hands bled. A woman fetched a shirt large enough to have sleeves that hung over Rachel's hands. She used the sleeves as gloves.

After supper, Billy came to the corn crib with a revolver in hand and dragged Rachel out kicking and flailing with her fists. She did not cry out. Her coworkers, especially the women, sucked their teeth and made other sounds of disgust. The men cursed under their breath. In the darkness, he took her inside the outermost of two cabins used by the Dukes before the war to house their enslaved hands.

Billy pulled Rachel and held her close to his chest. "Okay, Rachel, me and you are gonna have a little fun."

"No, we ain't." She punched him in the temple.

"Okay. Have it your way." Billy hit her chin with his fist. Rachel fell to the floor,

In excruciating pain, Rachel regained consciousness to find herself lying on her back with her hands tied behind her body and pushed to one side. The agonizing pain, like many needle sticks at once, was in her vagina. She twisted and turned but could not remove

276

Billy from between her thighs. Her anger made her head throb. She cleared her throat and spat into his right eye. He hit her again with his fist.

When she regained consciousness the second time, Billy was dumping her onto the floor of the corn crib, her hands untied. He threw her pantaloons in after her. After he was gone, she wept loud bitter angry tears. She tried to rip her dress, hoping to make a noose.

A hand caught her arm. It was the woman who gave her the large shirt. "Come here, honey." The voice sounded like her mother's. The woman sat on the floor beside Rachel and cradled her head in her lap. Rachel continued to sob. Her body shook with rage. The woman gently stroked Rachel's hair at her temple. She cried for a long time.

Rachel's voice was hoarse and weak. Her first words were. "Please give me water."

The woman with the voice like Edna's spoke. "Here, honey. I already fetched it for you."

Rachel drank. She handed the cup back. "Please give me more."

The woman turned her head toward their fellow inmates. "You mens face the wall. Don't look nowheres else till I tell you. Okay, honey, you scoot this way, in front of me. Now, move your dress aside so it won't get wet. Before I give you this water, you got to promise me you won't rub too hard."

"Oh, my God! How did you know what I wanted to do?"

"Oh, chile. I've been where you are." This time the woman's voice sounded sad.

"I must rub hard to wash away the filthy fiend that violated me." Rachel cried again.

The woman held her hand. "You will try. But you can't. You'll have to pray and overcome dis awful deed in your mind. I'll not tell you to forget it. 'Cause, I know you can't, nor should you. But you'll need to learn to live with it in its proper place in your head. You'll have to put it there. Then you'll see. Things'll be all right again."

Rachel thought, *I have heard the truth. But I don't like it.* In a whisper, she said to the woman, "I'll try not to rub too hard."

* * *

At three o'clock on Friday morning, it began raining. The corn crib door opened. Rachel slept beside her benefactor. A woman's voice whispered from the doorway. "Rachel."

Rachel's benefactor whispered back. "She's asleep."

"My brother and I have come to take her away."

"Lady, ain't you white."

"Yes. You'll have to trust me."

"No, I don't. Rachel is the one who'll have to trust you – or not. But, for me, I trust no white person – never have, never will."

Now Rachel sat up. "Who are you?"

"I'm a friend. Grady told me you were here. He was afraid of what might happen to you."

"Well, ma'm, you're too damn late. What I need now is a gun and two bullets – one for him and one for me."

"Oh, no. I'm so sorry, so very sorry. But we can't talk now. We need to go."

"Go where?"

"Me and my brother will take you to Natchez."

Rachel's head hurt. She said Natchez. Grady told her. Why? I don't know a soul in Natchez. I want to go home. If I return to the Bend, that son of a dog Billy will find me again. I can't go home and I surely can't stay here. God, it looks like I should go. Did you send her?

"Rachel, are you coming?"

"Wait. I'm thinking." God, I'm going. Please come with me. "Okay. I'm coming."

Rachel kissed her benefactor. "What's your name?"

"Ebony."

Rachel squeezed Ebony's hand. "Ebony, thank you so much for taking care of me."

"We will pray for you, chile."

Her coworkers said, "Amen. Fare thee well."

Chapter 20: Ciudad Chihuahua

By candle lamp, Alejandra wrote:

Wednesday, October 10, 1866. Dear Diary, Big news! My old schoolmate, Laylita, got married last Saturday. Yes, I saw Carlos at the wedding. He's still nice to me. More news: Ernesto is home until January. He and my schoolmate, Linda, announced their engagement. My eighteenth birthday is tomorrow. (I guess you knew that.) Last news: In the morning, I'm going to Ciudad Chihuahua with Mama to buy eyeglasses for her. It took two years, but we've finally saved enough money. No word from Papa since last month. That damn Torres is still hounding me and now he's harassing Carlos.

At sunrise on Thursday, Alejandra and Rocio walked to the El Paso-Chihuahua Road and met the freight master who had agreed to allow passage on one of his wagons. Alejandra's heart beat faster in anticipation of leaving Carrizal for the first time. She had heard Papa and Ernesto speak of the freight trains, but had not seen one up close. This train consisted of six large dark green freight wagons with red wheels. Alejandra marveled that the rear wheel stood taller than her, much larger than ones she saw on farm wagons. Each wagon had sides six feet tall covered by white canvas over arch-shaped ribs above the body and was pulled by eight burly oxen. A forty-gallon hoop barrel of water, lashed securely, rested on small platforms attached on both sides of the wagons.

A teamster helped Rocio climb the iron tie rods that held the tailgate of their wagon in place. Alejandra scampered up and into the wagon unassisted and sat beside Rocio on a sack of grain.

* * *

She had read a name carved into the tailgate on her way up. To the teamster standing on the ground, she asked, "Who is Hiram Young?"

"Oh, he's the black man whose company built our wagons up there in Missouri."

Alejandra and Rocio exchanged approving looks. They removed their bedrolls and gunnysacks from their backs and settled in for the ride. They rode facing the wagon traveling behind them.

Several miles south of Carrizal, Alejandra exclaimed, "Mama, I never knew there was so much sand and rocks this close to us!"

Rocio smiled. "The trail to my grandma's village near Casa Grande looks the same as this road. I'm so glad you're coming with me. Together, we can see the road traveled by your papa and brother."

Alejandra smiled, breathed deeply, and savored the crisp morning air. "Oh, I want to remember the details of this great adventure for a long time to come."

"Speaking of the coming time, most of your friends are married. I don't mean to push you, but I haven't heard you talk about the subject. I can see that for some reason you dislike Torres. But are you serious about Carlos?"

Alejandra sighed and swayed her head and shoulders from side to side. "Oh, Mama, do we have to talk about that now?"

Rocio smiled and spoke gently to her daughter. "Well, no, not exactly. But can you suggest a better time than when we're not pressured to get chores of the day done?"

"Okay. I bet you're thinking, She's eighteen now and one of the last of her schoolmates who's not married. Isn't that so?"

"Si, this is so. It is also true that a mother always wishes and hopes for a better life for her children than she has had. I am no different. Even so, I do not wish to interfere in your life. Though I have not said this to you before, for some time now, I've seen you as a grown woman. For the past year, I've tried to treat you like the friend I hope you will be to me in the years ahead."

Alejandra blinked back tears. She moved the bedrolls and gunnysacks aside, snuggled closer, and held Rocio's hand. "Mama, Laylita and Linda are my good friends. But, you are my best friend in the world."

"Gracias."

"Of course, you're right. The time we will have on this trip may be like no other we will have in our lives."

Rocio nodded.

"Mama, in time I want to marry and raise a family like you."

Rocio smiled and squeezed Alejandra's hand.

"But, Mama, in Carrizal I have not seen the man I want to spend my life with."

Rocio shifted about on her sack of grain. Alejandra studied Rocio's face. At length, Rocio spoke.

"What about Carlos?"

"Mama, I think he is a nice boy. But I don't think he's a person who will overcome the problems I have seen you and Papa solve time and again. He's too..., he's too soft, not resolute; too wishy washy. Do you know what I mean?"

Rocio nodded. "Yes, I see..." Her voice trailed off. She took another breath. "What about Torres?"

Alejandra shook her head and made her hair fly. "Never!"

"Why?"

"Mama, can't you see he's a scoundrel?"

"I see him when I work at the hacienda. He seems normal and it looks like he would be a good provider. What made you decide he's a scoundrel?"

"Mama, remember that night we left the spring festival early? Well, I asked you to take me home because I felt he was undressing me with his eyes. Ugh! He makes my skin crawl. Since then, he has done the same bad trick in the daytime right there in the village square. With that damned smirk on his face, he wants me to know he lusts for my body. Besides, I have it on good authority that Torres regularly sleeps alternately with the widows Durazno and Blanco."

Rocio nodded. "Hmm, I see... I felt you had good reason." Rocio was quiet for a time. "Allie, this is a dilemma. Are there other boys around that interest you?"

"Mama, I looked at every festival. No."

Rocio sighed. "Well, as you know, it is not practical to have a courtship with a boy from another village. That leaves reconciling your objections against Carlos or Torres."

Alejandra turned her face of incredulity to her mother. "Mama!"

Rocio ignored Alejandra. "Allie, you're so much smarter than Carlos or Torres. You can make this work for you."

"Mama!"

* * *

For their midday meal, they ate some of the machitos Rocio made before dawn from refried frijoles and blue maize tortillas. They finished the last of the machitos at supper time when the train stopped for the night near the village of Moctezurna. Early Friday morning, they ate beef jerky, dried purple prickly-pear fruit, and dried prickly-pear pads cut into strips like string beans. Both Rocio and Alejandra carried a supply of these foods in their gunnysacks.

They arrived on the shores of Laguna Encillias on Friday before sunset and the oxen were at last turned loose to graze. They ate supper beside the lake as Rocio answered Alejandra's questions about married life and how Rocio decided Papa was the man for her.

"Mama, are you thirty nine?"

"Si."

"How old were you when you married Papa?"

"Seventeen."

On Sunday, their fourth day on the road, they traveled a shorter distance. While the oxen grazed, the teamsters performed day-four road maintenance. That was when Alejandra learned that the short log that hung from the tail of each wagon was used under the axle while a wheel was removed. While a wheel was off, she assisted the teamster on their wagon in applying fresh grease and tar to the axle.

When they were done, Alejandra announced with her hands outstretched, "Look, Mama. I didn't get any on my clothes!"

Rocio smiled and applauded.

Tuesday, they arrived in Ciudad Chihuahua and spent the night in the travelers' inn with people going south to Delicias. By noon the next day, after four hours waiting their turn with the physician, they learned that Rocio's vision could be corrected with glasses, but they did not have enough money. Dejected, Alejandra sat beside Rocio on a bench by the busy street outside the doctor's office. They said nothing. With her face in her hands and elbows on her knees, Alejandra watched rich women in bonnets and holding parasols on the same wooden sidewalks with poor women wearing sombreros. She considered her sombrero decorated with worn green, white, and red ribbons. She thought, *which were the new rich? She wondered how they got their money. Had they compromised their principles for a comfortable life? Were the poor women people of uncommon virtue? No, it couldn't be that simple. She decided nether could be true of all the women she saw....*

Across the street, a crash of broken glass interrupted her thoughts. Alejandra looked up and saw a chair sail over the sidewalk from the saloon and land in the street. Then, two men with fists flying tumbled through the saloon's open doorway and onto the walk. More men followed, cursing loudly about cheating at cards. Women and children ran in all directions. Alejandra sat dumbfounded. When the first shot rang out, the street was already cleared of bystanders – except for Alejandra and Rocio. Before the sound of the second shot, Rocio grabbed Alejandra's arm and together they ran for the corner of the frame building and turned into an alley.

As they rounded the corner, Alejandra felt something tug at her boot. In the alley, she saw that a bullet had nicked the edge of the heel on her left boot. "Oh, my God. Look, Mama!"

"It's okay. I think it's over, now."

After the seventh shot, all was quiet for a few seconds. A man shouted, "Okay, men. Let's get these two over to the doc's place." Murmuring preceded louder talk. Only then did Alejandra and Rocio venture back to retrieve their sacks and bedrolls.

The gray-bearded doctor was in his doorway with a white apron over his pot stomach when the first victim was carried past him. He stared at the victim and then glanced up and down the street. Alejandra thought he was looking at them when he called out, "You senoritas, please come here." She thought, *he can't mean us.*

Before she could look for who the doctor could possibly mean, he called again, this time in an urgent voice, and beckoned. "Please come here. I need your help."

Alejandra was stupefied. "Do you mean us?" She pointed to herself, then Rocio.

"Yes. Please."

Inside, one victim was placed on a table, the other on a cot. They were bleeding profusely. Rocio looked away. The men who brought them in had disappeared. The doctor pointed. "Put your stuff in the corner over there." Pointing first to Rocio, then a direction, he said, "Run to the store down the street that way and buy a jar of honey. Get it in a clay jar. If that is not available, buy it in a blue glass jar – but not clear glass."

Rocio nodded and ran from the office. Alejandra gazed at the man on the table. He was quiet, eyes closed. The man on the cot held his arm and writhed and groaned. The doctor got her attention. Pointing to a sink, he said, "Go wash your hands over there."

When she returned in less than a minute, the doctor had cut the shirt from the victim on the table and was working on the trousers. "Follow me to the sink and wash your hands again when I finish mine. My apprentice went home for dinner and siesta. I will need you to help me remove the bullets from these men."

"But, but I know nothing...."

The doctor hurried past her. "Never you mind that. You will know quite a lot by the time we finish.

"You are Alejandra, correct?"

"Yes, sir."

"Alejandra, put this apron on and stand between the instrument cabinet and the patient on the table."

* * *

By the time of their departure on a northbound freighter that Friday with money in their belts, Rocio declared for what Alejandra thought was the hundred-tenth time, "It's miracle! God is great! With these glasses, I can see everything."

Chapter 21: Irene and Charlotte

On Wednesday morning, Isaac and Caleb arrived at the landing an hour early. They went to the site of the destroyed Hurricane Plantation house and sat on a bench facing the river. Isaac held his head down and did not talk to Caleb. They remained away from people lest their voices betray them. Though they were clean-shaven for the first time, their heads and parts of their faces were covered with their usual ponchos. Mrs. Mary Montgomery, Isaiah's mother, told them men or women could wear the ponchos. They wore Miss Mary's dresses, which Rebecca had lengthened the previous night. Thus, their scuffed work boots were well hidden.

Isaac was still at Davis Bend and he already missed Rachel. He reminisced about their spring meeting and sitting together on Saturday and Sunday afternoons on these same grounds with other young people who were courting – including Caleb and Ruth. The spring was great and the summer of love was even better. He savored his memories.

In the distance came a single long blast of a steam whistle. Isaac's thoughts of Rachel were replaced by images of his times during the war aboard the *John Adams* and the *Benjamin Franklin*. Those memories led to an idea that made him sit up straight. He thought, *if we can do this, there will be no need to be jobless in the coming cold winter.* He wanted to discuss his idea immediately with Caleb. But they had agreed not to utter a word until they were inside their cabin aboard the riverboat.

Presently, the *John D. Perry* came into view between the east shore and Hurricane Island. The pilot was moving the two-hundred-twenty-foot by thirty-three-foot *Perry* slowly in the narrow channel toward the landing. Most of the larger riverboats would not stop at Davis Bend because they preferred the safer wider channel between Hurricane Island and the west bank. The *Perry's* white exterior gleamed in the sun. Her deck rails, cabin window trim, and the molding about her side paddle-wheel covers were all painted blue. The pilothouse was trimmed in red. She sported two large black smokestacks and two smaller black chimneys, fore and aft, vented smoke from the coal-fired heaters located in her long parlor. She was slowing her approach for a bow-in landing. Already, Isaac could see her split curved stairs leading from the main deck to the first-class cabins above her four boilers. She docked and her paddle wheels turned slowly to keep her snug against the pier.

They watched as roustabouts unloaded cargo down a wide gangplank and onto two waiting wagons pulled by mule teams. At the same time, other roustabouts loaded shipments from three wagons over an adjacent gangplank.

When all the passengers had boarded, they heard Isaiah call from the gangplank, "Auntie Irene and Auntie Charlotte, please come this way. I'll help you aboard and get you settled in your cabin."

Isaac and Caleb nodded. Isaac remembered to stand and walk with difficulty. When Caleb leapt up, forgetting he was an old woman, Isaac whacked him with his elbow. He saw Isaiah cover his mouth and laughter. Isaiah conducted them directly to their cabin on the texas deck where the colored passengers and the mostly colored crew resided on riverboats. To avoid people, theirs was the last cabin.

Irene and Charlotte whispered their thanks again and bade Isaiah farewell. Caleb hugged Eight Ball, and then sent him with Isaiah. Before Isaac closed the door, Caleb was unfastening his dress. They wore their work clothes underneath the dresses. While folding and packing the dresses, Isaac said, "Miss Mary would be happy to know we've taken the first step to keep our promise and donate her dresses to a church."

"That oughta be an easy enough thing tuh do. I spects it'll make me feel better to help someone, even in de time of our troubles."

"Humph. Helpin' others is what got us in tuh this mess."

Caleb's laugh was short and sounded rueful. "Even though this sit'ation throws a wrench into the works, I've no regrets. I'm sure oonah don't either."

After a sigh, Isaac said, "Yep. You're right. 'Twas our duty. And I know both o' us would do it again tomorrow, if there was need in our faces."

Caleb sat on his bunk. "Yeah. But the thing on my mind right now is when and how I can get back to Ruth."

"Hmm-huh. When I finally found a woman who can take my mind off Bianca, some white sonovabitch steps in and wrecks my good fortune. But, this time, we have a better chance to see Rai and Ruth again than I ever had to find Bianca.

"I've got an idea."

"I was 'fraid o' what would hatch in yo' head when we couldn't talk for over an hour. Okay. Com'on wid it, let's hear this scheme o' yours."

Isaac sat backwards on a ladderback chair, with his chin resting on the top slat. "Yep. Oonah right again. Here's my scheme, as oonah call it. Unlike my case with Bianca, our Rai and Ruth are within reach. We know where they are. All we need is to be able to get back to the Bend."

"Okay, Mr. Wanted Outlaw. I want oonah to remember this: I like my neck."

Isaac was impatient. "Yeah, yeah. So what we do is take a job stokin' on dis nice riverboat. We have a ride back to the Bend and de means to feed ourselves. Dat also puts a roof over our heads and bunks under our butts. I like a warm place in winter."

Caleb's eyes brightened. "Hey, I almost like it."

"What part don't oonah like?"

"I guess I don't like the part about getting hung."

"Chicken."

"Yep."

"Well, I admit de danger part may need a bit more work."

"I'll tell you what, when oonah can convince me that Rachel will approve that part, count me in. Why? 'Cause, I don't want Ruth decidin' her man is gone for good from her life. I definitely wanna go back. But...."

"And I don't wanna lose Rai, either. She's some woman!"

With an impish grin, Caleb shot back, "How do you know? She didn't give you any yet."

"Gettin' some is all oonah ever think about. I know you ain't got any either. Yet Ruth is leadin' you 'round like she put a ring and chain in oonah nose."

They laughed together and were silent for a moment. Caleb broke the silence. "If I have daughters, I gonna raise'em just like Mr. John is doin'."

"Yeah, me too. But I'm real glad some girls don't listen to their fathers like Rai and Ruth do."

"Amen, amen. Say, did oonah find out from Rachel what Mr. John's rules are on marriage?"

"Whoa! Oonah dat far along with Ruth?"

"Well, I admit the thought crossed my little mind. 'Cose, I neber mentioned it to her."

"I didn't ask, but Rai up and told me that Mr. John won't let dem marry until they're eighteen."

"We both know girls back home who're as young as fifteen gettin' married to guys twenty-something. How'd Mr. John pick that number?"

"Rai told me dat eighteen was her mother's age when her folks agreed to let her marry Mr. John."

"Oh. So, Rebecca and Saul can get hitched any day now."

"Yep." Isaac paused. "But I haven't figured out what happens after I marry Rai."

"Oh, damn, Homey. You're in serious trouble. But lucky you've got me for a friend. I'ma school ya rat nigh!"

Isaac laughed. "Oh, shut your face. This is serious." He got up from his chair and paced to the window. For a minute or two, he gazed at the naked oaks and green pines of Louisiana on the larboard side. Finally, he began detailing his plan.

"Mr. Caleb, smithin' is fine work. A smithin' man could make a livin' for his family. Stokin' is work for a single man. So that's out. Two years ago, I decided I wanted to be a soldier and fight for our freedom. Now, the war is over and I still want to be a soldier."

Caleb took a deep breath. "Why?"

"I have unspoken feelings about why. Since oonah my comrade and brother, here goes with what's in my head – and my heart. So, no laughing. I think soldiers – in particular, soldiers who are leaders – can make a difference in how dey're seen and how our people are seen. I feel drawn to dis important work dat I sense I can do – atter I learn to read. I b'lieve my commitment and service will bring me dignity, make me somebody, and pass honor to my family."

"Wait. Let me ask you about the seen part. Do you mean as our people are seen by white folks?"

"First, I mean as we see each oder in dis generation. Second, I mean as the next generation sees what we 'complish or leave undone. Third, I hope among those of us who will prove to some whites that we're far more'n what they've been taught – more'n many of them."

"Whoa! Whew! Dis is way too deep for me on an empty stomach."

Isaac fetched cups of water from the cargo deck. They ate Rebecca's bacon and cornbread. He especially savored Rebecca's unique cornbread, for many times, like this one, her recipe included chopped red and green peppers. They agreed to save Miss Mary's fried chicken for supper.

"Now, Isaac, what is it about a black soldier dat's going to make coloreds take notice?"

"I think coloreds will come to see our soldiers as inspiring and proud dignified men contributin' to the value of our race."

"Oonah mean *some* coloreds."

"Yes, oonah right. That's what I mean. Oh, and did I say soldiers wear smart uniforms, ride gov'ment horses, get paid regularly, and are fed and housed? A man could put away a bit o' cash and, maybe someday, own a lil' piece o' land."

"All that sounds good to me. Makes me wanna join up too. Well, except for the part about white folks."

"What about white folks?"

"My pa told me that his grandpa was snatched in Africa and brung here. Since before my pa's grandpa was dragged here in irons, white folks have believed we're less than they are. I've gotta tell ya, I don't expect that my grand younguns will see anything different in what white folks b'lieve from what my pa's grandpa saw."

"Oonah may be right. My hope is if a few can be persuaded in our generation, perhaps, a few more can be persuaded by our children and so on."

"Homey, I got my doubts. Furthermore, I think if we join up, we'll have to keep an eye out for what the army is asked to do."

"What oonah mean?"

"I mean, it ain't our army. It b'longs to white folks."

Isaac nodded and fell silent. He went to the window again. It would be night soon. The whistle sounded announcing the *Perry's* arrival in Vicksburg. The pitch of the engine changed and the paddle wheels slowed. Isaac removed his boots and lay on his bunk with fingers laced under his head as he stared at the ceiling.

Finally, he spoke. "So, do oonah think soldierin' is a thing we should leave to whites?"

"No. I've come a long way with oonah. I now believe, as you told me, it is our country too. However, given *their* history, a man must remain watchful and take care of his family and himself."

"Caleb, the problem is you speak the truth. The truth complicates my vision. The war is over. We are free men. But I still feel it is my duty to serve *my* country. I know white folks don't think it's mine, but I insist on making it mine."

"I can join you in that service." Caleb sang the next sentence. "Brother Isaac, my lil' sister, Irene, I say your vision and my caution go together like a hand in a glove."

They laughed together.

"Oonah know what? I'm glad oonah my friend."

On his bullhorn, the *Perry's* captain, Alex Zeigler, announced that the boat would remain overnight in Vicksburg due to the number of sunken wrecks in the river between them and Memphis. Isaac and Caleb decided that they'd be safer remaining aboard.

Caleb said, "I ain't lost a damn thing in Vicksburg. And just in case somebody here read that cussed handbill, I'm not taking the chance on losing my neck in Vicksburg."

Miss Mary's fried chicken, accompanied by apple betty biscuits, was the star attraction at supper. They ate in their cabin by the light of wall-mounted candles. Isaac ate so fast that he bit his lip twice. "What's the matter, Homey? Didn't you get enough meat for supper?"

"Okay, smart alec. Tell me. Do I ask Rai if she wants a soldier-husband before I join the army or do I join and then ask Mr. John for her hand?"

"Yes."

"Which?"

"Both. Either will work. I've seen Rachel cast her dreamy hero-worship eyes up at you. Oonah can do no wrong!"

Isaac was surprised to feel himself blush. "Be serious."

"Lookin' down the road aways, it may be best to ask her now if this is the life she will accept."

Isaac pondered for a minute. "Oh, I get it. Thanks."

"Welcome. Good night."

"Good night."

* * *

After passing Memphis, Isaac proposed a demonstration to Captain Zeigler. He accepted, but sent his first mate, Allen, to observe Isaac and Caleb's work for show in the boiler room. Allen declared in five minutes that both were first-class stokers. Then Isaac told him stories of the *John Adams* and the *Benjamin Franklin.*

Allen pushed his hat back as they left the boiler room. "Okay, fellows. I'm hiring you straightaway. You go on duty when we next depart from our home in St. Louis. I'm going up and tell Cap'n Alex right now."

In unison, they said. "Thank you, suh."

* * *

It was cold in St. Louis on Sunday morning, December 10, 1865. Isaac wore two shirts under his poncho as he made his way with Caleb to services at the First African Baptist Church on Fourteenth and Clark Streets. Once inside, his fingertips and earlobes felt better. He knew Caleb was warm when he walked to the front of the church on their first visit and joined with the choir singing the spiritual "Heaven." His rendition was followed by much applause and a demand that he sing all five verses again.

Heav'n, Heav'n
Ev'rybody talkin' 'bout Heav'n ain't goin' there
Heav'n, Heav'n
Goin' to shout all over God's Heaven

They donated Miss Mary's dresses after the service and waited to meet the pastor, the Rev. Emmanuel Cartwright.

Isaac went directly to his problem and request. "Suh, my name is Isaac. I can't read or write yet. Please, suh. I need oonah, I mean, you to hep me write a letter to my girl down at Davis Bend in Mississippi."

"Why, I'd be happy to help. You did say you didn't learn *yet*. Is that right?"

"Yes, suh."

"I'm happy to know you intend to learn. Perhaps later I can help you find a place to learn. In the meantime, let's get your words on paper and send them off to your girl. Can she read?"

"Oh, yes, suh. She's a teacher."

"Oh, my! Maybe she's all the help you'll need. Follow me to my residence and let's get started.

"Now, what about you, my singing friend?"

"Yes, suh. My name is Caleb. I need the same hep."

"Of course, I'll help you, too. And I would surely like to hear you sing again."

Isaac beamed. "Don't worry, Rev. I'll bring 'im back."

* * *

"There. All finished and ready for the post office. I'll put your letters with my outgoing mail for this week. It will be okay for your girlfriends to write to you here in care of me. I'll hold your letters until you return."

They responded in unison. "Thank you, suh."

* * *

The *Perry* departed from St. Louis the following day, bound for New Orleans. During the two weeks before Christmas, the *Perry* made two round-trips between New Orleans and Natchez. She stopped again at Natchez on her homebound voyage.

During that stop Isaac and Caleb went up to the texas deck to survey the crowds that always gathered to watch the riverboats arrive and depart. From the starboard rail, they observed the saloons and shops in Natchez's under-the-hill district. The main thoroughfare was clogged with pedestrians, wagons with mule teams, buggies, and stylish coaches drawn by fine horses.

Two young women climbing down from a buggy driven by a well dressed white man caught Isaac's eye at the far end of the street, over three hundred feet away. About to look away, he snapped his head back for another look because they were an unusual pair – one black, one white, and both young. The short black woman reminded him of Rachel. "Hey, Caleb. Lookit! There goes a woman who looks like Rachel."

"Where?"

Isaac pointed. "Yonder. They're going into that store with the red sign over the door. Damn, sho' looks like'er."

"Okay, if oonah say so. I can only make out two blurry people in dresses. I think maybe my sight is gettin' worse. But oonah can stop eye-ballin' dat woman rat nigh. 'Cause you know Rachel ain't nowhere's near Natchez."

Isaac made a heavy sigh. "Yeah. True. We'd best be gettin' on back to the boiler room." He thought, *my sweet Rachel is making me see her where she ain't. My Lawd.*

* * *

On Sunday, December 24, Isaac and Caleb returned to the First African Baptist Church. After services, Pastor Cartwright gave them a warm greeting. Then he told them, "Boys, I'm afraid I have bad news. Your letters, and some of mine, were aboard the *Calypso* when she sank week before last, right here in St. Louis. When I read about the tragedy in the *Daily Missouri Democrat*, I thought of how disappointed you would be. But come Let's write new letters. You can show me if you remember how to sign your names."

* * *

Isaac and Caleb attended church services twice in January and once in February. Each time, there was no mail for them. They sent new letters in both months – addressed as before to their beloved in care of: Mr. Isaiah T. Montgomery, Davis Bend, Mississippi. When there was no reply by Sunday, March 25, 1866, Isaac dictated a letter to Isaiah. Pastor Cartwright marked the envelope: personal for Mr. I.T. Montgomery.

The letter to Isaiah read in part:

Thank you for your kind help over the months of our exile.

Please help us to know if our previous letters have been delivered.

Signed: Aunt Irene and Aunt Charlotte ☺

When they returned on the third Sunday in April, they had a single letter – their first ever.

April 4, 1866

Dear Aunties,

I just learned, and regret to report, that Rachel, Ruth, Rebecca, and John left the Bend within days after your departure last Dec.

I was unable to learn where they went.

Your Nephew, ☺

Isaiah

* * *

Chapter 22: St. Louis

"James, what the hell's wrong!"

James Darby sat under a shady maple with his face in both hands, elbows on his drawn-up knees. He threw his crumpled one-page letter at Barry's feet. James looked out at the gentle curve of the brown Missouri River between the lush green of each bank. A stern-wheeler appeared from the direction of Sioux City, Iowa. The Fifth Michigan Cavalry Regiment had arrived at Fort Leavenworth, Kansas, in late June 1865. Pearl's letter was waiting for him.

Barry finished reading and tried to hand the letter back to James, who would not take it. "Ol' buddy, I'm sorry. Is there anything I can do?" Barry held the letter by his side.

"Yeah. Trash the damn letter and leave me the hell alone."

"Gee, don't be sore at me. I didn't mean anything."

James sighed. "You're right. I shouldn't take it out on you 'cause Pearl up and ran off with pudgy-ass Reverend Arthur Smyth."

"The letter only said Arthur. So, you know this new boyfriend – I mean husband."

James let his chin drop down further. "Yeah. We were all schoolmates."

"I'm sorry, ol' buddy."

"Hey, some women do such shit."

"Are you still going to Springfield?"

"Naw. After this, I don't wanna see my folks right now. Sorry. I'll have to introduce you to my sister some other time."

"Well, okay. Sure, yeah, some other time." Barry walked away with his head down.

* * *

On June 23, the Fifth Michigan was mustered out of the US Army. James had no civilian clothes and no place to go. Without enlisting, he stayed in the barracks occupied by troops of First Michigan – and ate with them. They were not mustered out. Everyday, he sat under the same maple where he last saw Barry. The war was over. He had been a soldier for four years.

He thought, *I haven't enough money to amount to anything. No woman. No obligations. No plans. Damn. Doing nothing is awfully boring. I could hit the dice. Naw, then I could go to zero. I've never won at dice or cards. Skills stink. Zero stinks worse. Better keep what money I have. The First is getting an assignment soon. I can't stay here. One day, some officer is going to ask what I'm doing here. Where to go? What to do?*

Aimlessly, he chewed a twig. He dropped the newspaper he had forgotten he was carrying. He picked the paper up and examined it as if he had not seen it before. On the front page, an article about the Freedman's Bureau in St. Louis caught his eye. He read the article twice, sat up straight, and read it again. Maybe, he thought, *just maybe I could do something there until I make a plan. Best leave Fort Leavenworth before they throw my ass out.*

On the first day of July, James booked passage aboard a riverboat, the *John D. Perry,* and headed downstream to St. Louis. At half-past eleven that Friday night, he answered a knock upon his cabin door aboard the *Perry.* The *Perry* had stopped alongside the *Mars*, another riverboat, which had hit a snag and sank to the level of her boiler deck. James joined the men of both vessels to transfer all of the *Mars* passengers and almost eight hundred sacks of grain to the *Perry.* He worked side by side with two young black men from the *Perry's* boiler room and others from her roustabout crew.

When the *Perry* was under way again, James sat alone on the *Perry's* texas deck under a half-moon. He thought, *I've made a bad decision. I'm no teacher – not even I would hire me to teach children, let alone newly freed colored adults. What do I know? I know soldiering. The country always needs soldiers. So what do I need? Respect. Damn you, Pearl. A little respect and a regular payday will do nicely for starters.* He looked down at the uniform he still wore, though he was no longer a soldier. He remembered the cheers from the crowds lining Pennsylvania Avenue in Washington just six weeks before. *This uniform gets respect. It got respect for Major Augusta. Even President Johnson and General Grant saluted when we marched by. Respect. So I'll be a soldier – again.* Using both hands, he slapped his thighs. He stood and announced to the empty chairs around him, "Resolved!"

* * *

Over a year later, on September 10, James stood on the front steps of the Headquarters, Division of the Missouri at Jefferson Barracks, not far from St. Louis, and held his salute for the oncoming officer. It did not matter to James that Benjamin Grierson wore his regular army rank of colonel on his uniform. James thought him deserving of his temporary Civil War rank of Major General of Volunteers. "Good morning, General Grierson, sir!"

Grierson broke his stride, hesitated, and then returned the salute. "Good morning, Sergeant."

Still standing at attention, James announced with a smile, "Sir, Sergeant James Darby, Butternut Guerillas, Sixth Illinois Cavalry, at your service."

Grierson's grin showed his teeth when he heard his old command mentioned. He put his bag down and grabbed James's hand with both of his and pumped it vigorously. "Sergeant Darby! What a pleasant surprise. How are you getting on after your wound at Wall's Bridge?"

"Sir, I am very well. How are you?"

Smiling broadly, Grierson put his hands on his hips and looked James up and down. "I too am quite well. How did you know I would be here this morning?"

Standing at ease now, James's gaze into Grierson's eyes was steady. "Sir, the short answer is I read your mail." James hurried on, "Sir, I work in General Hancock's office. I saw his invitation to you and your response." James retrieved Grierson's bag. "Sir, I'll be brief. I know you have little time. I would like to work for you again as you get the new Tenth Cavalry Regiment up and going."

They took a few steps toward General Hancock's office. Grierson paused. "Sergeant Darby, thank you. I'd be happy to have you in any regiment of mine. As you may know, the Congress created six new regiments – all of them colored. So that means *all* the enlisted men will be colored."

James was crestfallen. He did not care if it showed. "But, sir, won't you need several experienced noncommissioned officers to help organize and train the recruits?"

"Yes, of course, I will. You know that, and I know that. But the Congress didn't think of that."

James sighed. "Oh, I see. Well, sir, here's General Hancock's office."

Grierson took his bag. "I'm sorry. If you're looking for a field assignment, I suggest you consider Colonel Graham's Fourth Cav Regiment. He's a fine commander. I'll even write a letter of introduction, if you wish."

James snapped to attention and saluted. "Thank you, sir."

* * *

Abigail screamed. It was too late to warn James. A shabbily dressed man struck James on the back of his head with the handle of a broken baseball bat. For James, everything went black. He collapsed forward, bruising his forehead from the impact on the cobblestones of St. Louis's Walnut Street. Abigail screamed again and shrieked, "Somebody help me!"

The robber scrambled over James's body and rifled hurriedly through his pockets. The man said over his shoulder, "If'n you scream agin, I'ma brain you!"

Abigail stood petrified, shaky hands covering her mouth. She looked up and down the street for help. A figure emerged from the Basilica of St. Louis and immediately retreated. She looked back toward Fourth Street and saw two men round the corner onto Walnut running and then stop. Abigail called out. "Help! Stop thief!"

The men hesitated. The robber grabbed James's wallet, stood, looked toward the two men, and ran in the direction of the church.

Abigail called again, pleadingly. "Please help us!"

Presently, one man approached. The second man followed and grabbed the sleeve of the first. "Com'on, man. Let's get the hell outta here. Dese people white!" Both men stopped again.

Abigail took a step toward them. "No. Don't go. Please don't leave us here."

The first man pulled free and advanced. He knelt beside James while his friend ran away. "M'am, do you have any liquid in your pocketbook?"

"Er, no. Oh. Oh, I just remembered. I have some smelling salts."

The salts aroused James. "Ooooh! Whaaat happened?" He tried to sit up, but collapsed against the man's knees.

"Hold it, boy! We gotcha this time!"

"Watch out – there's another nigger down there on the victim!"

The two policemen hit the second man with their clubs. A policeman shouted. "Git away from him, nigger!"

The man didn't move.

A policeman rushed forward, club raised. Abigail held up her hand. "No, please. He just stopped to help us."

The policeman ignored Abigail and struck the black man supporting James. The man keeled over on his side with James' head falling to the cobblestones again.

Abigail grabbed the policeman's sleeve. "Oh, my God. You've killed him! He only wanted to help."

"'Cuse me, madam, but niggers are notorious savages and brutes. God knows what could've happened to you if'n we hadn't come along. Anyways, he ain't dead – just out cold."

James struggled to sit up.

"Sir, who hit you?"

"I didn't see who hit me." James used his handkerchief to wipe blood from his forehead away from his right eye.

Abigail pointed. "We crossed Fourth and a white man hit James from behind. He robbed him and ran off yonder toward the church. If not for these men, he woulda robbed me too."

James felt his pockets. "My wallet's gone. Oh, he missed my father's watch."

The policeman holding the second black man patted the man down again. "This one ain't got it. Check the nigger on the ground."

His partner checked. "Hmm. He ain't got it either. Got his money tied in the corner of this old bandana just like the other one."

Abigail was kneeling and cradling James. She looked up. "I told you. They only stopped to help."

James stared at the black man on the ground beside him. "You know what? This fellow looks familiar. I know I've seen him somewhere...."

The policeman standing over the downed black man interrupted. "Now how likely is that? Son, where do you work?"

"I'm a soldier. I'm stationed at Jefferson Barracks."

"Well, these niggers don't look like soldiers. Maybe that bump on the head got you all mixed up. I think these niggers saw you down and smelled opportunity to take advantage."

James took the officer's hand and stood. Abigail held on to him. James draped an arm around her shoulders. He ignored the policeman. "Say, I'm okay after all. Abigail, why don't you pass those smelling salts under that fellow's nose?"

"Okay."

The man stirred and groaned.

The policeman exclaimed, "Well, I'll be doggone. It works on niggers, too." Both policemen laughed.

James looked carefully at them both, then the black men. He rubbed his chin. "As incredible as it seems, I have seen both of these men before."

The policemen looked at each other and shook their heads. One said, "It's the bump on the head."

James knelt beside Abigail and the black man. "Young man, have you seen me before?"

The man sat up on the cobblestone, held his head, and frowned as he examined James's face in the waning light of Friday evening. "Sir, maybe, maybe not. I work on a riverboat. Maybe you saw me there."

James' eyes widened. "The *Perry*?"

James thought the man's face showed surprise. The man sat up straight, staring into James's face. "Why, yes."

"Hell's bells! That's where I saw'em! Both of you're on the boiler crew!" James grabbed Abigail.

"That's right! When did you see us?"

"It was the night of the *Mars* wreck. Over a year ago."

301

"Oh, I remember! You were beside me passing sacks of grain off the *Mars*." The man staggered to his feet and joined James and Abigail.

The policemen started to walk away. "If'n I were you, I'd git on back toward Fourth Street and stay where there's light. And don't trust no niggers."

James waved to the officers. "Thanks." He turned back to the men. "And greater thanks to you for coming and helping us."

Abigail looked at the man who held his head. "You overcame your fear and helped. I'm very grateful." She paused, and then tilted her head to one side. "What is your name?"

"I'm Isaac Rice. Dis heah's my buddy and homey, Caleb Jenkins."

Caleb spoke. "How y'all doin'?"

James introduced himself and Abigail. He inquired, "Where y'all from?"

Isaac and Caleb answered in unison. "South Carolina."

Caleb glanced down. Then he touched Isaac's shoulder. "Man, I'm real sorry I didn't hang with you."

"Aw, that's all right. You could live to tell the tale. There wasn't any need for both of us to hang… together."

The quartet laughed.

Caleb changed the subject. "Hey Isaac, Mister James here is a soldier!"

* * *

On Monday morning, James met Isaac and Caleb at the entrance to Jefferson Barracks.

Chapter 23: Rachel's Second Ordeal

They rode in silence. Twenty minutes into their journey, they paused in the middle of shallow Bayou Pierre and allowed their two horses to drink. Light rain made a pitter-patter sound on the buggy's cover and caused the surface of the bayou to ripple. When they were under way again, Rachel asked, "Who are you?"

Her rescuer said, "My name is Mary Elizabeth Smith. Everyone calls me Mary Beth. This is my brother, Franklin. We came to Hinds County with our parents three years ago from Georgia."

"Why are you doing this for me?"

Over their left shoulder, day was breaking on Friday, December 8, 1865. Mary Beth turned her body on the single overstuffed seat the threesome shared and faced Rachel. "I have never believed that one human being has the right to own another. I am especially appalled at the way enslaved Negro women are treated."

Rachel's jaw dropped. In the dim light, she studied Mary Beth's face. "I've never met or heard of anyone like you. I would like to know more, but not now. I hurt and I'm angrier at anything white than I ever been in my life. I want to kill Billy Duke. Because I've met you, maybe I'll have to rethink some of that. But not now."

"Of course, I understand. Later, we can discuss anything at all."

"Where're you taking me?"

"Why, of course, we taking you to your Isaac in Natchez."

Rachel turned away and rubbed both cheeks with her palms. "And you know all of this about me from Grady? What is he to you anyway? He certainly doesn't look to be your type."

Mary Beth and Franklin laughed. "I met Grady at church and have been working on getting him to understand that Negroes are just people – though we've badly damaged y'all as a people. I think I'm beginning to reach him. That he told me about you makes me think I'm on the right track.

"You're perceptive. No, I wouldn't consider Grady as mate material. But since attraction is irrational, I have no idea what I was thinking when I fell in love with Billy Duke."

Rachel's jaw dropped again. Trapped! She tried to stand and leap out of the buggy. Mary Beth caught her. They struggled. Franklin stopped the horses and helped his sister restrain Rachel.

Tired and out of breath, Rachel slumped onto the seat. Her chest was still heaving.

Mary Beth blinked. "I'm sorry. I want you to understand that I know and appreciate more than meets the eye. I don't mind telling you in front of Franklin that Billy made a fool of me. He lied and told me he would marry me just to have my body." Mary Beth's anger began to show. Rachel could see her tears. "My mother was right. But I didn't listen. Even my younger brother here warned me. I was a fool."

Rachel put one hand on Mary Beth's hand.

* * *

It was midday. They munched pieces of dried apples. "What place is this?"

"Fayette."

"Forgive me, Mary Beth. But I must tell you the truth. Isaac is not in Natchez. I lied to send that lousy snake in the wrong direction."

"Oh, that's okay. I understand. You haven't misled me."

"But I have. I let you think I have someplace in Natchez I can go. I know not a soul in Natchez."

"Oh my. What will we do?"

"Well, I worked as a teacher for the Freedmen's Department at Davis Bend."

"Yes, Grady told me."

Rachel blinked. *Damn. Grady again.* "I heard there's an army man with the department at Washington, near Natchez, called, Major Reynolds. Perhaps he could help me find work and a place for me and my family."

"Your family?"

For the first time since she could not remember when, Rachel smiled. "So Grady didn't know about my two sisters and father back at the Bend. As you know, I can't go back there because of the damn guerillas. It seems to me that we should make a home in Natchez. Perhaps later I can get my sweet Isaac to live there with me."

"Oh, I'm happy to hear you have people in your life who love you. These days, there are so many displaced persons."

Rachel remembered her mother. *Where are you, Ma?* "We have much to talk about later. More than you can imagine...."

Mary Beth patted Rachel's hand. "Now that you've told me about family, I need to make sure you understand that you need to get them down here and settled with jobs before Christmas."

Rachel examined Mary Beth's grave face, drained and white. "Why? What's wrong?"

"The state legislature just passed, and the governor signed last week, a new comprehensive set of laws that will make Negroes all but re-enslaved. Negro men won't be able to change jobs, own land or guns – much less vote."

"What!"

"There's more...."

"So that's why y'all will need work contracts in place by January."

* * *

A week later, Rachel, John, Ruth, Rebecca, and her new husband, Saul, set up housekeeping in two former slave cabins with floors on a farm north of Washington, seven miles from Natchez. The trip from Davis Bend took three days in John's wagon – drawn by his two ancient mules. With assistance from Major Reynolds of the Freedmen's Department, John made a contract to sharecrop with the war-widowed landowner.

The family's plan called for John to manage the farm. Rebecca would cook and clean for the widow in addition to cooking for her own family. Saul and John did the field work. Ruth's job was care of the garden, pigs, chickens, and a cow. Ruth was also tasked with providing assistance in the field and house as needed. Rachel would clean both cabins, keep crop records, and hire herself out as a teacher for the Freedmen's Department or on her own. John convinced them to live frugally and save to buy a farm or the inn that Rebecca longed to own. In either case, it would be a family enterprise.

In mid-December, Mary Beth returned to shop with Rachel downtown and under the hill. During their celebrations of Christmas and New Year's, the family often debated how to find or be found by Isaac and Caleb.

They ate their meals in Rebecca and Saul's cabin. After breakfast on the third Sunday in January, Rachel vomited. After vomiting three consecutive mornings, Rebecca whispered, though they were outside, as she cleaned her sister's face with damp cloth, "Did you miss your menses?"

Rachel held her breath. Her eyes went wide. She remembered that her last menses occurred in the last week of November. The realization hit her and she fainted.

Rebecca revived Rachel by squeezing drops of water from the cloth into her nose. Rachel sputtered. Rebecca helped her stand. "Com'on, we need to walk and talk, sister to sister. Don't think I haven't noticed a difference in you since we moved from the Bend. And, I know it was not all your missing Isaac."

Rachel held her head down. She felt deep self-loathing and immeasurable hatred for Billy. Her temples hurt. She was nauseous again, but nothing came up. She felt no comfort from Rebecca's hug.

"Rai, look at me."

Rachel slowly turned and faced Rebecca. "Rai, I want you to know that whatever has happened, or will happen, I will always love you and be by your side – no matter what."

Rachel could no longer make out Rebecca's face. A flood of tears burst forth as Rachel reached out and draped her arms around Rebecca for warmth, comfort, and support. "Oh, Bec, it was the most horrible thing ever! How did God let this happen to me? I am undone. I know Isaac will never want to touch me now. Oh, Lawd, please have mercy! I can't take it no more!" Tears and mucus were smeared over her face. She put her mouth on Rebecca's shoulder to muffle her wailing and screaming at the top of her voice. Her body shook violently.

"Rai, I'm here. It's okay to cry. I'm right here." Rebecca guided Rachel onto the path that led to the spring.

"It isn't fair! Why did this have to happen to me? I love Isaac with all my heart. I found the man I allus wanted and then he's so ruthlessly snatched from me...." She screamed again and jumped up twice. Rebecca held on to her, lest she fall. "The same damn hateful ugly white bastard who ran my man off raped me! I'm gonna kill'im if it's the last thing I do. Mark my words. The bastard will die at my hand!"

Suddenly, Rachel was spent. She went limp. Rebecca kept her from falling on the rocks but stood motionless for a moment. Then Rebecca laid Rachel down and squeezed more water on her nose. She awoke with a start.

Rachel shook her head twice. Her tears started again. "Oh, Bec. This is gonna break Pa's heart. And look how I let you and Ruthie down."

"Rai, you haven't let anyone down. You're the kindest and sweetest sister I could ask for. I'll never forget what you did to save me from the same fate. I am and will be forever grateful.

"Pa didn't blame me. And I'm here to tell you, he won't blame you. Pa is a fine man and sees deep into people and how they behave. Trust me, he knows you well and will stand by you."

"But, unlike the thing with you, Pa will be dragged down because the day is coming when I'll not be able to hide the bastard's bastard inside me. Damn! Damn! Damn!" She began wailing again, this time applying her fists to her head and chest. Rebecca held her tightly.

* * *

Rebecca put Rachel to bed. She stared, for a moment, at Rachel lying in a fetal position. Rebecca walked to the school and told the headmistress that Rachel would be back tomorrow. Next, she found her father alone pulling fodder in a cornfield and loading it onto his wagon.

* * *

In the evening, Rachel took her supper in bed. John brought a chair and sat next to her. "Rai, Becky told me all about it." He paused. Tears welled is his eyes, but did not spill onto his cheeks. "Chile, I wantcha to know, I'm hurting inside, wishing I could bear your pain for you."

"Pa, I love you. Thank you.

"Did Becky tell you I promised to kill that bastard?"

"Now, calm yourself, chile."

"I'll be very calm after I kill'im."

"Remember: vengeance is mine saith the Lord."

"Then, I'm His willing instrument."

* * *

After supper the following evening, in the presence of John and Rebecca, Rachel told Ruth and Saul. "You can all know right now. You're my family."

Ruth cried and held Rachel's hand. "I'm so very sorry this awful thing happened to you."

* * *

In the spring of 1866, unusually heavy rains, along with the soggy ground that lasted long after the rains, had delayed planting of cotton and other crops. John told Saul they would do well to get half a crop out of the season. When they were finally able to plant, weeds grew faster than the young cotton plants. By late spring, Rachel's pregnancy was showing. She stopped teaching and joined John, Saul, and Ruth in the fields in the war against weeds.

A midwife, Naomi, whom Rebecca had found in the spring, attended Rachel when she gave birth in August. Naomi had visited in July to prepare the three women for the coming event. Naomi, with Rachel's permission, wanted Rebecca and Ruth to be present and assist when the baby arrived. She called it an educational and spiritual opportunity for women. Rebecca was two months pregnant when Rachel's baby arrived and she expressed gratitude for the chance to learn.

Rachel knew she had been crabby and out of sorts all spring and summer. She had no interest in anything but reading. She asked Pa to bring another book or newspaper every time he went to Natchez. After supper, Rachel would seclude herself and read by candlelight until she slept. She no longer discussed Isaac and Caleb with Ruth. She lost interest in going for drives with Mary Beth and carrying on her old tradition of banter and arguing with Rebecca. After the baby boy was born, the most time she spent with her child was to feed him from her breasts while she read. Ruth and Rebecca took care of the high mulatto boy's other needs. Even John and Saul helped with the baby.

At times, Rachel wished for her old Colt .44 revolver. She felt conflicted when it was time to feed her baby. She thought that she should love the child that came from her body but when she admitted the truth, she realized she loathed her baby. Rachel barely tolerated allowing the child to feed. After giving birth, she slept less, usually in a fetal position when she did, was tired, and had difficulty getting up for any reason but reading. She felt even more irritable and angry.

During the summer, they were hit by a drought that further stunted the cotton plants. In September, John all but lost hope when army worms invaded. Farms throughout Mississippi had the same problems. But, because the price for cotton was unusually high in 1866, their first crop paid their debts at the end of the year and cleared an unexpected small profit.

At the end of summer, Rachel experienced a moment that made her smile and think of Isaac. She found it exhilarating to read for the first time in a newspaper the name of a person whom she knew. John had brought home a discarded copy of the *New York Tribune* that he had found in a Natchez feed and seed store near the end of September.

"Pa, look! Come quick. I met this man!"

Smiling, John hurried to her side. The family followed. John looked over her shoulder for words he could now pick out. "Rai, honey, who is he? Where is his name?"

Rachel point to the name: Brigadier General Benjamin H. Grierson. "Pa, this is the man who was the boss of the Yankee soldiers that came to Bender's place in '63. Remember? I met him at the big house. Well, it says here that General Grant has nominated General Grierson to command a new cavalry regiment of Negro soldiers."

As they reminisced about the arrival of the first Yankees they ever saw and speculated on new opportunities for young colored men, Rachel smiled and thought, *I wish I could introduce Isaac to General Grierson.*

* * *

In October, Rachel withdrew further. One evening after supper in November, she called Rebecca aside and whispered. "Becky, last night, Isaac came by. We sat by the river at Davis Bend and had a long talk. He thinks I should get rid of the baby."

With her tears welling, Rebecca stood motionless and mute, with her mouth open, staring at Rachel's expressionless face.

Chapter 24: Alejandra Rejects a Suitor

Monday, October 29, 1866. Dear Dairy, Good news: Everyone is busy getting the house ready for the fiesta of Los Dias de Muertos – even Ernesto. Papa thinks he can come home for Christmas. They defeated the French again near some little village in the south that I never heard of. Bad news: I agreed with Mama to at least talk with Torres. Oh-oh, Mama is calling me to the kitchen. Bye for now.

In the afternoon on the day of Todos los Santos, Alejandra stood by with a tablecloth and marigolds in hand while Ernesto and Rafael put the finishing touches on their tabletop ofrenda. When they stood back to look at their work, she gave them scant seconds to admire it before covering the ofrenda with her decorations.

Ernesto protested. "Aw, Sis, you could give the men a chance to congratulate themselves. What's the hurry?"

"You're finished. A woman's work is never finished. Now I gotta hurry and help Mama make the pan de muerto. Besides, I only see one and a half men!"

Rafael looked at Ernesto and shrugged. "Betcha you didn't know having a big sister can be a pain."

"Yes. But I do know having a little sister is a bigger pain."

The siblings laughed.

* * *

Rocio and Alejandra had flour up to their elbows. Alejandra even had some on her nose. Rafael passed through the kitchen and noted, "My, my, aren't you two a pretty sight!"

Alejandra looked for something to throw. Finding nothing handy, she retorted, "How about we give all the pan de muerto to the neighbors?"

Rafael stopped in the doorway and looked back, laughing. "Well, gimme back *my* butter and *my* eggs from *my* cow and *my* chickens."

Rocio went into a fit of laughter and dropped her rolling pin on the table with a crash. "He got you, Allie."

Alejandra ignored Rafael until he cleared the door and then her giggles overcame her.

* * *

The festival began before nightfall. Rocio stayed at home with a headache. As the evening wore on, Alejandra and Linda danced and marveled and compared the various skeleton costumes. Alejandra announced, "I think your costume is by far the best one here."

Linda whispered, "Quiet, you'll embarrass me!"

A male voice spoke from behind a wooden skull mask. The man's costume was unbuttoned to midchest, displaying hair. "Oh, Alejandra is quite right. You're to be congratulated."

Startled, Alejandra tuned and was face to mask with Torres. She meant to be civil, but aloof. Instead, she made a backhand motion and said, "Go away! No one sent for the likes of you." She was surprised and taken aback by her tone. She saw Linda put her hand over her mouth.

Torres removed his mask and looked into Alejandra's eyes. She hoped he saw fire. He made a sweeping bow. "Senorita, may I have this dance?"

Alejandra put one hand on her hip and was pointing into Torres's face with the other when Linda pulled it down. Linda turned her back to Torres and whispered, "Allie that was uncalled for. It's not like you to be rude. It's just a dance."

Alejandra blinked. She already knew being rude felt uncomfortable. "Oh, all right."

"Thank you, senorita. I'm honored."

Alejandra didn't reply. Instead her eyes found Ernesto and Rafael. As they danced, she continued watching for her brothers and

Linda. Ernesto and Linda joined the dance late and swept past them. Alejandra wanted the music to stop. She glanced at Torres and flushed. Her anger was kindled again and she noticed that Linda was not near. Her brow furrowed as she spoke. "Don't you have anything better to do than stare at my tits?"

Torres lifted his eyes and met hers. His mouth was agape and he had lost his swagger. He recovered and said with a smile, "You know, I'm going to marry you."

"The way that works in my family is the man asks the woman and then her parents. You have done neither. So stop sounding like an idiot."

"Okay. Will you marry me?"

Displaying more exasperation than she felt, Alejandra drew her head back but never let her eyes leave his. "What kind of stupid question is that? You don't know me. All I know about you is your name. I have no interest in marrying you. Do you understand? Let me make this real clear: the answer is *no*!"

The music played on. For a moment, Alejandra thought Torres looked crushed. But then she saw the anger in his eyes. "Soon you will be happy to marry me and let me take you from your plow and horse."

Alejandra stopped in her tracks. Her hands flew akimbo. "This dance is over! Leave me."

Torres' mouth dropped open again. Again he recovered and moved closer. "Why you little...." Through his teeth he hissed, "Do not embarrass me in front of Carrizal. Dance with me until the music stops!"

Alejandra turned in a huff to walk away. Torres grabbed her arm and she snatched it away. He caught her and spun her around. The music stopped abruptly. Torres grabbed her collar and hissed. "You got what you wanted. Everybody is watching. Now you're coming with me!"

"Oh, no I'm not!" Alejandra delivered a fist to Torres's nose. He released her and held his nose. She stood before him with both fists ready. He reached for her again. A blur sped past Alejandra and crashed into Torres, knocking him to the ground. Ernesto then sat upon Torres's torso beating his face with his fists while Rafael beat his knees with a stick.

Alejandra saw Torres's cousin, Juan, running toward Ernesto's blind side. She timed his run perfectly, put her foot out, and tripped him, causing him to fall on his face.

"Ernesto, Raffy, let's go home! Quickly! Let's go before more Rodriquezes turn up. Please!"

* * *

Sitting on her bed, Rocio heard the story from the three of them. They finished each other's sentences. Rocio hugged her daughter. "I love you. I'm proud of you and your brothers. I'm sorry I doubted your understanding of Torres.

"Now, my children, unfortunately we've poked the hornets' nest. We must move quickly. You are young and may not understand that retribution is being planned with rage in the casa of Rodriquez. These are powerful people and will not allow unavenged shame to fall upon their family caused by commoners like us.

"We have little time. They will come for you. It will not be pretty. I have seen this before from such a family. Here's what we do. Ernesto, you are leaving tonight for the south with Allie. Give her some of your clothes to wear and carry. Allie, tie up your hair and wear Papa's old sombrero – not your pretty one. Both of you pack quickly. Raffy, fetch water for their journey. I'll pack some food. Everybody, move quickly. Now!"

Alejandra's eyes were wide as she stared in awe at her mother. She had never heard Rocio speak like this.

"Mama, where will I go? What about you and Raffy? What will you do?"

"Never mind all that. Get moving." Rocio hurried to the kitchen.

Rafael returned with water. "I'll keep watch under the tree out front."

Rocio ruffled his hair. "Good idea."

Ernesto stood in the kitchen doorway. "Okay, Ma, I'm ready."

"Here, take this money for the stage. Don't wait for a freight train."

Alejandra appeared with her bedroll and gunnysack. When it was full, Rafael burst into the room, out of breath. "They're coming! A lot of people are coming!"

Rocio commanded, "Quick. Get in the creek. Get out at the trail to Ojito. Going that way, with a little luck, you can make the Chihuahua road by dawn. Take Raffy's herding staff for snakes."

Minutes after two fast kisses, they were out of the house and in the water. Alejandra heard the mob coming.

* * *

They made Ojito at two o'clock. The Milky Way was clear, the stars bright, and the night was cool. They pulled their boots on and continued walking.

Ernesto spoke. "I will go to work in another mine in Zacatecas. Where will you go?"

"Mama said I should go to Dr. Sanchez. I will. You can find me there on your way to and fro."

Chapter 25: Loss

The whistle blew a loud and long blast.

Isaac and Caleb were already out of their cabin and standing on the texas deck, high above the Missouri River. They had boarded the four-deck riverboat, the *Ruth*, in St. Louis the day before, Monday, October 1, 1866. Now, Isaac stared at the buildings of Fort Leavenworth on the bluff above the river.

On the wharf, Isaac had stopped to check the rope he used to strap his bedroll and canvas tent half over his shoulder and across his back. The bedroll and gunnysack at his side contained all his worldly goods – including Rachel's Colt .44. The bedroll and tent half were gifts from James Darby. Caleb's bedroll was wrapped in another tent half.

After an hour or so of searching, they found Colonel Grierson in his small sparsely furnished office busy writing amid stacks of papers. At first, he peered at them over his spectacles and then he stood and greeted them warmly. There was no one else about. He read the letter they carried from James.

Grierson laid the letter aside. "So you've met my friend, Sergeant Darby. He's a good man and a fine soldier. I see he calls you two his friends. That must be why he has taken the care to provide you with bedrolls and a tent." Grierson smiled. "I'm afraid he's right to do that. You see, we will establish a new regiment and, at this point, we have nothing – even my office is borrowed."

Isaac and Caleb exchanged glances. Isaac cleared his throat. "Er, suh, you mean it's just us three?"

Grierson leaned back and laughed, holding his sides. "Don't worry. We have Private William Beauman with us." He laughed again. "And he's a little under the weather. Malaria, I think. So, with you three, I only need to recruit one thousand and eighty-nine more men. It'll take a little time. But we'll be in the field before you know it.

"In the meanwhile, we'll have to wait to start organizing and training."

Grierson looked at James's letter again. "So, Mr. Rice, you're the smithy, eh?"

"Yes, suh."

"Can you read and write?"

"No, suh." Isaac quickly added, "But I will learn soon."

Grierson looked at Isaac for a long moment, and then he turned to Caleb. "Mr. Jenkins, do you have any special skills?"

"Er, no, suh."

Before Grierson could speak again, Isaac interjected. "Suh, my homey is humble. He sings and plays several instruments. You should hear him. Why, he always has his harmonica in his pocket."

Caleb blushed. "Aw, the colonel ain't interested in that. He wants soldiers, not musicians."

Grierson dropped the letter. "Can you play 'Turkey in the Straw' for me?"

"Now, suh?"

"Yes."

Again, Isaac and Caleb exchanged glances. Grierson chuckled. Caleb pulled out his harmonica and held it close to his face and began tapping his foot. Then he stood and began playing a rousing rendition. At the end of the first verse, Grierson slipped his jew's harp from his pocket and joined in. Isaac's jaw dropped, but Caleb nodded to Grierson and kept playing.

Finishing, they laughed together.

Grierson folded his arms and smiled. "That was great. You two will make fine additions to the Tenth Regiment of United States Cavalry. I can always use soldiers who're also smiths and musicians. Welcome to the regiment."

"Thank you, suh."

Isaac asked, "Since there's no one else but Private Beauman, what will we do tomorrow?"

Grierson's brow furrowed. "Well, for a while, there won't be much we can do – not until we get more men and a few officers. As soon as I get a chaplain, you can start your reading lessons. But, for now, get Mr. Beauman to show you where you'll eat and sleep. Otherwise, stay in this area so I can find you if I need to."

"Yes, suh."

* * *

A week later, only one more recruit arrived. Isaac was tired of pitching horse shoes and playing checkers. Caleb said he needed to give his harmonica a rest. Isaac said to Caleb, "I'm goin' and to ask the colonel if I can go to Davis Bend for a few weeks. Sittin' here's a waste. I'll bet it won't be much different here by the end of the month. You wanna go?"

Isaac was back in twenty minutes, bursting with excitement. "Not only did he say we can go, he's leaving too!"

"Must be tired o' waiting, like us."

"Naw. He's going off to Washington. Gonna meet with some bigwigs and General Grant."

"So how long can we be gone?"

"Same time as the colonel. 'Til the end o' the month."

* * *

After three days on the Missouri and Mississippi, they arrived at Davis Bend by riverboat. Isaac and Caleb wore their hooded ponchos to conceal their faces. They found Isaiah at his father's store. Isaiah took them to the store's stockroom where they could talk.

After a few minutes, Isaac believed Isaiah had told them all he knew about the departure of Rachel and her family the year before. He borrowed two horses from Isaiah and went to visit the Freedmen's School. He learned from the headmistress that Rachel had been abducted by men who looked like guerillas.

The teacher returned to her class. Isaac felt weak and dizzy. "Homey, you reckon that leader fellow she described is Billy Duke."

"Sho' as shootin'."

"Let's ride."

* * *

They slept the next day near Hamer Bayou and, around sunset, planned a night raid on the Duke farm. At first dark, they rode on and hid their horses in a draw by a small stream close to the farm. Isaac put the .44 in his belt. Since they had only one weapon, they slipped into the farm together from the west. It took two hours to crawl to the first cabin.

By a window, Caleb hummed, "Steal Away, steal away to Jesus."

A woman inside sang, "I ain't got long ta stay heah."

She brought another woman out with her. Disappointed, Isaac asked, "Where is Rachel?"

The women looked at each other. After a moment, one spoke. "I knew her. She was heah last year 'bout dis time."

"Where is she now?"

"She left atter two days. White peoples came and took her to Natchez."

Isaac put one hand on his face. He thought, *this makes no sense but I can't stay here asking questions.*

"Do you wanna to ride outta here with us?"

They nodded.

"Can you ride bareback?"

They hesitated and then nodded again.

"Who's in the next cabin?"

"Two mens."

"Keep'em quiet and bring'em to me."

When the men arrived, Isaac went to the corral. There, he quieted two horses and two mules. He led the animals to his wards. Caleb took them away through the woods to their waiting horses. The second woman exclaimed, "Hallelujah!"

A dog barked. A second dog barked. The back door of the farmhouse opened and light streamed out. Two men emerged. Isaac felt the back of his neck tingle. He muttered, "Dammit!" He pounded the ground with his fist. Then he shook his head and thought, *I best be calm – if I can. I must try.* He rubbed his sweating palms in dirt.

One man said, "Git me my carbine! A couple of horses are missing."

Isaac watched both men head toward the corral while he ran to a tree at the edge of a cornfield. As he expected, they brought along the dogs. The men were mounted bareback. They checked the cabins and the dogs headed straight for Isaac. The men followed at a gallop.

Isaac waited for the lead horseman to come within range of the .44 he was pointing with both hands as he leaned against a tree to steady his aim. He guessed the dogs would reach him at almost the time he should fire. He was determined to concentrate on the lead horseman and not the dogs. The horseman leaned forward, his head barely above his horse's mane.

When the dogs were ten feet away and charging, Isaac fired. The horse and rider crashed through the dry cornstalks to the ground. Isaac fired again and the first dog yelped, whimpered, and fell. The second dog turned back. Isaac ran.

He heard the second horse stopping. Then, a voice shouted. "Billy, are you shot?"

There was no response. Isaac did not hear a dog or horse. He heard the voice again, asking, pleading, "Billy?"

Isaac trembled at the thought that Billy Duke might be dead. It felt exhilarating, scary, and sad all at the same time. He shook his head again and muttered, "Focus." He thought, *okay, I gotta remember I have only four bullets left.*

The two bullets he fired had killed a horse and a dog.

They mounted and rode in the stream. At the confluence with White Oak Creek, the group turned right and remained in the water until they reached Bayou Pierre. From there they rode south until they found a road that led west. That took thirty minutes.

His wards did not know the way to Natchez, but were happy to go there. Isaac guessed the next road they should take was south and had to be a well-traveled thoroughfare. He found it near Port Gibson. His travels on the river gave him a sense of about how far they needed to go to reach Natchez. On a wooded rise near Port Gibson, they rested.

* * *

At mid-afternoon the next day, they passed through Washington. An hour later, they arrived at the edge of Natchez. Caleb put his harmonica away. They said good-bye to their companions.

As the woman who sang in response to "Steal Away to Jesus" turned to leave, Isaac asked, "Ma'm, what's your name?"

"Ebony."

"Well, Miss Ebony, where will you go?"

"I don't know. But I'll have ta stay low, 'cause o' the strict laws 'bout us coloreds being in towns widout a job."

Isaac stuttered. "W-w-what did you say, Miss Ebony?"

After Ebony explained the new order of things under the Black Codes of Mississippi, Isaac and Caleb rode about two miles north of Natchez and camped in the woods near Mammoth Bayou. While Isaiah's horses grazed for several days, they debated a plan to find Rachel and Ruth in Natchez and not get caught by a lawman or angry white citizens.

At daybreak on Sunday morning, October 14, Isaac and Caleb rode into Natchez. They found a white frame church on Madison Street near Rankin that Isaac thought could have a colored congregation. When the first parishioners appeared at the Rose Hill Baptist Church, Isaac smiled and crossed the street while Caleb held their horses. The pastor, the Reverend Randall Pollard, and his wife had not heard of Rachel or Ruth or their kin, but would be sure and tell them to contact the church in St. Louis if perchance their paths should cross. The pastor suggested that they visit Zion Chapel A.M.E. Church at Jefferson and Pine Streets.

At Zion Chapel, Isaac met the Reverend Hiram Rhodes Revels, who told him, "I have not had the pleasure of meeting Miss Rachel Black or her family. I'm new here myself. But I've met a woman in the Zion Chapel congregation who seems to know everybody and nearly all the goings on in the colored community. Perhaps she can help you after services. She attends regularly, but comes in late."

"Thank you, suh. I'll get my friend, Caleb Jenkins, and we'll stay for your services. If you wish, I'll get him to sing a song for you."

"Well, thanks, Mr. Rice. I'll be sure to call on him."

Caleb sang "Nobody Knows the Trouble I've Had" amid shouts of "Amen!" and "Yes, Lawd!" and some weeping. Reverend Revels led the applause and asked Caleb to stand by to "sing another song to send us home at the end of service."

Isaac sat, mesmerized, listening to Reverend Revels's sermon and closing prayer. He thought, *I wish I could stand in front of people and speak like that.*

For the closing, Caleb sang another song popular among the enslaved in South Carolina's Low Country: "Fare Ye Well."

On the front steps, facing Pine Street, Reverend Revels introduced Isaac and Caleb to a silver-haired lady he called Auntie Martha Queen.

Isaac thought Aunt Martha's mind would pierce him as her clear eyes peered into his. He thought she had taken his full measure. "So, young man, whom do you seek?"

Aunt Martha listened and hardly blinked. "Son, you and yo' singin' friend best sit down. Let's go back inside." Inside, she began. "After freedom, a flood o' our peoples crowded into Natchez. I lost track. I don't know'em all. I know I don't know a Ruth. Others, I jes know of. Now I heard – mind you, I didn't meet her – last month 'bout a young gal like the one you described whose name was Rachel. But I don't know the last name."

Isaac's eyes brightened. He could see that Aunt Martha noticed, for she reached out and held his hand. He held his breath because she did not smile.

Aunt Martha blinked and said, "Be strong. The word was this Rachel died giving birth ta a high yellow baby."

Isaac stared in disbelief at Aunt Martha. She took Isaac's hand in both of her wrinkled hands. Caleb put an arm around Isaac. Isaac sat and wept. Silent tears flowed onto his shirt. He stayed in the pew while Caleb walked Aunt Martha out of the church. While Caleb was outside, Isaac pounded his fist into the pew in front of him. His knuckles bled.

* * *

Isaac looked down into the water of Mammoth Bayou. He did not remember the ride back to their campsite. He called to Caleb. "We need ta find Miss Ebony. I can see now there was something she didn't wanna tell me."

"Okay."

* * *

After six days of searching and avoiding the law, they discovered Miss Ebony working as a laundress in back of a hospital on Bowles Alley. They dismounted and Caleb held their horses.

Without an exchange of words, Isaac knew Miss Ebony knew something she had to relate from the shocked look in her eyes that immediately replaced her pleasant recognition of him as he strode briskly toward her. She was drying her hands on her apron and taking two steps back. They did not greet each other. She held up both hands. "Okay. Okay. But, first, let me sit down."

Isaac's voice was as steady as his gaze. "Did Billy Duke violate my Rachel?"

Ebony maintained eye contact but blinked several times. She stammered, "I-I-I didn't want to add to your hurt." Tears welled in her eyes. She spat her next words looking at the ground. "Yes! That devil took her the second night she was there."

Ebony looked up, her eyes pleading. Her tears spilled onto her cheeks. "Isaac, I'm so sorry. Later, I did all I could to comfort her."

Isaac felt sad for Ebony. They cried together. He sat beside her and held her hands. "Thank you very much for all you did. I pray that God will bless you for your kindness."

"Isaac, thank you. I hope you can heal soon. You done already killed Billy Duke. There's nothing else to be done but find Rachel. She needs you. I hope you can accept her as she is."

Isaac looked away and sniffed. He took a deep breath. "Last Sunday, I learned that she died givin' birth tuh a high yella baby."

Abruptly, Ebony stood. "Oh, Lawd, no! Not that po' sweet innocent chile!" She folded her arms and rocked from side to side. Her tears flowed anew.

Isaac stood. They embraced and comforted each other.

* * *

Isaac stopped talking for several days. He lost his appetite and would stare absently into space for hours on end. Caleb comforted and guided him from place to place. Isaac's grief was palpable. They waited three days for a riverboat that would both carry livestock and stop at Davis Bend. While waiting, Caleb carried on searching in vain for Ruth. After the stop at Davis Bend, Isaac began to eat and talk again.

They reported to Colonel Grierson at Fort Leavenworth on Monday, October 29.

Chapter 26: Rachel's Triumph

Rachel talked amiably at supper with John, Rebecca, Ruth, and Saul. She told them she could not remember when she felt as well. She held little seven-month-old Charles, whom she had named for Charles DeFaux, on her knee as she carried on banter with her family about prospects for Negroes since the passage of the Reconstruction Act by the United States Congress over the veto of President Andrew Johnson two weeks prior. Rachel credited her recent improved spirits to good news about the outlook for Negroes and loving care from Rebecca.

After the passage of the Reconstruction Act in March 1867, Rachel asked John to purchase particular newspapers, for she had tired of the lies and hate she found in Mississippi papers. Nonetheless, she continued reading the *Natchez Tri-Weekly Democrat, Natchez Tri-Weekly Courier,* and *Natchez Daily Courier* for local news. John bought subscriptions to the *Philadelphia Christian Recorder* and the *New York Tribune* for Rachel. When John brought these two papers home, Rachel felt she was almost her old self.

Change influenced Rachel to think about teaching again. The Black Codes of 1865 were rescinded by the new state legislature and, in the fall, General Ord issued an order for the election of men to a state convention for the purpose of creating a new constitution. The new constitution was one of the conditions set by Congress for Mississippi to be re-admitted to the union. Rachel thought this was the time to advocate for universal free education.

Early one morning after the election of convention delegates, Rachel made the six-mile trip to Washington and visited her former headmistress, Miss Samantha Thompson. Pupils had not yet arrived. Miss Thompson was writing lesson instructions on her blackboard and Rachel's voice startled her. "Good morning, Miss Thompson. I hope this bright fall day finds you well."

"Oh, good morning, Rachel." Her voice turned cold. "This is quite a surprise. I hope you understand the rules will not permit you to return to teaching now that you're a mother." Miss Thompson raised her face upward. "That is especially true for unwedded mothers. Such a pity in your case. You seemed to have such promise. So, if you'll excuse me, I'll get back to my preparations. Good day, Rachel."

Miss Thompson turned to her blackboard. Rachel took a deep breath. *I will not cry.* She made two fists down by her thighs and spoke through clinched teeth. "Miss Thompson, turn around. You will listen to me this morning."

Miss Thompson spun and faced Rachel. She put one hand on her chest. "Well! I never…."

Rachel cut her off. "When Major Reynolds sent me to you…."

Miss Thompson interrupted. "Well, there's no Major Reynolds or Sixth Artillery Colored Troops to help you now. They're all mustered out and gone home."

Rachel pointed to Miss Thompson's face. "Listen, lady. Stop interrupting."

Miss Thompson flushed and her face became bright pink. "Humph!"

"When Major Reynolds sent me to you, I had no idea that the white man who raped me just days before had planted his bastard in me. Now I have no job, no prospects, and, as black as I am, I have a little yellow bastard to feed!"

Miss Thompson's book and chalk crashed to the floor. Her face drained of color. "Oh, my God! I must sit down. I had no idea. Oh, I'm so sorry." She sat on the crude bench used by students and fanned herself with one hand.

Rachel ignored her apology. "The children in this state need universal free education. That's why I'm here. Now that the constitutional convention is coming in January, I see this as the time to make an alliance with a likeminded man elected as a delegate to the convention. Here's where I need your help. First, let's compare delegates. Second, when we agree on one, I'm asking you to write a letter of introduction for me."

"Oh, my, my. I've been so foolish to have judged you all this time. Please do forgive me."

"That's not important. Let's start with our own delegates. Of the three from Adams County, I think the Reverend Henry P. Jacobs is the best ally."

"Rachel, I agree completely. I've worked with the Reverend Jacobs on a city council project. I'll write the letter straightaway. Can you wait?"

* * *

In January 1868, Reverend Jacobs invited Rachel to travel to Jackson and remain with his family during the convention. Though all the delegates were men, she was able to attend sessions. She took notes and drafted resolutions for Reverend Jacobs, sometimes anticipating what was needed before he asked. For her work, he paid her $2 per day out of his $10 per day salary as a delegate.

When the convention ended in May, Rachel felt progress had been made toward universal free education. Though the proposed constitution was defeated in the vote that summer, it was again, with proposals on suffrage separated, on the ballot the next year.

In the November 1868 election, Ulysses S. Grant was elected president. Since the new constitution was not approved by the people in the summer, Mississippi was not re-admitted to the union and could not participate in the presidential election.

Sitting by the fireplace on a cold December night watching their two baby boys play, Rebecca said, "Rai, you've had quite a year. You must be proud of your work on the constitution. Are you satisfied with your progress?"

"No. The new legislature still has final say on the shape of education in the state. A lot more men need to be convinced – many more."

"Well, aren't you pleased about the nomination of Mr. James Lynch as secretary of state?"

John joined the discussion. "I'm real proud of Mr. Lynch. He could be the first colored man elected to a statewide office. I wanted to vote for both Mr. Lynch and General Grant. I guess I'll have to get used to calling him Mr. Grant. 'Twas sad to miss voting for him."

Rachel sighed. "I'll tell you when I'll be satisfied. That won't be until *all* adults of suffrage age can vote."

* * *

John put another log on the fire one night after the legislature convened in January. "Things are changing mighty fast. Just a few years ago, we were talking 'bout bein' free. Today, not only are we free, we're part of the government. Now, back then, who coulda dreamed Mississippi would send a colored man to represent her in the United States Senate. And I'm especially proud 'cause he's from right here in Adams County!"

Saul asked, "What's his name?"

Rachel announced with relish. "Reverend Hiram Revels. You know, some day, we oughta go to services at his church. I've heard he's one hellava preacher."

Rebecca feigned offense. "Rai!"

Ruth sat in a rocker holding Rebecca's baby. Rachel ignored Rebecca. She called to Ruth, "Hey, Ruth. What's on? Your mind?"

"Don't worry. My mind is switched on, never off. I was just wonderin' what Caleb is doin' tonight."

Chapter 27: "A White Man's Government"

"If y'all's on your way to vote the Democratic ticket and agin that abominable constitution, y'all's welcome to use dis here road. If not, turn 'round rat nigh and head on back home."

Billy Duke sat his horse in the middle of the road that led north to Carpenter. Cotton plants in the deep green fields on both sides of the road were more than waist high. He was flanked by the Avengers from the old days. Seven new men had joined them to help with the June 1868 constitutional election.

Halted before them were two wagons loaded with Negro men. One man stood and looked Billy in the eye. "Sir, if you please, let us pass. We wants ta vote."

"Y'all kin pass atter you promise to vote agin the constitution and for the Democratic ticket. If you promise and don't do like you say, we'll be seeing ya tonight. 'Fore you go taxin' yore lil' pea brain, lemme tell ya. We got people at the polls taking notes on which color ticket you vote. Yo' ballot had better be the right color."

The Negroes murmured among themselves. After a minute or so, the same man said to Billy, "Sir, it ain't right to deny us the right to vote."

Billy laughed. "Hey boys, we got us a proper-talkin' educated sambo here! Whata ya say we teach'im a lil' lesson?"

The Avengers shouted. "Teach'im!" "Silence the uppity nigger!" "What're we waiting for?" "Yeah, we got more nigger voters to find."

Bill turned his carbine on the driver of the first wagon. "Now, steady there. Don't move that team."

George lassoed the man standing in the wagon and snatched him to the ground. "Hey, Billy, I'ma drag Mr. Smart Mouth a ways up the road so he won't have so far ta walk to the polls atter his friends turn back."

"Good idea, George. When you finish with him, com'on and catch up to us."

Two more Avengers pointed weapons at the Negro men. Billy spoke through his teeth. "Okay, niggers. I've changed ma mind. No deal. The whole lot of you jes go on home. Now!"

The driver of the second wagon hurried and turned about. The first wagon sat with two passengers objecting. "Al, don't turn 'round. We've come dis far...."

The sharp report of Billy's Spencer carbine at close range startled the Negroes. Two leapt from the wagon and ran south along the road. Two ran into the cotton field toward White Oak Creek. The driver screamed, "Oh, Lawd, no! Not my best mule!" The mule lay dead with a bullet in its brain. The other mule was braying and bucking.

The Avengers guffawed.

Billy turned in his saddle. "All right, boys. I think these niggers done learn their lesson. Let's git on down the road to Dentv'le. We got us more work to do."

The Avengers acted in concert with the state Democratic Executive Committee, newspapers, other bands of intimidators, and white employers who threatened to fire colored workers caught voting for the constitution or for Republicans. Their work paid off. The constitution was defeated and Democrats won the governorship and four of five congressional seats. However, these men were unable to take office because the constitution was defeated.

The proposed constitution was on the ballot again in the fall of 1869. This time the controversial disenfranchising clauses were offered for separate votes, as suggested by President Grant. The constitution passed, Mr. James D. Lynch was elected Secretary of State, and Mississippi was re-admitted to the union.

Billy was not happy. "Henry, I told ya we shoulda been out there beatin' heads. Now we got us a nigger Secretary of State. Don't that beat all."

"Don't worry, Billy. This is still a white man's government, instituted for white people to run this state. I predict we'll be rid of niggers in politics in the very near future."

"Well, I'm ready and willing to do my part to make it happen sooner rather than later."

Chapter 28: **Ortega's Bride**

Ortega's shoulder burned under the blazing early August sun. Blood that had run down his biceps was dry and his wound no longer bled. The enemy's bullet had cut a horizontal groove across the vertical claw marks on his left shoulder made years before by a mountain lion. Blood had stained his breechclout and his moccasins. An ammunition belt and his blue headband were all else he wore as he watched the cloud of dust left by the attackers. Ortega tossed his carbine from his left hand to his right. He spat. "We're ruined. Look at this damned field. Yesterday it was our pride. Today it is destroyed. We have but a few animals left."

Dressed the same as Ortega, Jorge slumped and sat on the ground. He laid his rifle on his crossed legs. "We'll be hungry again this winter. Nantahe-totel said it's far too late to plant again."

Dejected, Ortega wearily sat beside his friend. "Where were the accursed Fort Stanton soldiers? They're never here to protect us when we need them. The White Eye citizens carry on the work begun by Carleton with zeal. It's very clear; they mean to kill all of us."

"You know, I'm beginning to think your solution is our only hope – kill every White Eye we can find."

"It's not my solution. It's our warrior's creed. It's the oath we took when we became warriors. It is the way of the great Chief Cochise."

Jorge pulled a weed from the soil and began winding it around a finger. "Yeah, but he's not our chief. Our leaders want to make peace with the White Eyes, again and again."

Grinning, Ortega looked about, checking over both shoulders. "Yes, like they're loco."

Jorge joined Ortega in a short grim laugh at the snide reference to the Chihenne Apache chief called Loco because he wanted peace and trusted the White Eyes.

Ortega gazed down the long rows of broken maze stalks without seeing them. "Cochise is right. Kill many, many White Eyes and do so with much brutality, showing no mercy, so as to make the living

White Eyes leave our land. It is our only hope, for they far outnumber us."

"I agree. But my agreeing doesn't matter. Our chiefs, both Santana and Cadete, still punish our warriors for leaving the reservation."

Ortega wagged a finger. "Wait. We actually don't have the reservation the White Eye Curtis promised Chief Cadete last summer when he returned with our people from Comanche country."

"You're right. So why do we continue to farm and camp here practically in the shadow of this fort? It is too much like being in a cage."

"We are in a cage...." Ortega's voice trailed off. After a moment, he spat.

They sat absentmindedly side by side, one wrapping weeds about a finger and the other picking tiny pebbles from the soil. Ortega's mood was again morose.

Before dawn that morning, Ortega and members of his grandfather's band had been awakened by the sound of rifle fire and galloping shod horses inside their camp. Another self-appointed posse of white New Mexico citizens was exacting revenge on the Mescaleros at Fort Stanton for depredations committed by other Indians – or by white men disguised as Indians. But since they could not distinguish one tribe or band from another, it only mattered to them that they attacked Indians. After all, Phillip Sheridan, the army's general-in-chief had said, "The only good Indian is a dead Indian." They fought a brief scrimmage with the band's few armed warriors while the women and children fled into the mountains. Some of the raiders torched wickiups while other attackers ran off the cattle, horses, and mules, driving them through the fields and destroying crops as they went.

Presently, Nantahe-totel approached with Klo-sen at his side. Out of respect, the two young warriors stood as their elders arrived. Ortega thought it curious that Klo-sen avoided his eyes, looking mostly at the ground. Nantahe-totel put a hand on Ortega's shoulder. "My grandson, be strong."

Immediately, Ortega's knees felt weak. He desperately tried to control the expression on his face. Straightaway, he recalled that his grandfather had used the same words the one and only time he mentioned the death of his parents. Ortega took a deep breath and braced for news that Jacali was dead. He locked eyes with Nantahe-totel.

With his hand resting on Ortega's shoulder, Nantahe-totel spoke. "Jacali's mother has left us. In accordance with our law, let her name be spoken nevermore. She died because she shielded her daughter as they ran from our enemies this morning. As they ran, she remained between Jacali and the enemy. She was a brave and wise woman."

Ortega's gaze was steady. In his mind's eye, he pictured the two women running and Haozinne being felled by a White Eye bullet. He wanted to spit. While he looked into his grandfather's eyes, he felt like screaming and renting his shirt – until he remembered he was not wearing a shirt. He acknowledged the news with only a grunt and a nod.

With the nod, Nantahe-totel dropped his hand from Ortega's shoulder. "Klo-sen wishes to speak to you."

Ortega turned to Klo-sen. He saw a defeated and bereft warrior. Sadness flooded Ortega.

Klo-sen raised his head and looked at Ortega for a long moment. Then he called Ortega by his Mescalero name. "Nah-kah-yen, though we have not left this place to raid and you have acquired no horses, if it is your wish and hers, you may wed my daughter, Sons-ee-ah-ray, when both of you are ready."

Ortega's jaw went slack. His mouth fell open, but he recovered quickly. He looked into Klo-sen's eyes. "Sir, thank you. Thank you for not requiring the traditional gift. I'll marry Jacali, if she will have me."

Klo-sen nodded, turned, and walked away with his chin up. Ortega thought he saw a hint of a smile on Nantahe-totel's lips before he turned and followed his friend.

Ortega sank to his seat on the ground. With his carbine propped on a thigh, he held his face in his hands. Jorge resumed his seat. "At last, the day you wished for as a boy has come."

"This joy arrived on a day of sorrow. My feelings are confused. Even more than you know. Before my grandfather and Klo-sen arrived, I was about to ask you to ride with me to join the great Chief Cochise on the warpath."

"What you ask, my friend, is no small matter. For death will do his best to follow our trail. Regardless, it will be my honor to ride with you on the warpath."

Ortega massaged his face with dirty hands. They sat in silence until the birds arrived to devour the not-yet-ready-for-harvest crop. It was then that Ortega realized that he had not eaten this day. They stood and stretched. "Did the White Eyes make a treaty and send the birds to make war on us?"

They laughed.

* * *

In the days after the raid, the people made new wickiups and repaired others. Jacali now lived with her sponsor and her sponsor's husband. Under the watchful eye of her sponsor, Jacali and Ortega talked quietly under a tree a few feet away. Their conversation ended after three minutes. Before he departed, Ortega shook Jacali's hand for the first time. He thought her smile was radiant. He felt warm inside and he walked away almost sure Jacali would accept his proposal.

In the week that followed, Ortega built a wickiup on the side of a hill overlooking the Rio Bonito, but not far from camp. He also made a deck of rawhide playing cards for Klo-sen. The deck consisted of four brightly painted ten-card suits. The suits were clubs, coins, cups, and swords. On the day he decided to make the customary proposal, he stocked the hidden wickiup with food, blankets, and the lion skin cover made by Jacali's mother.

At first dark, Ortega presented his gift of the card deck to a grateful Klo-sen. Then he led his horse and staked and tied her in front of Jacali's sponsor's wickiup. He retired to the wickiup he shared with his grandfather to wait for Jacali's sign that she would accept his proposal.

The next morning, Ortega's horse stood unfed and without water. Though already older than most brides at nineteen, it was clear to all that the beautiful Jacali was not desperate to be married. A second day passed. Ortega wondered if she could be considering another warrior. Custom held that the bride had four days to decide. If she accepted his proposal, she was to feed and water the bridegroom's horse and tie the steed in front of his dwelling. The night of the second day, Ortega had bad dreams and slept fitfully. Nantahe-totel had shaken him awake twice when Ortega cried out in his sleep.

Bleary-eyed on the morning of the third day, Ortega was afraid to look outside. When he did, he leapt for joy and hit his head on a small log cross member in the ceiling of the wickiup. His grandfather chuckled as Ortega rubbed the growing knot on his head. There in front of the wickiup stood his horse for all the people to see. Jacali would be his wife!

After two days of eating and dancing in celebration by the entire band, the newlyweds stole away after midnight, riding double on Ortega's horse, to their hidden wickiup.

* * *

At first dark, Jacali handed the reins up to Ortega. She touched his knee and dropped her hand and her head. Their three-month-old baby, strapped securely inside the hooded wicker and cloth *tsach* on Jacali's back, began to cry. Jacali ignored the baby and wiped her own tears with her hands and sleeves. Ortega looked down at her and blinked back water welling in his eyes. He reflected on the year that had passed since their wedding; Chief Cadete's unfulfilled prophecy of a Mescalero reservation, the stories brought in about Chief Cochise on the warpath, and living with Jacali and their new son. He wanted to dismount and hold her. Instead, he made a small wave of his hand. "Be strong. I'll be back by your side as soon as I can."

Jacali nodded and walked away.

Ortega took a long look at his son bobbing from side to side in rhythm with Jacali's stride. Then he turned his horse, nudged its sides with his heels, and joined Jorge and two warriors about their age, called Jarvis and Pedro, who had returned with Chief Cadete from Comanche country. He stopped beside Jorge. "It is time."

Jorge and their two comrades answered in unison, "Let's go."

They rode out side by side under a rustler's moon. Ortega looked back. Nantahe-totel and Klo-sen waved.

The foursome followed the crystal-clear waters of Rio Bonito's three-foot-wide South Fork glistening in the moonlight to a clearing where five canyons met. Large ponderosa pines and low growing junipers dominated the mountains rising from the sides of the canyons. They had traveled only fifteen miles and passed over a ridge from which the head waters of the South Folk flowed when they paused in the clearing and faced south to take in the sight of the peak of Sierra Blanca, the twelve-thousand-foot holy mountain. Ortega stretched his hands out from his sides and said a short prayer to Ussen. He looked back and found that his comrades did the same while their horses munched the tall grass beneath them.

Though Ortega had told each companion how to reach the place where they had heard Chief Cochise was camped, he led them by following his grandfather's directions. Out of the clearing, they went northwest for less than half a mile, found the headwaters of the Three Rivers River, turned sharply southwest, and followed it as it meandered through the canyon of the same name. Four miles on, they descended to the edge of the desert. They stopped and let the horses drink first, then, one by one, the young warriors drank.

Twenty miles later, they reached the U-turn where Three Rivers bent sharply south only to turn north again before continuing its southwesterly journey to the sand dunes. Ortega found the North Star and they left the river headed due west across the desert as Nantahe-totel had instructed. When they reached the small stream running southwest and parallel to El Malpais, they followed it until it went underground. There they entered the lava beds.

Ortega was surprised to find both tall scruffy pines and small saguaros in El Malpais growing through crevices in the rocks. At an hour after midnight, they made camp among the black rocks of the lava bed under an arch formed by the lava that had large pines growing on top. The archway was about thirty feet from floor to ceiling with plenty of room for the horses. The horses remained saddled. In the cave-like arch, Ortega felt safe from enemies – soldiers, Navajos, White Eye citizens, or Mexicans. They built a small fire and prepared their food. They would remain there throughout the next day to avoid passersby and rest their horses.

Sitting about the fire, the young men alternately complained and made jokes about farming. Pedro pounded a fist into his hand. "Never will I do this squaw work of scratching in the ground."

Jorge lifted himself from the ground and sat on a large black rock. "You know, I don't think it is a bad thing for men to work in the fields. Look at Nantahe-totel. He was a famous warrior. Now he leads men in the new ways of farming."

Ortega listened to his friend with surprised interest. Smiling, he asked, "Jorge, does the mere thought of farm work not hurt your back any longer?"

A raucous guffaw came from Jarvis and Pedro.

Jorge held his back with both hands and scrunched up his face in mock pain. "Why do you think I'm here with you idiots?"

More laughter.

Jarvis scratched his head. "Come to think of it, why *are* you going with us?"

Pedro broke in, "So he can rest his back!"

Ortega joined the guffaw.

Undaunted, Jorge replied, "I'm here to drive the White Eyes and Mexicans from our lands. Then we can live in peace and feed our children. Or, I will die trying…." His voice trailed off.

There was quiet for a long moment. Ortega held his head down and rubbed his chin. He had not thought beyond driving their enemies out of their lands. He simply wanted revenge. In deep contemplation, he wondered, what of my son's future? In the world of Jorge's thoughts, what would be the role of men in my son's generation? Or of my grandchildren? I know Jacali agrees with Nantahe-totel. He was aware that his comrades were talking, but did not allow their voices to distract him from new matters to which he felt he needed to give more serious thought.

Jarvis threw a pebble over the fire and hit Ortega's moccasin. "Hey! Say something. You invited us out here."

Ortega lifted his face. His serious look caused silence. "I'm not sure I know the answer to everything. But I do not believe there can be peace with respect from our enemies until we avenge the murder of our people and drive the White Eyes and Mexicans from our lands. Beyond that task, I don't know. Maybe Jorge and my grandfather are right about this farming idea. I don't know." He folded his arms and resumed his pensive mood.

* * *

The next afternoon, they cleaned and checked their weapons. First, attention was given to carbines and rifles. Next was the recheck of the security of their ammunition. Bows and arrows were carried primarily to hunt without attracting unwanted attention that would come with the sound of gunshots. Finally, each warrior re-secured the food in their cloth saddlebags and the emergency food pouches attached to their belts.

The sun was sinking behind the San Andres Mountains when they walked their horses to the edge of El Malpais. Suddenly, Jarvis' horse reared and snatched the reins from his hand.

Everyone gripped their reins tighter. Jarvis looked back and exclaimed, "Rattlesnake!"

He ran and his own horse galloped east away form the lava bed.

Pedro pulled his horse near and grabbed his rifle.

Ortega yelled. "Don't shoot! The echo could be heard for miles out here. Besides, that's not a rattlesnake. Look at its tail. Grandfather said that's a gopher snake. He tries to disguise himself as a rattler to fool his enemies. Why, he's not even poison."

Jorge quickly mounted and was off chasing the runaway horse.

Jarvis wiped sweat and adjusted his headband. "Well, he damned sure fooled me – and my horse."

* * *

From the end of El Malpais, they followed the setting sun. Ortega was amazed at the accuracy of Nantahe-totel's memory, for there in front of them were the two wide-mouth canyons he described. They were to take the one that opened to the northeast; it would lead them through the rugged San Andres without the need for climbing. Before midnight, they cleared the San Andres and crossed the desolate Jornada del Muerto. Once over the Camino Real-Chihuahua Trail and the low Cristobal Range, they camped on the east bluffs above the muddy Rio Grande, north of its confluence with the small clear Rio Cañada Alamosa. No fires were lit because of proximity to Fort McRae and the north-south trail used by merchants and settlers. Even in the moonlight, the bluffs and the river valley were lush and green.

Ortega had no trouble convincing his companions to wait for daylight to find a place to ford the famous river.

At daybreak, they crossed south of a lagoon and a bend in the river. Ortega and Jorge floated Jacali's painted gourds past the ducks in the lagoon. Alarmed at first, the ducks paid no attention by the third pass. Ortega and Jorge then donned large gourds over their heads and waded into the shallow lagoon from opposite ends, keeping their bodies concealed underwater. Jacali had made holes for the wearer's eyes. The men approached the unsuspecting ducks. Each reached underneath one, grabbed its feet, snatched it underwater, and stuffed it into a sack. As they climbed out of the lagoon with four bagged ducks, Pedro and Jarvis cheered.

By afternoon, they had made contact with Chihenne Apache warriors near Ojo Caliente in the San Mateo Mountains north of the town of Cañada Alamosa and its Mexican occupants. From them they learned that the Chihenne Chiefs Loco and Victorio had been in peace talks, first with President Grant's emissary, Vincent Colyer, then with US Army Colonel Gordon Granger near Cañada Alamosa, but the talks had ended in 1871.

Ortega, showing his disappointment, wanted to know, "Is it even true that Chief Cochise took part?"

The Chihenne warrior who reminded Ortega of Klo-sen spoke. "Yes, the great Chokonen chief was here six moons ago. Your information is old. The talks ended when the White Eye Granger refused to make treaty for a joint Chihenne and Chokonen reservation right here. Granger's agent even threatened to stop providing rations if we didn't move to Tularosa. Chief Victorio told the agent he could feed the government's rations to the wolves and bears. Chief Cochise walked out and departed for Janos."

Ortega smiled at Victorio's remark. Then he was serious again. "Where is Janos? How do we get there?"

"In northern Chihuahua."

The older man paused and looked Ortega and his companions over as if this was the first time he saw them. "You're young. Do you really know what going on the warpath means? Chief Victorio has fought beside Geronimo and Chiefs Cochise, Juh, and Coloradas against both White Eye and Mexican soldiers. Now, for the sake of our people, Chief Victorio is doing his best to give peace a chance – even if we, Chihenne, don't get our reservation at Cañada Alamosa. War, considering how few we are in numbers, is a most serious matter. Young men like you are the future of our people."

"If we fight, we may die. If we don't, all of us, Mescalero, Chihenne, and Chokonen, will surely die corralled like cattle on a reservation. Which way is best? Cochise's way or Victorio's?"

The older man and his Chihenne companions said nothing for many minutes. He stared at Ortega. Ortega stared back. Presently, the Chihenne blinked. "At sunrise, I will take you to Janos. By the way, I am called Ponce."

That night, four Mescalero and four Chihenne warriors shared roast ducks from an earthen rock oven and talked of joining the Chokonen on the warpath.

* * *

On the morning of their second day out of Cañada Alamosa, they were resting their horses on a slope south of Cooke's Peak, looking down at the desert floor, when Ortega pointed to a cloud of dust in the east. Ponce responded by waving for the warriors to follow him. The horses were coaxed down the rocky slope and past the cacti as fast as they dared, on a path to intercept the westbound travelers on the old Butterfield Overland Mail Trail below. Ortega rode beside Ponce, determined to exact revenge.

A short time later they joined the trail behind a fine black private coach pulled by three pairs of black horses. It was apparent to Ortega that the driver had seen them descending from the mountain, for he was driving his charges at high speed. Passengers began firing out the windows as the warriors overtook the coach. Ortega saw Ponce swing to the side of his horse, holding on with his left arm about the horse's neck, thus shielding himself from direct fire. He shot the driver off the box. Ortega copied the method by moving his horse left and firing his carbine from under his horse's neck. After the firing from inside the coach ceased, the black horses raced on along the trail. Ortega and Jorge rode past the coach on opposite sides, overtook the lead horses, caught their traces, and pulled them to a stop.

The Chihenne warriors immediately opened the doors of the coach. One male passenger was already dead, shot through the forehead. A second man was wounded and, in the doorway, held up his hands in what appeared to Ortega as an attempt to surrender. He had no idea what the man was saying, for Ortega spoke only Apache and Spanish. The man was shot twice before he had both feet on the ground. Ortega winced. He kept his feelings to himself that somehow this killing was not fair. He pushed aside his conscience and remembered that both Chiefs Coloradas and Manuelito were murdered by White Eyes while under a flag of truce. A trembling and crying woman in a long magnificent blue dress that opened at the top allowing her white lace ruffles to show stepped down from the coach with both hands up, one clutching a small handkerchief trimmed in delicate lace between two fingers and manicured nails. Though Ortega knew she must have been pleading for her life, his was one of three bullets that ended her days.

They took food out of the coach and removed the horses from their harnesses. Pedro and a Chihenne took clothing and watches from the bodies of the men. All the while, no one spoke. After setting the coach ablaze in the middle of the road, Ponce spoke. "We must ride like the wind." He pointed. "The soldiers over there at Fort Cummings may have heard our shots."

Nothing more was said. They led the black horses at a fast trot due south across desert country for sixty miles. Ponce called a halt at El Berrendo. "We are in Mexico. The blue soldiers will not follow us here. We can rest."

They watered the horses and ate cold food.

At sunset, they were welcomed by Cochise and his Chokonen warriors, camped in a canyon by a tiny stream in the small El Medio Range, a few miles northwest of Janos. Ortega was surprised that Cochise was over six feet tall and more than sixty years old.

* * *

For two weeks, Ortega and his Mescalero companions rode with Chokonen and Chihenne warriors conducting raids in Chihuahua, Arizona, New Mexico, and Sonora, killing White Eyes and Mexicans while seizing firearms, cattle, sheep, horses, and mules. On separate raids, Jarvis and one of Ponce's Chokonens died when they were shot from their horses. On their return to the El Medio camp, they learned that Cochise would go to his stronghold in the Dragoon Mountains of Arizona and meet with Brigadier General Oliver Otis Howard, a new emissary from President Grant.

That night at council, though seated far behind, first Chokonen, then Chihenne warriors, Ortega heard Cochise make the case for peace. Cochise told the assembly, in part, what he would say to the general. "Now, Americans and Mexicans kill an Apache on sight. I have retaliated with all my might. My people have killed Americans and Mexicans and taken their property. Their losses have been greater than mine. I have killed ten white men for every Indian slain, but I know that the whites are many and the Indians are few…. Why shut me up on a reservation? We will make peace. We will keep it faithfully. But let us go around free as Americans do. Let us go wherever we please."

Ortega marveled at Cochise's logic, eloquence, and that no one spoke in dissent. Ortega's chin rested on his collarbone as he sat and pondered what he should do next. *What of Jacali and our son? How can I live without acting to avenge the evil done to Apaches by White Eyes and Mexicans? To my own parents? Am I foolish? Am I* wrong, if chiefs so revered as Cochise or Victorio say it's time to try peace? Perhaps I should have listened to grandfather. These men are grandfather's age....

At the end of the council, Cochise asked for a halt to raids until he sent word to come in to a new reservation or resume raids. The next morning, in mid-September, Cochise and a party of Chokonen warriors departed for the Dragoons. In early October, a runner brought word that Cochise and Howard had agreed on the establishment of a Chiricahua reservation in the southeastern corner of Arizona. President Grant made it official two months later by Executive Order in December 1872.

While the Chokonen packed and left their El Medio camp, Ortega and his comrades discussed what to do next.

Ortega missed Jacali more than he thought he would, but did not say so. "I will take my share of the horses back to Fort Stanton and give them to my father-in-law."

Ponce shook his head. "There will be time for that later. You can leave your horses at the livery in Casa Grande. Come with me into the Sierra Madre and let's raid with Juh and Geronimo."

Jorge fidgeted with his bow and did not look up. "The Mescalero have no reservation. We may need to inflict more pain before the White Eyes will agree to a reservation for our people. I see riding with Chief Juh and Geronimo as an opportunity to learn tactics from two of the best."

Ponce grinned broadly. "Young man, you are wise." He put a hand on Jorge's shoulder and turned to Ortega. "Come with us. You will learn much and see the Blue Mountains, deep inside Sonora. Speaking of blue, I'll show you the blue waters of a lake that has no end."

Ortega thought there was truth in Jorge's words and recalled that Nantahe-totel had spoken in awe of a lake with no end. "I will go with my best friend."

Grinning, Ponce raised his lance. "We will ride at sunrise!"

* * *

On arrival at Juh's stronghold in the Sierra Madre, Ortega learned that Geronimo had met Cochise for the peace talks with General Howard and had actually ridden double with the general to Fort Bowie on General Howard's horse. Juh's Nednai Apaches welcomed the Mescaleros and Chihennes to their hideaway. Ortega and his comrades raided east and north of Juh's mountain stronghold.

By spring, Ortega longed to see Jacali. Returning from their first raid west of the Sierra Madre near the town called Ures, Ortega turned to Ponce. "I'm ready to see the lake with no end and return to my homeland."

Ponce looked at Jorge, who nodded. "I'm ready too."

Immediately, Ponce turned his horse about on the trail, telling the Chihenne and Nednai warriors, "Take these cattle to Juh." He called to Pedro, "Are you coming?"

"Yes."

The foursome skirted Hermosillo to the east and south. They saw several people on the trail. Ortega said to Ponce, "These people don't look like regular Mexicans. Who are they?"

"Their people are my neighbors. They are one with the Pima people who live near the Gila and Salt Rivers in my homeland."

"Oh."

They headed west, and, two days later, arrived on a Gulf of California beach near Bahia de Kino.

Ortega, Jorge, and Pedro removed their moccasins, stripped to their breechclouts, and waded into the surf up to their necks. Each tasted the water and spat it out. Jorge and Pedro were splashing each other when Ortega began pointing out to sea and backing toward the shore. He could only say, "L-l-look, look, look...."

Ortega turned and tried to run for the beach. But he found it difficult to run in the water and he fell several times. Once on shore, he turned to see two black and white killer whales leap from the water and splash down again, creating a geyser. He cupped his hands about his mouth and called to Jorge and Pedro. "Run! Run!"

They too saw the whales and tried to run and had the same stumbling results as Ortega. Fully clothed, Ponce was rolling in the sand, overcome with uproarious laughter. He was joined in that laughter by two passing Pima fishermen. The fishermen explained that the twenty-five-foot long whales were frolicking and having fun with each other and had no interest in humans.

The Mescaleros were still shaking. For the remainder of their time on the beach, they were content to collect small shells and unusual stones. He did not mention it, but Ortega knew he would create a necklace of shells for Jacali. Pedro made a tipi village in the wet sand to show Ortega and Jorge a model of his dwelling when he lived among the Comanche people.

* * *

A week later, the three Chihenne and three Mescaleros left Casa Grande with their horses and cattle and traveled east, then north paralleling the El Paso-Chihuahua Road. In the state of Chihuahua, they passed east of the village of Carrizal. Amused, Ortega watched as two unusually dark Mexican women herded three pigs toward the town. They reminded Ortega of Haozinne and Jacali. He thought the young woman was almost as beautiful as Jacali.

Suddenly, two mounted men rode from the mesquite near a stream and shot two of the pigs. One held the women at gunpoint while the other dismounted and tied the feet of the dead pigs. When he attempted to lift a pig to his partner's saddle horn, Ortega shot him. The surprised mounted man raised his rifle at the charging Jorge. Jorge shot him before the man's rifle was level. The man spurred his horse and raced away holding his shoulder. Ortega and Jorge let him go.

They dragged the pigs to the women's small adobe house. The young woman spoke. "*Gracias. Mucho gracias.*" The older woman, clasping her hands together, echoed thanks several times.

"You're welcome. Who were those men?"

The older woman spat. "They were revolutionaries who claim they help common farmers. I guess they were surprised that you would stand up to them."

The young woman smiled and changed the subject. "We are poor people and have but a few animals. We are too poor to be robbed. Thank you so much for helping me and my mother."

Ortega felt good. He and Jorge nodded. Ortega experienced a strange conflict within himself. He had been told Mexicans were their enemies. Yet these women's lives did not appear to be different from those of Haozinne and Jacali. Despite his feelings, he remained alert for threats. His eyes periodically darted to and fro and he said to Jorge, "Let's go. People are watching."

The young woman called after their backs as their horses trotted away. "Maybe someday, I can help your people. My name is Alejandra."

Chapter 29

Fort Leavenworth

"Dammit! Why the fuck do we have to move again?" Isaac was livid. Their tent and bedrolls lay in a heap next to the road with the belongings of their fellow Tenth Cavalry troopers.

Caleb hunched his shoulders. "Looks like ol' Gen'l Hoffman hates anything and anybody colored. He doesn't even like Colonel Grierson."

Isaac gathered his equipment. "Yeah. And another thing: in my book, the sonovabitch murdered that poor Thomas whatshisface. Ain't no young man like Thomas got no bitness dying o' no damn pneumonia."

"Williams."

"What?"

Charles Dougherty repeated, "Williams. That was Thomas whatshisface's last name. If we ain't careful, Gen'l Hoffman's gonna kill off more o' us before spring."

Charles and his bunkmate, Robert Johnston, were neighbors as their tent was next to Isaac and Caleb's. Charles and Robert were two of thirty-six new men who had joined the regiment while Isaac and Caleb were away in October 1866.

"Or, make us wanna desert. What was that boy's name who joined *and* deserted while Caleb and me were gone?"

Charles scratched his chin. "Dog, if I can remember. He was here only a few days – not even a week. Then, one evenin' atter supper, he said, 'I got treated better'n dis 'fore I joined – and I slept with dry feets.'"

They were still gathering their equipment from the pile along the road. Caleb grinned. "Hey, y'all. I kin feel a new song a comin'. When it's fully baked, I'll sing it for you. I'ma call it the 'Gen'l Hoffman cold, wet, pneumonia feet blues.'"

There was light laughter. Then quiet. The new soldiers trudged down the road to an isolated and damp low-lying place on the edge of Fort Leavenworth. As the western sky turned purple, they finished erecting their new tent town of nineteen two-man tents.

Isaac gazed at the spot on the horizon behind which the sun had just sunk. And then he looked down at the buttons bearing the letters US on his new blue cavalry uniform. He said aloud, but to no one in particular, "Ain't no gen'l or any other white sonovabitch gonna drive me outta the army o' my country."

Several comrades followed Caleb's "Amen!"

General William Hoffman, commander of the Third Regiment of US Infantry and post commander at Fort Leavenworth, made no secret of his opposition to the idea of Negro troops in the army. He decreed that colored soldiers be quartered and trained in areas separate and well apart from white troops.

* * *

Following their walk in a casual line from the mess area and supper, the men of the new Tenth Cavalry built two fires to ward off the chill of the coming evening. One of the recruits who arrived that day from the depot at Jefferson Barracks introduced himself. "Hey, boys. I'm Albert Jackson from the grand city o' St. Louie."

A man on the opposite side of the fire laughed. "I'm Dennis Rutledge. I came from the same place country-ass Albert came from – the woods o' Franklin County, Missouri!"

Hysterical laughter broke out.

Albert's nostrils flared. He looked about at the faces around the fire. Then, he singled out Isaac. "So, funny talkin' nigger, where 'bout you come from?"

Isaac chuckled. "Oh, from a wus place, I'm sure. I was born and raised in a swamp by de Pon Pon River in Colleton County, South Carolina. All de swamp folks back where I came from talk like me and my homey, here." Isaac slapped Caleb's shoulder.

The men told stories around the fire. Albert informed his new comrades that he had joined the army to rob the paymaster and then desert to St. Louis for "a big time."

"Yeah, man. I'm in wid som' bad-ass partn'rs on de outside. We gwine do the army. Dese white folks won't know what hit'em."

Isaac watched the dismissive response of the group with interest. Then he thought this Albert may be telling the truth – this time.

Caleb's story about the veteran Civil War soldier, Charles DeFaux, and their raid on a raider in Mississippi drew great interest. Their new comrade, Charles Dougherty, wanted to know more. "What happened after the wanted handbill?"

Caleb looked at Isaac. Isaac shrugged and then nodded. Caleb recounted the story. At the end of Caleb's rendition, every man was quiet. At length, Charles turned to Isaac. "My brother, I admire yo' guts and devotion to yo' woman. If she had lived, would you really have taken her back?"

Tears rose in Isaac's eyes. He blinked them back. In a firm voice, Isaac replied, "Yes."

Albert waved a dismissive hand. "Aw, hell no. I wouldn't have the bitch. I betcha she wanted that white dude."

Caleb pushed Isaac's shoulder down for leverage as he leapt to his feet and raised a fist. "Muthafucker, you'd better watch yo' mouf!"

"Hey, man, I was just sayin', you know, just my thought...."

Isaac felt rage building. He knew Caleb wanted him to remain seated. Isaac thought *I will be calm. I will think. I will control myself.* Isaac slapped the side of Caleb's boot and took a deep breath. "Hey, fellows. I've got a St. Louie story for you."

Slowly, Caleb resumed his seat.

Isaac continued. "Not long ago, a ho grabbed me off a certain street in St. Louie in front o' one them houses run by a madam."

There was light laughter that sounded like relief to Isaac.

"She had a nice shape, but her face was real ug-g-gly. So, I figured, what the hell, I can stand seeing her face for an hour. So I did her. Man, you shoulda heard her scream for more."

The group around their fire was laughing at Isaac's story. The group at the second fire listened to another tale.

"After we finished, we had smokes and a lil' talk. She told me her biggest regret in the world was not choking the life outta her lil' trouble-makin' bastard when she birthed'im. So I asked her what she named him. She said, Albert Jackson."

The laughter ceased. All eyes were on Albert. After a pause, a loud guffaw burst forth. There was backslapping all around.

In a second, Albert was up and jumped over the dying fire. He dove into Isaac, still seated, pinning him on his back. Albert's fists flew. Isaac felt pain in both cheeks and grabbed the larger man's left arm, turned on his elbow, and yanked Albert to the ground. Isaac rolled atop Albert and delivered a fist to Albert's nose. He felt the nose yield under his punch and Albert screeched in pain.

Albert shoved with both hands against Isaac's chest and sent Isaac backwards into the dwindling fire. Isaac rolled over twice and landed on the opposite side of the pit. Before Isaac could get to his feet, Albert was over him raising his foot to stomp Isaac's face. Isaac caught Albert's foot and twisted it, and Albert went down in a heap. Isaac leapt to his feet and rushed Albert, who had risen on all fours. Isaac laced his fingers together and brought his double fist down on the base of Albert's skull with all his strength. Albert slumped to the ground on his face, unconscious.

Isaac stood over his foe, chest heaving. Presently, Isaac realized Albert was not getting up. Isaac walked about the fire in an aimless circle. He could feel Rachel's Colt .44 strapped to his right leg inside his knee-high cavalry boot. He was amazed that it had not fallen out during the scuffle with Albert. Isaac wished again that Rachel was alive.

* * *

Several days later, Charles called to Isaac in the noon chow line. "Hey, Isaac. You've got a visitor."

Four men answered. "Which Isaac?" Laughter followed.

"Isaac Rice, the one from the swamps of South Carolina." More laughter.

"Comin'.

"Hey, James. Ain't you a sight for sore eyes? How the hell are you? Did you eat yet?"

Isaac saw Sergeant James Darby grin from ear to ear. "I'm fine and dandy. How's your new military life? No, I didn't eat yet. I'll get in line and join you and Caleb."

After dinner, James demonstrated the basics of drill for a single soldier. All the recruits of the new regiment watched as James put

Isaac and Caleb through attention, at-ease, salute, and facing movements. Then he taught them to respond to preparatory and execution commands, followed by marching as a pair. In the next hour, Isaac and Caleb gave commands and drilled two groups of six men. After a break, several of these dozen men drilled others. Sergeant Darby stood aside and chatted with Isaac and Caleb.

"This should help you overcome some of the criticism I heard when I asked about the Tenth Cav."

Caleb asked, "What criticism?"

"Some white soldiers said y'all move about like a mob. Never mind them. They'll always criticize. That's what soldiers do. But don't give'em free ammunition. March everywhere you go – even when you're the only person going. Put your chest out and march. And, without fail, when two or more of you are together going anyplace on this post, march. Drill at least two hours a day until you're comfortable with it. Pretty soon, your old man will have you marching in the regular parades held here periodically."

Isaac unfolded his arms. "Wait a minute, James. Who is our old man?"

James laughed. "Sorry. Soldiers generally refer to their commander as their old man."

"Oh."

"On my way out, I'll let Colonel Grierson know that you now know how to carry on among yourselves until he's able to get officers and sergeants of his own in here to train you.

"Oh, by the way, I'm leaving Jefferson Barracks in January. I'm joining the Fourth Cav in Texas. Perhaps we'll meet again in the field. Adios, amigos."

Isaac wondered, what manner of friend have we made in this strange white man?

* * *

The morning after a heavy frost in the second week of November 1866, Isaac, Caleb, Charles Dougherty, and Robert Johnston used folding cots to carry two recruits from their new round-shaped Sibley tents to the hospital. Two more men had fallen victim to pneumonia.

The Sibley tents were a major improvement in comfort. Each Sibley easily housed a dozen men. They slept on cots, arranged like spokes in a wheel, with their feet toward the fire pit in the middle of the round tent. The single pole of the tent stood in an iron tripod that was perched over a fire pit. They used the legs of the tripod to hang coffee pots above the fire. Sharpened wooden pegs held the sides of the tents in place.

With all the traffic of more and more recruits arriving almost daily, the low lying land remained soggy and muddy after each rain. General Hoffman ignored repeated requests from Colonel Grierson to move the Tenth or provide wooden walkways. Wet feet were common. Tent living with so many men presented a new challenge for Isaac to keep Rachel's Colt .44 hidden. He sometimes hid it in his shirt and when he could, in his boot.

* * *

Weather permitting, they drilled twice a day, taking turns as the sergeant leading and giving commands. The new recruits were taught the basics of drill as they arrived.

The night after the paymaster's visit in December, Albert Jackson was found near a road on the edge of the military reservation, dead of a gunshot wound in his chest. He was dressed in civilian clothes. The men of the Tenth noted that there was no investigation into his death.

* * *

In January, a few noncommissioned officers arrived. With satisfaction, Isaac noted these were the first colored men he had seen wearing stripes on their sleeves since his days at Davis Bend. The new sergeants took over drill, small unit tactical training, and discipline. As 1867 began, they still had fewer enlisted men in the whole regiment than Colonel Grierson's goal of one hundred to fill the ranks of the first company. Even so, Isaac imagined Colonel Grierson breathing a sigh of relief. Yet he still had not found clerical help.

Near the end of the month, the first officer to report for duty in the Tenth arrived at Fort Leavenworth. He was Captain Nicholas

Nolan. Other officers had accepted assignments in the Tenth Cavalry, but were elsewhere performing recruiting duties on behalf of Colonel Grierson. One such officer was Captain Henry Carpenter, Nolan's good friend from their days together during the Civil War.

Within three weeks, Nolan was directing training for the growing regiment. Soon Captain Nolan was feeling the long reach of General Hoffman. Officers of the Tenth Cavalry were directed to keep their troops ten to fifteen yards from white troops. During their first participation in a parade, General Hoffman would not allow the Tenth Cavalry to pass in review, but instead required the regiment to stand in place at parade rest. Colonel Grierson protested on the parade field to no avail.

Isaac remarked to Caleb and Charles, "Doggone it, I've joined the army and the first war I see is between a general and a colonel – about me and you!"

* * *

In the third week of February, Colonel Grierson told the men of the Tenth Cavalry that he had decided to create Company A, the regiment's first company, and that it would include only the eighty-four earliest arriving recruits instead of the one hundred originally planned. Colonel Grierson went on, "Men of Company A, you're making history today. Work hard and learn all you can as fast as you're able. Very soon, I will send you, Company A, to the field and in harm's way. I will not wait until we have enough recruits to fill Companies B through M. The eyes of our countrymen will be upon you. I salute you and your new commanding officer, Captain Nicholas M. Nolan. Carry on and Godspeed."

While Colonel Grierson returned Captain Nolan's salute, Caleb whispered without turning his head, "I love a short speech!"

Isaac whispered back, "Me too! Sh-h-h."

Captain Nolan marched the recruits to a new destination – the stables. On arrival, Nolan told two stories about the role horses played in his experiences with the Sixth Cavalry during the war. Next he demonstrated drill commands for horse soldiers, beginning with, "Stand to horse." Nolan's horse was already saddled. He gave and executed several more basic commands, riding his horse about on the field as he performed.

Nolan returned and dismounted. "Farriers, pick a horse. We will show the men the beginning of mounted drill."

Isaac hesitated.

Nolan approached. He was pulling his black goatee. "Mr. Rice, are you not a farrier."

Isaac snapped to attention. "Sir, I'm a blacksmith."

Nolan made a broad smile and turned away, saying to the assembled men, "I misspoke. Blacksmiths, join the farriers. Pick a horse."

Isaac entered the corral and stopped. He surveyed the fifty or so bay horses before him. All of Company A's horse were to be bays. None were saddled, but were fitted with bridles, bits, and reins. The two farriers and one other blacksmith walked among the horses. Isaac spotted a bay with a star face and high left-front stocking. Her ears moved to and fro, then stopped pointed toward Isaac. She was twenty yards away. Isaac took a step toward her and she met him halfway. When they were close, Isaac put a hand out. The horse did not back away. Isaac touched her muzzle, then the diamond-shaped white hair between her eyes.

Nolan called in a strong voice. "Stand to horse." Pause. The four men did as Nolan had demonstrated by standing to the left of their horse's head. "Prepare to mount." The men stepped back until they were beside the left shoulder of their horse. Pause. "MOUNT."

Isaac placed his left hand on the left side of his horse's withers, flexed his knees, and propelled himself up and onto the horse's back. The horse groaned. Caleb laughed, followed by a few others.

Nolan smiled. "Men, you'll have to remember, these horses are, like me, leftovers from the war. Several may even be as old as me."

Everyone laughed.

They tried to form a line with the horses the prescribed eighteen inches apart. Dennis's horse would not cooperate and tried to bite his left leg. Dennis jumped off the rear of the horse and landed on his butt. He promptly got up and kicked the horse. The horse then kicked Dennis and sent him sprawling.

The men laughed.

Nolan gave commands and had the three remaining riders perform as he had done.

As the threesome rode about the field, Isaac glanced back and saw Nolan, arms folded, standing toe to toe with Dennis. Dennis was standing at rigid attention with his chin nearly touching his collarbone. Isaac shook his head.

When the day was done, the sergeants, farriers, and blacksmiths had taught the men basic mounted drill without arms and how to wash, comb, curry, and feed the animals.

When the men were dismissed to prepare for supper, Nolan turned to Isaac. "Mr. Rice, I have a question for you."

Isaac's brow furrowed. He thought *now what did I do?* "Yes, sir?"

"I saw you select that horse. How did you decide? What did you say to the horse?"

Isaac's brow unknotted. "Oh, sir, I didn't pick that horse. The horse picked me. When I meet a new horse, I always put my hand on the muzzle and talk to'em. I don't remember what I said. That's not important. I want'em to hear my voice and tone. Then the horse understands that I want us to be friends."

"Amazing. I've met only one other man who can do that. He's a blacksmith too. Can you teach me how to do it?"

"Oh, no, sir. Sorry, sir. I don't understand how I came tuh do it. Somehow, I just sense what most horses need. But, I don't get through tuh some."

"Still, amazing." Nolan sighed. "Well, run along. See you tomorrow."

"Good night, sir."

They saluted.

* * *

The next day, the troopers were issued seven-shot Spencer repeating carbines and carbine boots that were purchased during the war by the government. Their leather carbine sling was worn like a diagonal sash and its metal hook attached to an O-ring on the left side of their Spencer. Noncommissioned officers were also issued a Colt .44 with holster and belt. In a side conversation, Isaac got Captain Nolan's approval for issue of a belt and holster for Rachel's pistol in exchange for fetching Nolan's mail and paperwork everyday. The same day, Nolan began armed mounted drill.

* * *

At first light on Tuesday, April 2, 1867, Colonel Grierson bade them farewell and, like a parent, watched their departure. Captain Nolan gave the command to march and Company A left Fort Leavenworth to General William Hoffman.

In fifteen minutes, when they were out of sight of the fort, Nolan called a halt. He rode up and down the line checking the men and the canvas-covered wagons carrying their company mess, rations, tools, clothing, and other equipment. Though Nolan had said he did not expect an attack by Indians between Forts Leavenworth and Riley, he organized an advance guard, flankers, and a rearguard so he would not miss the teaching moment. The wagons, each pulled by three teams of mules, were in the middle. Isaac noted every move.

Isaac and Caleb were in the rearguard. After thirty minutes, Caleb remarked, "Why is the captain taking so long? It's not like him to waste time."

"You're right. This is curious." Isaac looked around, trying to ascertain a reason for their delay. Teacher's ears were pointed to the rear. So Isaac looked back. "Hey, Homey. I think the mystery's been solved. Ol' Teacher told me to look back. Lookit, behind us."

"Well, I've gotta take it all back. Our captain's smarter'n that damn Hoffman!"

Laundresses, who had taken on work from Company A after the paymaster's first visit, caught up and climbed aboard the wagons. Their wash pots and scrub boards had been loaded by the troops the previous night. General Hoffman had forbidden the laundresses from following Company A to its new post – Fort Larned, Kansas. The men cheered. Nolan was all smiles. Again, he gave the command to march.

As they rode along, Isaac observed, "I think we're lucky to have Captain Nolan. We could've had much worse."

"Betcha the ol' man wouldn't pick worse."

"You know, I think you're right. Yes, I think we were first lucky to have the ol' man." Isaac nodded, reassuring himself. "Our leaders are good men who have had a lot o' combat experience."

"Do you think all that experience will help since we ain't gone be fightin' no Secesh?"

"Good question. Injuns damn sho' ain't no Secesh."

"Hey, Homey. I've been meaning to ask you, why'd you name that ol' hoss o' yours 'Teacher'?"

"Oh, that. Teacher's been to war, just like Captain Nolan. I ain't. I wanna learn everything I can from anywhere I can. I still remember everything Sergeant DeFaux taught us. I aim to let this ol' hoss teach me, too."

Caleb feigned sadness and shook his head. "Homey, sometimes, I think you're a tad touched."

They laughed.

They rode at a walk for several miles. Captain Nolan had the rearguard fall back a mile or so and instructed them to catch up again at a trot, then canter, gallop, canter, trot again, and finally resume a walk. When they caught up, Nolan called a halt. For ten minutes, Isaac lay in the grass with his campaign hat over his eyes. The trumpeter sounded "Boots and Saddles." Isaac pulled Teacher away from her grazing on wild rye and buffalo grass and stood by her head. After Nolan gave the command to mount, he switched the guards and both flanks. Nolan had them ride in a clockwise circle around the main body until the switch was completed.

Isaac and Caleb rode at the end of the advance guard and had the additional duty of preventing the guard from losing sight of the main body. Isaac admired the April wildflowers that stretched to the horizon on the open prairie. When he saw the bright blue prairie irid, he thought of his ma – he was sure she would want a cutting to take home. Isaac's heart ached for Rachel when they came upon a field of purple poppy-mallow mixed with pale orange flax blossoms waving in the breeze.

Under a cloudless sky, they traveled without creating a dust cloud, for it had rained the previous afternoon. From near the base of a roadside tree an alarmed speckled grouse flapped its wings furiously and flew off to the north. Isaac followed its flight and spotted a lone vulture patrolling high above the small wood north of the road and the prairie to the south. At that moment, he realized that all morning he had not seen small birds or animals – not even the yellow breasted western meadowlarks that were plentiful at Fort Leavenworth.

Isaac chuckled and listened to the sounds made by the advance guard. He thought their cavalry accouterments made enough racket to announce their approach a mile away. Isaac looked down at his equipment, which included his canteen, carbine, snug in its boot, saddlebags, lariat, tin cup, haversack, holstered sidearm, carbine sling, and cartridge belt and box. Inside one saddlebag, Teacher's nose bag, picket pin, curry comb and brush made their own special noises. In the other saddlebag, he carried his eating utensils, tin meat can, and personal items. He smiled as he thought the only way they would ever surprise an enemy was to arrive well in advance and set up an ambush.

Instead of grazing at lunchtime, Teacher stood behind Isaac and slept. Following the light lunch, Isaac and the advance guard took turns themselves dozing. Isaac and Teacher awoke with a start at the sound of "Boots and Saddles." Near a clear small tributary of the brown Strange Creek, they camped for the first night out of Fort Leavenworth. Company A had marched about fourteen miles. The first order of business was care of their horses and mules. The animals were unsaddled or unhitched and sent out to graze under the watchful eyes of an armed herd detail of six soldiers.

After their supper of bacon, beans, and coffee, Dennis stood and banged his tin cup with his spoon. "Attention everybody, this message just arrived from headquarters: men of Company A, Tenth Cavalry, I'm watchin' you! You are to move rat nigh half a mile back from that nice clear creek in case thirsty white soldiers arrive. Signed, Gen'l Hoffman."

Uproarious and sustained laughter followed from the soldiers and laundresses. Nolan laughed so hard that his hat fell from his head.

* * *

On Thursday of the following week, they arrived at Fort Riley having marched, with wagons slowing their pace, an average of thirteen miles per day. They spent the next three days on firing ranges, conducting their first sustained target practice with carbines and pistols.

Caleb whispered to Charles and Robert, "I'll betcha a whole dollar Homey won't miss a target while dismounted."

Isaac adjusted the rear ladder sight on his carbine and hit targets set out at fifty, one hundred, and two hundred yards. Isaac surprised himself by hitting targets at fifty yards while mounted.

Caleb won two dollars. But he'd have to wait for the paymaster's next visit to collect.

When practice ended on Sunday, Charles mopped his brow with a large red bandana and declared, "Man alive, Isaac is one shootin' fool! Ain't but two men mounted hit targets at fifty yards – him and that country-ass Dennis. I'm sho' as hell glad dey's on my side!"

Caleb was cleaning his carbine. "Well, with Isaac's hawk-eyes, I ain't the least bit surprised. My homey's good wid iron – bendin' it or shootin' it."

When the laughter died, Isaac gave credit. "I was real surprised to hit anything while moving. Teacher was the main reason I made hits at fifty yards. She's one steady customer."

"Yeah, Homey, we saw it all. We saw when ol' Teacher aimed and squeezed dat trigger for you."

It was a while before the repeating of Caleb's words and laughter stopped.

* * *

The next day, they began their march to Fort Harker, passing German and Irish workers building the Union Pacific Railroad along their way. They arrived at Fort Harker a week later. They camped outside the fort on the Smoky Hill River, across from a ranch. That same evening, the guards at the ranch were attacked by Indians or horse thieves. Men from Company A fired several shots and the would-be thieves fled empty-handed into the night. On arrival at Fort Harker, Nolan was asked to make a detour and escort an army-supply wagon train to Fort Hays, some sixty miles west.

Though the march to Fort Hays was uneventful, the advance and rearguards and flankers had to remain alert for Indians. From Fort Hays, they marched south for two days and arrived at their assigned post, Fort Larned, on the last day of April 1870.

* * *

Several days after arriving at Fort Larned, Nolan began aggressive patrols along the route of the Kansas Pacific Railroad, beginning with a few miles of laid track, passing the building site, and moving miles ahead of the workers along the route they would follow. Nolan told the men he was sure the Cheyenne and Arapahoe were watching, but not likely to attack their strong patrols. On each patrol, he would take about half of Company A. The remainder would perform garrison duties at Fort Larned. In the evenings, their patrols camped within sight, but ahead and west of the railroad crews. Each morning, the patrol packed before going out, for the railroad crews were laying track at a rate of one or two miles a day.

On his first patrol, Isaac noticed the looks of disdain and disgust on the faces of patrolling white infantrymen they marched past. He heard men of the Third Regiment of United States Infantry remark, "I still can't believe the government is arming more niggers." "Now we got the uppity-ass nigger cavalry." "And look at their nigger-lovin' captain ridin' so high and proud like he's leadin' some damn honor guard."

They topped a rise and Nolan, riding at the head of the column, pointed and called out, "Bison at nine o'clock!"

A gasp went up from the patrol. They stopped to take a long look. Isaac was excited. He blurted, "There must be hundreds and hundreds of'em! I've never seen that many of any kinda animal in one place – not even ants!"

* * *

Mid-June was hot. Isaac and Caleb were assigned to a garrison work detail, cleaning the stables. They worked side by side with pitchforks and shovels removing manure and soiled straw.

Isaac paused and leaned on his shovel. "Homey, I've been thinkin'."

"Oh, shit."

"Yeah, you're standing in it."

Both laughed.

"Pa died 'fore I let on I wanted to join the army. Mr. Luke, Uncle Jacob, and Uncle Theo told me to watch out, it ain't your army. White folks can have their army do whatever they want it to do."

"I know a young man who told oonah the same thing."

"Yes, I 'member he told me on a Mississippi riverboat. But, he didn't go on and advise me to find a way to get some land like dem three elders did."

"Hmm. I never thought o' that. Why oonah got that on your mind? Ain't oonah satisfied with the army?"

"Well, yes and no."

"Tell me about the no part."

"First, y'all were right. White folks will use their army however they want. What I've seen in eight months is that this army's job is to push the Injuns outta the way while white folks take over the land. Second, Mr. Luke and Uncle Jacob not only said find a way to get some land; they also said look at all the successful white folks. Now I can take that one step further – look at Mr. Ben Montgomery."

Caleb stopped shoveling and folded his arms. Isaac watched as his friend rolled his eyes upward. "I never stopped to think about the land part. Oonah one smart fellow not to be able to read."

"I don't feel smart. I feel I've not been takin' in what's in plain sight."

Caleb paused. "Well, I think that's true of a lot of coloreds – me included."

"Poor whites too. Some o' them ain't buyin' land either."

"I don't see how oonah or me can buy land on thirteen dollars a month."

"We have to look beyond the number thirteen. Let's say I make corporal before my enlistment is up. So, when I go re-enlist, my signing money will be based on years of good service and corporal pay. In the second enlistment, I make sergeant and de same thing happens with the numbers getting larger. Next, I add money made by helpin' de three blacksmiths at this post make hinges and the like for these buildings or doo-dads for the ladies. And last, I know I can live on seven dollars a month. The minimum a soldier can deposit with the paymaster is five dollars. So, if you throw in wid me, by the end of a second re-enlistment, we should be able to buy some worthwhile land. What do oonah think?"

"Damn, Homey. How long oonah been thinkin' 'bout all this?"

"Just since our first patrol."

"Did oonah see something to getcha started?"

"Yes. I saw why we're not too bad off being in the army. How many coloreds did oonah see workin' for the Kansas Pacific? Whose land was gettin' snatched?"

"Humph! It was all right there in front o' me and I didn't see a damned thing...."

"By the way, oonah can't withdraw no savings until the *end* of your enlistment."

* * *

The next day, Isaac knocked on the office door of Company A's Second Lieutenant George Raulston. "Suh, can we talk for a minute?"

Raulston pushed aside the mail on his desk. "Sure, Mr. Rice. Com'on in and have a seat."

Isaac knew he should not feel embarrassed, but he did. "Er, thank you, suh. The matter, plain and simple, is I can't read. Colonel Grierson said he would hire a chaplain to teach us, but I don't reckon he's going to send him way out here to Fort Larned for just one company. So, will you teach me?"

Raulston twisted his handlebar moustache one way then another as he gazed at Isaac. Finally, he spoke. "I'm game. But I want you to know, I'm hesitant because I'm not a teacher and know nothing about where to start. If you don't mind that I have no plan, we can start now."

Isaac's grin split his face from ear to ear. "Now, suh!?"

Raulston chuckled. "Yes. This minute. Oh, wait. I forgot to say, I'll do this only on one condition."

Isaac's countenance fell. "Yes, suh?"

"You have to agree to help me teach any of your fellow soldiers who want to learn."

Isaac's grin was back. "Oh, yes, suh!"

Isaac rocked from side to side on his chair in anticipation as Raulston cleared away more papers. "Okay. While I clean up, say this word for me. Listen carefully. 'Sir.'"

Isaac was puzzled. He turned his ear to Raulston.

Raulston repeated. "Sir."

Isaac said, "Sir."

"Great, we're off and started."

"Yes, sir. Thank you, sir."

"Bring your chair closer. Let's start with letters. I've heard that you're a blacksmith."

"Yes, suh, I mean, yes, sir."

Raulston drew a block letter A. "This is the first letter of twenty-six in our alphabet." Next to the letter, he drew an anvil. He pointed to his drawing. "What is this thing?"

"Sir, that's an anvil."

"So A makes the first sound in the word anvil. Repeat after me: A."

Raulston went to the next letter and asked Isaac to supply a B word and drawing. Isaac chose bed. In about four hours, they had finished the letters, drawings, and sounds. Raulston gave a homework assignment and they set a time for the next session.

In September, Raulston and Isaac opened their first reading class for a dozen Tenth Cavalry soldiers.

* * *

On patrol in October along the North Fork of the Smoky River, about halfway from Fort Larned to the Colorado border, Nolan called a halt to watch Cheyenne warriors ride into a herd of buffalo and cull their targets. Young boys followed on small ponies. Drawn by the rumble of what sounded to Isaac like rolling, but continuous, thunder, the patrol had stopped on a prairie knoll on the river's south side.

A Cheyenne boy of about twelve years old on a pinto that had become lame caught Isaac's eye. Isaac's peripheral vision noticed a subtle shift in the direction of the herd away from the whooping warriors riding at high speed within the ranks of the stampeding buffalos. Isaac guessed that the boy on the pinto would be trampled in less than two minutes. He nudged Teacher's flanks with his stirrups and said, "Let's go."

Teacher headed straight for the boy and the pinto without Isaac guiding her. In four steps, Teacher was galloping. Ahead, Isaac could see that the boy understood the threat and was desperately turning his crippled pony away from the herd. When Isaac and Teacher were about the same thirty yards distance from the boy as several bulls that were running in parallel to them, the pinto stumbled and fell. The boy bounced to his feet and ran toward Isaac and Teacher. Teacher came to a prancing halt as Isaac held out a hand to the fleeing boy. They grabbed each other's wrist and Isaac swung the boy onto Teacher's back atop his saddlebags. The boy held Isaac's waist and was still settling on the horse's back when Teacher leapt ahead and galloped forward among the oncoming bulls. One bull reached her side, lowered its head with its right horn, and ripped a gash where Teacher's flank met her belly. The horse screamed. Unbeknown to Isaac, Teacher's intestines were exposed. Teacher galloped in the direction of the herd and gradually slipped to the outside of the stampeding herd. Isaac drew rein halfway up the knoll and prevented Teacher from returning to the patrol with the boy. Teacher pranced in place, still charged up.

Soon, they were surrounded by several warriors. One grim-faced warrior pointed to Teacher's flank behind Isaac's spur. Isaac looked down. Blood had reached her hoof. "Ugh! My God, what have I done?"

The boy and Isaac dismounted. He took one more look at the gash in Teacher's flank and belly and protruding intestines. It appeared larger. He dropped his head and began removing his saddle and accouterments. Isaac blinked too late; his tears had spilled onto his cheeks. The whites of Teacher's eyes shone and he knew she was in great pain. He tossed his equipment aside and waved the boy and the warriors to one side. Isaac drew Rachel's Colt .44 and shot Teacher between her eyes at point-blank range. She slumped to the ground in a heap. Isaac knelt at her head and cried.

Presently, he felt a hand on his shoulder. The boy let his hand remain there. With his other hand, he offered his knife and elaborately decorated scabbard to Isaac. Isaac wiped his sleeve across eyes and looked up at the grim-faced warrior. The man nodded, almost imperceptibly. Isaac took the sheathed knife and immediately added it to his cartridge belt.

The boy smiled. Isaac smiled. The man's face was no longer grim. His face melted into a smile as he dismounted and handed the reins of his brown and white paint to Isaac. Isaac shook his head, but the man pushed the reins into Isaac's hand and closed Isaac's fist. Now Caleb was by his side, unarmed. He looked up at Captain Nolan and the patrol sitting their horses at the top of the knoll, carbines at the ready, but pointed skyward.

The Cheyenne man and boy mounted double behind two warriors. The man looked back and said, "You heap brave soldier."

* * *

In December, Isaac and Caleb were assigned to a detail assisting Lieutenant Raulston and Sergeant Augustus Wilson train new recruits arriving from Jefferson Barracks. Raulston and Wilson gave instructions. Isaac, Caleb, and four other men demonstrated the instructions and execution of commands – dismounted and mounted.

After supper on the first day of instruction, a smiling recruit, hat in hand, called to Isaac. "Hey, Mr. Rice, my name is Thomas H. Allsup. Can you help me learn this soldierin' business?"

Isaac stared at the recruit for a long moment, remembering the day he asked Lieutenant Raulston to teach reading. He smiled. "I'll do it on one condition." Isaac saw apprehension take hold across Allsup's countenance. "You have to agree that the next time we have new recruits, you will help train them."

"Oh, I will, Mr. Rice. I will."

"Where're you from?"

"Baltimore, Maryland."

"One day, you'll have to tell me about your city and why you're here. In the meantime, call me Isaac. Tom, what do you want to review?"

"I need to practice dem facin' movements. I'd like to learn to do them as I hear the commands. I messed up too many times today in front o' the lieutenant and that sergeant."

"Okay. Let's go outside and start."

Caleb found them and joined. When they finished, Tom asked, "Isaac, why do you ride that paint pony and everybody else has a bay horse?"

"Well, Cheyenne's just barely a pony. He's thirteen hands. My bay was fifteen hands. But the story of how I came to ride him is embarrassing. So I'll ask my homey to tell you."

When Caleb finished the story of Isaac and Cheyenne, Tom gazed at Isaac for a long moment. Finally, he said, "I'm gonna be like you – a real soldier!"

* * *

Over the winter, the library at Fort Larned became Isaac's favorite place. His preferred periodicals were *Harper's Weekly Magazine* and the *Army and Navy Journal*. He read the *Bible* and was struggling with Shakespeare's *Romeo and Juliet*. By the spring of 1868, he was in the middle of Alexander Dumas's *The Count of Monte Cristo* and was anxious to start *The Three Musketeers*.

For a change of scenery, Isaac requested and was assigned to a detail under newly promoted First Lieutenant Raulston escorting supply trains, stagecoaches, and the mail between Fort Dodge and Fort Larned. The escort duty became routine in 1868, as no contact was made with hostile Indians.

366

* * *

While Nolan had the entire company away from Fort Larned on patrol, Company A's barracks caught fire Saturday night, January 2, 1869.

Between shovelfuls of manure, Caleb fumed. "Dammit! It just ain't fair."

"Homey, life ain't fair. So why you think Third Infantry's gonna play fair when their plan all along was to drive us outta Fort Larned at any cost?"

Tom voiced disgust. "Bastards! I'm okay with leaving the sorry sonsabitches behind. But why did they see fit to blame the fire on Cap'n Nolan when he warn't even here? He's a fine man. Why they wanna destroy'im?"

Isaac sighed. "What I can't understand is not why they blamed Captain Nolan, but instead why the department commanding general would believe such a damn loony-ass charge. I cannot imagine what he's gotta go through to prove the fire wasn't his fault."

Caleb threw another shovelful. "Can you fuckin' imagine? The man's in de field wid us in the middle o' a cold-ass winter showin' white settlements we got'em covered and while we're gone, *they* set fire to our damn barracks and burn up all our shit, *and then* dey talkin' 'bout takin' two years o' money from de man to make him pay for what dey burned! Man, these 'bout some evil sombitches." Caleb slowly shook his head.

"You said it. There's evil aplenty in the world and Fort Larned has its share. From the start, Third Infantry wanted us out. They've won. We're gone."

Tom tilted his head and put a gloved hand on his hip. "So where're we goin'?"

"I heard we're leavin' for Fort Zarah in three days."

Caleb frowned. "Huh? What de hell kind o' name is dat for a fort?"

Isaac and Tom laughed. Isaac said, "Now don't start me to lying. That's all I know."

Grinning, Caleb asked, "Where de fuck is Zarah? And, is she givin' up any pussy?"

Tom laughed until he coughed. Isaac laughed so hard his sides hurt. When he recovered, he said, "She's up the road toward Fort Riley about a day's ride – that is, if you leave the wagons behind."

* * *

On arrival at Fort Zarah, exactly one week after the fire, they learned that Captain Nolan would also be the post commander.

They were surprised to find out that Special Order 183 was waiting for them. Holding the order aloft, Captain Nolan announced that Private Caleb Jenkins was directed to report to Colonel Grierson at the new Regimental Headquarters, Fort Gibson, Indian Territory forthwith to join the regimental band. The men applauded. Captain Nolan added, "He also wants you to bring your horse. You'll be detailed to patrol with whatever company may need your services."

Monday morning, Isaac and Tom prepared with half the company to go on a two-week scout to the confluence of the Sappa and Republican rivers in Nebraska. Since they were using pack mules instead of wagons, they knew this would be a rugged patrol. Caleb walked with them to the stables.

Isaac thought, *I cannot remember but one time going anyplace without Caleb.* Tom held his trumpet to his lips and sounded "Boots and Saddles."

Isaac shook Caleb's hand with both of his. "Fare thee well, my friend, until we meet again. How long will you be here?"

Caleb followed as Isaac "stood to horse." He said, "The Post Quartermaster Sergeant said an empty supply train will pass through tomorrow. So me and my ol' hoss will drow in wid dem to Leavenworth. Den, I'll catch another south to Fort Gibson."

Nolan: "Prepare t'mount!"

Isaac took two steps back. "When you get there, write and tell me all about it."

Nolan: "MOUNT!"

Isaac and the patrol settled onto their cold saddles, wearing overcoats split at the waist that covered their thighs and knees. Cheyenne's breath was snow white.

Nolan: "Forward!"

Caleb waved to Isaac, then Tom. "I'll write and tell you the happenin's at headquarters."

Nolan: "MARCH!"

* * *

Company A's mission at Fort Zarah was mostly the same as it was while at Fort Larned, except for the addition of scouting and mapping along the Republican River. As Captain Nolan carried on the paper fight to defeat the charge of responsibility for the barracks fire, Lieutenant Raulston led more and more of the scouts and patrols. Sergeants Wilson and Johnson also led small patrols and handled escorts.

In November, Phillip Sheridan, Commanding General of the Division of the Missouri, ordered Fort Zarah closed. Colonel Grierson redeployed Company A to Camp Supply, Indian Territory. The company's mission changed to include protection of Indians on nearby reservations from white intruders and livestock thieves as well as protection of settlements from the Indians – in short, they became a part of an army of occupation.

As Thursday, December 2, 1869, dawned over Fort Zarah, Company A stood to horse, with carbines in hand, every man at parade rest. On Captain Nolan's command, Tom sounded "Retreat." The men stood at attention. Nolan ordered, "Present arms!" Charles hauled down the stars and stripes into Robert's hands while the men held their salute. Each laundress held her right hand over her heart. It felt odd to Isaac. He smiled. He thought *the sun is on the wrong side of the fort for "Retreat!"*

Minutes later, they were under way. Isaac was in his usual new position at the head of the main body beside Tom. The pair rode between Nolan and the main body, within easy earshot. Tom used his trumpet to relay Nolan's commands to the entire company. Isaac was Nolan's courier and carried his instructions to the sergeants in charge of the flanks and advance and rearguards. Isaac was happy with the role the speedy Cheyenne had won for him. His six-year-old pony was faster by far than any of the fifteen- to twenty–year-old horses in the company.

They marched southwest, camping at Fort Larned, then Fort Dodge. From Dodge they marched south to Camp Supply, located near the confluence of a river and a large creek that formed the North Canadian River. Nine days after leaving Fort Zarah, Company A was deployed the first time on the same post with companies of the Tenth, namely, F, H, I, and K.

Camp Supply was established the previous November and was still a work in progress. It consisted of a log stockade that surrounded the quartermaster's stores and those of the Indian agency. Outside its stockade, large walled tents with stoves were used to house and keep warm the soldiers of the Tenth Cavalry along with three companies of the Third Infantry camped on opposite sides of the post.

After supper the next day, Isaac and Tom emerged from the mess tent with their tin cups filled with steaming coffee. They walked toward the corral. Tom looked about before he spoke. "Say, Isaac, what'd you think of the chaplain's sermon this afternoon?"

"Well, I think he wants us to think what white folks think."

"Huh?"

"Hey, I see no difference in his message that 'we' are destined to subdue the savages and civilize them than I saw in the sermons that a white preacher from Jacksonboro back in South Carolina fed us on the plantation. He told us, over and over, slavery was the natural order of things and that God put good white folks on earth to take care of us."

"Whoa! You mean you don't believe Injuns are savages?"

Isaac pointed to an animal feed house at the corner of the corral. "Suppose this was your private corral and feed house. So there you are all happy with your arms folded, looking over your stock. Suddenly I show up with Caleb, Charles, Robert, and Augustus. We tell you we're going to take your corral, but you can stay on in the corner over there – or die. So you're outnumbered and outgunned. You go talk it over with your one brother. He looks at our guns and says, let's give up and stay in the corner. After you think it over, you decide, hell no, I'll fight to keep my corral. We back you into that corner. You know we will keep our word and kill you. Do you fight gently or savagely?"

Tom stopped and leaned on the corral. He scanned the horses and took a sip of his coffee. "Isaac, my friend, you have a way with clarity. You know there is no question about what I would do. By any means necessary, any man would fight and struggle to the death. I see your point.

"Is that what you thought when you decided to join the army?"

"No. I'd never seen an Indian until I reached Kansas. At first, back in the spring o' '63 when the boys in blue were still gettin' their asses kicked all over the country, I thought the best course for a colored man was to stand up and join in the fight to end slavery. I couldn't imagine what enslaved life would be like if the Secesh won."

Tom nodded and took another sip. "Well, what about now?"

Isaac followed and took a big swig of his coffee. "Since '63, the many revelations before my eyes, and now from books and magazines, have all combined in my head and changed my views several times. I'm sure what I think will continue to change. But, to answer your question, now what I see is I have a mostly secure job. I will use what I earn from this job to make a way for my future family."

"But, you could do that as a blacksmith."

"Perhaps. Maybe the army will help me earn the investment to start such a venture and my travels help me find the right place where my enterprise won't be burned out."

* * *

Nolan's Fort Larned barracks fire trouble still dogged him through the winter. His letter-writing campaign continued in 1870. Isaac was happy to see Nolan engaged and almost his old self as the officers, noncommissioned officers, and old hands trained a flood of new recruit. In three years, Company A had lost about forty percent of its soldiers due primarily to disease and disability. Old hands, Isaac and Tom, assisted with mounted drill and marksmanship with the carbine.

In May, when the company raced to the rescue of an army paymaster and his escort, Nolan left many of the green recruits on garrison duty. A handful of the recruits sallied forth with the company in the late afternoon of June 11, 1870, to meet an attack on Camp Supply by about two hundred Comanche warriors. If the need arose to fight dismounted, the recruits would be the horse-holders. Isaac thought, *I guess they had to have their first taste of fighting sooner or later. So it may as well be today.*

The Comanche force was led by young warriors who believed they could drive the army from the region. They carried off three army horses and taunted the soldiers in English to be men and come out and fight. The attackers were deployed along the Beaver River and Wolf Creek, between which Camp Supply was located. The Comanche were west of Camp Supply. The river and creek met east of the post.

Nolan led the company directly at the Comanche warriors. They went west, and then northwest toward a large peninsular formed by a loop in Beaver River. More warriors emerged from the trees on the high ground to the south. Nolan, with Sergeant Wilson and half his command of about fifty men, wheeled left to meet the new threat while Sergeant Johnson engaged the warriors to his front. Isaac and Tom followed Nolan and opened fire on the warriors from their new right flank. Isaac combined the use of rapid fire from his repeating carbine with quick reloading from magazines in his cartridge box to help turn the Comanche warriors away from Sergeant Johnson's detail. He was sure he had shot one warrior from his saddle and that he missed another warrior and felled his pony instead.

The sharp exchanges were sporadic as combatants wheeled their ponies and horses about trying to take best advantage of the terrain. The high ground was ten to forty feet above the river valley. After almost two hours of hard riding and maneuvering, and with the sun low above the trees, the Comanches broke contact and retired to the west. On the field of battle lay six dead Comanche, a pony, and a cavalry horse. The engaged companies of the Tenth did not lose a man. No one was wounded.

Isaac saw that Charles was riding double with one of the recruits. "Tom, let's round up these loose ponies and rope one for Charles."

Tom secured his carbine. "Okay. I've got this side."

When they succeeded in pushing the ponies to the east, Tom lassoed one for Charles to ride back to the post.

* * *

The next day, Sunday, Isaac and Tom walked to Sudsville on the south side of Camp Supply, just above Wolf Creek, carrying their dirty clothes. Along their way, they dodged chickens pecking and children playing. Their laundress, Emily, was cutting a new batch of lye soap into bars and minding the fire under her wash pots. They were exchanging pleasantries Emily in front of her tent when a neighbor laundress interrupted everyone in earshot. "Get your hands off me!"

It appeared to Isaac that two Third Infantry soldiers were trying to drag a high mulatto laundress into her tent. Isaac hailed the soldiers with a raised hand. "Good morning, gentlemen."

The soldiers stood still for a moment, but held the woman by her arms. Then one grinned. "Look, Jake, a proper-talkin' nigger."

Snickers.

Isaac, unsmiling, dropped his laundry and moved in their direction. "The lady asked you to unhand her. Please release her." Smiles disappeared from the faces of the infantrymen. Isaac continued his approach. "Now."

Slowly, they released the laundress and began a retreat. "Okay, cav boy. You win this time. By the way, you're mistaken. She ain't no lady."

More snickers. Isaac saw the laundress flush. She muttered, "Bastards!"

Tom was at Isaac's elbow. Isaac looked at Tom's curled lip and chuckled.

Isaac touched the brim of his campaign hat and introduced himself and Tom. Isaac thought, *lady or not, this is one of the most beautiful women I've seen anywhere. What color is her frizzy thin hair? Copper? Brown? Tan? Hmm. She's taller than Rachel. Why am I comparing? Not fair.*

The woman did a curtsy and smiled. "I'm Francesca Dumas, late of New Orleans. Thank you, gentlemen, for coming to my rescue.

Now I need to change the subject." She turned to Isaac, ignored Tom, and did not speak again until she was toe to toe with him. She poked Isaac in the middle of his chest with a forefinger. "I want you to be my man."

Isaac's jaw dropped. When he recovered, he pushed his hat back and blurted, "Er, Miss Dumas, we just met. You don't know me...."

"Oh, but I know enough. I know you're Isaac Rice, unmarried, from South Carolina, ex-boatman, cav fellow, rides a paint, and brave soldier. I even know what you did in the battle yesterday."

Chapter 30: A Child Speaks

After dark, James Darby rode Danny Boy at a walk out of Fort Richardson, across Lost Creek, and headed for Jacksboro, less than a mile away. On his own, Danny Boy increased his pace to a smart canter as they approached the home of Josephus Smith, proprietor of Jacksboro's general store. In a few minutes, Danny Boy was foraging in his stall, inside Smith's barn. By lantern light, James wiped, brushed, and curried his horse. "I'll bet you're happy to have that saddle off."

James laughed and shook his head. I can't believe I'm talking to a horse again.

The mid-June night was warm. The crickets and frogs made sounds that filled the night. Fireflies signaled mates and prey alike. James slung his saddlebags over his shoulder and made his way to the three-room house he and Abigail had rented behind Smith's home. Before he set foot on the porch, the door burst open.

Abigail ran across the porch and leapt into his arms. "Oh, James! I'm so glad you're home."

After a long kiss, James spoke. "I've missed you, my love. Are the children asleep?"

She grabbed his hand and pulled him up the two steps onto the porch. "Yes, Jim and Catherine are asleep. Com'on in. Sit and read while I make your bath. Here's the mail."

"Oh, thanks." He dropped his saddlebags and gunbelt on the floor.

"Did you eat at the fort?"

"Yes." James began unloading his revolver and carbine.

She turned to go and he tapped her buttocks with his palm. She looked back at him by the light of their only kerosene lamp with her chin on her shoulder. In her best alluring voice, Abigail said, "Okay big boy! Don't start something you aren't ready to finish."

* * *

James lingered in the elongated tin tub Abigail had set on the back porch for his bath. She sat on a ladder-back chair beside him, massaging his scalp with her fingertips. "So, Sergeant James Darby, did Colonel Mackenzie lead you and the rest of the Fourth in the rain and mud for two weeks all over north Texas and half of Indian Territory and still couldn't find the murderers?"

James laughed. "I'm afraid that's right. It was just like last year and the year before when the Fourth went out under ol' Colonel Graham."

"I'll bet Colonel Mackenzie didn't think it was funny when y'all dragged yourselves into Fort Sill and found out they were there already in the guardhouse."

James laughed again. "You bet your sweet ass he didn't!"

"Is he really any better than Colonel Graham?"

"Too many people commend his war record for me to doubt that he'll be successful."

"Well, I know nothing about catching Indians, but I do know that half of 1871 is gone and the same Indian raiders are still running down here to Texas whenever they get the notion."

James turned his head and grinned up at her. "Say, are you nervous?"

Abigail paused and pursed her lips. "In a word, yes."

James changed his tone to a serious one. "Rest easy. Jacksboro is on the fort's front porch. The troops who are not out scouting can handle any raiders foolish enough to come here."

"Well, I hope you're right. Did you see anybody we know at Fort Sill?"

James stood. Abigail dried his back and he went on talking. "Sure did. I saw General Grierson for the first time since '66. He didn't have much time, what with General Sherman there for an inspection and the Fourth Cav turning up unannounced. But he did spend a few minutes with me. Oh, yes, he sends his regards."

Abigail smiled. "Why, that was thoughtful of him."

"Yeah, he's a decent officer."

"Why does he seem so busy?'

"Oops! I forgot to tell you, he's also the commanding officer at Fort Sill. Plus, his Tenth Cav is still building the fort. And he organized the regimental band."

"Oh, my. He really *is* busy. But the folks I want to know about are Isaac and Caleb. It's been five years and two babies since I've seen them."

James laughed. "You know, I don't recall hearing time measured quite like that before. Anyway, I was just getting to that. I chatted with Caleb. He's a leading performer in the Tenth Cav's band. He plays several instruments."

"What?" Abigail shook her head. "Will wonders never cease?"

"And, this is not new for him. He told me he has been performing – playing and singing – since he was nine years old."

"Whoa! Imagine Caleb singing at our wedding."

"Do you think your folks would've allowed it?"

"Humph! So, how's Isaac?"

"I missed Isaac. He's with his company up at Camp Supply. But Caleb said Isaac is well and doing well."

James put a finger to his lips and pulled Abigail close. "No more about others tonight. Come. Lie with me."

She embraced and kissed her husband.

* * *

The letter was postmarked Friday, November 1, 1872.

October 30, 1872

Dear James and Abygail,

This is a excitin time. I can hardlee wait for next wek when I can make my first vote! I am for Pres. Grant! I hope you and yor children are fine. I am very well. Hope to see you soon so we can talk about not killing Indians.

Your friend,

Isaac Rice

Tenth Cav

James handed the water-stained letter and envelope to Abigail. "Well, the election has passed before Isaac's letter arrived. I hope he's happy. He got his wish. Grant for four more years."

Abigail ignored James. "It looks like he heard about Mackenzie and y'all killing a bunch of Comanches. But, aren't Grierson and Isaac doing the same thing – trying to pen up the Comanches and Kiowas on that reservation at Sill and kill the ones who won't go?"

James dropped his shoulders and sighed. "We've had this debate dozens of times. It's a fact of life: Americans are going to settle in the west. And, yes, that means on lands the Indians call their home. They can make war and cause delays, but in the end, they will lose."

"So does that mean you have license to go out and kill people? Contrary to popular belief, they are actually people."

"Dear, we are on the same side of the argument. I don't want to kill them either."

"Then, stop. Oh, I know, it's your job." She threw dirty clothes into a tub in the corner of the kitchen. Abigail spoke sharply. Her tone dripped with sarcasm. "Get another job. I'm Pilate's wife. 'Wash your hands....'"

"No you're not. Pilate's wife was talking about a guiltless man. These murderers are...."

She cut him off. "Are they guilty of murder when they leave the reservation they've been promised because our government can't or won't provide the protection, rations, and annuities we committed in treaty after treaty? Maybe because we find something of value on the land we promised and make them move again and again. Or because they hit ranches and take cattle from whites. They don't know good white ranchers from the white cattle and horse thieves who enter reservations and raid their herds. I can't believe we're so surprised, and that our newspapers play the victim, when the real victim strikes back. Oh, what's the use of our arguing about any of this? You already know what I think. And you know that I know you can't change the world we live in. I'm just sick of it all." Abigail threw her broom behind the outside door.

James stomped to a chair and sat down at the kitchen table – hard. He buried his face in his hands, elbows resting on his knees.

Lil' Jim played in the front room with his red and white spinning top. Finally, the top wobbled and fell. Lil' Jim let it lay. He stood in the doorway and looked for a time at his father. "Papa, are you sad 'cause Ma fussed at you?"

In spite of himself, James chuckled. "No, son. I'm sad because soldiers can't fix the problem Ma is talking about."

"Well, you always keep your promises to me. Why don't you be the one who makes sure gov'ment keeps promises to the Injuns?"

With his mouth agape, James abruptly sat up straight, and then muttered, "From out of the mouths of babes...."

Abigail cried.

Chapter 31: Dr. Alejandra Luna

Monday, July 22, 1867. Dear Diary, Great news: Papa visited me yesterday! The French have been defeated and all their soldiers have left Mexico. Juarez is back! Papa is going home to Mama! I'm so happy! Alas, I decided not to go with him. As you know, Dr. Sanchez and his wife have been so nice to take me in and treat me like a granddaughter. They have no children. Dr. Sanchez thinks I should not interrupt my nursing and midwifery training. I think he's afraid that if I go home I won't return. Papa understands. He said he is so proud of me. PS: Papa also said I'm more beautiful than he remembered. I guess all fathers think their daughters are the most beautiful. What if he had two daughters...?

* * *

"Please don't tell Dr. Sanchez. He would fire me for sure."

"Alfredo, I will not tell Doc or anyone else. But you must never try to proposition me again. I really think you're a nice man. Though I am, frankly, flattered, I will not become involved with a married man."

"Alejandra, thank you for being kind to me even after I've made such a fool of myself."

"Dr. Diaz, it's okay. And hold your head up."

Alfredo raised his chin. Alejandra thought he tried to smile. He looked utterly depressed.

Alejandra looked about and then whispered. "The people in this restaurant may start to get ideas. Keep your chin up. You have done nothing so shameful. It's okay. Others have tried before you.

"By the way, I think you're an attractive man. But our timing was all wrong. You were married when I met you. So I marked you taken when I arrived in Chihuahua five years ago."

She rose to leave. "Get yourself together before you come back to the office. Doc may be old, but as you know he's not only smart, he's very perceptive. Adios, mi amigo."

"Thanks. I think I'll take the afternoon off and go for a long walk. See you tomorrow."

* * *

Dr. Sanchez had a wry smile on his face when Alejandra entered his private office. "Alejandra, you have done well in your studies. You have been an apt apprentice. The missus and I want to congratulate you on your progress."

Alejandra's smile brightened. She felt warm inside. "Thanks."

The door swung shut behind her. Senora Sanchez reached for Alejandra with open arms. They hugged and she said, "Child, you've been a God-sent blessing to us from the start. Now Tomas has a little surprise for you."

"This new medical bag is for you."

"Oh, Doc, thank you so much!" Alejandra lifted the bag from his desk and placed it on a chair. She began examining its contents as her adoptive grandparents beamed.

"Allie, as you know, we were to go this afternoon to Senora Gomez. She should go into labor this week."

"Yes, sir. Is it still on?"

"Oh, yes. It's still on. But I'm not going. You are."

Alejandra frowned, perplexed. Senora Sanchez chuckled.

Dr. Sanchez drew on his cigar and coughed. "You're going to make your first solo delivery."

Alejandra was dumbfounded. Her jaw went slack. She looked at the new bag and again at Dr. Sanchez, grinning with his cigar between his teeth. She stammered. "B-b-but, didn't you tell me it would be 1873 when I would go on my own?"

"Si. That is so. But I have the prerogative to say when a course of study is completed. And, you, my dear, have passed all requirements."

"You mean, I'm no longer an apprentice?"

"Si. You are your own nurse and midwife."

Senora Sanchez gave another hug. "Congratulations, dear Allie!"

With tears rolling down her cheeks, Alejandra sank onto a chair. "Oh, this is a huge surprise." She sniffed. "Thanks so very much for your every kindness – both of you."

Dr. Sanchez lifted a small glass of tequila from his desk and held it aloft. "Here's to you!" He took a swallow. "All right, all right. The party's over. It's time for you to run along. The Gomezes are looking for you before supper. I can't sit here and watch you blubber the rest of the afternoon."

They laughed together.

Alejandra sniffed, blew her nose, and sniffed again. Gathering the bag, she stood. "Yes, sir."

"Oh, I forgot to mention – take my horse and buggy. I'll see you in a few days."

* * *

Alejandra cried. "Oh, Doc, I couldn't save him. I did my best. I prayed for God to guide my hands. Oh, what a senseless death!" She sobbed and put her head down on Dr. Sanchez's pillow, tilting her chair forward.

"How many bullets did you remove from this fellow?"

"Four."

"Humph!"

Senora Sanchez massaged her shoulders. "It's okay, child."

Dr. Sanchez struggled to sit up in his bed. He coughed and his chest rattled. "I hope you realize that I couldn't save every man they dragged into my clinic shot full of lead. You do what you can. Some will live, some will die. You mustn't despair when a patient dies. Even with your very best effort, sometimes it just can't be helped.

"Now, Allie, I know my speeches won't make you feel better. But promise me you'll remember what I said when I'm gone, for you will see much death in your time. It comes with your chosen work."

Alejandra raised her head. "Doc, please don't talk of your death."

"Why, of course, I will. My days are numbered. I know that I have cancer in my chest. There's no denying it. Until my last breath, I'll do all I can to prepare you for the road ahead."

Alejandra broke into sobs again and buried her face in Dr. Sanchez's pillow. Senora Sanchez continued massaging her shoulders. "There, there, dear. I know Tomas has upset you. But we must be strong."

Between sobs, she managed to mutter, "Yes, Grandma."

* * *

Sunday, January 26, 1873. Dear Diary, Bad news: Last Friday, we laid Dr. Tomas Sanchez to rest. He was a good man and fine physician. He was seventy-one years old. May God bless his soul. Alfredo will take over his practice and the new apprentices. Senora Sanchez will go to live with her younger sister. More news: In a few days, I will take the morning stage home to Carrizal. Yes. I will go with no husband and no prospects. I can't wait to see Mama! Papa, Rafael, and Ernesto have promised to help me build a small clinic with the money Dr. Sanchez left for me. See you in Carrizal. Bye."

Chapter 32: **Fort Sill**

Isaac rolled and clamped his lips between his teeth in an attempt to muffle the primordial sound that usually accompanied his ejaculation. This time was no different. Some sound escaped, like low moan. Though he felt spent and sleep tugged at his consciousness, he heard Francesca's familiar screams of ecstasy through her clinched teeth as she bit the corner of the pillow she held to stifle her cries. He was aware of her legs, the same color of oak lumber and strength, and one arm holding him in a kind of silent desperation.

After a few moments, Francesca shivered. Isaac covered her with a blanket against the chill in her tent from the cool of Saturday night, November 11, 1871. Company A was transferred the previous month after two years at Camp Supply. Francesca had managed to get herself assigned to Fort Sill and followed him.

Isaac lay beside Francesca on her straw-filled cotton army-issue bed sack. By the light of a small candle, he appraised her face – again. They were close, for the bed sack was less than three feet wide. Isaac smiled. "Welcome to Fort Sill."

Francesca's grin displayed her perfectly even teeth. "Now *that* was a real welcome. You sho' know how to make your woman feel at home. This has been a wonderful first night."

Isaac thought for what felt like the hundred and tenth time, something is wrong here. "Fran, how old are you?"

Her brow furrowed. "Isaac, you know how old I am. We just celebrated my birthday two months ago. Why are you asking me stuff you already know?"

Sheepishly, Isaac said, "Oh, yeah. I remember now. I move ahead in spring and by late summer you try and catch up."

Isaac felt her stare. "Stop stalling, Mr. Rice. Why did you ask? Do you want to know if I'm feeling like an old maid? Well, the answer is yes."

Isaac blinked. How does she always know what I'm thinking? Do all women possess that ability? Or are all men as clueless as me? "Er, yes. You aren't getting any younger. Seems to me, your ruse to have

384

me as your man and guard dog has worked. Is it true you have no pursuers?"

Francesca raised her head and propped her jaw in her hand. Her gaze was steady and somber. "Isaac, I will confess. I admired you back there at Supply from the girl-talk going around the camp. It's simple. I wanted you – like a trophy. But I want you to know that although keeping our agreement is getting difficult, I'm keeping my word. I'm trying my hardest."

Isaac watched a tear slide down her right cheek. He looked into her eyes and thought, *I don't feel any closer than I did the first time I saw her. She is an interesting beauty and great company.* "Fran, our agreement was…."

"I know what I said. What I didn't know then was how difficult it could be. I thought I was strong and could easily handle our agreement that you're just my friend and protector. Please believe me. Still, I will do my best to reward you well every time and anytime you want me and still not violate our agreement."

Isaac lay back and stared at the flickering candlelight against the ceiling of her four-wall tent. He thought *well, what can I do now? I feel entangled, tied up against my will. Sleeping with Fran is great. But this has to end. How can I do that? She, it is clear to me now, will not end it. On the contrary, I think she has just begun her effort to make our agreement permanent.*

* * *

Departing dinner mess the next day, Isaac was all smiles. "Hey, Tom, watch this." He grabbed Caleb's sleeve and poured water from his tin cup on Caleb's two new golden yellow chevrons.

Caleb looked down too late to pull away. "Hey, Homey, what the hell are you doing?"

While Tom laughed, Isaac intoned, using his best command voice, "Corporal Caleb Jenkins, consider your stripes duly baptized according to the customs of your ol' Company A."

Caleb shook his head. "I never heard o' that. Did y'all jes make that up?"

Tom put a hand on Caleb's dry sleeve. "Congratulations, music man. Isaac couldn't wait to see you since we heard on Friday that you got promoted." They shook hands.

Isaac offered his congratulations. "Yeah, we made up that fool ritual last winter when we got promoted to corporal on the same day."

Caleb sighed. "I miss Company A. We had some great times together. All I can say about headquarters is it is different. We do everything you do, but less. Of course, we have our music lessons from the ol' man himself and practice."

Isaac was surprised. "The ol' man actually teaches music?"

"Yeah, Homey. Before the war he was a music teacher."

Tom shook his head in amazement. "Will wonders never cease?"

"Yeah, we have a hellava band. We're gettin' ready for our Christmas concert. Last year's was great. This one will be even better."

They were walking toward the corral. Caleb pointed to the unfinished stone stable. "Here's another way we headquarters guys get detailed. Not only do we scout with one company or another, we've toiled many a day over the years building Fort Sill from nothing. This stone stable is kind of the crown jewel o' our building. All the companies, except for you way-out field guys, have had a hand building barracks, officer's houses, and everything you see."

Isaac looked from the stable to other structures. "I salute you guys. This is great work."

Tom nodded as he appraised the scene. "Who's the overseer?"

Caleb beamed. "My fearless leader and your ol' man is the boss man builder."

Isaac muttered, "Well, I'll be damn."

They continued walking. Sudsville came into view. Caleb changed the subject. "Hey, Homey, when you gonna introduce me to your laundress?"

Tom laughed. "Maybe he don't wanna take a chance on having a music man steal his woman."

"Well, that's all right. I know which one she is. I can't miss her. She's the only high yellow woman on post."

Isaac stopped walking. He grinned and his hands went akimbo. "Say, didn't I see you yesterday after supper slipping into a tent down there in Sudsville?" He jerked his head toward Sudsville.

Tom said, "Uh-oh! Music maker, you been holding out on us."

Caleb held up both hands. "Yeah, I got me a cute lil' thang down there by the name o' Louise – beautiful and black as midnight and as sweet as her apple pies. We met at Fort Gibson. She moved on over here tuh Sill with the headquarters."

Isaac raised an eye brow. "Oh, with all that long time, this must be a serious thing. What about it, Homey?"

Tom chimed in. "I heard the part about the pies. I've seen how much this ol' boy loves his tummy, so it sounds serious to me."

Caleb demurred. "Well, you know, a man needs a good woman to keep'im going. So, Homey, I'm glad you found somebody. Maybe we can have a double wedding."

Isaac held up an arm as if to shield his face from Caleb's missile. "Sorry, Homey, this one ain't *the* one. I won't know until she comes along. But I do know this one ain't it."

"Damn, Homey. Fran sho' is a fine-lookin' female." Caleb shrugged. "But, I've heard beauty ain't everything."

Suddenly, he changed the subject again. "Hey, I meant to tell you. Speaking of pies, James and the Fourth Cav visited Sill two months ago! It was great to see'im again."

Isaac frowned. "Yeah, I would've wanted to see'im. But what does a pie have to do with James?"

"Oh, Colonel Mackenzie, James's ol' man, was amazed when our ol' man and Captain Carpenter had a full-course dinner ready for him and his staff – including prune pies. Colonel Mackenzie was surprised and pleased. The Fourth had rode in all muddy and dirty after chasing Kiowas with no luck. I think he and our ol' man are going to be good friends."

Tom looked puzzled. "Where do you guys know this James from? Isn't he white?"

Isaac told the story of their friendship.

Tom raised his brow and sighed. "Like I said, will wonders never cease?"

After a pause, Caleb invited Isaac and Tom to sit with him on a log bench across the road from the stable. Isaac knew the serious look on his friend's face and hoped the matter was not about his newfound love. Caleb spoke looking out at the rows of red-wheeled canvas covered army wagons. "Sometimes it seems to me like we're wasting our time, and potentially our lives, for all the good we do. Yet, at other times, I'm having so much fun I don't care about the whole picture."

"Hey, Homey, have your fun, man. We're not about to change a picture we didn't draw."

Tom looked at Caleb. "What picture are you guys talking about?"

Caleb removed his face from his hands. "I guess I'm thinking, in part, about progress made by white people. Now I don't see anything wrong with that. It just seems to me we're helping them overcome their Injun problem and they get all the benefit."

Tom frowned. "What benefit?"

"Well, the biggest benefit they get is the land."

Isaac stood. "Agreed!" He sat again. "Once you have the land, you control everything that follows. Look at the railroad crews we guard. They work for big men who take control of broad swathes of public land and create towns along their tracks. In the library back at Larned, I found out from *Harper's Weekly* that these bigwigs and their friends in Washington are making a killing off lands taken from the Indians."

Tom nodded. "This is land that's taken at the point of our Spencers and Colts."

Isaac put a hand on Tom's shoulder. "The men who made these fine weapons earn their keep by knowing there is a need for instruments to enable those who will resolve disputes by violence."

Caleb was still staring ahead. "So now that we know a few things, what do we do?"

Isaac began to pace before his friends. He hit the palm of his hand with his fist. "I think we are too poor to do anything. For example, we don't have the means to buy the inferior half-weight blankets merchants are selling to Indian Agencies at the full price of our army blankets."

Tom chimed in. "Nor can we supply diseased cattle for Indian rations."

Caleb chuckled. "Of course, we could. We could raid the thieves and sell their booty – including whiskey."

Tom and Isaac laughed. Isaac said, "Sure we could. And we could sell the loads of arms, ammunition, and rations on the supply trains we escort."

They laughed together.

Caleb turned somber. "Homey, we haven't talked about this matter in a while. But James got me thinking about it again. By the way, here's a little headquarters news for you. Captain Cox and Captain Graham were court-martialed for selling government property. Cox is going to jail at Leavenworth."

Isaac was still pacing. He raised an eyebrow. "Now, that's what I'm talking about. Even cavalry officers are too poor to play this game."

Tom rubbed his stubble. "So what's the answer?"

Isaac stopped in front of Tom. "Actually, I don't know. But my idea is to figure out how to do what my elders told me – buy some land, no matter how small. That'll be my beginning. I'll use my time on this job to figure out what the next step is so I'll know where to look for land. In the meantime, I'll continue living on less than half my army pay."

* * *

At the end of the month, Isaac was accompanied by Tom and Caleb when he went to Captain Nolan's office and re-enlisted for another five years. Then Isaac and Tom stood beside Caleb in the Regimental Sergeant Major's office while he signed his re-enlistment papers. When the paymaster arrived, Isaac deposited all but seven dollars of his pay and bonuses with the United States Army.

* * *

On a cold December morning, Captain Nolan got the Kiowa chief's agreement to keep his warriors on the edge of the reserve and promised to chase thieves and stolen horses. From the Comanche,

Kiowa, Southern Cheyenne reserve, Company A marched southwest at a trot, then canter. Isaac and Tom rode near the head of the column near Company A's two Tonkawa scouts. Since Charles was discharged the prior week, Tom was astride Charles's pony and Isaac rode Cheyenne. The scouts rode ponies.

At Nolan's command, Isaac and Tom, along with the scouts urged their steeds into full gallop. Periodically, they slowed to give the animals a breather and to ensure they were still on the easy track of a horse herd. After a dozen or so miles, and still short of the Red River, they topped a rise and saw the horse herd. The thieves were filling their canteens from a creek.

Isaac's eyes widened. "Hey, I've got an idea. They haven't spotted us yet and don't know how far back the company is. Let's spread out in a charge line and sit our horses with carbines in the ready position. And then you blow 'Boots and Saddles'. If we have to ride down on them, let's go between them and the herd."

Tom nodded. "Okay."

Isaac used broken English and pointing to position the scouts, Cisco and Alfredo. Then to Tom he said, "Okay, blow it."

"Boots and Saddles" never sounded so good to Isaac. The eight thieves looked up at the ridge occupied by the four uniformed men and quickly mounted. To Isaac's surprise, they did not attempt to move the herd. Instead, they fled south for the river and Texas soil.

Isaac sighed. "Let's ride down and turn the herd and head for home."

Tom announced, "Company A strikes again!"

The foursome drove the herd back along the same track and into Nolan and their comrades.

* * *

Over the holidays, Isaac and Tom were the talk of Company A and Fort Sill. In February, both were promoted to sergeant. Caleb was on hand to "baptize" the stripes of the new sergeants.

* * *

Building projects, reservation policing, patrolling crossings on the Red River, and garrison duty filled most of Isaac and Company A's days in the spring of 1872. Isaac and his comrades were enthusiastic about chasing down a party of Indians who jumped from the reservation adjacent Fort Sill in July. Three days into the chase, Nolan camped and rested the men and animals a few miles south of the Red River, close to the eastern edge of the Llano Estacada, about one hundred thirty miles west of Fort Sill.

At dawn the next morning, Company A successfully drove off an Indian attack. They resumed the chase and on the morning of the second day after being attacked, Company A surprised and routed the Indians in their camp. Their supplies and rations destroyed, the Indians returned to the reservation. Company A had marched two hundred and sixty-seven miles on beans, bacon, and coffee.

* * *

It was early on the morning of April 28, 1873. "Fran, are you home?"

"Come in, Isaac."

Isaac stepped inside Francesca's tent and saw that her cheeks were wet. "Fran, this is painful for both of us. I will simply tell you good-bye and wish for you a happy life."

Francesca sobbed and, before Isaac could turn to go, she ran and buried her face against his chest. "Please, please take me with you. I'll be good. You'll see. I'll do anything you want; be whoever you want me to be. Just don't leave me here without any hope. Please."

She squeezed him in her arms. Isaac wanted to hug her, but his hands only hovered in midair behind her back. "Fran, perhaps we met too soon. I know it is years later, but I still grieve for Rachel. I haven't any room left in my heart for another love. Not now. Not yet."

Francesca sobbed louder. "Please, please take me with you. Let me be there when your heart can take me in. I'm so sorry about not keeping our agreement. I love you more than I can find words to say. I commit my life to you. I will be nothing except what you want me to be. Please take me with you, please."

"Fran, I can't. What I want more than anything is for you to find the right man and have a happy life. I'm sorry. Now I must go. The trumpet will sound at any minute. We will march within five minutes after 'Boots and Saddles'."

Francesca looked up into Isaac's eyes. For him, her eyes confirmed the deep love she professed and it wrenched at his heart. She released him. He felt her trembling fingertips brush across his hands. She grabbed and kissed his hands, turned and walked to her bed, her breath coming in uncontrolled jerks. Isaac could not bear to watch. He turned and walked out of her tent and her life.

* * *

Isaac knew there was no time for breakfast. He wanted to kick himself for not rising early enough to eat and tell Francesca good-bye, for he knew it would be a long march to their first camp. His stomach growled. He went directly to the stable and Cheyenne. He thought *it is good to be here before the boys arrive*. Isaac leaned against Cheyenne's shoulder and cried. Cheyenne turned his head and rubbed his muzzle against Isaac's arm. Isaac faced and patted his pony's muzzle while Cheyenne licked his hand.

Isaac untied his bandana and wiped his eyes and face. He checked and rechecked his accouterments, rations, and ammunition. Twice, he checked the security of his saddlebags, tent, and bedroll.

Soon, Tom appeared. His face was somber while he handed an extra haversack to Isaac. Isaac's mouth dropped open. Tom said, "Shut your fly trap. You gotta eat too. Here, put it over your shoulder; you can eat during the march. Be careful when you open it. There's an extra canteen of coffee in there."

Isaac's tears welled again. He blinked them back. He managed to mumble, "Thank you."

Momentarily, Tom blew "Boots and Saddles."

Minutes later, Nolan gave the command and Company A began its three-hundred-mile march to its new duty station at Fort Concho, Texas.

* * *

The first night, they camped on the south bank of the Red River. As usual, tall tales, women stories, and gossip were heard around the supper cook fires.

Isaac sat cross-legged on the ground. "Hey, Tom, I got a letter from my homey. He said the ol' man and his missus are all moved in and enjoying St. Louis."

"Never mind reporting on all the good living, when is he coming back?"

First Sergeant William Umbles kicked a twig aside and sat with them. "You mean, *if* he comes back."

Isaac felt alarm rising within. He must come back. "Oh, I think he'll keep his word. His recruiting assignment is for only two years. We'll just have to be patient."

Tom wrapped his arms about his drawn-up knees. "Yeah. He's always kept his word."

William wagged a finger. "You can hope. But, remember, this ain't his army. Even though he's a colonel and a brevet major general and all that, he's still a soldier who's not to reason why, but to do and die like the rest of us."

Isaac and Tom exchanged glances.

William changed the subject. "Hey, Ike, the word's going 'round that you fired your laundry lady. Now I know that can't be true. That Miss Dumas is the finest female flesh to ever grace Fort Sill. So I know somebody musta lied. Right?"

Isaac stood and stretched. "Mr. Umbles, my name is Isaac, not Ike. It's time to visit the latrine. See you fellows later."

Without waiting for a reply, Isaac departed. As he walked away, he heard Tom say, "William, you don't want Isaac to put you in the dozens. If he does, you'll wanna fight. And that won't be good. I think you'd best leave his business off and not mess with him."

Chapter 33: Old Maids

When young Charles and his cousin Fred were nine and eight years old in the summer of 1875, riots based on race politics were common occurrences across Mississippi. John, now balding with salt and pepper hair, had mourned the passing of James D. Lynch in 1872 at age thirty-four due to a kidney disease. The family had moved into Natchez. There Rachel taught in a school established for colored pupils by Robert H. Wood, Natchez's first black mayor. Rebecca cooked and managed the family business – an inn in the under-the-hill district. Ruth was the face of the eatery and Saul supervised the ten-room upstairs hotel. Rachel kept the books and, on weekends, helped Rebecca in the kitchen. John assisted Ruth in the dining room.

For their quarters, the family used three rooms on the second floor at the back of the two-story brick building. Rebecca and John purchased the building on a five-year note with a balloon at the end from an old Confederate who had no heirs. The building, with a Georgian roof, featured a second-floor sun porch above the sidewalk. It provided a view of Vidalia, Louisiana, across the Mississippi River. Rachel spent a part of the time she devoted to her studies on the sun porch with her books, as she prepared to enter the new college for colored led by Reverend Revels at Alcorn the following year.

Sunday morning, October 31, 1875, was bright and pleasant at about sixty degrees Fahrenheit. Rachel was feeling satisfied with her work on the campaign of her mentor, Robert H. Wood, who was running for Sheriff of Adams County. She worked with the former mayor's friend and supporter, Congressman John R. Lynch. She stood at the door of the room she shared with Ruth. They were almost ready to walk up the hill to St. Mary's Cathedral on Union Street, the church Wood attended. "Girl, com'on. Let's not be late for mass again."

"Comin'. Just let me pin this side of my hat."

Outside on the sidewalk, Rachel caught a glimpse of a reflection of herself and Ruth walking together. "Hey, look, Ruth. We're not a bad-looking pair of old maids."

"Well, you don't need to be an old maid. All you need to do is say yes to that handsome preacher, Arthur Roberts. Girl, whatcha waitin' for?"

"Frankly, dear, I'm trying my best to find room in my heart and head for Arthur. With Isaac in both, there ain't much room left."

"Oh, that problem. Honey, I know where you are. I know that place very well. It took me so long trying to fit Claude in alongside Caleb that when I looked up one day, a gal from Morgantown done snatched him up."

"Humph! Well, what happened to Marion?"

"Same thing. My fault again. Say, I didn't see Arthur at the rally yesterday. Where is he?"

"Oh, he left Thursday on his way to Jackson. He's preaching up there today.

"Stop trying to change the subject. What went wrong with Richard?"

"Why, landsakes! I cannot abide Richard Johnson, for I fear he's a Democrat like his late pa, the barber."

"Oh, me. Oh, my. I didn't know." Rachel pursed her lips and choked a smile, looking sideways and winking at Ruth. "However-r-r, what I do know is a little something 'bout why *you* don't have to be an old maid."

"Do you know something I don't know?"

"Oh, you know all right enough who I'm talkin' 'bout."

Rachel sensed Ruth was feigning protest. "I don't know any sich a thing, either."

"After John R. made that great speech yesterday up on Main Street, I saw the way you two were eyeing one another."

Ruth gave a little wave of her hand, brushing Rachel's claim aside. "I don't think for a minute Congressman Lynch is the least bit interested in me. To him, I'm just another Wood campaign worker."

"Ruth, I'm here to tell ya, you're one hellava great-looking campaign worker!"

"Oh, stop." Rachel thought Ruth was growing pensive, but Ruth continued with a big grin breaking out. "Besides, he's too young for me."

"Ha! He's the same age as Isaac. And don't forget. I know how old you are. That excuse ain't gonna work."

"Actually, I feel he would like to lay me down just like any other female that catches his handsome eyes. I took a serious look into those eyes, and I regret to say, I didn't see me in there when he looked back. Just lust."

"Whoa! I knew I didn't have to worry about saving you from yourself – or any man either. I love you, sis."

"I love you too."

Chapter 34: The White Revolt

Billy gritted his teeth. His upper lip curled into a snarl. He twisted in his saddle and called over his shoulder, "Okay, boys. Form a column o' threes and follow me. We're gonna run these niggers down!" He paused and watched the men behind him maneuver their horses and cover the whole road in the formation he commanded. Raising his new 1873 Model Colt .45 Peacemaker, he spurred his horse and yelled, "Charge!"

Behind him, the thirty-five men of the Avenger Gun and Rifle Club responded with a bloodcurdling rendition of the rebel yell. Billy led them at a gallop down the road and into a group of about fifteen Negro men on their way to a polling station. First, the startled pedestrians froze, then scattered in all directions. The men in the middle and those who moved too slowly were run down and trampled by the horses. Three of those who managed to get off the road were felled by five shots from Billy's Peacemaker.

Billy thought, *we live and learn. We shoulda done more of this last year during the congressional election. Funny thing 'bout niggers; hardly ever find one who'll fight back. The fuckin' rabbits. Oh, well. On to the next bunch.*

The Avenger Club rode out from Raymond and crossed Snake Creek along their way to Clinton. It was Election Day for state and local offices that fateful Monday, November 1, 1875.

In his mind, Billy reviewed the cavalry tactics that he had taught the new club several times on their ride to Clinton. He had been in the number of whites who formed an impromptu militia in Clinton back in August, just one of many riots leading up to the next task in the execution of the Democratic Party's Mississippi Plan. He admired the plan's simplicity: win at the polls by any means necessary. Riots over the summer in Vicksburg, Austin, and Yazoo City yielded similar results with the loss of few white lives, if any. In Clinton, more than twenty Negroes had been shot dead. As one of the leading clubs in the state, Billy was proud to have been invited back.

As planned, Billy and George met Henry on the western edge of Clinton at the railroad tracks that led to Vicksburg. "Hey, Billy. Hey,

George. I'm afraid there's not much going on here. Of course, that's because y'all did such a number on the niggers in August that today they're hiding in their cabins."

Billy and George shared a big laugh. When Billy recovered, he said, "It's just like the *Register* says in every issue, 'A white man in a white man's place. A black man in a black man's place.'"

George waved his hand. "Well, it looks like when that happens, there'll be no fun left to be had."

Henry said, "Don't worry. You'll have plenty o' shootin' and ridin' to do today."

"Hot diggity dog!"

Billy nodded in satisfaction. "All right, Mr. Democrat, what do you have for us?"

Henry pulled out a map. "Ride through, to and fro, and keep niggers in their communities from Clinton down to Taylorsville along this route. Keep 'em reeling. And if you see any carpetbaggers, shoot 'em."

"Yes, sir, Captain Carter!"

Billy led the club south through colored communities, running down any black men who assembled on the roads. They encountered no resistance. Crossing the Jackson-Raymond Road, Bill spotted two well-dressed riders coming out of Jackson. He halted the club and waited.

The riders were about a hundred feet away when Billy decided. "All right, boys. Let's surround these fine gentlemen."

What followed was the sound of commotion as the entire club yelled and maneuvered their horses on the road. Billy urged his horse up nose to nose with the black rider's mule. Billy thought the young man's eyes had grown to the size of hen eggs. Billy chuckled. "Well, you dressed up mighty fine for a nigger. Where 'bouts you from?"

"Er, Natchez, sir."

"Oh, my. Why, that's true uppity country, if you ask me. I guess that's were you learned to talk all proper."

Billy laughed and glanced at the men around him. The response was loud, derisive laughter.

Billy continued. "So where you gonna preach, all duded up like that?"

He watched the man's face twitch with a nervous laugh. The man spoke. "Well, sir, er, t-t-that was yesterday."

"You hear that boys? We got ourselves a nigger preacher heah."

The club shouted back. "Amen, brother." and "Pass the bread and wine." and "A nigger preacher is an abomination."

Billy turned to the man's white traveling companion. He wanted to hear the companion's accent. "Good afternoon, sir. Is this nigger your prisoner?"

The white companion stuttered. "W-w-why, er, no. A-a-allow me to introduce myself. I'm Horace Jackson III from Boston. I'm on my way to settle in Natchez."

Billy spat and, meeting the eyes of several members of the club, gestured toward Horace Jackson. And then he hunched his shoulders.

The club responded with a chorus of, "A fuckin' carpetbagger." and "String'im up!"

Billy watched both riders squirm and perspire. "Nigger, do you have a name?"

"Yes, sir. I'm A-A-Arthur R-Roberts."

"Well, Reverend Roberts, looks like this is your unlucky day. You see, I don't think it's fair to hang Mr. Jackson and let you jes ride on off. So, tell ya what we gonna do. We'll leave the two of you hanging 'round here like the friends y'all are."

Billy waved to George and pointed into the woods. "All right, haul'em over to that big-ass oak yonder. I'm sure it'll support the both of'em."

George made two nooses and draped them over the heads of the frightened victims. He tied their hands behind their backs.

Billy rode over and took the reins of Jackson's horse and Roberts's mule. "Fellows, I plan to visit your fair city in a few weeks. I'll give the good folks down there your regards."

Reverend Roberts's lips were moving in an apparent prayer when Billy turned and pulled the two animals after him. The nooses tightened and the large limb on the ancient oak held, supporting the combined weight of Horace Jackson III and Arthur Roberts, hanging by their necks.

Chapter 35: "Revenge is Mine…"

Rachel thought, *okay. I'll tell Arthur I'm open to seeing him socially. I'll tell him that depending on how I feel at some later time, he can court me. Lawd, I've tried every way I can think of to find Isaac or be found by him. Sometimes, I wonder if he's tried as hard as I have. Now, here's another attractive man – but, Lawd, we both know he ain't no Isaac. Hope you're smiling, Lawd.*

"Rachel, com'on. Who's late this time?" Ruth called from the stairs.

Rebecca walked past the open door to Rachel's room. "Rai, give it up. That mirror's lying. You ain't lookin' no better'n when you started on that face that nobody loves but Charles. We're leaving."

"Comin'."

They caught up with Saul on the sidewalk. "It's my special pleasure to escort three of the loveliest women in Natchez to the celebration ball."

Rebecca held her chin up and put a hand on her hip. "Humph! That's because I made you do it!"

They laughed together.

* * *

The foursome was in a gay mood when they walked into the inn shortly after midnight that Saturday, November 6, 1875. John shushed them at the door. He pointed first to the ceiling, then put his hands together beside his tilted head and closed his eyes.

Rebecca whispered. "How long have they been asleep?"

John whispered back. "Half-hour." He cleared his throat and spoke in a low voice. "I have a feelin' some bad news is comin'." John sat at one of the inn's dining tables. Hushed, his family gathered around him.

He held up a hand. "Now, mind you, nothing is known for sure yet. Arthur's brother, David, came by shortly after you left to ask if Rachel had heard from him. It seems Arthur is missing." Rachel stared into John's eyes. He was looking at no one else.

Rachel felt a deep foreboding creep in and replace the happy spirit of Robert Wood's victory ball.

* * *

Ten days later, word came from Jackson that Arthur's body had been found. Rachel went into mourning with the Roberts family. She noticed that Rebecca and John watched her every move and reacted with keen attention to her every utterance. Rachel thought, *I'm okay this time – even in the face of all the fighting and blood that's been shed in the revolt of the white man. I'm holding on. Lawd, please give me strength.*

Days after the closed-casket funeral for Arthur, Mary Beth and her new husband arrived in Natchez with her mother to visit friends. Rachel was happy to spend an afternoon with Mary Beth. It lifted her spirits.

* * *

About a month later, on the third Sunday in December, Rachel and Ruth decided to attend services at Zion Chapel A.M.E. Church. Rachel was glad they heard a message about gifts. As parishioners filed out of the church, Rachel noticed a woman with gray strains in her hair who looked at her several times, but turned away in time to avoid eye contact. The woman remained in her pew. Rachel and Ruth were near the exit of the small church when Rachel heard, "Lawd, Ebony, chile, it's so good to see you out again. How are you this blessed day?"

Rachel froze. She thought, *that's it. Ebony! She looks so much older than I remember. That's why I didn't recognize her. But she apparently recognized me. Why did she avoid me? I better find out.* "Ruth, wait up. See that lady over there? That's the Ebony I told you about. She's the one who took care of me."

"Are you sure?"

"Yes. Com'on, I'll introduce you."

"Hello, Miss Ebony!" Rachel thought, *why is she ignoring me?* "It's me, Rachel. Don't you remember me?"

The woman standing beside Ebony looked down at her. "Why, Ebony, it's not like you to ignore people. Speak to this nice young lady."

Ebony burst into tears and wailed aloud. Exiting parishioners turned to see what the matter was. She rocked back and forth in her seat and would not be consoled. After a few minutes, Ebony spoke. "Lawd, I'm so sorry! Please forgive me! I only tried to help!"

Rachel's heart melted. She put a hand on Ebony's shoulder. "Miss Ebony, it's okay. You did everything you could've done. I'll be forever in your debt."

In response, Ebony wailed louder. Reverend Revels, who was visiting from Alcorn, arrived and sat beside Ebony. She leaned on his shoulder and screamed, "I need forgiveness! I thought I did the right thing."

Rachel stepped back and looked on in bewilderment. She said to no one in particular. "I'm sorry. It seems I somehow upset her. I'll take my leave now."

Ebony reached out with a frail-looking hand and caught Rachel's coat. Hoarsely, she declared, "No, you can't go. First, you must forgive me."

Rachel was thoroughly perplexed. Her purse dangled on her wrist as she held out her hands, palms up. "But, Miss Ebony, there's nothing to forgive. You did fine by me – just like a mother."

Ebony wailed again, louder still. She held onto Rachel's coat and Reverend Revels' robe. Finally, between gulps for air, Ebony said, "You don't understand. Me and Auntie Martha, God rest her soul, told that fine young man you were dead!"

Rachel couldn't feel her legs. The room spun counterclockwise. The floor tilted up ten degrees in front of her and she saw Ruth reaching out. She was going down.

Ruth caught and eased Rachel into the pew beside Miss Ebony and held her against her shoulder. "Rai, what is it?"

Rachel's voice was barely above a whisper. "Isaac."

Miss Ebony still rocked back and forth. "Yes. That's him! Isaac."

Ruth's eyes went wide, but she held onto Rachel. "Oh, my God! Isaac was here in Natchez? When? Was a man with him named Caleb?"

Reverend Revels spoke for the sobbing Ebony. "I remember almost ten years ago two young men came here looking for a young woman. I sent them to Aunt Martha, who has since passed away."

Ebony broke in. "Aunt Martha got you mixed up with another Rachel who died birthin' a yellow baby. So, I too thought it must have been you. I'm so sorry."

Rachel looked at Ruth. Her voice was still barely above a whisper. "Well, our love for them was not in vain. My heart is, at the same time, so sad and yet very grateful. Sad that I will never see my love again, grateful to know that he loved me enough to come back and search for me. He was this close...."

Ruth stammered. "B-b-but, where did they go?"

Ebony blew her nose. "I'm sorry. They didn't say. And I didn't think to ask. I'm so very sorry. Please forgive me."

Rachel sat up. "Like I said, Miss Ebony, there's nothing to forgive. You did your best for me and then Isaac. Be at peace."

"Thank you, Rachel. Thank you. Reverend, that's the sweetest gift I'll get this year."

Rachel kissed Ebony's wet cheek. Somewhat unsteadily, she walked out of the church holding Ruth's hand. They turned left and headed for the inn, walking on Jefferson Street. She thought again and again that *if Isaac had not been told I was dead, somehow he would have found me. He was so determined; he got so close....*

From the upstairs veranda of a rooming house near Wall Street, Rachel heard a familiar voice. She touched Ruth's arm and put a finger over her lips. They stopped and Rachel listened more closely. The voice continued. "Now, Mr. Corbett, I see no reason why you fellows down here in Adams County can't have the same success we've had with the Mississippi Plan across the rest o' the state."

Rachel signaled to Ruth and they walked again. When they were out of earshot, Rachel said, "I need a small gun. Do you know anyone, other than Sheriff Wood, from whom I can borrow one this afternoon?"

Ruth's mouth dropped open. She recovered and sputtered, "R-r-richard Johnson. Why do you need a gun?"

"I think guns are great for killing snakes without getting too close. Show me, dear Ruth, the way to Richard's house."

Ruth pointed south. "We turn left here and it's just a few blocks on."

* * *

With Richard's four-shot Allen & Wheelock .31 caliber Pepperbox Model 1857 snug in her corset, wrapped loosely in a handkerchief between her breasts, Rachel mounted the stairs of the rooming house at first dark carrying a tray of steaming fried catfish and a bowl of rice and beans. She had learned the room number from the desk clerk.

At room number thirty-six, Rachel took a deep breath and knocked. She announced, "Catfish supper, compliments o' Massa Corbett!"

A man, with his black and white galluses hanging at his sides, opened the door with a curious look on his face. His expression changed into lust that he did not try to hide. "Well, what have we here? Old Corbett is a gentleman after all. Never woulda thought he would send me supper and, my, my, brown sugar for dessert. Well, don't just stand there, gal. Com'on in before that good-smelling food gets cold."

"Yessuh. All right, if I puts it on dat table yonder?"

"Sho'. Then you can make yourself comfortable over there on the bed while I eat. Now you just rest easy. I won't be long."

The blond man sat at the table and began to devour the catfish. "Hmm! This is real good. Hope you already et."

"Yessuh. I did."

Rachel sat on the bed long enough to complete her survey of the room, including the window and fire escape beyond. She saw his Peacemaker on the dresser. I will remain calm. I will not rant and rave. First, confirm. Presently, she walked in front of the apparently ravenous man.

She put her hand between her breasts. "Suh, Massa Corbett said Massa Duke be a mighty handsome man and I oughta be reel nice to him. Dat is yo' name, ain't it, suh? Wants to be sho' I 'members right."

With his mouth full, the man spoke. "Yeah. That's me. Billy Duke at yo' service. What's yo' name, sweet thang?"

Rachel removed the handkerchief from her corset. She took her time unfolding the handkerchief, one corner at a time. She was surprised that her hands did not tremble. The man could not see the two-and-seven-eighths-inch barrel of the tiny pistol in her left hand. "Oh, my name is Rachel."

At the sound of a different voice coming from the small woman before him and hearing her name, Billy stopped chewing with a cheek still full of catfish and stared at Rachel's face. She saw in his eyes the moment he recognized her. She grasped her little pistol in her right hand. "Yes, Billy Duke. *That* Rachel. The mother of your bastard."

With his jaw slack, Billy looked back at his Peacemaker lying out of reach on the dresser.

"Look at me when I'm talking. I'm going to shoot you four times." Rachel pointed and fired a bullet into Billy's right shoulder. "That was for Mary Beth."

Billy grabbed his shoulder and fell backwards, upsetting the table with his feet as he hit the floor. He scooted toward the dresser.

Rachel thought the look on his face was more total surprise than pain. She thought it was almost comical that he was still holding a bite of catfish in his cheek. She shot him again in his left thigh. "That was for Reverend Arthur." Billy yelped and stopped scooting.

"Any last words?" Before he could speak, she shot him through the top of his sternum. "That was for Isaac."

He blew out the catfish onto the floor and coughed up blood. His blood continued trickling from the corner of his mouth. His lips quivered. "Oh, Lawd, please don't let me die."

Rachel heard footsteps on the stairs. She propped the chair under the doorknob. Then she moved and stood at Billy's feet. "You leave the Lawd be. This last one is for me. Now you will die." Rachel took careful aim with both hands. She held the gun sight between his eyebrows and fired. Billy lay still, his blue eyes stared at the ceiling. Blood oozed from his forehead, into his left eye, and down his left temple into his hair.

Rachel returned Richard's Pepperbox pistol to her corset and ran for the window. It was dark outside. She opened the window, stepped onto the rusty iron fire escape and hurried down the steps to the landing at the second floor. There she boarded the vertical ladder that extended down for a few feet and learned that the ladder required weight greater than her one hundred five pounds to cause it to extend to the ground. The tail of her dress was on the landing; her waist was at floor level. Rachel tried jumping on the bottom rung where she stood to no avail.

Rachel decided she would have to jump and hoped she could walk after hitting the ground. She turned herself about on the rung, faced forward, and leapt. The hem of her dress had caught between the corner of the ladder and the landing. Her dress ripped and then gave way, but not before rendering Rachel upside down. She landed on her head, breaking her neck.

As the darkness around her grew deeper, she heard people running. They sounded far away and were fading. She could just make out Isaac waiting for her in the darkness on the bench where they spent so many wonderful hours at Davis Bend beside the Mississippi River holding hands and dreaming the same dream of their future.

Then, the scene changed. Rachel saw Isaac emerge from a building with two men. His hat blew off and he did not chase it. He stood with his eyes closed. The scene grew dim. She felt panic when the darkness covered Isaac and he disappeared from view. She thought, *Isaac, my sweet love, I'll see you tomorrow when the sun shines for us.*

Rachel died Sunday evening, December 19, 1875.

Chapter 36: The Lost Command

Five days into the march to Fort Concho, Isaac still had not paid attention to the blossoms of Texas bluebonnets waving in the breezes that swept across the plains. He was acutely aware of the fine-powdered gray-taupe dust that clung to his face and his uniform. He spoke through his bandana. "Tom, we're gonna fail in our new assignment for lack of good horseflesh."

"What're you talking about? Me and you're sitting on the fastest animals in the company."

"Naw, I'm talking about the whole company. I guess you noticed that the ol' nags they sent us after we got the last batch o' recruits were throwaways from the ever-wonderful Seventh Cav."

"Oh, you're right. Colonel Custer must be in thick with the quartermaster general. Of course, they're the first to get new Springfield carbines and Colt .45s."

"Guess who'll be last? But, you know, I think I'd rather keep my Spencer. I heard you can only hope to fire that damn single shot trapdoor Springfield ten times in a minute – if you're good. Without being good, the average trooper can fire twenty rounds a minute with a Spencer."

"Now, Isaac, you know it don't have to make sense for the army to buy the Springfields."

Though Isaac was still feeling grumpy and generally unhappy, he chuckled. "Now, I wouldn't mind getting my mitts on that Colt .45 peace disturber. That's a sweet-looking toy."

Isaac thought, *hmm, I'll buy a Spencer for myself when the army discards them.*

* * *

"Hola, Sargento Darby. Bienvenido a Fort Concho. James, it is good to see you."

"Hola a ti también. Es bueno verte, amigo mío. Congratulations, Sergeant Rice."

"Thanks. And congratulations to you on your promotion to First Sergeant."

"Thanks."

"How're your missus and children?"

"All are well and roasting in the heat of South Texas."

They laughed.

James pushed up the brim of his dusty campaign hat. "So where'd you learn Spanish? Laundress? Bar girl?"

Isaac laughed. "Actually, not from a female. Cisco taught me the few words I've learned. I'm still learning. Cisco's one of our Tonkawa scouts. How about you?"

"Our Texas-Mexican laundresses at Fort Clark taught me."

"What do you mean, Texas-Mexican?"

"These are people who proudly want you to know that they were here on this land before whites or blacks came to Texas."

"Oh."

"So, are you ready for war? Who started this mess anyway?"

"Yes, I'm ready. The main warmonger is a Kiowa chief by the name of Lone Wolf. He's been trying to start this war for years. Since we killed his son and nephew on a raid they made into Texas back in '73, he's succeeded in getting Comanches to join'im on the warpath. They've jumped from the reservation in Indian Territory and are raiding somewhere in North Texas."

"Why were they raiding?"

"Oh, many reasons. The younguns don't like the white man's road. Horse and cattle thieves continue raiding their stocks. Rations our government promised them in a treaty don't show in quantity or on time – if they show. Revenge. So, mark this year, 1874, as the year war has come to the Red River Valley. Do you need more reasons?"

"No. I'm sure there're more. But that's quite enough for us to go on killing each other – this year, or any year."

"Are you guys in the Fourth ready to march?"

James laughed. "We marched two hundred fifty thorny miles just to get here and you're ready to push us out already? But we'll be on the march before the end of August."

"Yes, now that you mentioned it. It's not a bad idea for you to go first. Bad joke. Actually, the Ninth and Tenth won't be ready to march for another five or six weeks."

"Oh. Why's that?"

"Our supplies will arrive late. And, as always, we're in bad need of horses that can hold up in a long campaign. Most of the ol' nags we get are castoffs from certain other regiments."

"Oh, I get your drift. What a way to run an army!"

Isaac pointed to a bench on the porch of the commissary. "Let's sit here until it's time for supper. I heard you guys in the Fourth went into Mexico again and kicked some Lipan and Kickapoo butt."

"Yeah, we surprised'em. They never expected us to cross the border. But, you know, Indians are not the only problem we have down in our neck of the cactus patch. Depending on which side of the Mexican revolution is winning at the moment, the losers run north of the border to resupply by raiding."

"Sounds like you have your hands full like we do up here with the horse thieves, bootleggers, and arms comancheros."

James removed his hat and used it to beat the dust from his sleeves and the front of his shirt. "That Lone Wolf fellow is going to be in for a big surprise. For the first time I know about, we're combining nearly every cavalry and infantry regiment in Indian Territory, New Mexico, and Texas for this effort. I predict they'll be happy to return to the reservation when this operation is done."

"Once back on the reservation, are we gonna continue to starve 'em?"

"After we shoot enough of 'em to make some surrender and go live on reservations, the civilians will keep right on lying and cheatin 'em outta everything our treaties promise. The paradox makes my head hurt."

Isaac frowned. "What's a paradox?"

* * *

As planned, the Fourth Cavalry, commanded by Colonel Mackenzie, marched in late August from Fort Concho with supporting infantry and Seminole and Tonkawa scouts. As Isaac

410

predicted, it was near the end of September when the Ninth and Tenth Cavalry with Tonkawa scouts and the Eleventh Infantry marched from Forts Concho, Richardson, and Griffin.

Isaac could see only a small part of the five-pronged search and assault into the Stake Plain. What he did observe was five companies of cavalry and two of infantry in the column that included Company A. Captain Nolan commanded Companies A and C for the campaign. From the heat in the waning days of summer to the blizzards of November through January, soldiers and animals suffered. They lost no men, though more than twenty suffered severe frostbite. And more than a hundred animals froze to death.

By March, the last of the Comanche, Kiowa, and Cheyenne holdouts surrendered and returned to the reservation at Fort Sill. The Indians lost over six hundred lodges and nearly two thousand ponies. Many had to walk back to Fort Sill. The Red River War of 1874-75 was at an end.

* * *

"What the hell do you mean, *relieved*?" With vigor, Isaac pushed off the cottonwood tree on which he was leaning, hiding from the scorching heat of Monday, August 16, 1875 and stood up straight, glaring at Tom. Company A was one of six companies of the Tenth, two of the Twenty-fourth Infantry, and one of the Twenty-fifth Infantry out since early July with Seminole and Tonkawa scouts sweeping the Llano Estacada of pockets of Comanches.

"Bunkie, this is serious. Colonel Shafter just got the word from General Ord that he has permission to go ahead and relieve Captain Nolan of his command." Tom made a chopping motion, pointing a forefinger.

Isaac stomped the ground with the heel of his right boot so hard that he spilled water from his tin cup. "This is powerful wrong! We went out there in this damn waterless God-forsaken place and found two Indian camps. They saw us coming and skedaddled. We were so close the cook fires were still going. They ran, leaving all their supplies and rations. It took us most of the day to destroy all that stuff, plus the seventy-four lodges. Captain Nolan decided we would pick up the chase early the next morning. Bad luck. Wouldn't you know it? The first time we've seen rain since we left Concho, we get a gulley-washer at first light. As soon as it's over, we saddle up and head off in the direction of the tracks we saw the day before. After eight or ten miles, the captain realizes that we have about a snowball's chance on the Llano Estacada in August of catching up to Indians with a day's lead on our sorry-ass nags. Hellfire, we only got close to'em in the first place because they were camped. Damn that fucking infantry shit Shafter. What more could the man have done?"

"Well, Bunkie, you understand, I see absolutely nothing wrong with the captain's decision. Both of us would've done the same thing."

"Aren't you glad you stayed in the supply camp this time?"

"That was Captain Nolan's decision too. He said since he would also have Company C under his command for this operation, he would use C's trumpeter and give me a break. He told me to enjoy this cottonwood grove. But, you know, you're right. Shafter ain't no cav man."

"Colonel Grierson's back. He shoulda been in charge. Who's dumb-ass idea was it to put Shafter in command of what is clearly a cav operation?"

"It was General Ord. I heard he said Shafter was more familiar with the area than our ol' man."

Isaac shook his head. "Sure. This smells. He had to have some other reason."

"Well, never mind that. This thing ain't over, yet. The worst for our favorite captain will come at a court-martial."

Isaac banged his empty cup against his holstered Colt .45. "Are you shittin' me? Shafter's actually bringing charges?"

Tom shrugged. "Yes. Calm down. We need to talk and act quickly."

As Tom spoke, Isaac remembered and realized he was not living by his new creed: I will remain calm. I will think. "Okay. What?"

"Shafter is sending Captain Nolan back to Concho right now."

Isaac was further annoyed. But, he thought, *I will remain calm.* "Now?"

"Yes, now. Here's what I have in mind. I'll get to Shafter with some made-up report on the stock and, while I have his ear, I'll suggest to him that he designate a sergeant and a detail to escort Captain Nolan back to Concho. I'll suggest you. You can pick your own detail."

"Aw, Bunkie, that's a great idea. I'll ask 'em. You knew I'd go for it, huh?"

Tom caught Isaac by his shirt. "Oh, no, hell you ain't. Not with that short fuse o' yours. You could cause big trouble. With the mood he's in, Shafter ain't looking kindly at Company A for anything – especially if you were on this scout with Captain Nolan."

Isaac blinked several times. He considered the truth of his friend's assessment. He nodded and said, "Okay."

* * *

"Mr. Rice, this must be the hottest day of August. Would you rather travel at night?"

"Yes, sir. I'll have the detail ready to ride after supper mess."

"Very well, Mr. Rice. Oh, there's one other matter we should discuss." Nolan reached out and turned Isaac by his shoulder. They walked close together toward the picket line. "Though we're approaching a full moon, I won't be able to see where I'm going. In the dark, I can barely see my hands. I will be of no help getting us back to Concho."

Isaac thought *oh, shit. I don't know precisely, but I'm sure the fort is more than a hundred miles due south.* Isaac smiled. "Don't worry, sir. I'll get us there."

"That's good to hear. Now, remember, you're the only person in the detail who will know the way. I'll give you my compass once we leave camp. And, by the way, I need you to keep my little disability to yourself. The fewer people who know the better."

"Sir, your secret is safe."

* * *

Isaac never considered himself much of a tracker. The trail created by the seventy-five wagons brought by the column was five weeks old and not a consideration for night travel. There were no roads. Isaac set a course by memory for an opening in the low mountains he recalled from a previous expedition as situated north of the Colorado River. Up front and leading two privates, Isaac and Nolan rode stirrup to stirrup. He thought, *damn, this is like leading a blind man.*

Isaac figured the mountains would be only slightly west of due south. So, he used one hundred eighty-five degrees. That worked. In the rolling hills approaching the mountains, the trees and scrub cedars were far apart. Though he had hoped to reach the Colorado River before sunset, he was forced to make a dry camp on a ridge with trees and grass. By midnight of the second night, they reached the river. Isaac breathed easier, for he knew he could find the Concho River from there using only the North Star. Their second camp was made on the Colorado, followed by a third on the Concho. From the last camp, he followed the Concho River and guided Nolan and the detail into Fort Concho at dawn on their fifth day. They did not see any Indians during their trek.

Grierson had moved his headquarters to Fort Concho when he came back to the regiment in April. Grierson intervened with Shafter upon his return from the field in December and, to Isaac's relief, Nolan only received a reprimand and was again given command of Company A.

* * *

On Sunday, December 19, 1875, Caleb and Tom were walking out of supper mess laughing and talking with Isaac when a sudden gust of warm wind blew Isaac's campaign hat from his head. He didn't look back for his hat. He stopped and stood in stunned silence, sniffing the air. He saw Caleb and Tom look back at him with question marks on their faces. Isaac knew he smelled Rachel, a scent he would never forget. He closed his eyes. The warmth he felt that cold December evening surrounded him. He sensed it on his front and back. He thought he heard her say, as only she could, "Isaac." Then, as suddenly as it started, it was over. The cold resumed. Isaac blinked several times and sniffed again. But now all he smelled was Fort Concho.

"Hey, Bunkie, go get your hat and com'on. Let's not make the music maker late for his concert."

Isaac planned to go to the concert, but suddenly wanted to be alone. "You guys go ahead. I'll catch up." He thought, *what just really happened?*

* * *

From his sentinel's position, prone in the shadow of a scrub cedar, Private Green Johnson called over his shoulder toward the camp to the south behind him. "Horsemen at twelve o'clock!"

Isaac was sitting on a rock at the north edge of Company A's scout supply camp located at Bull Creek, on the headwaters of the Colorado River. As he lifted and checked his carbine, Isaac called out to the eighteen troopers and two civilians encamped with them. "Horsemen at twelve o'clock."

That Wednesday morning, August 1, 1877, the men were especially watchful because they recently had more than once put to flight several Comanches trying to steal horses or mules from their remuda and picket line. Isaac ran to a preselected position to cover the withdrawal of his north sentinel. He was the sergeant in charge of guards and defense of the supply camp while the main body, commanded by Captain Nolan, was out on a planned twenty day scout for a large party of Comanches on the loose from the reservation adjacent to Fort Sill in Indian Territory. The supply camp was under the command of Sergeant Tom Allsup. Two of twenty-some odd bison hunters, Hiram Bickerdyke and Billy Devins, remained with their wagons and equipment in the camp. Their comrades had joined forces with Nolan, Lieutenant Cooper, and forty troopers of Company A on the scout.

From his forward position, Isaac called to Johnson. "Okay. Pull back."

Johnson acknowledged. "Aye."

Isaac removed his hat and peered around a mesquite bush. He saw men whose clothing and faces were the same color as the earth around them. Though they moved with deliberate speed, they held no weapons at the ready. Isaac stood and watched their approach over the muzzle of his carbine, pointed at the leader. Soon, Isaac identified the riders. "Hey, Tom, friendlies coming in. Looks like some o' our boys. Stand by."

Tom's response was, "Barney, go ahead and start another breakfast for about fourteen or fifteen head."

In a moment, Isaac recognized First Sergeant Williams Umbles. "Okay. Everybody, you can go back to your posts. Confirmed. Friendlies." Isaac lowered the hammer on his carbine and let it hang at his side. He gave hand signals directing the riders to the picket line.

Once dismounted, William went directly to Tom. Tom was smiling. "Hey, William, are you guys the advance? How'd it go out there?"

"Hell, no, we ain't no advance! All o' us here under these trees may be what's left o' the company."

Isaac and Tom exchanged glances. Isaac read William's face and realized he was very serious. His anger flashed. Where was his friend, James Jackson, another blacksmith? Isaac thought *there is something wrong with what I'm hearing. I will be calm. Best keep my mouth shut until Tom....*

His thought was interrupted by Tom. Isaac heard Tom suck in air as he folded his arms and looked straight at William's eyes. "William, I need you to explain what you just said."

William glanced at Isaac for the first time. "Mr. Rice, will you 'cuse us a few minutes?"

"No. Isaac stays. Anything you have to say to me can be said in front of Isaac."

William frowned and then shrugged. "All right. Have it your way. Our pigheaded captain has the men and animals up there dying o' thirst. Men are monkeyin' and fallin' like flies. Before my little group o' stragglers were left behind, we had I don't know how many horses drop dead. They would snort and stagger all which ways and then fall head first into the ground and make a single heavy moanin' sound. And that'd be it. They never stirred again.

"The reason me and my little bunch made it here is 'cause we listened to some o' the hunters. They told us – and the captain – we could find water at Silver Lake. We did find water near Silver Lake at Casa Amarillas.

"What I want you to do is pack up and let's go back to Fort Concho and get an officer to take over the company. He can organize an expedition to recover remains and equipment."

Tom glanced at Isaac. Tom lifted one folded arm and rubbed his stubble. "William, are you telling me Captain Nolan and everybody up there on the Llano Estacado are dead."

William blinked. Isaac saw his Adam's apple move up, then down. William spoke. "Damn, right. That's what I said. Now let's get moving"

Tom refolded his arms. "No."

William glared. "What? That's an order, Mr. Allsup!"

"That's an order I will disobey."

William stamped his foot. "Damn your time!" He turned to Isaac. "Okay, Mr. Rice. You're takin' over from Mr. High and Mighty. Let's get this show on the road."

Instinctively, Isaac's right hand slid down his shoulder sling to steady his carbine. He thought *I will be as calm as Tom*. Isaac let his gaze into William's eyes remain steady. "I will stand with Tom, no matter what you order."

Isaac heard Tom inhale. Tom took a step closer to William. "You're free to leave with who ever will follow you. Take two day's rations and be gone."

William bristled. "Mr. Allsup, you haven't heard the last o' this. That goes for you too, Mr. Rice."

Tom walked past William and spoke to the men who were pretending not to listen. "Men, stand by for action. Shortly, we'll be getting a relief operation ready for our comrades. Somebody, sound 'Boots and Saddles'."

Several men cheered. Two of the men who rode in with Umbles followed him to Fort Concho.

Tom whispered to Isaac, "Come with me. We need to figure out where the most likely place is to find them."

"Right. There won't be time to random searchin' up there. The Llano's much too big and it's much too hot on our guys up there."

They huddled with Hiram and Billy. Tom wanted to know, "If you were way up in the northwest close to the New Mexico border and you hadn't found water, where would you go?"

Hiram pulled at his beard. "Hmm. That's a tough question. Well, I, right off…, I'd say they would have three choices. They could go back to where they last found water – Cedar Lake, I'd guess. Or, they could press on to Silver Lake. I think that's what I'd do. The only other place I'd look would be the Double Lakes."

Isaac hit his palm with a fist. "I can feel it in my gut. That's where we'll find them – Double Lakes. If we hurry, we may even get there ahead of'em."

Tom's eyes were blinking rapidly. "Why there?"

"Because William and the boys went to Silver Lake and didn't see the company there or on their way here. Plus, you know the captain likes a sure thing. From far away, he could miss Silver Lake with a compass – plus, as far as I know, he's never been there. With Double Lakes, the two lakes together are so big, he can't miss. And he's been there before."

Hiram was pulling his beard and nodding. "That's pretty good figurin'. I'd bet wid Isaac."

Tom stretched. "Okay, that's where we're going. Hiram, if anybody asks that's where we'll be. Now I need to borrow one o' your wagons."

"Hep yourself. And good luck."

* * *

Isaac and Green scouted ahead to the east and up the Tobacco Draw. That Saturday, August 4, with a wagon loaded with rations and barrels of water, they reunited with their comrades at Double Lakes. When Nolan heard what Sergeant Umbles had reported and that Umbles was on his way to Fort Concho, he wrote a message to Lieutenant Smither, the officer he left in charge on July 10, and asked Tom, "Who would you send to deliver my message to Lieutenant Smither?"

Tom pointed to Isaac. "Sir, I'd send Mr. Rice."

Nolan handed his paper to Isaac. "Indeed, so be it. Mr. Rice, before you go listen to this announcement. Mr. Jim Thompson and everyone need to hear this. Mr. Jim has served us well as acting first sergeant for a trying few days that felt like weeks." There were shouts of "Amen." "Today, I'm announcing our new first sergeant is Mr. Thomas H. Allsup."

Isaac led the applause and then offered his hand. "Congratulations, Bunkie!"

Tom shook hands with Isaac and Nolan. Then he held up both hands. "Thanks, Captain Nolan. Thanks, Bunkie. I ain't much on speeches. Let's just hang tough and make Company A healthy again."

More applause.

Tom gave his first order as first sergeant. "Mr. Rice, pick a riding partner and let's get you started."

Within the hour, Isaac and Green Johnson were in their saddles and, since they did not have a wagon to contend with, headed down Yellow House Draw. They stopped at the supply camp for rations. They soon left, each leading a spare horse. The morning of the third day and one hundred eighty miles later, they rode into Fort Concho with the good news that the command had lost only three men dead and one missing – not the whole command.

Shortly, Isaac learned that his and Green's trail had not crossed that of Lieutenant Smither who was on his way to the rescue with the post surgeon and Caleb and members of the regimental band. On hearing the news of gloom from Umbles, Lieutenant Smither had sent word of Fort Concho's troubles by telegraph and requested troops be sent from elsewhere to protect the post during his absence. About twenty troops from the Tenth Infantry and two officers arrived from Fort McKavett. Isaac gave Nolan's message to the new temporary post commander, Lieutenant John J. Morrison, who quickly had the good news out on the telegraph. Morrison had Umbles and his two companions placed under guard.

* * *

Isaac spent the fall caring for Cheyenne and a new government horse issued to him. As usual, he did overflow work with James Jackson for local blacksmiths trying to fill Christmas orders. While he attended to these mindless tasks, Isaac daydreamed about Rachel. Once in a long while, Bianca came to his mind. Meanwhile, Umbles and three troopers were court-martialed, dishonorably discharged, and sentenced to serve jail time at Leavenworth. By December, Companies A, G, and I had orders to move back to Fort Sill in January 1878.

Within the hour of hearing the news, Isaac requested and got a transfer to Company H, commanded by Nolan's close friend, Captain Henry Carpenter. Company H was assigned to Fort Davis, Texas, further from Fort Sill and Francesca than Fort Concho.

"Bunkie, I'm gonna miss you. But I understand why you're not returning to Sill."

Isaac listened to Tom but sat with his down and hands folded, looking at his boots. "Yeah, ol' friend, I'll miss you, too."

Isaac and Tom stood and applauded the regimental band as the band finished the last piece in rehearsal in preparation for the coming Christmas concert. Isaac said, "Be sure and tell me in your letters how Company A and others receive the army's first colored officer."

Caleb arrived with a trumpet and a banjo. "Yeah, send me the same inside news while it's hot. This has got to be the biggest colored news in the west. How do you see this whole thing unfolding?"

Isaac shrugged. "I believe he'll get on well with Captain Nolan and Colonel Grierson. However, I fear that outside the Tenth, Lieutenant Flipper will just be a nigger with gold bars on his shoulder boards."

Tom put a hand on Isaac's shoulder. "Bunkie, I sure as hell hope you're wrong."

Isaac and Caleb said in unison, "Me, too."

* * *

On a cold morning, two days after Christmas, Isaac bade farewell to his best friends and climbed aboard a Wells Fargo stagecoach beside the driver, who handed him a shotgun. Isaac secured his carbine to his sling. Caleb checked the security of Isaac's saddle and accouterments on his new government horse. Tom tightened the tethers of Cheyenne and Isaac's new horse to the back of the stagecoach. Isaac's footlocker was tied down in the rack atop the coach. When they were satisfied, Caleb and Tom stepped aside. Tom gave the driver and the soldiers escorting the coach the high sign.

Isaac looked back and waved as he thought, *I've never been without at least one of those two turkeys – ever.* He smiled and sniffed.

Chapter 37: **Ambushing Ambushers**

Jacali stumbled and fell as she ran from the wickiup carrying her two-year-old son in her arms. Looking back, Ortega saw her roll over to protect their child. A rancher drew rein and lifted his rifle toward her. Screaming women and children ran for their lives past Jacali. Ortega dropped his saddle and ran like the wind to his enemy. In milliseconds, he covered the fifteen feet separating him from the raider. With two final bounding steps, he leapt and grabbed the rancher above the waist before he could take aim. The startled rancher fired into the air as Ortega's momentum carried both off the horse and onto the ground.

Ortega rolled him over, held his enemy about the neck with one arm, snatched his long hunting knife from its scabbard, and in one swift motion plunged the blade through the rancher's sternum. The man gasped for air and wore a surprised look on his face as Ortega yanked his knife from the man's chest.

Jacali had recovered and now blocked their son's view of the dying man. The sound of gunfire continued, echoing through the canyon where they camped. She stood, mouth agape, looking at Ortega rise from their fallen enemy.

Between deep breaths, Ortega glanced at his wife and pointed to the mountain. His voice was low, but emphatic. "Go!"

Jacali fled.

Ortega grabbed the reins of his enemy's horse and ran to his dropped saddle, retrieved his carbine, mounted, chased, and fired at the withdrawing ranchers. During the running battle, he shot two from their saddles. At length, he turned the confused horse and returned to the Mescalero camp. There he heard much moaning from the wounded and wailing for the dead. He spat.

* * *

Almost a year later, in the fall of 1877, Ortega learned on his return from a short hunting trip with Jorge and Pedro that the camp had been dispersed due to a raging smallpox epidemic. He searched for Jacali in a wickiup community she had built with the wives of

Jorge and Pedro. Ortega didn't know which wickiup was theirs, so he called out her name. Jacali and their three-year-old son, Edgar, ran out of the first wickiup to meet him.

Jacali stretched out her arms as she ran. Ortega dismounted from behind the carcass of an elk tied over his horse's shoulders. After a quick embrace with Jacali, he lifted and held Edgar.

Later, while they toiled together to butcher the elk before nightfall, Jacali asked, "Did you hear that we moved out here on this mountain because of the fever that killed so many people?"

"Yes. Is it true that only children and teenagers died?"

"Oh, no. It seemed that way at first. But many adults also died — even our old chief."

"What? Chief Cadete?"

"No. Not the son. He lives."

Ortega looked about. Then he whispered. "Do you mean Chief Santana?"

Jacali glanced over her shoulders too for anyone in earshot. "Yes. We will speak his name nevermore."

For a few minutes, they worked in silence. Ortega reflected on Chief Santana's desire to live in peace and the old chief's newfound White Eye friend, Dr. Blazer. Maybe the old men are right....

Jacali broke his thought. "While you were away, the *Tejanos* returned and took more horses from our dwindling herd."

Ortega's shoulders sagged. Barely above a whisper, he said, "Oh." He turned away and spat.

Jacali stopped her work and looked with pleading eyes at Ortega. "Husband, I am afraid for Edgar. Please, let's go away. Let's take Edgar from this place of fevers and death. Let's go see the lake with no end."

Ortega smiled. "Did you talk to the wives of Jorge and Pedro?"

He looked into her eyes. She spoke without blinking. "Yes. They think of their children and the fever the same as I think of Edgar."

"My wife is wise. We will go when the moon is at one-quarter."

They hugged. Jacali's necklace of beads and small shells from the Gulf of California clanked softly.

* * *

A few weeks later, led by Ortega, the entourage of three men, three women, and four children slipped into the abandoned Chiricahua Reservation and rested for two days. Ortega offered a prayer to Ussen for the spirit of Cochise and the Chokonen people.

Jacali demanded, "How can the Great Father of the White Eyes in Washington give his word to the Chokonen people twice that this land was their reservation for all time and then both times take it away?"

Ortega shrugged. "Only the Whites Eyes know."

Jorge turned to Ortega. "Remember, they will kill us for these lands."

"Yes, though these lands are ours and not theirs to give, they claim to give us a corner to be our prison and call it a reservation."

They all nodded in agreement.

* * *

In mid-October, they camped for a time with Juh's people in the Blue Mountains. Ortega, Jacali, and Edgar walked hand in hand in the peace and quiet of the Sierra Madre. Ortega wondered if this could be the place for his little family but concluded that he and Jacali would soon enough want to live again among their Mescalero people.

During the winter months, they camped among the Pima along Sonora's coast. Occasionally, they took Edgar to the beach to build sand villages and play in the surf of the Gulf of California.

By March, Jacali and her women friends missed their ponderosa-pine-covered mountains. Instead of returning by way of the abandoned Chiricahua Reservation, they passed south of Casa Grande and west of Carrizal. From their overnight camp in the hills above Carrizal, they traveled to a path parallel and west of the El Paso-Chihuahua Road.

Suddenly, as they reached the old Indian trail, Ortega called a halt and sent the women and children to the rear. Jorge hurried to

Ortega's side. Pedro gave the lines of the pack animals to the women and moved them to the mouth of a canyon. He stood guard.

Ortega gazed ahead to the north and kept silent. Jorge put his right hand over his eyes to block the sun. "Ortega, my friend, what do you see? As usual, I see nothing."

"There are a dozen Mexicans hiding in a draw ahead on both sides of the trail. They have prepared an ambush for six vaqueros traveling south."

"Oh. Highwaymen?"

"I suppose."

"Can we surprise the bushwhackers?"

"I'm sure we could. But let's not. We cannot risk a fight, for we are too few and can barely defend our families."

"I agree."

"Ride back and remind everyone that we scatter in different directions if I give the signal. And make sure all know where we agreed to rendezvous after we escape."

Jorge turned his horse about in the desert sand. "Okay."

Ortega was alone with his thoughts. He could see himself as the ambushers and as the ambushed. He slowly realized that his sympathy lay with the six southbound riders. That did not change his resolve to stay out of their fight – no matter their fate. But he wished he could help.

Presently, Jorge materialized at his side, dismounted. "Our people are ready."

Ortega did not move his eyes from the men in the draw. "Thanks."

The vaqueros drew nearer. Ortega removed his carbine from its saddle boot. Jorge did likewise. Ortega led his horse ahead and then out of sight of the ambushers lest they looked toward them. "Come. I have an idea."

Jorge followed Ortega as he climbed the side of the mountain by their trail. They separated and hid behind boulders. "Can you see the ambushers?"

"Yes."

The ambushers opened fire.

Over the den of gunfire, Ortega called to Jorge. "Shoot the ones nearest us. I will get the ones further away on the east side of the road."

"We'd better do it now. The vaqueros are down."

"Fire!"

Seconds later, several of the ambushers stood and ran for their horses. The vaqueros had lost their hats in the fight. Ortega saw a black vaquero's hand move for his dropped weapon. He was shot again. The white vaquero threw himself over his black companion and took the next bullet. Ortega reacted to the heroism and uncommon sacrifice in front of him by shooting the shooter and the man next to him. Jorge's fire downed two more.

The surprised ambushed ambushers fled, taking one of the vaquero's pack mules. Ortega and Jorge ceased firing. Because they hit their targets with each shot there was no dust to help the trapped ambushers determine the direction from which the lead came. Ortega waited. He saw a hat rise above the lip of the draw. He held his fire.

Minutes passed. No movement. Five minutes later, the last of the ambushers ran for their horses and galloped up the draw away from the road, leaving six of their men lying in the sand and rocks.

After five more minutes passed, Ortega ventured down to aid the fallen. The Mexican, Tonkawa, and White Eye vaqueros were dead. The black man was bleeding badly and barely conscious. While Ortega labored over the man to stop the bleeding, he raised his left hand and pushed his hair behind his left ear. The black man's glazed eyes followed Ortega's hand. With Ortega bending above him, the man raised his hand toward Ortega's ear and touched his face near his blue headband. The man's hand fell to the ground as he passed out.

* * *

Within the hour, they arrived in Carrizal at the home of the women who drove pigs when they last passed by Carrizal. Using their makeshift stretcher, Ortega and Jorge lifted the victim into the house. Jacali held his head steady. The pretty young woman in the house hastily prepared a bed for the wounded man.

426

Ortega watched as the woman, without a word, expertly cut away clothing with scissors, cleaned the man's four gunshot wounds, and carefully rebandaged him, keeping bleeding to a minimum. When she finished, she said to no one in particular, "I must remove the bullets before nightfall."

Ortega and Jacali looked at each other and headed for the exit. Once outside, Ortega described the ambushers and asked the older woman who they might be. The woman spoke sharply. "They are the same revolutionaries you saw last time you were here – Lerdistas!"

With his rifle cradled in the crook of his arm, Pedro kept watch, riding his horse back and forth in front of the adobe house creating small dust swirls. Ortega was anxious to depart the Mexican village, no matter how friendly the women were. Their neighbors were in their dirt yards and watching with large eyes.

* * *

They reached the Mescalero Reservation in early April. Ortega was surprised to see his old Chihenne friend Ponce living at Mescalero. He wanted to know the news then, not later. But instead Ortega worked with Jorge and Pedro to curry and brush their horses and pack animals. They were finished building new wickiups by the end of the second day and anxious to hear Ponce's stories.

Ortega invited Ponce to join him and his friends for the evening meal. Adding wood to the fire as first dark approached helped ward off the cool spring night in the mountains of Mescalero.

Ortega noticed a large new scar on Ponce's forearm. He pointed. "Say, you didn't have that a few summers ago when we went to Sonora. What happened?"

Ponce held his arm out for the others to see. "So, it is little wonder that your name is Nah-kah-yen. You see what many miss. That mark was caused by the bullet of a White Eye citizen two summers ago."

Jorge craned his neck to see in the dim light. "Did it hurt much?"

Ponce laughed. "At first, it felt like a bee sting. The next day, it felt like a toothache!" He opened his shirt and exposed his shoulder. "This scar was made in the same summer by the bullet of a blue soldier who has hair like that of a buffalo. His bullet felt like a red branding iron and a fall from a horse at the same time."

Jorge and Pedro marveled and said, "Oh."

Ortega made no sound. He thought, *hmm. He had hair like that of a buffalo....* Ortega rubbed his chin and wondered if the black man near Carrizal, who was dressed like a vaquero, was really a vaquero. Or was he soldier? He thought *no matter. He was a man in trouble. Why did he touch my face?*

Ponce continued. "Enough about me. What have you three done since I last saw you – except make babies?"

The four men laughed together. Jorge and Pedro told the older man about using his trails to return to the Blue Mountains and the Gulf of California. Pleased, Ponce smiled a lot.

Ortega listened and waited. After a time, he changed the subject. "Ponce, tell us about what you were doing when you were shot. Why did it happen? Whose shot hit your arm?"

The older man's face went grim. Jorge and Pedro shifted in their seats.

Ponce cleared his throat and toyed with a twig. Ortega thought Ponce suddenly looked older and very tired. Ponce held the end of the twig in the flames until it was ablaze. He pulled it out of the fire and let it burn. "Just as the flame consumes this twig, just as surely as I sit with you, the White Eyes are consuming the lands of the Apaches and all Indian nations."

The young men nodded.

Ponce tossed the twig into the fire. "Since I last saw you, my great chief agreed to move our people to the arid San Carlos Reservation and share it with the White Mountain people, though he argued for a reservation to be established in our homeland at Ojo Caliente. He soon regretted that decision. After that, we broke out of San Carlos. To re-imprison us, the White Eyes *gave* us the reservation Chief Victorio requested in our homeland. We came in. We were happy to have a place of our own. Then, without any provocation, a stupid White Eye army officer called Lieutenant Wright led his black soldiers and Navajo scouts in a raid and burned our main rancheria, home to twenty-seven of our families – including mine. My mistake was firing back instead of running. That's when I was hit in the shoulder.

"I guess I'm a slow learner. Just one moon later, I made the same mistake again when White Eye citizens raided our reservation and drove off a herd of our horses. That time, I was hit in the arm."

The young men sat wide-eyed and listened.

Ponce leaned back and stretched his arms. "Of course, since I arrived here, I've heard about White Eyes raiding on your reservation. The real question is, Why am I here? Well, I'll tell you why. But, first, I need a drink of water."

The foursome stretched their legs and each man drank water. Ortega's mind went back to the twig consumed by fire. *What kind of a future would little Edgar have? Would there be grandchildren? Or, like the twig, would the future of Indian nations be ashes? What can I do now to save the twig? Or at least save some of the twig? Is it true that we will die whether we fight or farm? Is there a way to fight without killing or being killed? Oh, how little I know.*

Ortega's head hurt. Ussen, please help us!

They gathered around the fire again. Ponce sat erect like the warrior he was. He began again. "Last summer, the White Eyes in Washington changed their minds and closed our reservation."

In unison, Jorge and Pedro expressed disgust. "Oh, no!"

Ortega slapped both thighs and spat into the fire. Rage was clear in his voice. "That's the same thing they did to as great a chief as the Chokonen leader!"

Ponce pointed out, "At least, the White Eyes did wait and change their minds after the great Chokonen chief died. Now they have done this twice to Chief Victorio and us Chihenne in just two years."

Ortega seethed. He demanded, "What did Chief Victorio do?"

"Five moons ago, before the troops came to force us to move, Chief Victorio broke out with a sizable number of warriors. I went with him. Now he has more warriors and is raiding against the army, White Eye citizens, and Mexicans. He has killed many. I'm here for a rest. I'll return to my chief soon."

"If your chief is committed to fight to the death, I'll join him too."

"Actually, he is periodically sending messengers to tell the White Eye Indian agents and army officers that he will come in again and keep the peace if the Ojo Caliente Reservation is restored. Victorio wants peace. He has even considered living here at Mescalero."

Ortega was flabbergasted. "Really?"

"Yes. Victorio knows, as the great Chokonen leader knew, and I finally know, we are too few to hurt the White Eyes enough to even make them grant concessions, much less defeat them."

Staring into the fire, Jorge said what all were thinking. "There are too damned many of them...."

Pedro added sourly. "Plus, they hire black soldiers, Apache scouts, and Navajo scouts."

Ortega made a deep sigh. "My grandfather was right." He spat again. "Dammit! What will become of us?"

Chapter 38: Isaac and James

In the spring of 1878, Colonel Mackenzie and the Fourth Cavalry were reassigned from Fort Sill to Fort Clark. The old troubles of two and four years before had returned. The Kickapoo, Lipan, Southern Mescalero, and revolutionary Lerdistas were again raiding into Texas – areas assigned to both the Fourth and Tenth Cavalry Regiments – the Military District of the Nueces, commanded by Colonel Mackenzie and the Military District of the Pecos, commanded by Colonel Grierson. The new Porfirio Diaz government in Mexico was again asserting its sovereignty and required prior approval for future cross border strikes by the United States Army. Companies of both the Fourth and Tenth had previously made successful separate strikes into Mexico.

In March, two troopers and four scouts dressed as vaqueros departed from Fort Davis with the mission of scouting and mapping new routes for possible retaliatory strikes into Mexican territory. While none of the six were cartographers, they were to provide their report to the Tenth's Ordinance Sergeant, Robert F. Joyce at Fort Concho, who had demonstrated some significant map-drawing skills. Their plan was to cross into Mexico behind the old abandoned Fort Quitman, go west to the Candelaria, then southwest to Casa Grande, southeast to Babicora, east to the Rio Conchos, and cross back into the United States near the Rio Grande's big bend.

Their march to Fort Quitman from Fort Davis provided team members a period to become familiar with each other's skills. Fort Quitman was a few minute's walk from the Rio Grande. They carried surveying equipment atop the pack animals' cargo. Before they arrived at Quitman on their third night out of Fort Davis, they had already supplemented their rations with roasted antelope. One of their number always stood guard and watched their six horses and two mules graze.

The stars were so bright and distinct that Isaac paused to admire their beauty and wonder. He dropped the wood he had collected near the fire and sat beside James Darby. A Tonkawa stood guard. On the other side of the fire, a Mexican guide and two Tonkawa tribesmen told tall tales in Spanish. Isaac was surprised that he could follow most of what was being said. He shook his head as if to clear his thinking. "James, I'll remember our conversations from these nights for a long time to come. Around fires on the trail, one gets to know another."

"Likewise, I've gained insight into what makes you go that I never would've learned in casual conversation."

"Let me ask you, what advice would you give me about choosing a mate?"

"Whoa! I have no idea what to tell you. But I'll let you know that Abigail was not my first choice. That was a girl back home during the war. She sent me a 'Dear James' letter that caught up with me just as I was mustered out at Fort Leavenworth."

Deep in thought, James chuckled. "I used to pick wildflowers on the battlefields of Virginia and send them in letters to her."

"Did you plan to marry her?"

"Oh, yes. We promised each other we would get married as soon as I returned."

"What happened?"

"I don't know. Maybe she got tired of waiting."

"But she sent that letter at the end...."

James interrupted. "My guess is, she ran off with my classmate some time prior and just couldn't write the Dear James thing until she absolutely had to."

"Oh. That makes sense. Where'd you meet Abigail?"

"Funny you should ask. I met her in St. Louie just a couple of weeks before you came to my rescue."

"You mean me and Caleb."

James paused and tilted his head, examining Isaac's features by the light of the fire. "There always was something about you that nagged at me. Now, I can put my finger on it. You're loyal to a fault. You gave him credit – even in his absence – and Caleb didn't do a damn thing to help me. How do I know? Abigail later told me everything that happened while I was unconscious. So, I know that Caleb, bless his heart, tried to get you to run away and leave me on that sidewalk."

Isaac dropped his head. "Oh."

"I guess the answer to your question is you'll know when you met *the* one."

* * *

They crossed the Rio Grande at first light. The night creatures were still making their sounds. In a distant village, dueling cocks crowed again and again, one after the other. Two nights later, they camped on the south slope of the southern tower of the Candelaria Mountains. Again, at dawn they moved out.

By late afternoon, they were skirting the southeastern edge of the Santa Maria Mountains in an effort to avoid the village of Carrizal. Isaac was thinking about the contrast of desert sand and cacti as they crossed below Candelaria and now they were approaching a draw, down which flowed life-giving water, nourishing trees, and larger and larger mesquite bushes. The first bullets felled the four scouts. The Mexican guide screamed, "Lerdistas!" That was his last word.

Before Isaac could remove his carbine from its saddle boot, Cheyenne was hit in his chest and right cannon. He screamed in pain and went down on his right side, pinning Isaac's right leg and fracturing his tibia. Isaac's pain was excruciating as he pushed with his left foot against Cheyenne's croup. The horse tried to rise. Cheyenne's movement was enough for Isaac to pull his leg free before Cheyenne took a bullet in his head and went down again.

Isaac had so much pain in his leg that he did not notice blood inside his left arm until he was hit a second time in the same arm. He rolled himself into a position with his back against his saddle. It was no use – he realized he was in the middle of a well-planned ambush. Bullets came from both his left and right. Suddenly, a bloody James was at his side. New rifle fire now poured from above. At close range, revolvers still fired into their position. A pack mule stampeded past. Isaac's carbine remained pinned under Cheyenne. Isaac saw movement to his right and fired his revolver. A man wearing a sombrero tumbled from behind a mesquite bush. James fired with the same result.

Now, war whoops sounded from the ridge above the draw, along with more rifle fire. James was hit again. Isaac could not see where, but heard him groan. The ambushers were hurriedly mounting. A man grabbed the lines of one of their mules and rode north. Isaac realized that he and James lay in the escape path of the Lerdistas and that the Lerdistas were now under attack by Indians. Isaac thought, unbelievable. As the Lerdistas rode his way, they continued firing. Isaac was hit again, this time someplace in his trunk. The pain was so great he could not determine where. He was sweating profusely. He tried to wipe his vision clear with his bloody left sleeve. When he looked up to fire, it was too late. An ambusher had paused and pointed his revolver and fired into Isaac's left shoulder, cursed that he missed his mark – the heart – and prepared to fire again from his prancing mount. Just as he fired, James rolled onto Isaac, taking the bullet. Under the impact, Isaac dropped his .45. Isaac heard someone else close by fire. By the sound, Isaac thought it was a Spencer. He blinked and the shooter lay two feet from James with the blank stare of death replacing the surprise on his face.

With pain coming from his trunk, arm, shoulder, and leg, Isaac could not move James. He called, but James did not respond. Presently, two men stood over them. A wave of nausea swept over Isaac and he lost consciousness. When he drifted back, he heard an unfamiliar language. He could not see James. A man bent over him and checked his vital signs. The man said, "Hmm." And then he called a friend. They applied a tourniquet to his left upper arm. One pressed on his shoulder while the other pressed on his right side. The man on his right wore a headband. Below the headband, Isaac saw that the man's left ear was torn by three gashes in parallel. The marks, plus a fourth, continued down the man's cheek. Isaac reached up and touched the man's scarred face just below the blue headband. The man smiled.

Isaac drifted out and back again. This time he saw and recognized the men to be Indians of a tribe he had never encountered. They were hurriedly rigging a stretcher using two spears, rope, and a blanket. The next time he regained consciousness, he was in a bed. He did not see the Indians. A face appeared over him, the most beautiful he could remember. It was framed by shiny black hair. He felt his brow furrow, but not from pain but confusion. The woman's scent was Rachel's – or was it? He felt the warm breeze again that accompanied the last time he smelled Rachel. He smiled, and then lost consciousness.

Chapter 39: **Saving Isaac**

"Papa! Papa, come get Ida!"

Alejandra left her horse, Ida, hitched to a plow in the field and ran, then tripped over her long calico work dress, but regained her balance without falling. She paused, gathered her dress at the sides, and pulled it up to her knees. And then she ran as fast as she could to intercept the two men trotting toward their house bearing a stretcher. Trailing behind the men was another man on a horse cradling a carbine. That man was followed by three women, each with a child behind her on her horse. They led four pack mules.

Without breaking his stride, the man in front said, "Hola, Alejandra. We need help for this man. Where is your shaman?"

Alejandra smiled and slowed to a trot beside the patient. She thought, *Hmm, I've never seen a black man close up. I wonder if Orestes looked like this man.* "Take him to my house." Still trotting beside the stretcher, she lifted the blanket covering the patient and saw blood-soaked clothes and a tourniquet. She let the blanket down gently.

Running again, she asked. "You're Ortega, right?"

"Si."

"Even like this, it's good to see you again, my friend. I will prepare a place for him." She ran ahead and entered the house through the kitchen.

Alejandra washed her hands in a basin on the wall near the door. Panting, she said, "Mama, please help me! Ortega is bringing in a wounded man."

In the warm kitchen, Rocio's brow wrinkled under beads of sweat. "What do you want me to do?"

Alejandra was dipping from one of their water supply buckets and filling a kettle. "Boil this, and put on two more pots of water to boil." She pushed aside Rocio's supper preparations and set the kettle on the hot part of stove. She ran to hold the door open, gave the open door to Rocio, and said to Ortega, "Follow me."

In her room, Alejandra snatched off her colorful spread and pointed to her bed. The woman who followed them inside held the

436

patient's head steady. They set the makeshift stretcher and the patient on the bed.

Ortega began untying the rope and removing the spears. "This is my wife, Jacali, and my friend, Jorge."

Alejandra glanced at Jacali and Jorge. "Hola."

In unison, they replied, "Hola."

Alejandra removed her medical bag from behind her bed and placed it on a chair next to her. From the bag, she selected a sharp pair of scissors and began at the foot, cutting away the patient's clothes. In less than two minutes, the patient lay nude on what remained of his clothes.

When Alejandra looked up, Ortega, Jacali, and Jorge were all trying to move through the doorway at the same time. She was amused at the look of surprise on their faces. She covered the patient's genitals with a white cloth.

"Don't go yet. I need you for a few more minutes." From another valise, Alejandra took out a large white apron to cover her clothing. In a small white porcelain basin, she soaked a large bandage with hydrogen peroxide. "Ortega, come and place your hands here and here. When I give you the word, raise him gently about this much. I need to find any exit wounds." Ortega lifted the patient a few inches as instructed and Alejandra checked the wet bandage.

"His right leg looks strange. Cut his boots off – gently, very gently."

While Ortega and Jorge slowly cut away the boots and socks, Alejandra moved quickly to find and stop bleeding from all of the patient's wounds. When she had pressure bandages in place and strapped down on the patient's left shoulder and right side, she loosened Ortega's tourniquet. And then she bandaged the wounds in his biceps and forearm.

Ortega pointed to the patient's right leg. "Trouble."

She glanced at Ortega, standing at the foot of the bed. "Oh, my." She took a closer look.

"Si, trouble. His tibia is broken. And, I have nothing… Wait! Measure his left leg from here to here and cut four shafts the same length from those spears." She nodded. "Yes, of course, that'll work."

Neither man moved, except to exchange glances. Alejandra's hands flew out and her face changed to exasperation. *"Well?"*

Ortega nodded. "Jorge, my friend, I'll make a new and better spear for you when we get home. We can keep the heads."

While Jacali returned to her child and Ortega and Jorge fashioned splints outside, Alejandra covered her patient with Ortega's blanket and one of hers. She returned to the kitchen and washed her hands again.

Rocio asked, "How is he? Will he live?"

"Mama, the answer to both questions is I don't know. I just hope he didn't loose too much blood."

"My child, I'm proud of you." Rocio's smile vanished. "Why do you look so troubled?"

"Thanks, Mama. I'm troubled because I just decided I must get those bullets out of him now – right now. That will mean the loss of more precious blood. I could kill him." Alejandra shook her head.

"Oh, my!" Rocio put one hand over her mouth.

"Okay. We need to get moving."

"We? Me? Oh, no." Rocio held her hands up and shook her head. "You know I can't look at blood without fainting."

"Mama, you and me are the only chance that man in there has to live."

Rocio bit her lower lip and wiped her hands on her apron. Alejandra saw her mother's hands tremble. Rocio's voice was weak. "Okay."

Ortega knocked and laid the splints on a kitchen chair. "We must go now. We need to find a camp before the sun sets. Sorry for our behavior. We did not know that you are the shaman here. Please take this for your services." Ortega pressed three gold coins into Alejandra's hand.

"Oh, no, this is not necessary. I may never be paid for all my services. It's okay."

Ortega held his hands up as Alejandra tried to return the coins. "We go now."

Rocio interrupted. "You can camp here."

Ortega stopped in the doorway and smiled. "Thank you. But we must find a defensible place. Here, too many people are about. We trust you, but not your villagers." He trotted to his horse.

"Oh." Rocio spoke to Ortega's receding back.

Alejandra dropped the coins into the pocket of her apron, thinking that one of these coins is way more than Dr. Sanchez would charge. She washed her hands, yet again. She grabbed the kettle. "Mama, please wash your hands and bring that pot of water."

Rocio looked at her clean hands, fingers spread.

"Mama, I know your hands are the cleanest in this family. But, please, wash them again. Please."

Rocio smiled. "Okay. You're the doctor."

"And bring a jar of honey."

"Honey? Oh, never mind. I remember. Dr. Sanchez used honey."

Alejandra set out more white porcelain pans. She poured scalding water on the instruments she selected and used forceps to fish them from the water and place them on a hydrogen-peroxide-soaked towel.

Rocio lit two candle lamps, though there was still some fading daylight left. After they tied their hair inside bandanas and Alejandra wore one over her mouth and nose, she was ready to begin.

Her father, Manuel, appeared in the doorway. "Will he live?"

"Papa, I don't know. Sorry. I had to borrow Mama. Supper is on the stove."

"Gracias." He disappeared.

Alejandra operated on the shoulder wound first. With her knees on two pillows, she probed gently, noting the torn tissue in the entry wound. Minutes later, she felt the piece of lead. From her experienced touch, she had not mistaken bone for bullet. She thought, *God, please let it be in one piece.* She reached for her smallest forceps and extracted a jagged misshapen bloody mass of lead and dropped it into an empty pan with a resounding clank.

When Alejandra had stopped the bleeding, she applied hydrogen peroxide, followed by honey over the wound. And then she rebandaged the shoulder wound Rocio rearranged the sheet in which Alejandra had cut out a square so that the opening was now over the wound between the patient's ribs and his pelvis. Rocio moved Alejandra's pillows to the opposite side of the bed. And she put a blanket back in place on the patient.

This time, Alejandra had to make an incision and it took more than several minutes to find the bullet – almost an hour. All the while, she thought, *hurry, for he cannot abide the loss of more blood. Focus on the probe and my fingertips. One thing at a time. God, please help me. Please, please don't let me puncture something. Oh, I feel so warm.*

The candle lamps flickered. Alejandra felt a warm breeze on her forehead. Just then, her probe touched something solid where there was no bone nearby. Aloud, Alejandra said, "Thanks be to God." The breeze stopped. The air was cool again.

After her sutures held together the incision and the bleeding was stopped, Alejandra was ready for the arm. She did not suture the wound. She moved on to the biceps and tightened Ortega's tourniquet. Alejandra found the third bullet quickly. The forearm wound was a groove carved by a bullet on the underside. She sutured and bandaged it. To each wound, she applied honey. She removed Ortega's tourniquet.

When they were done, Alejandra slumped exhausted on her pillows and leaned back against her bed. Rocio knelt beside Alejandra and mopped her daughter's brow. "Come, Allie. You must eat."

"Okay, Mama. You go ahead. I'll be there in a minute."

* * *

After supper, Alejandra, and her parents worked together to fashion what Rocio called "a most excellent splint." Alejandra set the bone. They made the splint from four shafts of Ortega and Jorge's spears, a pair of Alejandra's pantaloons, twine, and the top of the patient's right boot.

They were in the kitchen putting away the scraps from the split when Ernesto and Rafael arrived with their wives, Linda and Patricia. Ernesto whispered, but so they all could hear, "Hey, Sis, I heard you have a man in your bed. Are you gonna keep him?"

Alejandra bared her teeth and growled to keep from laughing. She grabbed Ernesto's ear and twisted. He whispered, "Ouch!"

Smiling, Rocio hugged Manuel. "Honey, I guess they'll always be our children."

Manuel nodded. "Reminds me of days gone by...."

In hushed tones, they laughed together.

Alejandra held her hands up. "Papa, Mama, everybody, let's pray all at the same time for the patient, whoever he is."

The seven people circled the kitchen table and held hands while they whispered prayers.

* * *

Though Ernesto and Rafael had homes of their own and no longer lived in their old room, Alejandra only used it for her bath. She felt refreshed, but still tired as she sat by her bed and for the first time looked at her patient's face. She thought, *under that stubble, he does have a nice face. I wonder if he's another handsome Torres.* She shook her head. *I must be getting desperate for a husband. How dare I gaze upon a patient and think of him as a potential mate? They don't know how I hurt inside, especially my beloved brothers, when they tease me as their old maid sister.* She smiled. *Oh, well, all in God's good time.*

Alejandra slept on the floor beside her bed. At five o'clock, it was still dark. She awoke when the patient whispered, "Water."

She leapt to her feet and leaned over him. Alejandra did not know the English word "water." She ran and lit the candle lamp. The man's eyes were closed and he appeared to sleep again. She checked his pulse at the carotid and radial arteries. Alejandra could not decide if his pulse was stronger than in the evening. She sat and watched his chest rise and fall for thirty minutes. He made not a sound.

Alejandra dozed in her chair until the cocks began to crow throughout the village of Carrizal. As was her morning habit, she gave thanks aloud. She whispered, "God, thank you for the present of Wednesday, March 27, 1878."

Her patient whispered, "Water."

Alejandra at once was over him, listening and studying his face. With his eyes closed, he repeated, "Water."

Rocio appeared in the doorway. "Good morning."

"Mama, come quick. He's saying something that I can't understand."

His eyelids fluttered. "Agua."

Alejandra's jaw dropped.

Rocio looked from the patient to Alejandra. "You don't understand agua?"

"Mama, I declare, he said a word I don't know."

The man's eyes closed again. He repeated, "Water."

Pointing to the patient, Alejandra said, "That word."

Rocio said, "Oh, it's English for agua. I'll get some." Rocio ran to the kitchen and returned with a cup of water and a spoon.

Alejandra dipped and dripped several drops onto the man's parched lips. His eyes opened, but did not appear to be focused. She fed drops of water into his mouth. Only his lips, tongue, and throat moved.

"Mama, let's give him spinach and chicken soup."

"Okay. I'll make some."

* * *

The third evening, Alejandra washed the patient's body and covered him with a clean sheet. At nine in the evening, she read by candle lamp next to her bed. His eyes opened and he said, "Please give me soup."

She leaned over him and asked, "Can you speak Spanish?"

The sleepy-eyed man smiled and said, "Un poco. Por favor, dame, la sopa."

Alejandra beamed and clasped her hands together. "Oh, good! I'll get some soup for you."

She fed him while she asked questions. Rocio and Manuel stood in the doorway. Alejandra asked, "What is you name? Where did you come from? Where are you going?"

The man smiled and said, "My name is Isaac. I hurt all over – even my hair. Tomorrow, talk tomorrow."

Rocio and Manuel laughed. Alejandra smiled and fed her patient. When he had eaten his soup, she stood on a chair and reached a high shelf. She brought down a brown bottle and poured a small amount of laudanum into a spoon. "This is for your pain. I warn you, it is very bitter. Also, I have to ration it, for I have very little."

He blinked. "Gracias."

* * *

Though he was reluctant and appeared to be highly embarrassed because he needed assistance with the elimination of body waste, Isaac gradually stopped protesting. In a week, he struggled to sit in a chair and no longer allowed Alejandra to bathe him. Now he wore Ernesto's clothes. Over his protests, she still sniffed him as she checked for signs of infection. Finding none, she credited Dr. Sanchez and the honey.

Alejandra waved her hand across Isaac's line of vision. "Isaac, where are you in your thoughts?"

"I'm in the ambush. I saw the men in front of me go down. Did they die?"

Alejandra moved closer and spoke softly. "Yes. They died. A Mexican and three Indians."

"And what of the white man?"

"Ortega told me...."

"Who is Ortega?"

"Ortega is the Mescalero Apache whose people drove off the Lerdistas who ambushed you and he brought you to me. Anyway, Ortega told me that the white man with you saved your life. Ortega said the man deliberately took a bullet for you from a Lerdistas. An instant later, Ortega killed the same Lerdistas. He could not reload his carbine fast enough to prevent the man from killing your white companion. Ortega was deeply touched by your companion's sacrifice of his life that you might live. So am I. I'm sorry to be the bearer of bad news."

They were quiet for a time. Alejandra kept her eyes on her fingers. Finally, she asked, "What was his name?"

"James. His name was James. He once told me he wanted to leave the army and be an honest Indian agent because his son, at age five, inspired him to do so. The son said, 'Pa, you always keep your word.' Now, the son is fatherless and dear Abigail is a widow."

Alejandra touched the single tear on Isaac's face.

* * *

By the end of April, Alejandra allowed him up to hop about on his left foot within her room on one of the crutches made by Rafael and Manuel. Between what Alejandra called laudanum naps, they talked – day and night. At times, they drew pictures for each other to compensate for Spanish words Isaac did not know.

The moon was full on Saturday, May 16 and Isaac wanted to go outside after supper to see it. With his left arm still in a sling, Isaac sat in Alejandra's chair and Ernesto and Rafael carried him to the front yard.

Manuel asked, "Did Allie tell you I stored your saddle and equipment in the barn?"

"No, sir."

"Oh, my, she's becoming quite forgetful. I put your guns under my bed."

"Thank you, sir."

Manuel winked. "I've been exercising your mule in front of my plow. Is that okay?"

They laughed. "Oh, yes, sir. Of course, it's fine."

As the family sat together, Alejandra remembered that it was under the same large tree that Rafael stood watch years ago for her and Ernesto the night they escaped to the south. She thought of Isaac's stories of escape ordeals from slavery in a canoe, a cyclone, buffalos, and war to ultimately come and sit in peace with her and the people she loved. She smiled and thought, *I really admire this man.* She sat quietly while Ernesto and Rafael asked Manuel and Isaac many questions about the combat they had experienced. Rocio moved from beside her husband and sat next to Alejandra, holding her hand. They smiled at each other. *I wonder if Mama is thinking what I think she's thinking.* She blushed at the thought.

* * *

In June, Alejandra moved into Ernesto and Rafael's old room. Rocio noticed right away. That same day, they were out tending the garden. Grinning, Rocio asked, "So, Allie, I noticed you moved. Why?"

"I thought you'd never ask. It's simple. Mama, I love Isaac. I need some space from him before I lose my mind."

Rocio dropped her hoe and hugged Alejandra. "Oh, I'm so happy for you."

"Mama, don't be too happy. I have no idea if he loves me or not. I see no sign."

* * *

The next month, they sat under the stars at full moon. While they were out in the warm evening, Alejandra felt a warmer breeze pass over. Isaac's collar blew in the gust. He leaned back and smiled. He touched her forearm briefly. Alejandra looked around, for she felt the presence of something or someone else. She saw nothing. She looked again at Isaac. His eyes were closed and he was still smiling. She was puzzled.

Under Alejandra's watchful eyes, Manuel let Isaac lean on him with his damaged left arm and shoulder to walk, with his crutch under his right arm, from the yard back to her room.

Once inside and alone, a sweating Isaac told Alejandra he needed a bath. She prepared the bath for him in her room and turned to leave. Isaac touched her hand and whispered, "I need your help."

She closed the door and bathed him as he sat on a ladderback chair.

Lying beside Isaac as he slept, Alejandra studied his physique with new eyes. She committed to memory the curves of his shoulders and biceps revealed as art by the silver moonlight streaming through her window. She thought, *If I'd known it would feel this great being loved, maybe I would have married Carlos all those years ago! No. I'm glad I waited for this man.*

It was this great delight in finding the love of her life that she savored then and later alone in her brothers' room when sleep would not come. She relived the experience in her head until she finally slept not long before dawn.

After breakfast, when Alejandra and her mother were alone in the kitchen, Rocio whispered, "How was it?"

Alejandra felt warm and sweaty. She blushed. "My God, Mama! How did you know?"

"Your face is radiant. I've never seen you so happy."

Sitting at the kitchen table, Alejandra buried her blush and a huge smile in her hands.

Chapter 40: Isaac's Bride

Still holding his letter to Captain Carpenter about his health status, Isaac sat staring out the window. He could hear Rocio and Alejandra making kitchen noises and giggling. He smiled and thought, *I'm as sure as it is morning of two things. Last night, I know I felt Rachel's presence and heard her say, "This is the one." I also know that for some time I have loved Alejandra. It's been just four months since we met, but I believe it's time to ask.*

Alejandra appeared in the doorway, dressed for fieldwork. "Knock-knock."

"Buenos dias." Isaac called cheerfully from the chair beside Alejandra's bed.

Alejandra met his eyes, but looked away when she blushed. "Buenos dias."

She entered the room with Isaac's breakfast. She carried his plate of two open-face burritos made from blue corn tortillas topped by scrambled eggs cooked with milk and onions. The next layer was crumbled sausage and salsa; the top was melted queso de país. She used a rough vegetable cutting board, made by Ernesto, to carry the plate and a cup of coffee. She set his breakfast on a crude bedside table, another product of Ernesto's youth, and moved it close to Isaac.

Isaac thought there will be no better time than now. He took a deep breath and spoke in the most serious tone he could muster. Inside, he was actually bursting with joy. "Allie, we need to talk."

He watched her bright smile fade. She fidgeted with the fingertips of her left hand. She didn't say a word, but immediately sat on her bed. Her face was cast down, yet her eyes still met Isaac's.

Isaac began. "Some day, when I can walk again, I will return to my work as a soldier." He watched Alejandra's face fall further. Now she looked only at her moving fingers. Isaac thought, *I can't stop now.* He went on. "I have three more years left to serve the army. At the end of that time, I hope to start a business and a family. I will need a wife by my side. Will you marry me?"

Alejandra cried covering her face with both hands. Isaac thought, *this is curious. She is really crying. Her face is all screwed up and she is boo-hooing. What do I do now? I sure as hell can't outrun Manuel or her brothers. They're going to think I've harmed her. Oh, my God! What if she tells them about last night?*

With thoroughly wet hands, Alejandra covered all but her eyes and ran to the kitchen. Isaac could hear her. "Mama, Mama, he asked me! Is it okay?"

"Oh, my baby, I'm so happy for you. This is such great news!"

There was a pause and much sniffing. Isaac was still not sure what would happen. He shrugged and bit into his delicious breakfast while straining to overhear the conversation in the kitchen. At times, he stopped chewing to focus on listening.

"What was your answer?"

"Oh, Mama, I was so excited I didn't answer. But, you and Papa have to approve. I can't just say yes. Isn't that right?"

"Si. That's true enough, but did you tell him this is our rule?"

Sniff. "No."

"Well, I don't guess he will know until you tell him."

Isaac smiled.

Sniff. "But at least tell me what you'll say. Please."

"Of course, I'll say whatever you want."

More crying. "Oh, Mama, thank you. Thank you so much. I'm so happy I could scream!"

Isaac shrugged again. He thought, *I guess that means two yeses.*

He looked up from another bite and Alejandra was in the doorway. She was wiping her face. "You'll have to ask my papa." She disappeared before Isaac could respond.

Isaac heard Alejandra outside yelling. "Papa, Papa, come back to the house." In his mind's eye he could see her waving frantically. He smiled.

When Isaac finished his breakfast, he heard a family conference under way in hushed tones outside beyond the kitchen. He could not make out what was being said.

Presently, Manuel stood in the doorway. "Did you want to see me?"

Isaac struggled to his feet and held onto the chair. The men faced each other without a hint of a smile. Isaac responded. "Yes, sir. I love your daughter. I want her to be my wife. Is this okay with you?"

Manuel beamed. "If Alejandra will have you, yes, you can marry her."

Smiling, Isaac offered his hand. They shook hands, using their left hands to cover their joined right hands. And then they hugged, using both arms. Isaac winced as he felt a pain stab his left shoulder.

Rocio and a dry-eyed Alejandra entered the small room. Alejandra took Isaac's right hand in both of hers. "Isaac, yes, I will marry you. We will live together wherever life takes us."

Isaac saw with his peripheral vision that Rocio and Manuel were smiling and holding hands. He kept his eyes on Alejandra's eyes. "Thank you."

* * *

That evening, Isaac lay awake imagining the future with Alejandra. When the house was quiet, he saw her tiptoe into the room and close the door without a sound. In the moonlight through the curtain at the window, he watched Alejandra change her clothes. For the first time, he saw her perfectly round small breasts. He lifted the sheet and she slid in beside him. Tenderly and slowly, they repeated the intimacy of the previous night. Though it caused pain in Isaac's abdominal wound, he did not tell her.

* * *

"What? Are you sure? Wait a whole year?"

"Darling, that's what I read. Of course, it's an average. We both wanted to know. So I looked it up. I've never treated a broken leg before – really, a broken tibia. It says here that it can be as little as six months for a fibula."

"But, Allie, the wedding is next month – though I still can't believe it's the end of August already."

"Do you miss the army?"

"Yes. It's been my life for almost twelve years. That's not the thing on my mind. You're telling me I'm going into your church in front of Carrizal on crutches."

Alejandra nodded. "Uh-huh. That's not so bad. But, Isaac, we need to talk about a much more serious matter."

Isaac smiled and shook his head. He thought, that sounds familiar. "Okay. Come and sit on my good knee and tell me what's on your mind."

She sat on his left knee and planted a kiss on his lips. Then, face-to-face, eyes locked, Alejandra whispered with a forefinger in front of her lips, "I'm pregnant."

"Are you sure?"

"I haven't had my menses since late June."

They kissed again. Isaac said, "I'm the happiest man on earth."

"And I'm the happiest woman." Again, they kissed. She tried to stand but he held her. With a big grin she said, "Let go of me before you make me do something we'll both regret – right here in the broad open daylight."

They guffawed. She rose from his knee and fell on the bed laughing.

* * *

Isaac feared that he would trip and fall during the wedding or reception. He was relieved that it did not happen. When he reflected on Alejandra's big day some time later, he remembered with amazement the curiosity seekers. He was sure they were there to see the only black man in Carrizal or, as Alejandra once said, to "see who would marry the old maid."

Throughout the summer and fall, Isaac had difficulty using both crutches because of the pain in his shoulder. The thing Isaac and Alejandra feared above all else was a fall that could re-injure his leg. To make himself feel useful, he assigned himself as Rocio's chop chef and Manuel's assistant implement mechanic of farm equipment that Rocio would allow into the kitchen.

By the fall, Isaac had not received a response from Captain Carpenter. So he sent a second letter updating his health status. He was careful to make no mention of the mission.

After the crops were gathered, Manuel put a canvas cover on his wagon and took Rocio and the newlyweds to Casa Grande to visit their relatives. Isaac was amazed that some of Rocio's cousins were darker in complexion than Rocio or Alejandra. Isaac considered Manuel a light brown, more like the Mexicans he had seen in Texas. Speculation abounded on whether Alejandra's handsome husband resembled their seventeenth-century patriarch, Orestes. Casa Grande was only the first stop of a journey undertaken for the additional purpose of helping Isaac fulfill his mission. He was no longer the vaquero, but a surveyor making a field trip for a cartographer. The foursome traveled by wagon over the route in Isaac and James's plan. When it was not possible to use a hotel, Isaac's new family learned much from him about camping along the Rio Concho in eastern Chihuahua. Rocio and Alejandra saw the Rio Grande for the first time and the United States across the river from Ojinaga. They did not cross the river. Five weeks later, they were back in Carrizal and preparing for Christmas.

* * *

Alejandra continued delivering babies in and around Carrizal until February when she was eight months pregnant. Manuel drove Alejandra to her midwifery appointments in his wagon. Aunt Nina and Rocio helped Alejandra deliver her baby in April. Alejandra and Isaac named their daughter Julieta.

* * *

Isaac returned to Fort Davis in May without Alejandra and Julieta. When he reported for duty, he was arrested for desertion, thus delaying his search for a place for his family to live. Captain Carpenter, the only person in Company H who knew Isaac was on a special assignment, was away in the field the day Isaac reported for duty. While confined in the guardhouse, Isaac wrote a complete history of his scout and unforeseen consequences resulting from the ambush. He added the new pages ahead of his report, mapping notes, and sketches.

For the remaining three weeks of Captain Carpenter's absence from the fort, Isaac lingered in the guardhouse. Two days after Carpenter's return, Isaac was taken to his office in the same Mexican clothes he had worn for three weeks. Carpenter recognized him as the new arrival from Company A the year before who came with a stellar recommendation from his friend, Nolan. Isaac was not invited to sit. He watched his company commander leaf through the first two pages and look up. Carpenter dismissed the guards and told Isaac to sit. After several more pages, Carpenter asked Isaac to remove his shirt and show his scars.

When he finished reading, Carpenter, a veteran of recent strikes into Mexico, stood and apologized for the reception Isaac received. He noted with great pleasure that Isaac had completed the mission, though his comrades had died in an ambush. Carpenter offered his hand. "Mr. Rice, I'm recommending you for a promotion. And don't worry about your back pay. I'll see to that detail. Welcome home."

"Thank you, sir."

"Here, take this note to quartermaster and get yourself outfitted and a barracks assignment."

"Yes, sir. Thank you. I'll need all of that except the barracks assignment. I have a wife and baby daughter." The new father beamed.

"Well, I see you weren't completely disabled all those months down in Old Mexico!"

The two men shared a bonding laugh.

"By the way, Mr. Rice, we'll need to take care of your medical expenses."

Isaac beamed again. "Er, no, sir, that won't be necessary. My wife is a nurse and midwife. She's really a doctor, but she doesn't have the proper papers. She removed three bullets from me, fixed my leg, and nursed me back to health."

"Wow! Mr. Rice, it looks like you've robbed Mexico of a valuable citizen. You'd better not let their government find out."

They laughed again.

"I hope she's interested in practicing in our post hospital."
"Thank you, sir."

Chapter 41: The Victorio War

A Ninth Cavalry Regiment bugler at Fort Stanton sounded "retreat" shortly before sunset on Tuesday, August 20, 1879.

Ortega paused with the entourage following Victorio when he stopped walking and held up a hand. He watched Victorio cock his head to one side, as if to listen intently. They stood a short distance from Indian Agent Russell's office on the fort side of the Mescalero Reservation. After the bugle call ended, several mounted soldiers rode by, escorting a wagon in the direction of Tularosa.

Victorio did not move. His eyes and head turned to watch the soldiers until they were out of sight. Then Victorio turned to Kaytennae and Nana, his two main war leaders. "I think the time has come. Get our people ready to ride within the hour!"

Neither Kaytennae nor Nana asked a question or offered a counter suggestion. They said in unison, "*Enjuh!*"

Ponce, standing beside Ortega, repeated, "*Enjuh!*"

Ortega walked rapidly, trying to keep pace with Ponce as he headed for his arbor. "What did your chief mean, 'it is time'? Where are you going?"

Ponce stopped walking. "I do not have time to explain. But I will tell you: there will be war. We are going to the place where you and I met for the first time. If you wish, join us in that place at the harvest moon. Now go ask your grandfather to explain the matter." Ponce turned and left Ortega to ponder.

Ortega stood and watched as Chihenne men and women scurried about, leading horses to their arbors and packing everything they could carry on the animals. A small boy followed Nana and his horse. The boy smiled at Ortega.

When the boy was nearer, Ortega squatted and sat on his heels. He smiled at the boy. "What is your name, little warrior?"

At the word warrior, the boy's smile broadened. "My name is Torres. What's yours?"

"My name is Ortega. Who is that man you're following?"

Torres glanced toward Nana. "Oh, he's my grandfather. I gotta go now. Bye." Torres waved and ran to catch Nana.

Ortega waved and sprang to his feet. "Bye, Torres." He said to himself, I'm going to see my grandfather, too.

* * *

Nantahe-totel sat on a stool fashioned from a pine log. The chunk of log stood on end, just the right height for a seat. Ortega and Jorge sat at his feet. Nantahe-totel smiled and folded his arms. "Now what's so important that you tried to interrupt my supper?"

Ortega and Jorge laughed. Ortega rushed ahead. "Grandfather, I heard that Victorio is a man of peace. But I also heard that he broke out of the Ojo Caliente Reservation and raided in Mexico. I am also told he is as brave as any of his warriors in battle. How much of this, if any, is true?"

Nantahe-totel's smile vanished. He took a deep breath. "All of it is true."

Jorge looked perplexed. "How can he do all of these things?"

Ortega put in, "What battle is he famous for?"

Nantahe-totel held up both hands, leaned back, and laughed. "Hold on, now. One question at a time. Listen carefully."

Ortega and Jorge nodded. Ortega knew that meant his grandfather would not repeat.

Nantahe-totel continued. "When Victorio was a young warrior, the great Red Sleeves was his chief. Red Sleeves joined his warriors with those of his son-in-law – whom you know, the former splendid leader of the Chokonen – anyway, his warriors fought against Carleton's blue soldiers in a major battle at Apache Pass when you both were about eleven summers old. I was told by many who were there that Victorio acquitted himself very well. So, brave, he is."

Ortega nodded thoughtfully. "If he came here one moon ago seeking peace, why is he breaking out tonight? Doesn't that mean war since the soldiers are ordered to shoot any Apache man found off a reservation?"

"That is complicated. But I'll offer you this. For eight summers, the poor man has sought peace with the White Eyes. Time after time, a White Eye representing Washington showed up and made an agreement for peace. Then another would arrive and say that

455

agreement is no good, let's make a new agreement for a reservation farther away. Last year, the White Eyes took away the reservation at Ojo Caliente that Victorio argued in favor of for so many years."

Jorge looked up. "Sir, is that where the Chihenne were raided by black soldiers one moon and by White Eye citizens the next?"

"Yes, just like we experienced."

Ortega hit a palm with his fist. "Why didn't Victorio get revenge before he came in to Mescalero?"

"I don't know."

Jorge frowned. "Is it true that he does not drink?"

"True. Nor does he allow his people to drink when they are on the warpath."

There was a pause. Ortega and Jorge glanced at each other.

Ortega wondered, "Without a council, why did he suddenly leave tonight?"

"Word is local White Eyes have put a price on Victorio's head. If I was in his moccasins, I would expect the arrival of soldiers at any minute to attempt an arrest. Though innocent, that would mean death. I have never heard of an Apache being let go by the White Eyes."

Ortega and Jorge listened intently, eyes wide. Ortega remembered the look of concern on Victorio's face when he heard the bugle. "What did the bugle call at sunset mean?"

"Oh, that call is just part of a ceremony the soldiers make every day before they take down their flag. I witnessed this several times when I happened to be at the fort just before sunset."

Ortega and Jorge looked at each other.

Nantahe-totel continued. "But, I am almost sure the answer to your earlier question is, when the White Eyes send their soldiers to force Victorio to return, there will be war. They have run the man's patience into the ground. That is all I know to say." Nantahe-totel folded his arms and lapsed into silence, looking up into the night sky.

Ortega realized that his grandfather had correctly anticipated questions about whether he should join Victorio or not. He understood not to ask. He tugged at Jorge's sleeve. They stood and offered their thanks.

Nantahe-totel responded with a grunt.

* * *

A week later, Ortega, Jorge, and Pedro bade farewell to their families. They set out on the same trail Nantahe-totel had described for them several years before when they rode and offered their services to Cochise. This time, Ortega was sure they would join Victorio while he was already engaged in a series of battles with the US Army. Ortega hoped the outcome would result in a homeland for Apaches and the freedom to move about the countryside as Americans did. In the meantime, he thought, revenge will be sweet.

At first dark, the full moon rose in the east and hung like a shiny golden disc above the trees. The harvest moon arrived on Sunday, August 31, Ponce and his Chihenne companions were waiting for them in the spot where they met eight years earlier.

Ponce stood and held up a hand in greeting. "Welcome to our homeland."

Five days later, Ortega and his Mescalero comrades rode with a large contingent of warriors that Victorio led on a raid of the US Army's horse herd near the former Ojo Caliente Agency. They surprised the five soldiers and three civilians on herd duty. Ortega fired only one shot. A black soldier fell. In five minutes, all the guards were dead and forty-six horses were driven off – to a canyon near the Chihenne camp.

Ortega made note of the way Victorio time and again outmaneuvered the army just as Victorio must have done as a warrior learning from Mangas Coloradas. Victorio chose campsites from which it proved to be impossible for the army to dislodge the Chihenne. Each time there was a battle, Victorio's warriors thwarted the army. Many times, Victorio, assisted by his sister, Lozen, anticipated the army's next move and abandoned campsites hours or a few days before the army arrived to attack. All the while, Chihenne women and children traveled with the warriors.

Throughout October, Victorio defeated attempts by Major Morrow of the Ninth Cavalry to subdue his people in New Mexico. Near the end of the month, Ortega was surprised when Major Morrow led his soldiers and scouts across the border into Old Mexico in pursuit of Victorio's band. He saw Victorio skillfully use

457

terrain, leave a spring dry, and employ tactics to defeat Major Morrow again in mountains near Rio Corralitos. Major Morrow was forced to withdraw.

A few days later, Victorio moved ninety-five miles eastward to territory very familiar to Ortega. They established a longer term camp in the Candelaria Mountains of northern Chihuahua. From the mountaintop, Ortega looked for, but could not see, Carrizal directly to the south. Sitting among the rocks on watch duty, his thoughts turned to his last visit in Carrizal. First in his vision came Jacali, then the black vaquero and Alejandra.

Jorge's face was covered with dust as he sat down beside Ortega and Pedro. Pedro was as dirty. Ortega's reminiscing ceased. Jorge was grinning from ear to ear. "Mon amigo, you should have come with us. There were just six of us on the raid. Look at all the horses we took."

Ortega pointed. "I saw you far out there in your dust. Didn't you know? We have enough – we don't need your sand and dust up here!"

They laughed together.

Pedro peered to the south. "It would be nice to visit Carrizal again."

Jorge pushed Pedro's shoulder. "Why? Weren't you the one who was the first so ready to leave the last time we were there?"

They laughed again and the threesome looked longingly to the south.

Ortega said, "Uh, oh!"

Jorge looked at Ortega, then the El Paso-Chihuahua Road, and back to Ortega. "Do you see something?"

"Yes. I see twelve to fifteen horsemen coming up from the direction of Carrizal. Get Kaytennae over here."

Pedro was back in less than a minute with Kaytennae and Victorio in tow.

Ortega gave his report and ended with, "Sir, I believe they will find and follow the trail of our just arrived raiding party. That will lead them to us, passing between the two peaks over there on the north side."

Victorio put a hand on Ortega's shoulder. "Well done, my son." He turned to Kaytennae and they walked away together. Victorio was saying, "Let's get ready. Here's what we'll do...."

The Mexicans from Carrizal were led by two of their most prominent citizens, Jose Rodriguez and his nephew Torres. The hidden Chihenne and Mescalero warriors waited in perfect silence. As Ortega predicted, the posse of fifteen men spotted and followed the trail left by the returning raiders. When the posse's last rider was between the twin peaks, Victorio shot him from the north peak. That signaled his best marksmen on the north side to open fire. Just as Victorio knew they would, the survivors dismounted and ran for cover behind the low-lying boulders on the south side. Before the posse could return fire against the marksmen on the north slope, a volley rained down on them from south crest.

Ortega heard the clatter of hooves in the rocky draw, men and horses screaming, rifle fire, and double echoes against the mountains of all of the mixed sounds. So perfect was the ambush that Ortega fired just twice from his perch on the south crest and in seconds fourteen of the fifteen-man posse lay dead. A single marksman continued firing at one Mexican, who hid most, but not all, of his body behind a small boulder. He fired until the victim no longer moved. The Mexicans' surviving horses that did not die from gunshot wounds stampeded and fell to their deaths when they raced off a cliff into a deep canyon.

A few days later, a second posse was sent from Carrizal. They fell into the same trap.

Later, when Victorio decided to move his people, Ortega and Jorge rode side by side away from the Candelaria Mountains. In a deep reflective voice, Ortega said, "I don't know why, but, I hope Alejandra's kinsmen did not enter our ambush."

459

Chapter 42: Ortega Goes to War

As moon after moon passed, Ortega and his friends rode with Victorio's band carrying out his policy of killing almost every American or Mexican they found. Only selected Mexican sheepherders in northern Chihuahua in the vicinity of Casa Grande and Janos were spared on the condition that they continue providing food and ammunition.

By July 1880, people on both sides of the Rio Grande had seen a year of Victorio's vengeance; he was pursued by elements of several United States Army regiments, Texas Rangers, white citizens of New Mexico, and the Mexican Army. Victorio's main problems were that each of his fallen warriors was irreplaceable and his supply of ammunition was dwindling. On the other hand, the clamor from newspapers as far away as New York City asked that more and more troops be sent to make Arizona and New Mexico safe for white Americans. However, the *New York Sun* pointed out that the greed of settlers and the incoherent and corrupt Indian policies of successive administrations in Washington were to blame for causing Victorio to go to war.

Ortega, Jorge, and Pedro were riding side by side in their usual place on the right flank of the main body. Having convinced Victorio that more warriors would join their ranks, the Mescaleros were happily on their way back to their reservation. As usual, Victorio deployed his most experienced Chihenne as scouts in the advance guard, while Nana and Kaytennae led the rearguard. They were three of more than one hundred twenty-five warriors with Victorio departing the spring at Ojo del Pino in the Sierra de los Pinos of Mexico. Their vaqueros kept the band's cattle and other horses moving within the main body.

Shortly after sunrise, July 23, Ortega spotted Colonel Adolfo J. Valle's Mexican cavalry approaching from the south on his side of the main body. A dozen or so warriors in two coordinated squads split off the right flank to meet and engage the threat at a distance from the women and children. The encounter was brief. Ortega was sure they killed at least six soldiers and wounded several others.

They lost three warriors before the Mexicans disengaged. Back in their usual formation, he called out to Jorge. "Hey is that blood on your sleeve?"

"Yes, elk face. What'd you think it was?"

"Do you need a tourniquet?"

"Nope. It's only a flesh wound."

About a week later, they were nearing the Rio Grande. On their approach, Ortega used the time to build his courage for fording the river. He thought *will I ever get used to crossing this accursed river? The current does something different every time and I'm never ready.* He had lost count of how many times they had crossed the Rio Grande, which in his mind was significantly more dangerous than the numerous smaller streams they crossed.

As the right-flank warriors forded ahead of the main body, Jorge laughed and asked, "Do you need me to hold your hand while we cross?"

Ortega thought Jorge and Pedro would fall into the water as they laughed and slapped they sides. Hoisting his carbine over his head for the crossing, he made an obscene gesture at Jorge, and then held onto his saddle horn for dear life. Jorge and Pedro laughed until they were under way again.

By nine in the morning, they were approaching the Eagle Mountains. Gunfire rang out. Victorio directed a squad from the left flank to move forward and assist the advanced guard in attacking the black soldiers blocking their path forward. After hours, no forward progress had been made. Ortega thought, *hmm. These soldiers have a different approach from the ones in New Mexico. They are succeeding in making us use up our resources while blocking our way.* At about that time, more troops arrived and joined the fray.

Victorio committed men from Ortega's side. Jorge and Pedro rode on either side of him. After another hour of stalemate, yet another unit of blue soldiers was seen arriving. Victorio disengaged and immediately turned south to the river. Pedro's mount turned the wrong way as the rearguard passed through their ranks to hold off a possible charge by the soldiers. Before Pedro could regain control of his frightened animal, he was hit in his chest.

With his back to his enemy, Pedro slumped in his saddle, his face in his pony's mane. Ortega and Jorge turned their horses twice and arrived on both sides of Pedro's horse. Jorge took the reins and Ortega held Pedro's belt to keep him on the horse. They stopped briefly at the river. Pedro was coughing and spitting blood. Ortega and Jorge were still beside him when Nana and Kaytennae arrived with the rearguard. A few minutes later, Pedro died.

Ortega and Jorge did not talk as they buried their friend, his saddle, and personal effects with him on the Texas side of the river. They mounted to cross the river leading Pedro's pony when Ortega paused to ask Ussen if they were doing the right thing.

Victorio ordered a camp set up in the Sierra San Martin del Barracho, about fifteen miles southwest of the Rio Grande.

The next day, Ortega and Jorge were on sentry duty. While they talked, they scanned the horizon in all directions for anyone approaching their camp – American or Mexican.

Ortega absentmindedly flipped the O-ring on the left side of his 1865 Model Spencer carbine back and forth as they talked. "I've been thinking. How many people and soldiers do you think we've killed?"

"Do you mean me and you or all of us together?"

"All."

Jorge paused and took a deep breath. "Oh, I'd say about four hundred people – pretty evenly split between Americans and Mexicans."

"I agree. What about soldiers?"

"Hmm. Say a little over a hundred?"

"Yeah, I'd guess that's about right."

"What have we gained?"

"We haven't. We've lost."

"True.

"We lost a good friend. We've lost the future we wanted. We've won so many unbelievable battles. But already we've lost the war. I've had my revenge many times over."

"Satisfied?"

"At first, I was. Now, no. I've grown numb with all the killing. We kill every person in sight. Not all of them deserved to die."

"What about your folks?"

Ortega took a deep breath, looking up at passing puffy white clouds. "Of course, they deserved to live and see me grow up and give them grandchildren. They tried to live simple lives in the tradition of our people. They, like all Apaches, were in the way. So the powerful sent soldiers to get rid of us."

"I agree that this thing is all over. The last chapter just hasn't been written yet."

"Do you think Victorio knows?"

"Victorio is a wise old man. I think he knows, but is out of options. Neither the Americans nor the Mexicans will make peace with him after all the mayhem we have caused. Not possible. But I'm sure he'll fight to the death."

Ortega heaved a big sigh. "We wanted killing. We got killing. Now what do we do so that our families can live?"

There was a long silence. Finally, after several minutes, Jorge answered. "I don't know."

"Me either."

After a few days, they crossed into Texas again. Victorio needed new recruits, now more than ever, from the Mescalero Reservation in New Mexico.

By two o'clock, the August 6 sun was high and hot. They had nearly reached Rattlesnake Springs when the advance guard was stopped by hostile fire. Again, the actions of the black soldiers blocked their way and denied access to water. Ortega thought *that's what I would have done in their boots last year in New Mexico.* Ortega waited while the advanced guard was pinned down in a stalemate with the soldiers.

Two hours later, he was brought back to reality when Ponce called his name. Ponce pointed to approaching wagons from the southeast. The right-flank units swung to attack the new target. They rode hard toward the wagons with Ponce in the lead. Instead of the goods or much-needed ammunition Ortega expected, the wagons were transporting more black troops – infantry. The infantrymen leapt from the wagons and in the first volley Ponce and his horse were killed.

Ortega was hit. He turned his horse and galloped southwest. Out of the range of fire, he stopped to examine his wound. He could not ascertain his condition, but the throbbing pain was subsiding. Now he felt dizzy and nauseous. He stopped his horse and slid from his saddle, still holding his carbine. He looked down and noticed that his shirt and breechclout were bloody. So was his carbine.

Jorge appeared and knelt beside him. He felt so sleepy. He thought Jacali poured water on his lips. He moved his tongue from side to side. Then he slept. He awoke when Jorge and three black soldiers lifted him into a wagon. The pain was now excruciating.

Chapter 43: Company H, Fort Davis

"Hey, Charles, tell me somethin'. I know yore sharpshootin' ass is from Louisville, Ken-damn-tucky. But have you ever been ta Washington, DC?" David D. Givens, from Spartanburg, South Carolina, was digging into his noonday meal and talking with food in his mouth.

Charles answered with a mouthful of beans and canned tomatoes. "Naw, I can't say that I have. Why you wanna know?"

David looked up, still chewing. "I'm tryin' ta fine out if'n it's somethin' in the water up there in Washington that makes white people so foolish."

There was much laughter around the mess table for noncommissioned officers that day at Fort Davis, Texas. Isaac was enjoying listening to his new friends in Company H. To keep the hilarity going, Isaac asked, "David, are you reporting them for doing yet another foolish thing?"

"Yeah, new man."

Charles pretended surprise. "Aw, man, don't you go lying on them people again."

Snickers.

"It's the God's honest truf. Even some sensible newspapers say folks up there in Washington done screwed the Indian Bureau up so bad that we got us another war on our hands."

Charles turned serious. "That ain't funny. This time they messin' wid the Apaches. That Victorio's gonna rack up some serious revenge before we hafta put his ass down."

David pointed his fork at Charles. "I see you got two things right in yo' little Kentucky head. Number one, Victorio's proven he's nobody to be trifled wid. Number two, they gonna send our asses after this hornet now that they done kicked his nest over and thoroughly pissed him off."

Laughter.

"Seriously, why couldn't they just keep their word after they finally gave the man the reservation he asked for in the first place."

"Now, hold on, Charles. Me and you both know that'd make too much damn sense. They ain't got no where's near enough sense to figure somethin' so simple."

More laughter.

"So, how long has it been since ol' Vic jumped outta that Mescalero reservation?"

"What's this, nearly the end of November? So, it's been about three months."

"And the Ninth ain't caught'im, yet?"

"Oh, hell no! This here is 1879. What year you want 'im cotched? Sheeeet. What do you expect the Ninth can do ridin' them ol' gov'ment nags?"

Guffaw.

Isaac finished his canned peaches. "Now, David, I'd spread some o' that blame around and splash a mess of it on thieving agents, ranchers, and merchants in competition with horse thieves and worse to see just how much money they can make off what the Indian Bureau has created."

"Hey, new man, you nailed it. Don't get me started on they asses."

* * *

With Captain Carpenter vouching for him in June, Isaac had rented a three-room cottage from a nearby rancher. The little house had most recently been used as a guard station by cowboys on the ranch. He had returned to Carrizal the same month on a stagecoach by way of El Paso. He was by Alejandra's side at the going away festival hosted for her by Ernesto, Linda, Rafael, and Patricia one Saturday night. After a tearful good-bye with her parents, Alejandra and Julieta boarded a stagecoach with Isaac for the trip to Fort Davis.

On arrival at their new home, Alejandra giggled as she held Julieta and Isaac lifted them both across the threshold. "Oh, honey, I expected bare walls. Thank you so much for beds and blankets for all of us. You are so thoughtful." She kissed Isaac. "Oh, and look, there's a stove too. Querido, you're the bestest husband I ever had!"

They laughed together.

She hung out her midwifery shingle in July. In September, when a local midwife had two births expected within days of each other, Alejandra had her first customer. Her reputation as being more than just an ordinary midwife spread rapidly and new patients came to visit. Isaac bought a used one-bench buggy from an officer who was in need of a two bencher for his growing family. Next he bought an ancient surplus government horse at auction. Alejandra was in business, carrying little Julieta on her back in an Apache tsach.

The newlyweds were very happy.

Bad news arrived in early December in a letter from Rocio. In November, Manuel had died in an ambush set by Victorio and his warriors in the Candelaria Mountains for a posse of Carrizal citizens. Alejandra cried for many days. Isaac took time off from patrolling and mapping water holes to care for Julieta.

Chapter 44: **Grierson's Strategy**

In the spring of 1880, Captain Carpenter relayed to his noncommissioned officers that the strategy of the Tenth would be different from that employed by the Ninth Cavalry. "Men, Colonel Grierson's strategy is simple. When Victorio comes through West Texas to get back to his friends at the Mescalero Reservation, we'll be waiting at every water hole and in every mountain pass. The colonel has no plan to go chasing ol' Vic – unless he's in plain sight. We'll use some of those telegraph wires we strung last year between forts for communications in addition to couriers and stagecoaches.

"Since we'll be waiting for Victorio, you see how important it is for us to map every pass and water hole. Check the springs that Mr. Rice has already mapped periodically for water flow and report your findings. That's all. Good luck with your patrols. And, as Mr. Rice can attest, beware of the ambush."

On the way to the stables, Sergeant David Givens caught up with Isaac. "Hey, new man, I'm short-handed today. Too many o' my guys are on sick call. How 'bout we combine our guys for patrol this week."

"It's okay by me. See if it's okay with the ol' man."

* * *

On Monday, May 10, 1880, Isaac and David drew rations and ammunition for their combined patrol of nine privates and two corporals. As the senior sergeant, Isaac took command. The first day, they marched thirty-eight miles and camped on the southeastern end of the Sierra Vieja Mountains.

"Damn, Homey, you're a hard task master. My ass is plum woe out. Oh, is it okay for me to call you 'Homey' being as I talk hillbilly and you talk geechee?"

"Sure, Homey. That's fine with me."

David smiled big at the reciprocation. "We don't hafta march so far tomorrow, do we?"

"Yep, I'm afraid so. The sooner we make our rounds and get our notes over to Sergeant Joyce, the sooner I can get home to my sweet wife."

"O-o-oh! So, dat's what's drivin' you. I just took you to be a hard-ass soldier 'cause o' your combat reputation. Newlywed, I hear."

"True, if you call folks married for over two years newlyweds."

"So we gotta go see Joyce all the damn way over to Concho 'fore we can git back?"

"Yeah. But we don't need to go over to Concho every time. I got a telegraph message from Joyce. He wants to discuss where we go next and places he needs filled in on the new maps he's making for Colonel Grierson and General Ord."

"How soon you think the regiment's gonna need this stuff?"

"I think Chief Victorio will be here giving us a hard time in our patch before the harvest moon rises."

"Damn, Homey. I think I'ma like soldiering wid you. You know what needs to be done and you gits on wid it."

* * *

At Fort Concho, Isaac talked Caleb into getting the band to practice for the men in his patrol the one night they were at the fort. After the concert, Caleb followed them to the barracks. A grinning Caleb said, "Okay. Last time you were over here, my sweet Louise made her famous apple pie for you. So hand over the daguerreotype. Lemme see this wife person of yours."

David waved both hands. "Uh-mm! Ain't no need lookin' at no pictures. She's the purtiest woman in Texas – or, for that matter, the whole darn country!"

"How do you know?"

"I seed her wid my own eyes over at the post hospital. She works there since April. One o' my sick guys saw me gawkin' at her and he said, 'There goes that new Sergeant Rice's wife.' Saved my ass from a whole mess o' trouble."

Isaac smiled. Sheepishly, he removed a locket hidden under his shirt and handed it to Caleb. Caleb took a long look at the tiny facing pictures of Alejandra and Julieta. David looked over Caleb's shoulder.

Caleb exclaimed, "Wow! Homey, she's a beauty."

"See, you oughta listen to ol' David. I knows what I seed."

Caleb ignored David. "Do you think Rachel is okay with this?"

"I'm completely sure of it."

* * *

Before "Taps" was sounded, Caleb's face looked troubled. Isaac reached out and touched his friend's shoulder. "Hey, Homey, what's going on in your ol' big head?"

"Man, I don't know how to feel about the death of James. He was a mighty good man. I regret not helping him that night in St. Louie. And to think he gave up his promising life so you, my best friend, could live. Of course, I'm most happy to still have you. And, at the same time, I'm sad that we lost him."

Isaac thought for a few minutes. It was quiet in the barracks. David and Caleb sat on bunks looking down at their socks. Finally, Isaac spoke. "Homey, I think your feelings are well expressed and not in conflict. You're proof that it is possible to be sad and happy about the same person. We share the same feeling. Ever since Allie told me the story of my rescue, I have at one moment grieved for James and the next felt deeply grateful for what he did. Allie convinced me that it is perfectly okay to have both feelings at the same time."

Caleb nodded. "Your Allie is a wise woman. You should treasure her."

"I do."

David sighed. "I hope I kin fine me a woman like her." Then he slapped his hands together. "I didn't get to meet your friend. I'll bet you homies know some good stories 'bout him. Tell me one 'fore the trumpter blows out the lights."

Caleb chuckled and nodded. "Good idea. Isaac hasn't heard this one. I forgot to tell 'im.

"James told me when he was in Company B of the Fourth, one night two buddies got beat up by local thugs and thrown outta a ho house in Jacksboro. Seems a local was sweet on a certain ho who was happy to do tricks for soldiers. These two soldiers got beat bloody – I mean real bloody. Well, they dragged their asses back to Fort Richardson and got their carbines and six shooters and some buddies. Then they decided they needed some tactical smarts. So they went by James's house in the middle o' the night and convinced James to join them. Abigail was steamed but James went anyway. He owed one o' the guys a favor. They found the thugs still there. James and his boys shot their way into the ho house and beat the crap outta 'bout five locals in front o' several naked-ass ho's."

David and Isaac were holding their sides laughing. When David could speak, he asked, "And what happened then?"

"I'm so glad you asked. Our man, James, and his boys *burnt* that damn ho house to the fuckin' ground! I'm talking ashes *to* ashes!"

The guffaw was joined by troopers who overheard the story.

Taps sounded.

* * *

"Mr. Joyce, may I have a word with you?"

"Sure, Mr. Rice. By the way, your notes and sketches have been most valuable in the development of our new maps. Thanks for your work. Now what can I do for you?"

"Thanks. When the Springfields arrived a while back, I bought my Spencer. In your travels, do you still see ammo for it?

"Yes, from time to time."

"Please collect four to five hundred rounds for me."

"Oh, of course, I'll take care of that for you. There are times such items pass in the local market. I'll get some for you and send them over to Davis."

"Thanks."

* * *

Isaac and David returned to Fort Davis after a patrol of three weeks. They learned that two days after they departed for their patrol, Captain Carpenter and most of the rest of Company H had trailed eight Mescalero warriors to the Rio Grande. Carpenter was certain the warriors were on their way to join Victorio. Nodding, David gave Isaac an admiring glance.

* * *

With their mapping chores done, in June, Carpenter began leading the company on full-scale patrols. In early July, Colonel Grierson brought in four more companies to Fort Davis, including Nolan's Company A. Isaac was happy to spend some time with his old friend Tom and former comrades. But there was not much occasion for garrison duties and casual activities. On July 10, a telegraph message arrived from Mexican Army Colonel Adolpho Valle informing Grierson that he had skirmished with Victorio's warriors and they were likely to cross the Rio Grande into Texas near the Eagle Mountains. All of the Tenth's five companies at Fort Davis were ordered to the field, manning sub camps, supply stations, and passes to block probable routes from the border to the Mescalero Reservation.

Old Fort Quitman was activated by the arrival from Fort Sill of Nolan's Company A and Lieutenant Henry O. Flipper. It was Lieutenant Flipper who, on July 30, led Company A's couriers ninety-eight miles to deliver the word to Captain Gilmore of the Twenty-fifth Infantry at Eagle Springs and Colonel Grierson near the water hole at Tinaja de las Palmas that one of Company A's patrols had learned that Victorio and his warriors crossed the Rio Grande into Texas southeast of Fort Quitman. Lieutenant Flipper and his couriers made that ride in just twenty-two hours.

Grierson guessed that Victorio would come to Tinaja because it was a smaller water hole and not likely to be heavily guarded. Grierson took his party of eight troopers atop a steep rocky ridge and prepared to confront and delay Victorio. By a passing stagecoach driver, he sent word for Nolan to bring his company at double-quick time. Grierson sent the same message to Companies C and G at Eagle Springs.

On arrival at Tinaja, Victorio's warriors engaged and they were stalled by Grierson's small contingent with the help of Companies C and G. When Victorio saw the cloud of dust made by Company A coming from the west, he disengaged and made a run for the border, leaving seven dead warriors on the field.

Isaac moved with Company H to the Eagle Springs supply camp. He learned that Grierson had ordered four other companies to the same location. Isaac thought, *hmm, good move*. They were positioned to block access to the spring at the Van Horn Mountains. But Victorio guessed that blue soldiers would guard that spring and he moved his force west of the Van Horn Mountains and pressed northward and west of Sierra Diablo. Grierson's scouts and patrols reported Victorio's change and Grierson made his move. He ordered a forced overnight march to the next water hole, Rattlesnake Springs.

In the middle of the sixty-five-mile march to Rattlesnake Springs, David said, "Hey, Homey, thanks to marchin' wid you, I'm ready for anything."

Grierson laid his ambush with C and G forward in Rattlesnake Canyon to await Victorio's force. Grierson put Carpenter in command of his two companies in reserve, hidden close to the eastern side of Sierra Diablo. Isaac and David waited and watched from their perch. At two o'clock in the afternoon, the warriors appeared. Victorio may have sensed a trap, for he halted. C and G opened fire and Victorio approximated the number of troops as small and attacked because he needed the water. When Grierson saw Victorio's move, he countered by sending Carpenter into the fray with B and H.

Isaac led his men at a gallop to the warriors as they swayed under the soldiers charge. The warriors scattered. Isaac reacted to prevent his men from getting in front of the line made by B and H. Shortly, Grierson's supply train of covered wagons, guarded by black soldiers of the Twenty-fifth Infantry's Company H, came into view, rounding the corner of a mountain to the southeast. The right side of Victorio's force swung to attack the new target. Carpenter led B and H after them. The infantrymen dismounted from their wagons and fired a volley into the oncoming warriors. Men and ponies went down and were left on the field. Realizing his mistake, Victorio turned his warriors southwest and raced for the Rio Grande.

Isaac was riding on the left flank of H, holding his carbine at the ready, urging his panting and coughing horse to get close enough to be in range. On either side of his path lay fallen warriors. His horse and the rest of the company's horses were tiring and losing ground on the fleeing warriors. Isaac spotted a wavering warrior who looked vaguely familiar who was guiding his pony out of the race for the river and drawing rein. Isaac was pointing his carbine when the lone warrior seemed more to slide from his saddle than dismount. Isaac approached with caution. Slowly the man rolled over onto his back. Isaac thought *I have seen that blue headband before. Where?*

In his peripheral vision, Isaac saw David approach aiming his carbine at the downed warrior. "No! David, no!"

Isaac wheeled his tired horse into David's line of fire. David raised his weapon and drew rein beside Isaac. Isaac said, "Cover me." And then he dismounted and approached the man on the ground, carbine ready. The man was bloody and did not see Isaac approach. When he noticed Isaac, he instinctively moved his carbine. It was too late. Isaac grabbed the barrel and easily pulled it from the weakened man's bloody hands. Isaac turned to the man's head, knelt, and moved the head full to the right, exposing a torn left ear and four parallel scars on his cheek.

Isaac exclaimed to David. "Oh my, God! This is Ortega. This is the man who saved my life!"

Ortega had fainted.

David's jaw dropped. He looked bewildered. "Huh? You know this Injun? For real, you know him?"

Isaac let his carbine hang from his shoulder sling. "Yes, dammit! Throw me your kit. I've gotta stop the bleeding. Double-quick, man!"

David complied as other members of Company H rode up. David explained the unusual scene before them. Their mouths dropped open. When they recovered, they clamored. "Amazing!" "Unbelievable!" "Now I've seen it all!"

Isaac shouted. "Stop blabbering! Get an ambulance from that train over here."

"Hold it right there, fellow." It was David's command voice.

Isaac looked up. David was pointing his carbine at a lone warrior who had his hands up, still mounted.

Isaac stood hands bloody and blinked. There was plenty of daylight left, for it was only about five o'clock. He frowned. "Are you Jorge?"

Jorge looked astonished. "Si."

David shook his head and said, "Homey, don't tell me you know this one too."

Isaac kept his eyes fixed on Jorge. In English, Isaac said, "Yes, I know him. I only know two Indians in the whole world." In Spanish, Isaac said, "Jorge, I'm the vaquero you and Ortega saved in Carrizal."

Jorge smiled, looked skyward, raised his hands even higher, and exclaimed, "Thanks be to Ussen!"

David still pointed his carbine at Jorge. "What the hell did he say?"

"I think he said 'thanks be to his god.' I don't know that word."

Isaac spoke again. "Jorge, listen to me. Leave your carbine in your saddle boot. Dismount and stay close to me before some eager soldier shots you." Isaac then translated for David.

After some initial confusion about "not hauling dirty Indians in an army vehicle," Captain Carpenter arrived after Company H failed to catch Victorio before he crossed the Rio Grande and solved matters. Instead of the ambulance, Carpenter ordered the use of an army wagon for Isaac and other materials that needed to be transported back to Fort Davis. With Ortega's wound bound tightly, Isaac, David, and a light escort were on their way to the fort before first dark.

* * *

They traveled overnight and arrived at Fort Davis around noon the next day. As they approached the fort, Isaac hurried to fetch Alejandra while David and the escort took Ortega and Jorge directly to the post hospital. Isaac smiled as he watched Alejandra drive her buggy out of their yard, past the pink blossoms of her transplanted glory of Texas cacti, and turn toward the fort as fast as her ancient horse could go. He thought, *soon I'll put her up to race against Mr. Luke*. He laughed at the thought.

Isaac yawned and went to the kitchen. There, he used a fork to mash string beans and peaches for sixteen-month-old Julieta's midday meal.

* * *

Ten weeks into Ortega's recuperation, Ortega and Jorge mounted their ponies with a pass in Ortega's saddle pocket from Captain Carpenter, acting in his capacity as post commander, to travel to the Mescalero Reservation without interference from military units they might encounter en route. With hung-down heads, Ortega and Jorge repeated their thanks to Alejandra and Isaac, who bade them farewell from their porch. Both understood the sadness in Ortega and Jorge, for word had come the day before that the Mexican Army had killed Victorio and sixty of his warriors, their former comrades, at a place called Tres Castillos in the state of Chihuahua on October 14, 1880.

The Victorio War was over.

Chapter 45: Entrepreneur

"Isaac, I had my chance. I could've killed Ortega on that operating table."

"Allie, my love, you didn't. I know you wouldn't do such a thing – not for revenge. That's just not you."

"Sit, please, so I can rest on your knee." Isaac sat on an old ladderback chair. Alejandra sat on his good knee. "Please hold me." They cuddled and were quiet for a time. Isaac inhaled her scent and smiled. He gave thanks for his good fortune.

Alejandra rested her chin on Isaac's shoulder. Presently, she whispered, "Sometimes life's twists and turns are so confusing. Papa went to war against his will and fought the French. Ortega saves your life. Then it could have been his bullet that killed Papa. These damn wars continue to reach out and kick me in the gut! What can I do with my anger?"

"Perhaps the bullet came from one of more than a hundred others on the mountain that day following the orders of Victorio. That happened a year ago. In time, the pain will be less. Let me massage your neck and shoulders while I tell you a story about Aunt Ella. Maybe you'll feel better."

She caressed his hands. "Okay."

* * *

While Alejandra and Julieta took a Sunday afternoon nap, Isaac settled at the kitchen table and pushed Tom's letter aside. It read in part:

Lt. Flipper's trial
for embezzlement
will likely last for weeks.
Will keep you posted.

With a sigh, Isaac said aloud, "It is time to turn the dream into a plan. Let's get on with it." He cut a section of brown butcher's paper and sketched from memory a steam water pump he had seen in

Harper's Weekly Magazine. He added to the sketch the edge of a river, a cutaway of a shed to house the engine and pump, and a section of a rice field. After two hours of enhancing his drawing, he labeled it "Manuel's Rice Farm." Then he signed it and noted the date: October 2, 1881.

After rubbing her eyes, Julieta climbed onto his good knee and grabbed a pencil. "Let me, Papa. Let me, Papa."

Isaac moved his drawing, out her of reach, stood and tacked it on the kitchen wall. Sitting again, he lifted Julieta onto his knee and gave her a piece of paper. "Julie, Papa needs a horse. Can you draw a horse for me?"

"Yes, Papa. I make a horse for you."

Isaac watched. When she finished, Julieta marked all over her horse. Isaac exclaimed, "Oh, no! Julie, you're ruining your nice horse."

"No, Papa. I make him black like my hair!"

* * *

Alejandra took one look at the caption and kissed her husband. "Oh, this is so good. Now I see your dream more clearly. I had trouble making a picture in my head of rice growing in a field and being watered by a river when the rains don't come."

"Do you think Caleb will like it?"

She laughed and raised a fist. "He'd better, if he knows what's good for him! Oh, and thanks for remembering my papa. Let's leave it up. This will be a good memorial for Papa when we celebrate the fiesta of Los Dias de Muertos in a few weeks."

* * *

While Isaac gathered mustard greens from their tiny garden behind the kitchen, he thought that perhaps if Manuel had lived, he would like to return to Veracruz with us and make a go of it as rice farmers. He reflected on the army adventures Manuel had shared with him, Ernesto, and Rafael about his times in the state of Veracruz fighting against the French. Even with the fighting all around him, Manuel had admired the countryside for its beauty and rich agricultural possibilities. Isaac savored his two-year-old memory of the beginning of his dream business when Manuel had mentioned his first time seeing rice growing in a field in Veracruz.

He looked up as a buggy arrived. "Hey, Homey, com'on outta that garden. I'm starving! Let's get this dinner on the road!"

Louise landed a playful slap on Caleb's arm. "Stop talkin' like that! You'll make Isaac and Allie think I haven't fed you this week."

* * *

Isaac sat with Caleb, helping Julieta eat her guisantes verdes con pinones. With enthusiasm, Alejandra and Louise were still discussing Isaac's dream and drawing as they cleared away the remains of their dinner's antelope pot roast, greens, jalapeno cornbread, and frijoles refritos.

Caleb leaned forward and put his elbows on the table. "I really see it now. This is a great drawing. I had trouble imagining how we could control water on a rice field without doing it the old way with trunk docks. Since it won't be on swampland, this farm is going to be a lot less work – especially with the mules that we couldn't use much before."

* * *

Three weeks later, Isaac and Caleb were discharged. David hosted a going to Mexico fete for them. The Tenth's band played in honor of one of its original members. By November 10, Isaac and Caleb began their reconnaissance journey to Veracruz with a Raramuri guide who was a former scout for the Mexican Army. Isaac rode his second surplus army horse. Caleb had bought one too.

Beside the cook fire the first night out, Caleb chuckled and asked, "Hey, Homey, what the hell are we doing out here sleeping under the stars again instead o' sleeping beside our wives?"

"Didn't you tell me you missed those long gone nights when we slept on the ground in Kansas?"

"Smart alec."

* * *

They went first to Ciudad Tuxpan, on the Gulf of Mexico, about one hundred sixty miles northwest of Ciudad Veracruz, almost five hundred miles south of Brownsville, Texas. Isaac thought the water in the broad Rio Tuxpan was too brackish near the city. They followed the river inland to the small town of Alamo where the river tasted fresh. Isaac and Caleb marveled at how the wide river reminded them of the South Edisto. At a bend in the river two miles northwest of Alamo, they found a farm for sale that was surrounded by woods. They made an arrangement with the owner, a bank in Ciudad Tuxpan, to purchase the farm without an interest payment for twenty-five percent down and a six-month balloon, due May 1, 1882. They took an option on the wooded land for future expansion of their farm. The partners were back in West Texas by mid-December.

* * *

The morning after his arrival, Alejandra handed Isaac a letter.

Thursday, Dec 8, 1881

Dear Bunkie,
This is just a quick note
to give you & Caleb bad news.
Yesterday, they found Lt. Flipper guilty
of conduct unbecoming and
dismissed him from the army.

Tom

* * *

The next day, Isaac began writing letters to procure equipment, implements, supplies, and a sales agent. He celebrated Christmas with family and friends, and then participated in the New Year's celebration. Two days into January, Isaac and Caleb departed for the

Mescalero Reservation, riding their ancient former government horses.

Several days later, Isaac was reunited with Ortega and Jorge. Caleb was embraced as a friend of a friend. After some time, Ortega accepted that his friend was no longer in the army. Ortega pointed out that Isaac was using the same civilian saddle he used when he was disguised as a vaquero. Isaac showed them small watercolor paintings of the Rio Tuxpan. Ortega inhaled audibly when he saw the large river. Isaac also showed them rice plants he had brought from Veracruz as well as his drawing. Many hours later, Isaac and Caleb invited Ortega and Jorge to join their family enterprise.

The two Apaches looked at each other. Isaac thought they seemed stunned.

Ortega folded his arms. "This is an honor and an important matter. We will discuss. Please meet us here at midday two suns from now."

It was Isaac and Caleb's turn to look at each other. They shook hands all around.

Two days later at noon, Isaac and Caleb arrived at the fire pit in front of Ortega's arbor. They waited two minutes. Ortega arrived leading a three-year-old solid black pony, thirteen and a half hands high. Jorge followed, arms folded.

Ortega stood toe to toe with Isaac. Isaac thought *I believe I'm not supposed to take a step back.* Ortega spoke. "My good friend, you are a brave and generous man. Please accept this pony as a token of my esteem." He thrust the reins into Isaac's hands.

Isaac felt surprised and overwhelmed with gratitude. He remembered to accept any gift presented without protest. He simply said, "Thank you." He thought, *I guess this is a fare thee well.*

Ortega and Jorge stood together again. Their wives, Jacali and Tina, emerged from an arbor and joined them. Ortega folded his arms. "We have decided. We will go with you and grow rice for two years. If we like, we stay in Veracruz by the second lake with no end. If no, we will return again to these mountains. I have spoken."

Jacali and Tina served lunch: blue cornmeal-chile verde enchiladas made with chopped elk shoulder and spices.

* * *

After arriving back in West Texas, Alejandra shared the news from their letter-writing campaign. "Rafael and Patricia will remain in Carrizal. Mama, Ernesto, and Linda have decided to go with us. They especially like the idea of a family enterprise. Honey, I have a really good feeling about this. And, don't worry. I have completely forgiven Ortega for what he may or may not have done."

Isaac kissed her. "You're the bestest wife I ever had."

They laughed.

She took Isaac by the hand and pulled him into the kitchen. "Please tell me if these English letters are good news too."

Isaac opened and read each letter aloud. They were offers for equipment and implements. The last letter was postmarked in South Carolina. In turn, Isaac read it.

Charleston

December 31, 1881

Dear Isaac,

My husband, John, has passed on. I am writing to let you know again how grateful I am for your benevolence toward me in '63 during that awful war. I have not forgotten.

Further, I will be happy to represent your product in the capitals of Europe as you asked.

Please let me know if the enclosed contracts are satisfactory.

Respectfully yours,

Mrs. Margaret Tinsley Tiffany

"Isaac, who is she?"

Isaac explained.

Alejandra sat with wide eyes, both hands covering her mouth. Into her hands she said, "Incredible."

* * *

Because they waited several days for Abigail, Isaac rode ahead on his new pony, Midnight, to Fort Bliss to meet Ortega, Jorge, and their families. Caleb agreed to bring the wagon and livestock and their families along when Abigail and her children arrived at the town of Fort Davis. While waiting at Fort Bliss, Isaac calculated a date at which he would take the money and ride ahead to ensure that they make their balloon payment on time. His target arrival time was noon, Friday, April 28, 1882.

By the time Caleb arrived at Fort Bliss, they were ten days behind the original plan. The six mules could not pull the large industrial wagon loaded with household and farm items faster to make up lost time. They crossed the Rio Grande at El Paso and drove on toward Carrizal. Passing the Candelaria Mountains, Isaac carefully watched Alejandra. He noted her forlorn gaze at the mountain range. She did not make a sound. Once past, she did not look back.

Rocio had already moved out of her rented house and they found her with Ernesto and Linda, camped at El Ojito. Manuel's old farm wagon was loaded and ready to go. They departed with the four former warriors on horseback. The women and children rode in the wagons. Rocio and Caleb led them singing road songs for several miles. The children sang with gusto.

Isaac noticed Ortega frowning and realized he was concerned about noise. They passed Ojo Caliente and the sands slowed them before they reached the Chihuahua-El Paso Road. Suddenly they were surrounded by fifteen horsemen. The singing ceased.

The horsemen encircled their train and halted. Isaac picked the man he believed to be the leader, a man dressed in black riding a white horse with a long scar through his neat black handlebar moustache. Ortega moved beside Isaac. He whispered, "The one on the white horse led the attack on you and your comrades at Carrizal."

"Thanks."

Isaac nudged Midnight with his stirrups and maneuvered him nose to nose with the white horse. Isaac wore a straw sombrero, a Colt .45, and chaps with his vaquero clothing. He looked the leader in the eye and asked, "How can we help you, sir?"

The leader answered, "We could use your women. Isn't that right, boys?"

A cheer went up.

Speaking softly, Isaac ignored what he had heard. "Señor, my name is Isaac Rice. Who are you?"

"I am Ricardo Lopez, Lerdistas Military Commander for the northeast of the State of Chihuahua."

Isaac made his gaze fast and steady. "Señor Lopez, we're just poor farmers on our way to new work we heard about in Veracruz. Sir, we'll all be much obliged if you will let us pass."

"Señor Rice we're all poor. But we still look to the people to support us – voluntarily or otherwise. I'll make you a deal. Stand your menagerie of women over there on that sand dune. I'll have my men search your wagons for money. If we find any, you can keep your women. If not, we take them with us to a place where women and children bring good prices – even after we slightly use them before we sell them."

Isaac expected Ricardo to end with an insidious laugh or make a show in front of his men. Instead, Ricardo struck a match against his gun belt buckle and lit the cigar he held between his teeth, and went silent. Isaac had taken the measure of the man and believed Ricardo would not make idle threats. Now, he thought, *what do I do? I am responsible for bringing these innocents out here and I am asking what I do now. Fool, there's only one option. Okay. I will not come down on myself. I will be calm. I will hear Aunt Ella's voice. I will think before I act.*

"Señor Lopez, it will not be necessary for your men to search our wagons and disturb our women and children. I see you're a man of few words and a man who means what he says. Therefore, I will turn our money over directly and only to you. I believe you will keep your word."

"Well said, Señor Rice. I will keep my word. Will you keep yours and hand over *all* the money?"

Remembering the years of sacrifice and scrimping to save the money they now carried to complete their land purchase, Isaac's gut cramped. He took a deep breath. "Yes."

"Then, it's a deal."

Isaac turned Midnight and rode over to the large wagon where Alejandra held the reins. In a calm voice, he said, "Dear wife, please hand to me the old Pony Express mail pouch behind you on the floor."

Alejandra screamed, "No!"

Isaac did not blink. He sat his horse watching Alejandra's eyes cloud with water and spill onto her cheeks. He made no move and offered no words. He continued looking into her eyes, without repeating. He saw her lower lip quiver, then make an upside-down U. She reached back and handed the pouch that contained the money for their dream and that of all those assembled in their train.

"Thank you."

Isaac had Midnight retrace his steps. Isaac handed the pouch to Ricardo, who attached it to his saddle horn without opening it. "Gracias. Adios, amigo."

In seconds, the Lerdistas were cantering south, ahead of a cloud of dust. All the adults of the train gathered around Isaac behind the lead wagon. He saw them look to him for some sign some hope that all would be well. He said nothing. Isaac removed his sombrero and climbed inside the wagon.

A column of soldiers were riding south. He heard Rocio hail them. "We were robbed by Lerdistas! The dust has not settled there to the south. It is they. If you hurry, you can catch them."

The captain said, "Señora, we can try. But we have been riding since dawn. Our horses are tired. We will try." He gave the order and they galloped south.

Isaac emerged from the wagon wearing an extra ammunition belt, his old campaign hat, sling, and carbine. He heard a gasp and saw smiles from his loved ones. He ignored them. They stood aside as he checked the assembly of his old Spencer and loaded it. Next, he spun

485

the cylinder on his revolver and holstered it. Then he attached an ammunition box to his belt that contained eight preloaded tubes with seven rounds each for his carbine.

For the first time since the departure of the Lerdistas, Isaac spoke. "Caleb and Ernesto please drive the wagons south and camp at El Vado. I'll meet you there."

Isaac turned to Ortega and Jorge. Isaac nodded briefly, for they were already checking their carbines and ammunition. Utterly dejected, he looked up at Alejandra where she still sat on the driver's seat of the wagon. She made a fleeting smile under wet cheeks and threw her full canteen to him. Her gesture of support reassured him. He perceived that Alejandra knew what he needed and she gave it to him in that quick smile; Isaac was grateful. He mounted and turned Midnight south. As he did so, he heard Julieta ask, "Mama, where are Papa and Midnight going?"

"Your papa is going to get our dream back." Isaac thought, *Alejandra sounds as if she really believes I will succeed.* Then he said to himself, "I will, or die trying."

* * *

Soon, Midnight overtook the army patrol. As he passed the captain, Isaac saluted. The captain, mouth agape, returned the salute in slow motion. Ortega and Jorge's ponies were at Midnight's heels. Once completely clear of the patrol, they rode three abreast. The road was wide and flat. Ahead, Isaac could see the dust cloud made by the Lerdistas as they continued at a canter. Patches of blue grama grass amid the yucca on both sides of the road were sending up new green shoots amid the brown grass of the previous season. The clumps of brown became less of a blur as he slowed Midnight to a canter. Ortega and Jorge slowed their mounts.

Because the road was straight and it was a bright sunny day, Isaac could see more than a mile ahead. He thought that if they were to look back, we would be hidden by their dust cloud. More likely, they don't expect to be chased by three farmers. There's no time to discuss what we will do when we're in carbine range.

After giving Midnight a breather for more than a mile, Isaac urged him back to a gallop. As they closed the gap, Isaac signaled Ortega and Jorge to disperse further to the flanks. The warriors and cavalryman brought their experience as mounted marksmen to bear in their first and second volleys by reducing the number of Lerdistas to nine. Isaac slowed Midnight to remain out of the range of the revolvers the Lerdistas were using to fire over their shoulders. Then there were six Lerdistas.

Less than a mile north of El Vado, Ricardo turned east and headed for low mountains that had draws, trees, and boulders. Isaac realized they would lose the advantage of long-range fire. As he urged Midnight to gallop faster, Isaac thought it would have been a waste of time to stop and discuss an attack plan with Ortega and Jorge. They knew what to do. They kept pace and made the turn to the east with him for the same reason. Isaac was determined to reduce the number of Lerdistas again before they could use the mountainous terrain, boulders, acacia trees, or creosote and mesquite bushes to hide in. They fired two more volleys, but only brought down two more Lerdistas before the rest reached cover.

As they drew rein and tied their mounts, Isaac thought, *if I was in Ricardo's boots, where would I hide to make a stand?* Then, he noticed Ortega beckoning. Isaac followed to the side at about fifty feet from Ortega. He reasoned, of course, Ortega and his comrades have done many times what Ricardo is trying to do. Isaac could not see Jorge, but heard a carbine fire twice from the direction Jorge walked. He thought, *are we going the wrong way?* Ortega beckoned again. Isaac followed, this time understanding that Jorge was shooting the Lerdistas' horses.

A bullet kicked up dirt between Isaac and Ortega. The sound from the revolver shot rang out from the side of the mountain and gave them a fix on where the Lerdistas were hiding. Ortega directed Isaac by hand signals to cover him while he advanced. Isaac fired twice and then reloaded in three seconds and fired again, while Ortega scampered forward and ducked behind a boulder. From his new position, Ortega opened fire. A scream from the mountainside followed his second shot.

Isaac took that second to run forward to a new position.

From directly above on the mountainside, Ricardo called out. "Señor Rice, you lied. Your men are not farmers."

"We are committed farmers who once were warriors."

"That you were warriors is painfully clear. I made a big mistake."

"Señor Rice, let me make you an offer."

"Speak, Señor Lopez."

"I offer you half your money for the lives for my remaining men and me."

"No. Return *all* of our money and you're free to go. You don't have long to decide. There is an army patrol behind us."

"Señor Rice, I know you to be a man of your word. I will return all of your money if your men will stop killing our horses and let us go."

Isaac thought, *I know Ricardo realizes he has no choice. What is he saying? Perhaps he needs to think he negotiated a deal or needs his men to think he did so.* Isaac said to himself, "Screw that. I want you dead, Señor Ricardo Lopez." Then he remembered Aunt Ella's admonition. *Is that revenge? I guess Aunt Ella would say yes.*

"Okay, Señor Lopez. It's a deal."

Epilogue

On April 27, 1882, the seven women, five men, and their children arrived at their farm near Alamo, Veracruz, and made camp. The proud members of the new family enterprise, Manuel's Rice Farm, spent the afternoon joyfully exploring and romping over their new homeland. The next morning, Alejandra, Julieta, and Caleb accompanied Isaac to the bank in Ciudad Tuxpan to complete their purchase. In a review of the Spanish language documents, Alejandra discovered an error that resulted in a price reduction of one hundred thirteen dollars.

Once outside the bank, Isaac declared, "Well, my love, the purpose of these new-found funds is to build your clinic."

Alejandra was gleeful. "My thoughtful husband, I thank you so much for all you do! Now I have news for you! Your reward is another offspring. I'm pregnant."

Isaac hugged his wife. "I'm so glad. I've waited for this. Let's call her Ella."

Julieta said, "Mama."

Grinning, Caleb asked, "Who told you you'll have another daughter?"

Again, Julieta said, "Mama."

Isaac told Caleb and Alejandra, "Oh, it's just a wish and a feeling."

"Honey, Ella is a fine tribute and a great name."

Isaac looked down at Julieta pulling Alejandra's green, red, and white skirt at the knee. "Allie, I think Julie's calling you."

Alejandra lifted and held Julieta. "I'm sorry. What is it, Julie?"

"Mama, what's peg-nate?"

#

A partial list of famous and not so famous historic people in this novel.

The bibliography is located at: <u>bobrogers.biz</u>

Harriet Aiken, wife of William Aiken, Jr.
Henrietta Aiken, daughter of William Aiken, Jr.
William Aiken, Jr., Governor, US Congressman, South Carolina
Thomas H. Allsup, First Sergeant, Company A, 10th Cavalry
Alexander T. Augusta, surgeon, Major, US Army, Howard University Medical School
Griffin M. Bender, Owner of Bender Plantation
Wash Bender, Slave, Bender's valet during the Civil War
William Blackburn, Colonel, Battalion Cmdr, 7th Illinois Cavalry
Cadete, Chief, Mescalero Apache
L. Henry Carpenter, Captain, Company H, 10th Cavalry
Emmanuel Cartwright, Pastor, First African Baptist Church, St. Louis
Cochise, Chief, Chiricahua Apache
George Crook, General, US Army
George A. Custer, US Army, 7th Cavalry
Jefferson Davis, President, Confederate States
Joseph Davis, Jeff's older brother
Charles Dougherty, Private, Company A, 10th Cavalry
Henry O. Flipper, Lieutenant, Company A, 10th Cavalry
Ulysses S.Grant, General, US Army, President, US
Alice Grierson, Colonel Grierson's wife
Benjamin H.Grierson, Music teacher, Colonel, 7th Illinois Cavalry, 10th Cavalry
Charles Jackson, Slave (William Aiken, Jr.'s Coachman)
Henry P. Jacobs, Natchez City Councilman
Andrew Johnson, President, US
Richard Johnson, son of William Johnson (the barber of Natchez)
Robert Johnston, Company A, 10th Cavalry
Robert F. Joyce, Ordinance Sergeant, 10th Cavalry
Kaytennae, War Leader, Chihenne Apaches

Abraham Lincoln, President, US
James Lynch, Secretary of State, Mississippi
John R. Lynch, US Congressman, Mississippi
Ranald Mackenzie, Colonel, 4th Cavalry
Ben Montgomery, Slave, manager of Davis Plantation
Isaiah Montgomery, Slave, Son of Ben Montgomery
Mary Montgomery, wife of Ben Montgomery
Nana, War Leader, Chihenne Apaches
Nicholas M. Nolan, Captain, Company A, 10th Cavalry
E.O.C. Ord, US Army, General, Civil War, Indian Wars
John C. Pemberton, General, CSA Army
Randall Pollard, Pastor, Rose Hill Baptist Church, Natchez
William Prince, Colonel, Qmasters, 7th Illinois Cavalry
George Raulston, Lieutenant, Company A, 10th Cavalry
Hiram R. Revels, US Senator, Mississippi
Don Jose Rodriguez, Carrizal citizen; uncle of fictional character Torres
Rufus Saxton, General, US Army
Philip Sheridan, US Army, General, Civil War, Indian Wars
William T. Sherman, General, US Army
Richard Surby, Sergeant, Scout, 7th Illinois Cavalry
William Tunnard, Sergeant, 3rd Louisiana Infantry Regiment
Victorio, Chief, Chihenne Apaches
Robert Wood, Mayor of Natchez, Sheriff of Adams County, Mississippi
Hiram Young, Slave, entrepreneur, wagon manufacturer